METAL DRAGON

WARRIORS OF GALATEA #2

LAUREN ESKER

Metal Dragon
Published by Icefall Press, March 2019

Warriors of Galatea

Metal Wolf

Metal Dragon

Metal Pirate (forthcoming)

Metal Gladiator (forthcoming)

ONE

SO THIS WAS the planet that its inhabitants called Earth.

On the ship's forward viewscreens, it looked much like other planets Lyr had seen, a marble hanging in space, swirled with white and green and blue. Beautiful in its way. But not unique, as its people believed. He'd visited many others like it, most of them populated with people and animals taken from the mysterious planet called Birthworld, the legendary birthplace of humanity.

If rumor was right, Birthworld had been found at last, right here in the vast sweep of stars that the Galatean Empire claimed for their own.

Which mattered little to him. *His* people, the dragons, weren't from Birthworld. He was here only because he was ordered to be, and only for the purpose his masters commanded.

And yet the planet pulled on him, in a way he couldn't quite understand.

Idly, he flexed his hands so the battle spines in his arms slid in and out. Although slaves like Lyr were not normally allowed on the bridge, no one tried to remove him, and the bridge crew avoided him nervously. Slave collar or not, no one bothered an agitated dragon.

He made a striking figure, he knew: bare to the waist so his shoulder, back, and wrist spines and the implanted blades in his forearms were not impeded. The silver cuffs he wore—energy weapon and ship link all in one—slashed across the gleaming, iridescent skin of his arms just below his wrist spines.

Compared to an average Galatean soldier, he had very few implants. The only ones visible at the moment—with his arm blades hidden—were a faint tracery of silver on his forearms to help him use the cuffs, and the glint of the translator implant just below his ear. Human soldiers for the Empire used modifications to give them strength and speed, to help them survive in deep space, and otherwise to be more dangerous and effective warriors.. But Lyr was a dragon at the height of his ability and power. What need had *he* for the technology of lesser species?

And this kind of thinking is why you're currently a war-slave to the Galateans, he told himself darkly.

Around him, feet whispered on polished deck plates as the furred, catlike Galatean crew went about their duties. Slaves like Lyr normally went barefoot, while Galatean citizen crew wore slippers with their dark blue and gold uniforms, except when they put on boots for planetside duty.

And there was the sound of boots now, marching toward Lyr in a brisk and uncompromising line. He knew those footsteps, and tore his gaze away from the cloud-swirls of the planet below them. "Lieutenant Tamir."

Tamir of House Kynn was a tiger-type Galatean, his thick orange-and-black hair threaded with silver. Although in late middle age, he was still heavily muscled. His blue uniform left his arms bare, the powerful shoulders and biceps covered with soft tawny fuzz, marked with darker stripes leading down to the gold citizens' cuffs at his wrists.

"Lyr," he said, not bothering with formalities. "I heard you were brooding up here."

Lyr bristled—literally, the spines sliding partway out of his arms. "Come to throw me off the bridge?"

"No. I came to tell you they're prepping the chaser ships for drop. Time to go catch some pirates." Tamir dropped his gaze to Lyr's bare feet, and raised a shaggy eyebrow. "You're supposed to be geared up."

"I'm going like this."

Tamir's look said *What the hell.* "No you aren't."

"I'm more comfortable this way."

Tamir dropped his voice so the conversation wasn't broadcast across the bridge. "You're punishing yourself again, and I won't allow it. Lyr—" He smiled quickly, a flash of fangs in his tiger-striped face. "Don't make me *order* you to put boots on."

"If it's obedience you want, you could use the collar on me."

That scored. Tamir flinched, a quick shudder twitching his fur. Lyr stared back at him impassively, and Tamir jerked his head at the door of the bridge. "Come with me," he said with a hint of impatience. "And yes, that *is* an order."

Lyr refused to allow his reaction to show on his face. He set his shoulders, sheathed his spines, and obediently followed the commander who had once been father and older brother and mentor, all in one.

They went down a level, through the ship's utilitarian corridors to the lockers. Tamir leaned against the wall, arms folded, while Lyr pulled on the boots that had been designed for his long, narrow feet.

"Lyr—" he began, with a gruff note of apology in his voice.

"How many pirates?" Lyr interrupted, not looking at him.

Tamir sighed and let himself be redirected to work. "It looks like a typical trafficker ship. They've dispatched a chaser-class vessel on a scouting run. We're going down after them."

A fight sounded pleasing. Lyr felt the spark in his chest growing hotter, filling the emptiness inside him as his dragon-half roused with the urge to draw blood. He'd been trapped for too long on blockade duty, hiding behind Earth's moon, able to bleed off his energy only by sparring with other soldiers. He'd bloodied a few faces, broken a nose or two, but if he allowed himself to really let go, he was going to land someone in the infirmary.

There were times when he didn't care.

It had gotten to the point where the only person on the ship willing to spar with him was Tamir, and Tamir had the scars under that buff-and-black fur to prove it.

"They're getting bolder about the raids," Tamir added, as Lyr laid his wrists in a charging station to top off the energy cuffs that were both gun and shield. "Word's getting out on the galactic black market about Birthworld, I think. We're going to have our hands full if this sector gets really busy."

Human DNA from Earth/Birthworld was a hot commodity in a galaxy where most intelligent races—aside from a few who had evolved independently, like Lyr's people—were descended from a relatively small stock of humans who had been taken from Earth a very long time ago and genetically modified by the long-vanished aliens dubbed the Founders. Birthworld was an untapped wellspring of vast genetic diversity, a source of salvation for people like the Galateans who struggled with birth defects and low fertility—and all of it controlled by primitives who didn't know the first thing about the galactic battles taking place above their heads.

"I'm surprised you people haven't just swept in and taken over," Lyr remarked.

"Above my pay grade. Come on, you don't want to miss the fighting, do you?"

"You know what I like," Lyr said as they left the locker room, and Tamir actually laughed. Lyr hadn't meant it as a joke, but he was taken off guard by the twitch of his mouth upward before he caught himself and forced his face back to impassivity.

Tamir grinned at him, and Lyr resented it. *You have no right. You are not my friend, even if you pretend it.*

You could not save Rei and Rook when they died.

"Is this a redemption for you, Lieutenant Tamir?" he asked softly. "You've spent your life helping the Empire take and train slaves, so you think you can make up for it by saving a few?"

The smile fell away, and Tamir gave him a steady look from his calm gold-green eyes with their cat-slitted pupils. "Someone has to," he said quietly. "You're right, it won't change anything. The Empire I serve will still take children from our subject worlds and turn them into slave-warriors, like they did with you and your friends. But I'm going to do what I can to help the rest."

Lyr's lips curled back from his teeth. For an instant he was tempted to lash out with his mind—*I could show you all the anger inside me, Tamir; I could show you what it is to truly "serve" this Empire.* But he hadn't used his telepathy in the better part of a year, not since Rei and Rook, the last two surviving members of his training sept, had died in battle.

Broken and bleeding from the psychic backlash of their deaths, he had locked down the telepathic part of himself to survive. He would never reach out for another person's mind for the rest of his life; he had sworn it.

"Help," he spat. "You could have *helped* years ago, but you didn't." There was always something about dealing with Tamir, the only person still living who had watched him grow up, that seemed to turn him back into a petty teenager instead of a grown warrior. "Rationalize all you want. You're as guilty as the rest of them."

Tamir had always let Lyr's anger roll off him, back when Lyr and the rest of his sept were children and Tamir was the adult Galatean charged with training them. A lot had changed since then, but that was still the same. He didn't bristle, just looked at Lyr with eyes that were sympathetic and tired.

"What's happened to you, Lyr? I asked for you specifically for this duty; I thought it might help you to move past ..." Tamir paused before going on. "You used to be gentle and kind—proud, yes, but ... you weren't like this."

"Your Empire *made* me like this," Lyr snarled. "What did you expect?"

Just outside the hangar bay, Tamir stopped abruptly and caught Lyr by the arm. In his surprise, Lyr nearly drove his spines straight through Tamir's thick palm. He wasn't used to being touched, not anymore. Everyone on the ship was afraid of him, and he'd done his best to keep it that way.

"Lyr, listen." Tamir's voice was quiet; his calm gaze searched Lyr's face. "With your sept ... gone, things are different now. You could contact your people and see if you can get your indenture lifted. I could help you do that. You can go home—"

"You think my people would *take me back*?" Lyr laughed

then, for the first time in months, a bitter laugh with no trace of amusement. "I can see you never listened to a single thing I told you, in all these years."

With exquisite control, he extended his spines just far enough to prick Tamir's palm, and also allowed the tip of the knife-sharp metal blade to tear its way out of his forearm, a thin line of pinkish-silver blood tracing its way down his skin. Tamir might not be able to take a hint, but he could read a threat; he let go, and Lyr pulled away and strode into the hangar bay, wiping away the trickle of blood with a swipe of his thumb.

Even after spending his entire adult life among the Galateans, he still found their ships harsh and unwelcoming. The sharp right angles, gray metal with stripes of vivid paint, and too-bright lights were nothing like dragon city-ships with their gracefully curving interiors and gentle mother-of-pearl colors. The hangar bay echoed with loud voices, the clank of metal on metal, the clashing of equipment as gear was loaded onto the ship—all of it an assault on his sharp ears.

He hung back as Tamir greeted his crew, staying apart from the shared camaraderie of the Galatean marines, and they made no move to welcome him. They didn't like him any more than he liked them. Normally slave-soldiers would be required to ride out a short hop such as the flight to the planet on fold-down seats with locking restraints in the cargo hold, but Lyr, without speaking, took a seat in the back of the crew compartment, what might be termed the bridge on a larger ship. If Tamir didn't want him here, he was going to have to throw him off.

No one said anything about it. But of course Lyr was not, had never been, a typical slave. The Galatean Empire collected slaves from their subject peoples to use as cannon fodder in their wars, but the arrangement they had with the dragons was something different. It was draconic honor, more than the collar, that had kept him tame and chained for all these years. He was vow-bound to his Queen to serve the Galateans as part of the treaty that kept them away from dragon space.

Lyr was legally a slave, but in reality, he was a hostage, a high-ranking dragon prince from one of the ruling families of the Well of Stars.

For the good of his people, he could never go home again. They would not welcome him if he did.

He noticed a couple of Tamir's men glance nervously at the collar that kept him from shifting and could bring him to his knees at the touch of a button. As a dragon, uncollared and free, he could have destroyed this ship easily, and they all knew it. Lyr smiled at them darkly as he pulled down the seat harness.

You have nothing to fear from me, he could have told them. The only thing he hoped for now was a swift and honorable death.

Perhaps this battle would provide one.

TWO

"I'M *SO* glad you're moving to Kansas City, Mer. It'll be great having you close again. I've missed you so much since college."

Meri Rowland turned away from her own reflection in the dark window to smile at her best friend in the driver's seat. If she kept smiling, maybe she'd eventually be as happy about it as Cora was. It would be good to live somewhere she had a close friend. She wouldn't miss Columbus; she hadn't been that attached to it. Cora and Dave had a pretty little house in the suburbs, and they'd set up the guest bedroom for her. Only temporary, of course– as a nurse, finding a job shouldn't be *that* hard, and then she could get a place of her own.

A new start. A new life.

Shouldn't she be looking forward to it?

"It's a good thing we finally convinced you to move down," Cora went on, chattering to fill the silence as the radio station they'd passed awhile back faded to static. Had her best friend always talked this much? Meri wondered. Back in the old days, when they were young college girls in love with their boyfriends and inseparable from each other, the two of them used to chat about everything and nothing; there were no awkward silences. Now Cora had been doing most of the talking since they left Ohio.

"It's not good for you, Meri, rattling around alone up there. You can get to know the kids, and Dave'll be thrilled to see you. It'll be just like old times, back when it was just the four of us—I mean, the three—oh—"

Cora broke off, and even in the glow of the dash lights, Meri could see guilt written clearly across her friend's face.

Sometimes it felt that the grief of losing Aaron was compounded a hundredfold by other people's inability to deal with Meri's widowhood. All too often, it seemed, she ended up soothing their feelings instead of being comforted herself. And it wasn't like it was new, this well-worn sorrow. Aaron had died almost ten years ago, which made her realize—not for the first time—how little she'd seen of Cora since college, and how much they were strangers to each other now.

"It's all right," she made herself say. "Don't worry about it."

What was I thinking? she thought to herself, looking out the window at the pitch-dark rural countryside. Her face floated ghostlike across the blackness of the night and the lights of distant towns, dark skin and the glimmer of the lighter tips of her bleached and dyed twists. Seeing herself like that made her feel even more insubstantial, like she wasn't really here at all.

This was going to be a disaster. She didn't even know Cora and Dave anymore. She wasn't sure if they had pets, she couldn't remember where Dave worked, and she'd embarrassingly misspelled the name of their eldest daughter, who she'd never even met, in her last email. She tried to keep up with Cora on Facebook, but it was a completely different matter to insert herself into their lives, moving into a spare bedroom and becoming a guest in someone else's life instead of wandering like a ghost through her own.

Kansas City is going to be just like Columbus, and just like Atlanta before that. I'll get a job, and I'll do all the things you're supposed to do, and Cora will probably talk me into trying to date again and I'll hate every minute of it ... and I'll think of Aaron every time it rains or whenever a song comes on the radio that he used to like ...

To her dismay, and even a little anger, she found herself blinking back tears. Wasn't this supposed to stop? How much time to grieve was too much time? Wasn't there going to be a time in her life when she stopped feeling as if the biggest and best part of herself had been buried along with Aaron all those years ago?

"—Mer? Did you hear me?"

"Yes," she said quickly, blinking fiercely until the stinging in her eyes went away. "I'm listening. Uh ..." She cast her mind back, trying to remember what they'd been talking about.

"Mer, are you okay?"

"I'm fine." She took a deep breath, scrambling for another conversational topic. "How are *you* feeling? Do you need another allergy pill?"

Cora rubbed at her eyes with the back of her hand. "That obvious, huh? I was trying not to sneeze. I can't believe I forgot my meds back home. It's not so bad in KC, but as soon as I hit the Illinois border, it was like the waterworks turned on. You said you still had some allergy medicine in your purse, right?"

"I'll get you another pill." Meri twisted around into the backseat to get her purse. It was jammed between a suitcase and the purple flowered car seat where Cora's baby daughter Toni slept, her head tilted alarmingly to the side in the way of sleeping babies and her dark hair twisted up in little pink butterfly-shaped clips.

"Don't wake up the baby, Mer. It's not that important."

"I did two years in the neonatal ward. I have a lot of experience at not waking up babies." Meri wriggled the purse free of its prison and pulled it into the front seat with her.

She loved this purse. She'd always liked large, colorful handbags, and Cora had given her this one for Christmas a few years ago. It looked like an enormous clownfish—the orange and white fish from *Finding Nemo*—and it was full of pockets. It didn't match anything else she owned. Though half the reason why she liked it so much was because of people's faces when she went out with the clownfish hanging from a strap over her shoulder.

"I can't believe you actually take that thing out in public," Cora said, right on cue. She eyed the purse as Meri briskly extracted a tiny flashlight from one of the pockets and began to rummage around with the bag held between her knees. "I just wanted to imagine your face when you opened the package. I kept the receipt so you could pick out a purse you actually *liked.*"

"I like this one. It fits everything I want to carry with me and it's solid enough to take down a mugger if I need to." Meri knew exactly which pocket the allergy medicine was in. She knew which pocket everything was in. It was just a matter of shifting enough items to be able to reach it.

"That's because you have everything but the kitchen sink in there."

"If I find a travel-sized kitchen sink, I just might put it in there too. Oh!" She'd had the pill bottle for a minute, but the car jolted and it slipped down into the depths.

"There's an exit up ahead. Let me pull off, and I can take my pill and call Dave to let him know where we are."

"Sounds good." Having found the bottle of antihistamine tablets, Meri held it up and checked it with the flashlight to make sure they were non-drowsy. She shook out a pill into her palm, and got out the little bottle of water tucked into the end pocket. "And I didn't wake up the baby."

There was a quick flash of a bright smile, so reminiscent of those college days that it made Meri's heart ache. "She's handling it so well. She's really good in cars. Just goes right out." Cora smothered a yawn. "Okay, let's stop talking about falling asleep."

"I can spell you on the driving when we leave the rest stop."

"It's just a yawn. I can still drive fine." She smothered another yawn. "Okay, maybe I am tired. It's probably a good idea to trade off soon."

They took the exit for a town that Meri immediately forgot the name of. They were mostly interchangeable anyway, these little roadside towns in the cornfields, the ones that consisted mainly of a gas station and a couple of restaurants at the freeway exit, and scattered farmhouses and maybe a county road or two. She had grown up in a town like this farther south. As a girl, she couldn't wait to get out of it, though now she found herself missing it vaguely, in that wistful way you miss a place you know you can never go back to.

Cora parked near the bright lights of a gas plaza, and they both got out to stretch their legs. Meri handed over the allergy pill and bottle of water.

"I love how you're still prepared for everything," Cora

said after knocking back the pill. "I remember back in college if anybody needed an aspirin or a screwdriver, you were the one to talk to."

Meri patted her purse. "I still have both."

"The original mom friend, right?" Cora said, grinning at her. "You always took care of us."

Yes, but who took care of me after Aaron died? Bitterness welled up in her. She pushed it down as she always did and turned away, leaving Cora looking up the route ahead on her phone, and went in to use the restroom.

Under the harsh restroom lights, she looked faded to herself in the mirror, her shoulders hunched and her skin wan with undertones of gray. Her hair, in springy short twists, was bleached at the tips and dyed coppery red, a new thing she'd decided to try just recently after noticing the first threads of silver beginning to curl and twist among the black. Cora had laughed and said it looked like her hair was rusting. (That was a lot of shade from a woman who used to get her hair straightened and dyed purple in college.)

She found that she was restlessly turning the wedding ring around and around on her finger. Ten years she'd been a widow, and still she wore that ring. It had always seemed wrong, somehow, to take it off. It meant letting go of Aaron, moving on, making decisions about a future without Aaron in it.

I'm 35 years old. The future is coming for me whether I want it or not.

Well, that was the problem. She had things she wanted; her entire heart, it seemed, was a bruise that ached with vaguely defined wanting. She *wanted* Aaron back. She wanted to have the money and leisure time to travel and see things; she wanted, maybe, to take up a hobby like pottery or writing poetry, something fun and creative. But there was nothing she wanted enough to get fired up for it. Not like she'd wanted things when she was a young woman, with the heat and passion that had driven her to work her way through nursing school, to marry Aaron after a whirlwind courtship, to throw herself wholeheartedly into work and friendship and love. She remembered that young woman like a stranger, that woman who was full of energy and life.

Somehow she didn't think Kansas City was going to feel like starting over any more than Columbus had.

What's that old saying? Wherever you go, there you are ...

But at least it would be *something*. She'd have Cora and Dave and their kids to help her stop getting lost in her own head. She could explore the city, go for walks like she used to. Maybe she could take a college class, or take up jogging.

With a firm, decisive twist of her fingers, she pulled off her wedding ring. There was a paler band of skin where she'd worn the ring for most of her adult life. Meri stared at it for a moment, her hand already feeling naked, and then thrust the ring into a pocket of her purse.

New city. New start.

Her eyes stung with tears again. She blinked them firmly away.

I'm 35, not 92. I'm not dead. Aaron wouldn't have wanted me to spend my whole life grieving.

She bought herself a cup of coffee in the convenience store and tried not to feel too self-conscious about her empty ring finger.

A little boy clinging to his mother's hand giggled and pointed at her purse with a happy cry of "Nemo!" The boy's mom tried to shush him, but Meri smiled at both of them.

It was why she liked wearing this purse even though it was ridiculous, she reflected as she pushed through the door into the warm humidity of a Midwest summer night. It made people smile. It made *her* smile, and not many things could do that anymore. As a young woman, she used to love bright things, flowers and jewelry and colorful skirts. There hadn't been a lot of brightness in her life lately.

Maybe she would treat herself to a pretty skirt when she got to Kansas City.

Cora was leaning against the car and just finishing up a conversation when Meri reached her. "Love you too. Bye." She looked up at Meri. "Dave says hi. He's pretty much talked me into getting a hotel for the night before we get too tired. What do you think?"

"I think that'd be a good idea," Meri admitted.

"He said he'll make us a pot roast tomorrow. I told him he didn't have to, but he said if we're driving all day, it's the least he can do to welcome you to Missouri. He said to text him if you had any special requests for dessert."

"Tell him ..." Meri hesitated. "Tell him thank you for me," she said absently. Something had caught her attention; she just wasn't sure what.

Cora looked up from texting. "Mer? What's the matter?"

"I don't know." Meri looked around the parking lot. It was just an ordinary freeway stop at night. There were a dozen or so other cars, a couple of 18-wheelers and an RV pulled into the truck parking area. Traffic hummed along on the interstate. Her gaze skimmed past a couple giving their dog a travel break on the gravel beside the convenience store, an old guy with teenage grandkids by the doors, and the lady with the little boy ...

But the cicadas weren't chirring anymore. *That* was what she'd noticed, the sudden cessation of that constant soundtrack of Midwest summers.

And there was ... something else. A strange heaviness in the air. It made her think instantly of tornadoes, and she looked quickly upward, but there was nothing to see except stars winking through patchy clouds in the sky. This wasn't tornado weather, and there was no wind except a light breeze, neither the hard gusts of wind that heralded a storm, nor a sudden deadly stillness.

"Meri, you're worrying me."

"Check your phone," Meri said, still staring at the sky. "See if there are any weather alerts." Would they get warning sirens out in the country like this? She'd never actually seen a tornado, and it wasn't an experience she cared to have. *I wouldn't mind excitement in my life, but not that kind!*

"It's all clear on the radar. What's the matter, did you hear something about bad weather up ahead?"

"No, I've just got a bad feeling. I think we should get back in the—"

She stopped.

"Meri?" Cora said nervously.

"Get in the car," Meri said. Her own voice sounded hoarse and strange.

There was something ... *big* landing on the edge of the parking lot, blocking the freeway exit ramp.

She hadn't seen it because it was completely dark, making it almost invisible in the darkness of the rural night; something about it seemed to swallow light instead of reflecting. And it made no noise. It was like a huge ... balloon? Yes, maybe that was it, a long balloon like a dirigible, setting down at the parking lot's edge.

—no, that was stupid, it *wasn't* a balloon, balloons didn't look like that; she had no idea what it was.

A sudden, powerful gust of wind flattened the grass, blew leaves off the trees along the edge of the parking area, and made Meri stagger back as the—balloon? helicopter?

whatever-the-hell-it-was settled to the ground. With a sudden screech of tires, the nearest tractor-trailer skidded sideways, having caught the gust broadside, and teetered for a moment on the verge of falling over.

Meri was only distantly aware of panic breaking out around her. She couldn't take her eyes off that big dark thing. Now that it had settled to the ground, completely blocking the exit ramp and crushing brush on both sides of the parking area, she could see it a little better in the lights of thee gas plaza. It appeared to be dark, dull silver, like some kind of unreflective metal, pewter or lead or something. The gas station floodlights lit it up enough that she could make out its general shape: tapered at one end, flaring slightly at the other, maybe thirty or forty yards long and about twenty feet high.

It was as big as a *house*, and it hadn't made a sound except for the crackling of the brush as it set down. Now it was utterly motionless, just sitting there across the end of the parking lot.

Cora had her phone in her hand, but all she could do was stare, her eyes huge. "Should I ... should I call 911, do you think?"

It looked like several other people were already doing that. Meri glanced through the car window at Toni sleeping in her carseat. "I think you should get in the car with your little girl."

A streak of light appeared low on the silver thing's curving side, opening rapidly to reveal a block of bright silver light with incredibly, inhumanly weird-shaped figures standing in it.

And finally Meri's rational mind managed to come up with an explanation, as little sense as it made.

This is a UFO.

These are aliens.

We are being attacked.

"Get in the car!" she snapped, and Cora fumbled with the door, staring in wild-eyed panic. Meri reached into her purse and got out her key chain with the pepper spray on it.

The door of the UFO was flush with ground level, and as the aliens marched into the parking lot, the two leading ones each pointed at one of the onlookers, most of whom now had their phones out. There were two quick flashes of green light, and the two targets, a trucker and a tourist-looking woman, went completely limp and crumpled to the ground with a pair of painful-sounding thumps.

The aliens didn't seem to be carrying weapons. None of them had anything in their hands. They just pointed and people fell.

They were a motley assortment; the only thing they all had in common was that they were clearly not human. The majority of them were covered in fur, at least seven feet tall, with pricked-up cat-ears. All wore pants and boots; most were shirtless. One of them was shorter, with purple skin and—*Heaven help us,* Meri thought. The purple-skinned man's hands ended in *claws*, long and curved, making him look like a mole or something.

And he wasn't even the weirdest of the bunch. That had to be the actual, honest-to-God, am-I-freaking-seeing-this *centaur*, a broad-shouldered man with flowing chestnut hair that matched the hide of his horse-half, clattering along on dinner-plate-sized hooves like a Clydesdale's.

Meri stood frozen, clutching her little tube of pepper spray like it could do anything at all against *that.*

Panic spread; people began to run. The aliens were in no hurry. They pointed and zapped, pointed and zapped, and each target crumpled to the ground. One woman managed to get into her car, but as she veered around in a squeal of tires, aiming for the wrong-way ramp leading back to the freeway, the centaur pointed at her tires. The car swerved wildly and jolted to an abrupt stop, the rubber stripped off all four tires and paint blistered as if someone had raked a flamethrower across the side.

Meri didn't know if the people who had been zapped with that terrible green light were alive or dead. Alive, she thought maybe, because the aliens were starting to drag them back to their ship. But maybe they just wanted to eat them. *What the hell, what the hell, what the hell!!*

They weren't waiting until all of them were stunned, either. They seemed to enjoy grabbing screaming, running people and hauling them, struggling, toward their ship.

"Meri, get in!" Cora cried through the half-open car window. The baby was awake now, starting to cry.

I don't know if it'll help, Meri thought. Any of the cars that tried to drive away were disabled with stabbing bursts of light so that the aliens could drag the people out of them. They seemed to be having fun; it was like sport for them.

"Meri!"

"Stay in the car. Get down and see if you can keep Toni quiet. Maybe they won't see you." It seemed hopeless. Meri clutched the pepper spray tighter.

Cora leaned between the seats to try to calm the wailing baby. "Hush, baby, hush. Meri, get in!"

"Shhh! Get down! Hide!" Meri stepped forward, standing between the car and the oncoming aliens. Maybe if they were busy with her, they wouldn't notice anyone in the car.

She wasn't sure what made her do it. Meri had never thought of herself as a brave person, or a heroic or self-sacrificing person. But Cora had her kids and husband. Meri was alone. It made sense for her to stand here and try to stop them from taking Cora, who had so much to live for, when Meri had so little.

The centaur galloped ahead of the others, clattering up to her. Despite her terror, she couldn't help being fascinated. The man's muscular torso blended seamlessly into his horse half. He wore a loose leather vest, silver bracelets on each wrist, and strands of beads woven into his hair. There were tattoos on the light skin of his human arms, and on his horse half a complex brand of a similar design, a bold swirling pattern, weaving its way up his back leg and across his flank.

Meri still hadn't managed to see what the aliens were shooting people with, but as far as she could tell, he didn't seem to be carrying any weapons except for a knife in a sheath at his human waist. He grinned at her, a flash of broken teeth in his chestnut beard, and reached for her.

Meri squeezed the pepper spray and unloaded the little canister into his face.

Alien or not, he wasn't immune. He let out a bellow of pain and clawed at his face with his hands, coughing and choking.

If Meri was going to run, this would be the time to do it. But ... how could she leave Cora? She looked over her shoulder and saw that Cora had taken her advice and crawled into the backseat to get Toni out of the carseat. She was trying to get them both down on the floor in the backseat, hiding beneath one of Toni's blankets.

The alien was starting to recover from the pepper spray, squinting at her furiously through streaming eyes. He made a grab at her and missed.

Meri wanted desperately to run away. Instead she ran forward and punched him in the stomach as hard as she could. It had been a very long time since she'd been in a fight—not since grade school. She was distantly surprised to discover that she still remembered those long-ago playground brawling tactics.

The punch made him huff out a startled breath, and Meri, confident that she had his attention, turned and ran a few steps before stopping to see if he was chasing her rather than paying attention to the car.

She *definitely* had his attention. He started to point one hand at her, the fingers curled down, and she realized suddenly that maybe those silver bracelets *were* the weapon. Then he changed his mind. His reddened eyes still streaming tears from the pepper spray, he broke into a gallop, coming after her.

Meri cried out and began to run. She was hardly even thinking of getting him away from the car anymore; she just wanted to escape.

THREE

TAMIR CURSED SOFTLY from the pilot's seat. "They're not just scouting. It's a raid, and they're already on the surface."

Lyr said nothing. It wasn't the sort of comment that required a response.

They came in low over dark fields and scattered clusters of lights that marked villages and towns. Slender strings of light connected the bright clusters like a softly glowing spiderweb: those would be roads for land vehicles. Most of this planet's travel still went on by ground transport.

Initial visuals were coming in on long-range sensors from the mothership overhead, and suddenly the main screen's view of the dark countryside was replaced with a scene of chaos in front of a roadside complex of buildings. The pirates were rounding up terrified humans. Some of them had been stunned, perhaps killed. One of the vehicles was on fire.

This was the most public pirate raid they'd had to deal with. Previous attacks had taken place in remote, rural locations. The pirates were growing bolder now that they'd realized Earth humans, in a one-on-one fight, were largely defenseless against them, lacking personal shields and or combat training.

"Useless," Lyr muttered aloud in contempt, causing the rearmost of Tamir's complement of space marines to glance back at him. It was galling, having to fight to protect people who weren't even prepared to fight on their own behalf ...

As if in rebuke, memory sucker-punched him. He remembered teaching kids to fight, the motley bunch of younger fellow slaves that he, as the older child, had been put in charge of. Telling them, *You fight not to kill, but to protect. You are strong and fast and well-armed. It's your duty to use the weapons that you have, the ones the Galateans gave you and the ones the Founders made you with, not to bully or hurt without reason, but to protect others weaker than you. Protecting others is your greatest responsibility.*

He'd really believed it, then. Young. Idealistic. Stupid.

Anyway, some of the humans *were* fighting back. Lyr's gaze was drawn to a fight going on outside one of the vehicles in the roadside parking area. The human woman was dwarfed by the huge Hnee warrior looming over her, a man with the upper body of a human and the lower body of a hoofed beast. He could have trampled her to death without breaking a sweat. And the woman had no weapons. There was no gleam of gold or silver cuffs at her wrists, not even any sign of the handheld weapons that were used on the galaxy's more primitive planets.

But still she fought, hopelessly, courageously. She used some kind of small chemical weapon on the Hnee, and when that didn't work, attacked him with her bare hands. She started to run, but only a few steps, and then looked back to see if he was chasing her.

It was evident to Lyr that she was protecting something in that vehicle, maybe a child or another member of her family. Like a mother bird pretending to have a broken wing, she lured the Hnee warrior away, even though it would likely mean her capture or death.

That woman had the courage of a dragon.

He unfastened his seat restraint and stood in a single swift motion.

Tamir glanced back, noticing the movement. He was a good commander, always conscious of what his men were doing. "Where are you going?"

"Tell me when we're over them," Lyr said, and turned toward the back of the ship.

"Lyr, dammit!"

"The jump won't hurt me." Lyr looked back over his shoulder, mouth twisting in a humorless smile. "I'll clear the way for your *non-expendable* crew."

Lyr heard Tamir curse as he went into the back of the ship, but he wasn't ordered back to the bridge. The only way to really force Lyr to do anything was to use the collar on him, and so far, Tamir hadn't done that.

Tamir would have the collar controller with him, though. By law he wasn't allowed to leave the cruiser with a slave-soldier on his team and not bring the means to punish him for disobedience.

Lyr opened the cargo door. Wind whipped at his hair as he leaned out. Despite the immediacy of the visuals on the ship's screens, they hadn't reached the battlefield yet. Instead they were flying low over a dark field of some kind of crops. It had been a while since he'd been on a planet. He'd forgotten how much sensory input there was, so many smells and sounds, even in a place like this. They passed over a cluster of houses, marked with scattered lights, probably giving the inhabitants a story to tell their grandchildren if they happened to be looking up at the wrong moment.

Lyr smelled smoke, but he didn't see the battlefield until their ship came upon it abruptly, and suddenly it was beneath them. The scene was even more chaotic in person than through the ship's sensors, with the screams of the fleeing humans, the rough shouts of the pirates, the roiling smoke from flaming vehicles filling the night.

He found himself scanning the battlefield for the Hnee warrior he'd seen on the ship's long-range imaging. The Hnee had hold of his captive now, but she was struggling and kicking like a cornered wildcat.

Lyr had felt little except anger since his last septmates had died, but this was, at least, a new *kind* of anger, a surge of protective fury that rushed through him and made his dragon flare inside him. A woman with that kind of fighting spirit deserved better than to be taken by filthy pirate slavers. He would help her first.

He jumped.

There was a brief surge of exhilaration, his dragon rising in him only to be thwarted by the collar. He landed with a painful shock, rolled, sprang to his feet and slashed with his arm blades at a startled pirate.

His blades glanced off a shield. Lyr hissed in frustration. The pirates must have stolen Galatean weapons, giving them the ability to form shields around their bodies as the Galatean marines did.

Lyr himself hadn't bothered raising his shields. The idea of being shot didn't bother him, and it was easier to fight without it. You had to either deal with losing the effectiveness of your edged weapons, or constantly drop and raise your shields.

Instead, he grabbed the pirate's head in both hands, his

fingers slipping on the shield, and fired full blast. The energy wave seared Lyr's hands as it rebounded from the shield, even on stun, but the pirate was momentarily blinded, and before he could recover, Lyr picked him up and threw him at the Hnee who had captured the human woman.

There was nothing quite like the element of surprise.

MERI HAD no chance to escape. The centaur ran her down easily and grabbed her arm in a bruising grip. She was dragged off her feet, stumbling along for a few steps before she lost her footing. She couldn't understand the vicious words he hurled at her in his strange language, but she could guess the gist of it. His curled lip and sneering tone suggested that what was going to happen to her once he got her onto his ship wouldn't be pretty.

Cora, stay down, stay hidden, please ...

Meri hadn't lived in cities most of her adult life without developing a few self-defense tricks, but they simply didn't work on someone who was half horse. There weren't any balls to dig her knee into. She remembered a female friend at her previous workplace telling her that the neck was as good a target and often easier to hit, but he was too tall. Meri wasn't short herself, but even standing on tiptoe she wouldn't have been able to reach the neck of a man whose torso was mounted on a horse body big enough to ride, let alone while being dragged along, struggling to keep on her feet.

So she twisted around and sank her teeth into the meaty part of his forearm.

She had never bitten another person before, but she

ground down with all her strength. He bellowed in pain and she tasted blood. (Ew! Ick!)

But to her dismay, he didn't let go. Instead he smacked her hard across the face, and as she reeled, hauled her off her feet by the strap of her clownfish purse. Meri was too dazed and scared to think of squirming out of it. Instead she tried to kick at him, but couldn't get a good angle.

Spitting angry words at her, he held her off the ground and placed a fist under her chin. She almost went cross-eyed trying to look down and see what he was doing. There were green sparks glimmering on his silver bracelet. She'd seen what those green bursts had done to that car, and panic surged through her. At least she had the satisfaction of seeing the half-moon imprint of her teeth on his skin.

She grabbed his powerfully muscled arm and tried to push it away, but he was much too strong.

And then, out of nowhere, something slammed into him.

The impact knocked him down. Meri went sprawling as he released her, and a bolt of green energy sizzled past her ear and spent itself harmlessly on the night.

The centaur thrashed around, his hooves slipping on the pavement. It was one of his own men who had landed on top of him. As Meri pushed herself up to her hands and knees, she realized that while she was engaged in her own life-and-death struggle, a new kind of chaos had broken out around her. The night had erupted in yelling and cursing and sizzling green bolts of energy. Everywhere she looked, the aliens seemed to be fighting each other.

No—a new faction had arrived on the scene, and they were attacking the others. The newcomers were also cat-people, but they were all wearing dark blue sleeveless uniforms with gold piping. Some kind of alien cops or military?

The centaur heaved off the limp body of his companion, just as someone else came out of the night. From her position on the ground, all Meri could see was a fast-moving shape, intercepting the centaur as he tried to reach for her again.

She was shocked at how fast they moved. Green blasts of light dazzled her, and then the centaur was down on the ground, still thrashing, with her ... rescuer? ... on his back. The newcomer seized the centaur's tangled chestnut hair and pulled his head back. He laid his other arm across the centaur's neck, and Meri stared in shock as a blade appeared directly out of his forearm, tearing through the skin to press against the centaur's neck.

The newcomer wasn't a cat-person like most of the others. His skin was a gleaming golden bronze that shimmered with hints of other colors. He looked like a metal statue, but was clearly made of flesh and bone. And he was about to kill another person in cold blood.

"Stop!" Meri cried.

He couldn't possibly have understood her—but he did stop, and turned to look at her. His face was beautiful, if that was indeed a word that could be applied to those sharp features, so hard and still that he might have been a gorgeous metal statue. The blade pressed against the centaur's throat. Chest heaving, the centaur stared wildly around with white-rimmed, terrified eyes. Spittle flecked his lips and beard.

"Stop," Meri said again. She pushed herself up to her knees. Her legs were shaking so badly she wasn't sure if she could stand. "I—I know he's an evil man. I know what he was going to do to me. But please don't kill him like that."

The beautiful stranger with the cold bronze-statue face stared at her. Then the blade slid back into his arm. He shook the centaur's head roughly by the hair and placed a hand against the man's temple. There was a quick green flash from his bracelet, and the centaur's eyes rolled up as he slumped to the ground. The flanks of his horse body heaved as he breathed.

"Thank you," Meri said shakily.

The stranger vaulted off the horse-man's back. He took hold of Meri and set her on her feet with strong hands so gentle, now, that it was hard to believe he'd been about to cut a man's throat a minute ago.

She stared up at him, amazed to find herself unafraid. He looked nothing at all like the others—nothing like anything she'd seen or imagined before.

Soft iridescent colors chased each other across his golden-bronze skin whenever he moved, as if his body was made of light. He was bare to the waist, and short spikes curved from his shoulders and the backs of his forearms, sharp and glistening under the parking lot's floodlights. His hair was a blue so dark it was almost black, oddly spiky, more like feathers than hair; it flowed in a loose mane past his shoulders.

Most striking of all, he had *horns*. Not big ones, just small golden horns sweeping back from his temples and curled slightly at the tips.

He looked down at her with tilted silver eyes above high cheekbones. His masculine beauty took her breath away, and somewhere inside her, something stirred—something that had been frozen to ice and walled away since Aaron's death.

"Who are you?" she asked, forgetting he wouldn't be able to understand her.

He answered, but the language he spoke was incomprehensible, musical and lilting, sounding almost like a symphony with the resonance of his deep voice. Then his head snapped up and he looked past her and brought an arm down across her back. As he did so, Meri felt tingling across her body, like a sudden rush of static electricity, raising the hairs on her arms. There was a green flash and when she looked around, she saw one of the cat-men lowering his hand with green light glimmering on his bracelet, looking furious. Her bronze-statue alien had just shielded them somehow.

The alien stranger gripped Meri's shoulder and said something to her urgently. The words might be unfamiliar, but she understood the gist of it. *Get yourself somewhere safe!* For a moment it was almost as if someone had spoken those words directly into his mind. His silver stare on her was so intent that she could believe, for an instant, that he'd somehow imprinted the words on her brain.

Meri nodded and, when he released her, she hurried behind a parked car, the only shelter nearby.

LYR HADN'T INTENDED to use telepathy on the Earth woman. He just needed her to understand, to get to safety, and then suddenly she *did* understand and was scrambling for a hiding place.

He had never heard anyone mention telepathy as a quality of ordinary, unmodified Earth humans, but he felt as if she had used it on *him* earlier. He had been about to kill the Hnee pirate. He knew Tamir would disapprove, but Lyr felt no sympathy for the pirate; he was a slaver, most likely a killer and rapist as well.

But the woman had asked him not to. He couldn't understand her language, but the meaning came through loud and clear.

And he'd stopped.

He still wasn't sure why.

Having raised his shields to protect both himself and the woman, he left them up and closed the distance between himself and the pirate who'd shot at them. The man was shielded, so any attempts to shoot him would be deflected by his shields just as his plasma burst had bounced off Lyr's. Instead, Lyr leaped and kicked him with all his considerable draconic strength. Most of the force of the blow was absorbed by the shield, but the physical impact still knocked the startled pirate to the ground. He clearly wasn't expecting it. By now, these pirates had probably had some experience with the Galatean military, and Galatean soldiers weren't normally trained to fight up close. They would stay back and shoot from a distance, as Tamir's troop of soldiers were doing, trying to keep the pirates away from their ship and herd them into a group. Shields dulled the impact of blows on both sides, so hand-to-hand combat was generally considered ineffective against a shielded target.

Lyr had no patience with that. He jumped on the pirate and stomped him, kicked him again when he tried to get up. His attacks slid off the shield—it felt like fighting someone who was covered with soap—but the pirate was too confused to know what to do. He couldn't get up because every time he tried, Lyr knocked him down again.

There was something very satisfying about being able to stomp him as much as Lyr wanted. Of course, it would be infinitely more satisfying if he were actually doing damage to the pirate's face. Lyr looked around for something that might be heavy enough to drain and eventually collapse the shield.

One of the wheeled human vehicles was nearby, this one damaged by the pirates; it was flipped on its side, with its tires sliced through by the pirates' energy weapons, smoking faintly. Lyr braced himself and lifted it with a grunt of effort. The pirate tried to shoot him in the back; Lyr felt a dim burst of heat as his shield absorbed the plasma attack.

He turned around, holding the vehicle over his head. The pirate stared at him, too shocked to keep shooting. Even Galateans weren't strong enough to hold a couple tons of metal over their heads. But they weren't dragons. No one was as strong as a dragon in his prime.

Lyr grinned savagely. His arms ached from the strain, but it was worth it for the look on the pirate's face as Lyr swung his arms over and down, and brought the vehicle down on top of the pirate as hard as he could. The pirate's shield managed to absorb enough of the impact to keep him from being splattered, but it shimmered and then popped like a soap bubble as the vehicle's metal body bent around the shield's former span.

Pinned and hurting a lot, but not dead, the pirate struggled feebly. Lyr stunned him in the face with a blast from his cuffs. At this close range, there might be brain damage. Good.

"*Lyr!*" Tamir's voice spoke into his ear through their communication link via the cuffs. "*If you're done playing with your prey, we're pinned down over here. We could use an assist from the rear.*"

"I'm not *playing*," Lyr grumbled. "I've taken out two by myself. How are *you* doing?"

"*Feeling glad we brought you along.*"

Tamir's voice was light, teasing. Lyr locked down his feelings. He was not *enjoying* this. Of course not. It didn't remind him at all of training exercises long ago, of fighting side by side with Tamir and with his sept-siblings—

They're all gone now. And Tamir is one of the enemy who enslaved you. Don't forget that.

He fired at the group of pirates who'd pinned down Tamir's team, then ducked behind one of the human vehicles. He only realized as he dropped into a crouch that it was the same one the human woman had taken shelter behind. She stared at him, wide-eyed, and Lyr had a strange urge to offer her some words of comfort, perhaps tell her things were going to be okay. Instead he settled for giving her shoulder a rough pat before he leaned around the end of the vehicle and fired at the pirates again.

Strangely enough, they didn't shoot back. Instead they started falling back, not to their ship, but in the opposite direction, running for the open grassland beside the road. Some were dragging human captives with them; others just ran.

As if they expected something extremely bad to happen in the middle of the parking lot ...

"Tamir!" Lyr shouted, over the radio and across the space between them. "Get out of there!"

Tamir looked up, cursed, and began snapping orders at his team.

Lyr had a feeling what might be coming. He curled his body around the human woman, arms wrapped loosely around her, and raised his personal shield at full strength, extending it to cover them both.

Tentatively, he felt her arms reaching back, a light and cautious touch, almost a hug.

He hadn't been hugged since—

A beam of searing light, impossibly huge and bright, stabbed out of the sky, hit the Earth structure Tamir and his marines had been using for cover, and instantaneously turned it into a fireball. Lyr tightened his grip on the woman as sparks and debris rained around them.

The light winked out an instant later, leaving orange and yellow afterimages blazoned across Lyr's retinas. The pavement was buckled and bubbling where the laser had raked across it.

That was a ship-to-surface gun, one of the big ones. Their personal shields wouldn't have stood a chance. If any of Tamir's men had been caught in that, there wouldn't be enough left of them to put in a very small box.

Lyr uncurled from his protective clench around the woman. Immediately she tried to pop up and look out. "No!" he snapped, jerking her down.

She said something in her language, and he realized he'd clamped a hand on her arm and quickly let go.

"Just stay here, all right?" He stabbed a finger down at the pavement. "Hide."

Her stare was uncomprehending, and she tried to look around the vehicle again, perhaps looking for the companions she'd been protecting. Before she could put up more of a fight about it, another beam stabbed out of the sky and struck Tamir's ship. The small ship's shields shimmered into visibility for a moment, an opalescent gleam turning a brilliant, shivering violet before the beam winked out again. The woman gasped and clutched at Lyr.

Can't take another of those, Lyr thought. *And if that ship goes, we're stuck here and pinned down, at least 'til the cruiser gets around to sending someone to pick us up.*

He gently detached the woman's grip. "They're not

shooting at you, understand? Stay here and you'll be safe." As safe as anyone could be in this mess.

She shook her head and grabbed at him. Somehow she seemed to have latched onto *him* for safety. He could have laughed at that, but instead he jerked away his arm from her attempt to touch him, suddenly hating the gentleness of her touch, the trusting way she looked at him.

Another eye-searing beam stabbed from the sky and raked across Tamir's ship. The shield failed; the ship's skin split and peeled, and the engines went up with a *whoomp!* that shook the ground. The beam winked out again, leaving Lyr's vision dazzled with afterimages and the troop transport a smoking wreck.

So much for their ride home.

This time, he was able to trace the angle of the beam to see what was shooting at them. Like the smaller ships, the pirate mothership was running dark; little of it could be seen except for a great black shape blotting the stars. But it was big. Not as huge as the Galateans' orbital battle cruiser, but built along similar lines. There could be an entire complement of chaser-class ships in its spacious cargo bay.

They couldn't fight a ship that size, even with backup.

Well ... most of them couldn't. He might be able to.

"Stay here!" he ordered the woman, and backed it up with a mental command this time. She seemed to understand, or at least she didn't try to follow him as he bolted away from the vehicle, staying low as he darted toward the last place he'd seen Tamir and the rest of their squad.

He found that Tamir had rounded up most of them under some trees that provided limited shelter from the air —not that anything would help if one of those beams hit them. Tamir's fur was dirty and singed, but he didn't appear to be hurt. He was crouched beside a badly injured soldier, tending the other's wounds. The smell of scorched fur and flesh was strong in the air.

When Lyr dropped into a crouch beside him, Tamir looked up quickly and his face relaxed in relief. "You all right?" he asked, clapping a hand on Lyr's arm.

Lyr didn't bother dignifying that with a response. "Where's our backup? Are they coming to get us or not?"

Tamir wouldn't meet his eyes. "They're staying concealed behind the moon. They'll take on the pirate ship once it breaks orbit—"

"But they're perfectly willing to let us get slaughtered down here."

Tamir's lip curled, exposing his fangs. "Our orders are to avoid discovery. That's more important than—"

"What the hell do they think is happening down here?" Lyr stabbed a finger above them, pointing at the vast bulk of the pirate mothership. "Unless these humans are blind *and* stupid, that egg has already hatched."

"Think about it," Tamir shot back. "Can you imagine the consequences of a full-scale aerial battle right over a populated area? There'll be mass casualties."

"So we cower like frightened hatchlings and let them pick us off?"

Tamir shook his shaggy head. "They're not really trying. I think they're simply covering the others' escape."

Lyr looked out. Tamir was right; rather than pressing their attack, the pirates on the ground were retreating to the grassy verge of the road, along with their handful of captives.

Tamir hissed through his teeth and checked the charge on his cuffs. "We might be able to get the rest of the prisoners back before the ship can pick them up. Selvyn, Zain." He pointed to two of his men. "I want you to circle around, get behind them. If we can flank them, trap them between us—"

"It's not going to matter," Lyr interrupted.

He felt the wobble first of all in his inner ear, a sense of dizzy unease as if gravity had stopped working properly. The group of pirates at the road began to rise into the air, floating, tumbling. So did every nearby human and everything small and light that wasn't tied down.

Tamir cursed. "They're not landing at all, they're using a tractor beam!"

Set on low power, the beam wasn't moving the cars or anything else heavy (it would probably have crushed the humans had that been the case). But all the nearby humans, anyone who hadn't managed to hang onto something, were dragged up toward the ship's slowly opening cargo door. Lyr was incensed to see the woman he'd rescued among them, looking terrified and flailing at the air. He hadn't saved her just so the pirates could get their hands on her again!

Without thinking, he started to lunge forward. Tamir caught his arm, heedless of the deadly spikes that could extend with a stray thought. "What are you going to do?" Tamir demanded. "One of you against all of them? What's that going to accomplish?"

Lyr turned on him. "Then help me," he snarled. "You know I could do it." He touched a finger to the cold metal of his collar. "Without this, I could do it. You've seen what I'm capable of, as a dragon."

"What am I supposed to do about that?"

"I know you have the controller with you! Unlock my collar! Or at least turn off its energy-damper. Let me shift!"

Tamir didn't move.

"Unlock it, damn you! I can take them."

Tamir shook his head slowly. "Is it them you want to kill?" he asked softly. "Or yourself?"

Lyr cursed at him, and then tore away from him and ran into the beam. Behind him he heard Tamir shout an order at his men, followed by the pounding of boots on pavement.

He felt the beam catch him, the ground fall away beneath his feet. It was unexpectedly disconcerting, tumbling through the air with no control over it, no sense of up and down. Nothing at all like flying.

"You son of a bitch," Tamir's voice yelled at him.

Lyr looked down. Tamir seemed to be having even more of a problem than Lyr at getting himself oriented in midair. Under other circumstances it would have been hilarious watching the Galatean soldier tumbling with all his limbs flailing, but it only reminded Lyr how high up they were. If they fell from this distance, they'd be killed.

And the cargo doors above them were closing. They weren't going to make it.

"Your cuffs!" Tamir shouted up at him. "Use them to magnetize yourself to the hull—"

Anything else he was saying was lost in the clang of the doors closing, and suddenly there was no more lift.

With the speed of thought, Lyr ordered his cuffs to magnetize themselves. He hadn't even known they could do that, but it worked. He slammed into the nearest part of the hull, not the cargo bay but an external tank of some kind. He looked down the side of the ship to see that Tamir had not only managed to do the same, but had also grabbed onto an access ladder meant for working on the outside of the ship.

Show-off.

The ship vibrated against him, and wind screamed across him, tugging at his hair.

"They're headed for space," Tamir called, crawling up the ladder toward the access hatch. "Get over here, you idiot."

"Turn off my collar! If I can shift, it won't be a problem. I can survive in deep space just fine as a dragon."

Tamir just shook his head.

Cursing furiously, Lyr made his way across the tank, with only the tenuous grip of the magnetic cuffs to stop him from tumbling into the void below. Streamers of clouds trailed across the ship's exterior. The air was growing noticeably colder. Lyr raised his personal shield again, and noticed the opalescent gleam around Tamir that meant the Galatean had done likewise.

By the time Lyr reached him, Tamir was cutting his way through the hatch with a controlled beam from the cuffs. "Basic boarding training," he said over his shoulder. "I've never done it on a ship that was actually flying before." He started to look down and then wrenched his gaze away; they were high in the air now, roads and towns dwindling to a hair-fine web of light against the world's dark nightside. "Give me a hand with this. If we're still out here when our ship starts firing on them, we're twelve kinds of screwed."

Lyr clung to the ladder beside him and started cutting the other side of the hatch. "You didn't have to be here, so shut up and quit complaining."

"It's *your* recklessness that got us into this."

"There is no *us*!" Lyr snapped.

The hatch gave way. They tumbled into the small airlock. Behind them, the ship's automatic vacuum-sealing system diverted a part of its shields to seal the leak; it glimmered brightly against the star-studded darkness outside the ship.

"They'll know they have a breach," Lyr said. "We'll have company in a minute. Do you have a plan for *that*?"

The inner airlock wasn't locked; it slid open on a dark hallway. "Run?" Tamir suggested.

"A prince of the Well of Stars does not—"

Tamir grabbed him by the arm and hauled him out of the airlock. "That's an *order*, you stubborn ass. Besides, we have to find the prisoners."

FOUR

MERI LANDED in a bruised heap on a metal floor. There was a tremendous clang as the doors slammed shut.

She was in a large, echoing space, an enclosed hangar with girders overhead. There was an entire row of sleek, teardrop-shaped ships parked side by side, as well as a dozen or so people picking themselves up off the deck, pirates mixed with terrified, crying, and in some cases unconscious humans.

As she huddled on the deck, clinging to her clownfish purse because it was the only thing she had to hold onto, Meri reassured herself that Cora and Toni were still down there in the parking lot, hopefully okay.

She had to believe that.

It was easier than thinking about where *she* was.

At least the terrifying flight through the air was over. She still didn't know what had happened, though advanced alien technology was obviously involved. It had felt like being sucked up by an enormous vacuum cleaner. Gravity had restored itself again as soon as she was through the big metal doors, and she'd fallen several feet to the deck.

As the initial panic began to pass, leaving her able to think sensibly again, she started to pat herself down for anything worse than bruises. But she didn't get a chance. Rough hands seized her, dragging her to her feet.

She and the other captives were marched out of the big open space and down a hallway with scarred, filthy metal walls. So far this place was living up to every space pirate cliché in those ridiculous science fiction movies Cora used to liking watching. Meri wasn't at all a science fiction person, herself. Oh, she'd watched *Star Wars* when she was a kid, like everyone did. But she always preferred to keep her feet on the ground. She liked reading romances about bosses and their secretaries, and mysteries about little old lady sleuths, nothing with aliens or superheroes or wizards. She didn't even like those werewolf books that were so popular now.

It seemed completely unfair that she, of all people, had just found out that spaceships were real and was now being kidnapped by one of them.

I can't believe those stupid supermarket tabloids with their abducted-by-aliens stories were right!

The captives were dragged into a room with long worktables, cabinets, and large pieces of equipment bolted to the floor. The place looked sort of like a machine shop, although Meri didn't recognize a single thing she saw around her except some coils of cable.

Before she had a chance to do more than glance around, her captor flung her through an open door into a tiny closet-like room. The door slammed shut and Meri was about to start yelling for someone to let her out when a weird pink powder, like a cloud of talcum powder, poured down from the ceiling. She accidentally inhaled some of it and started coughing. It didn't really have a taste or a smell. As she tried to stop coughing long enough to hold her breath, more of it settled on her clothes and shoulders and hair, and then fans kicked on suddenly, whipping it up into a whirlwind around her. Just as suddenly, the blowing turned to suction and it was all sucked back up. The door opened and Meri was dragged out, still coughing, as two more captives were thrown in. She guessed she'd just gone through some kind of alien de-lousing process.

Wheezing and giving off clouds of pink powder whenever she moved, she was hauled to one of the workbenches, where another pirate picked up a gun-shaped thing off the bench. Meri sucked in her breath, inhaled more pink powder, and was coughing too hard to put up much of a fight as something cold was jammed behind her ear. There was a hissing noise, and a sharp pain spiked through her skull.

She was handed off to another pirate and a new captive dragged to take her place. It was all done with rough, fast efficiency. They tried to take the clownfish purse away from her, but Meri kicked one and bit another, and possibly at that point they decided it was some sort of strange pet and let her keep it. She got a series of bruising shots in her arm and then she was dragged out of the room, stumbling along as she tried to keep up with the longer legs of the pirate who had her arm in his callused fist.

I'm not supposed to be here! she thought dismally. *I thought I wanted to go new places and see new things, but I changed my mind! I just want to move to Kansas City with Cora and Dave, and settle down in the suburbs, and maybe go out to a jazz club every now and then ...*

Instead, she was flung through another door into a new room. She got a brief impression of a whole bunch of people packed into a small space, standing around or slumped hopelessly on the floor. Several of them stood up or looked around when she and the new captives were dumped among them. Then the door slammed shut and they were left alone.

Meri sat up slowly, shivering and clutching the purse to her chest. She still shed pink powder every time she moved, and her skull throbbed in time with her heartbeat.

The nearest person to her was a delicate alien woman with green skin, long fingers, and huge violet eyes. She reached a hand toward Meri and said something in a light, musical voice. At the same time, Meri thought she heard a faint shirring of whispers, just below the edge of hearing. They seemed to echo painfully through her head and stopped when the woman stopped talking, but started up again immediately when two other alien captives near her, a furry man and a woman with purple skin and pointed ears, began talking quietly between themselves.

"I'm okay," Meri said shakily, mostly to herself. "I'm okay." She brushed at her clothes, trying to get the powder off. The green woman smiled and brushed at some of it for her, saying something that sounded sympathetic. This time the echoes beneath the speech were frustratingly familiar, as if she could almost understand them, but not quite. The pain in her head spiked, and Meri grabbed behind her ear, moaning. Her fingers found a hot, painful nub. There was something under her skin. That gun-shaped thing had implanted something in her.

"What did they do to me?" she asked. "Where are they taking us?"

The woman shook her head. She had silver hair that whispered over her shoulders, so light and fine it almost seemed to float, and a silver collar around her neck. She touched behind her own ear, then touched her lips and reached toward Meri.

Meri jerked back as the woman's dry, cold fingertips brushed across her lips. "I don't understand," she said helplessly, and looked around.

The room was no bigger than her old apartment in Ohio, and there were, she guessed, probably about fifty people crammed into it. Most of them, including the green woman, wore loose gray coveralls, and most of them also had silver collars like the green lady, which Meri was starting to get a sinking feeling were more than just a fashion accessory. There was nothing to sit or lie on, just the bare floor. The room was lit by white light strips in welded metal cages, resembling fluorescent lights but without the characteristic flicker.

Meri took a deep breath that threatened to set her coughing again and turned toward the other Earth captives who had been thrown in with her. "I'm a nurse," she said. Her voice came out shaky and weak. She cleared her throat and tried again. "Is anyone hurt? Can I help?"

"I can't wake up my wife." The speaker was a man about ten years older than Meri, with silver streaks in his hair and a cheap houndstooth sport jacket over his soft gut. "They shot her with something, and I think she hit her head when she fell."

Meri didn't try to stand up—her legs still felt too shaky to hold her. Instead she scooted on her butt over to him. There were five other human captives besides herself, two more unconscious women besides the one with the attentive husband and one woman who didn't seem to have been knocked out, but was hysterical and crying. To Meri's vast relief, Cora and the baby were not among them. She could only hope Cora was still where Meri had last seen her, safe in the car.

"See if you can calm her down," Meri told the man. One thing she'd learned about dealing with crises as a nurse was that giving people things to do helped keep them steady. When he hesitated, she patted his arm. "I've got your wife. What's her name?"

"Pam." His voice wobbled. He cleared his throat. "Pam Sears. I'm Frank. We've been married thirty-two years and I don't know what I'd do without—"

"Listen to me, Frank." She gripped his arm firmly. "She's going to be fine. Now you help me and see if you can get the young lady settled down, and I'll have a look at her, okay?"

To her relief, it seemed that she hadn't lied to him. Pam and the other unconscious captives really did seem to be basically unhurt. Their color and respiration was decent. Whatever the aliens had done to them, it didn't appear to have injured them, and one of the women was already stirring weakly, looking like she might be about to come around. Meri loosened their clothing and rolled them onto their sides in the recovery position. It was all she could really do.

The deck shuddered suddenly and the lights flickered. Some of the captives cried out, and the hysterical woman, who had just been starting to calm down with Frank's arm around her, burst into loud sobs again.

"What's happening?" Frank asked Meri.

How should I know? she wanted to scream. *This is all just as strange to me as it is to you!* But she couldn't admit that when she was trying to keep people calm. "It might be someone coming to rescue us," she suggested.

Maybe it was, she thought wistfully. Maybe her beautiful bronze-statue rescuer was here. He seemed like the kind of person who wouldn't be stopped by a few pirates.

LYR AND TAMIR ran into the first defenders on the metal ladder leading up the maintenance access tubes to the next level of the ship. There were two pirates, both with their shields up and weapons armed. Lyr kicked the first into the second, then grabbed him and jumped down to the nearest landing, where he slammed him repeatedly headfirst into the decking until his shields failed, then a few more times for good measure, and snapped his neck. *Honorless, murdering bastard.*

There was a startled yell as the other pirate lost his balance fighting with Tamir and plunged down the access tube. Far below them, his shields flickered. He wouldn't have been killed in the fall, but it would take him a while to climb back up.

Tamir glanced at the body of the pirate Lyr had killed. "Do you think you could do less of that and more capturing?"

"These people are trying to kill us. We don't have time for squeamishness—"

"I was thinking interrogation. We could search this whole place by brute force, or we could simply ask one of them where the prisoners are."

"Ah." Lyr looked down at the dead pirate at his feet. He considered taking the man's cuffs for spares, but there was no point; they were completely discharged.

"You really have changed," Tamir said quietly. Lyr looked up to see Tamir looking down at him from higher on the ladder, wearing a hard-to-read expression. In the dim light of the maintenance tube, Tamir's eyes were reflective as a cat's. "You never used to be like this."

"Maybe I used to believe in things I don't believe in now."

"Like what? Honor? Compassion?"

Lyr stood in a quick, fluid motion. "I still have honor. Honor is *all* I have."

He meant to say more, the anger in him flaring beneath his self-control, but he was interrupted when the ship shuddered around them. The lights flickered.

"And that'll be *our* ship, right on cue, shooting at us." Tamir hooked an arm around the ladder to avoid falling as the ship continued to shake. "We can probably steal a transport to escape with the prisoners if there aren't too many of them. Now we just have to figure out where on this ship they are."

"I ... think I might know a way," Lyr began reluctantly.

Tamir was no idiot. "Are you talking about telepathy? But you need someone whose mind you're familiar with to connect from a distance, don't you?"

Having known him since childhood, Tamir had a better idea of how Lyr's abilities worked than, probably, anyone else in the Empire. What Tamir didn't know was that using telepathy right now was like tearing the scab off a wound that had just stopped pouring blood.

But he didn't have a choice. They could wander around in the pirate ship for hours, and all the while the ship would be engaged in combat with a Galatean warship and probably preparing to jump out of the system.

As if to underscore the urgency, the ship shuddered violently again.

"I connected with one of the captives on the planet's

surface," Lyr admitted. "I think I might be able to find her mind again, if she isn't too far away."

"Do it, then." Tamir glanced down the shaft. "They'll have reinforcements here soon. We don't have much time."

Lyr closed his eyes. On the planet, it had happened spontaneously, in the heat of the moment; it was much harder to make himself do it with time to think about it beforehand. Opening up to let someone else into his mind *hurt*. He couldn't even tell if the pain was emotional or physical. He'd felt his septmates die, felt them ripped away from him forever, and had temporarily lost himself in a madness born of grief and despair. Now he felt himself teetering on the edge of that abyss once again. He felt, again, the warm sparks of Rook's and Rei's minds flaring and dying in his awareness, felt the way his dragon had risen inside him to take over and save him from a grief so terrible he thought he would die from it—

"Lyr." Tamir's voice was low and near, his hand warm on Lyr's arm. Grounding him. Pulling him back.

And Lyr didn't *want* it. He yanked his arm away. He was alone, always alone. If he stayed open like this, the next thing would be feeling Tamir in his mind again, and with that sense of connection would come all the memories of those early years with his sept-siblings, when they were all together and alive—

No. *No*. He couldn't survive the loss a second time.

Lyr snarled wordlessly at Tamir, who pulled back, his face sympathetic. But his touch had helped pull Lyr out of his own head, and when he reached out with his mind this time, his barriers were firmly in place. He groped for the warm touch of the woman's alien mind.

When he used to touch his septmates' minds, werewolf Rei had been moonlight and snow and fleet-running paws;

winged Rook was the rustle of feathers and the smell of high mountain air; Skara was the sharp smell of soldered circuit boards and the flicker of lightning in a storm. When he reached for the woman, he thought of candlelight, and the lightly spicy-sweet smell of her skin, and the way that it felt to wrap up in a warm knitted fabric blanket.

And he found her.

AS THE SHIP SHUDDERED AGAIN, the door to the captives' holding area burst open and two pirates stormed inside. One was a cat-man with leopard spots on his tawny fur. The other was the centaur. He was limping and looked like he had the world's worst headache; the lights in the room made him squint. He also looked deeply pissed. Meri found herself wishing that she had let her beautiful bronze savior kill him, and then felt sick at the thought.

Both of the pirates were wielding short baton-shaped sticks, and the centaur carried something else, a small box like a garage-door opener.

One of the captives, a slight man with blue skin and claws, lunged at the pirates. The leopard-spotted one jammed the stick into his attacker's chest. There was an audible crackle, and the man went down with a cry. He struggled to his knees, but the centaur turned and pressed a button on the gray remote-control thing in his hand.

The blue-skinned man screamed. His hands went to the collar at his throat, tearing at it as if he could rip it off, but he couldn't get a grip. He fell to the floor and began to convulse.

Meri couldn't help herself. She was a nurse; she had to do something. She flung herself forward, trying to reach the writhing man on the floor, but she was driven back by the leopard-man. His baton smacked into her arm.

It felt like being electrocuted. Her arm muscles knotted up violently, and a scream tore from her throat. Clutching her arm, she fell to the floor and crawled blindly away until her shoulder slammed into the wall, where she huddled as the pain faded until she could think again. She flexed her hand carefully. It tingled, but didn't seem to be damaged.

And then a voice said clearly, **Can you hear me?**

Meri jerked violently, banging her tingling elbow against the wall.

Sorry! the voice said.

"Who," she whispered, looking around wildly. It wasn't words, not really. It was something happening entirely within her head, unfolding like the memory of a conversation, where the specific words didn't matter so much as the meaning.

I'm speaking to you inside your mind. Don't worry, I can't read your mind,* the unseen voice added, which only panicked her more, because she'd just been thinking that. *I can only feel your emotions. I can tell that you're frightened.

"How—what—"

The leopard-man snarled something incomprehensible and jabbed at her with his pain stick. A sharp burst of agony made her cry out again.

Don't speak aloud. She sensed regret for her pain in the stranger's ... mental? ... voice, and that was what made her decide that perhaps she could trust him. And it *was* a him. She could tell that much, though she wasn't quite sure how. **If you want to talk to me, focus on the words inside your head. I'll understand their meaning if they're close to the surface.**

Like this? She closed her eyes, and found herself

moving her jaw and tongue with her lips closed, forming the shape of the words even though no sound emerged. **Can you hear me?**

I can! Nicely done. Most people don't get it on the first try.

As oddly pleasing as it was to be praised by someone who was only a voice in her head, there was just one thing she really wanted. **Please get me out of here,** Meri thought at him, silently shaping the words with great care. **Please, help me. Can you help?**

I will. This came with a sense of determination and a kind of ... she could only think of it as supportive warmth, like the mental equivalent of a hand on her shoulder, holding her steady.

Who* are *you?

You met me earlier.

And with that, a picture came into her head, her silver-eyed friend from the planet with his hands on her shoulders.

Oh, it's you!

Her body and emotions both betrayed her with a sudden flood of delighted warmth. Surely he had to have felt that through whatever link connected them. Meri felt her cheeks grow hot, especially when she caught a flash of his answering reaction, warmth and a startled, reciprocal delight that was far more endearing than his cool, marble-statue beauty.

I meant to say, thank you for helping me earlier. It was getting easier to talk to him this way; she didn't have to concentrate quite so hard at forming the words without opening her mouth.

For all the good it did. Disgust, directed at himself.

It's not your fault. Er ... where are you now?

The answer was a picture: Silver-Eyes crouching in some kind of stairwell. She could dimly make out scarred, bare metal behind him. She had a vague sense of someone else with him, but couldn't see the other person clearly.

Are you on this ship with us?

Affirmation answered her, not quite in words, and then: *I need to know where you are.*

I don't know. We were in some kind of warehouse-like place, and then there was a hallway—

Don't describe it in words. Give me pictures. Here's where I am.

What followed was a dizzying three-dimensional series of images, not just flat pictures but a visceral sense of depth and motion, like moving around in a video game. She saw a door in the side of the ship, saw and felt Silver-Eyes catch hold of the ship itself, and had a general sense that he'd entered the ship below and to the side of that door.

She had been so disoriented when she was first brought on board that it was hard to visualize the turns they'd taken, but she tried to send him her memories of the hallway, the processing room where they'd deloused her, and the direction they'd taken her to get to the cell where she was now.

It was hard to concentrate. The deck kept shuddering under her, and she thought she could smell something burning, which seemed like a deeply bad thing on a spaceship. Although she couldn't understand what the pirates were saying, they seemed agitated and angry. The leopard man kicked some people out of the way and grabbed hold of a frightened-looking young woman, little more than a teenager. She had cat ears and fur, like him. He dragged her to the door. Meri leaned forward, her hands curling into fists.

*I think they're doing something. They're taking some

*people out of here. Should I—?**

No! You can't fight them. You'll just get yourself hurt.

But where are they taking them? Are they going to kill them?

Probably not yet. They might want hostages, someone they can take up to the bridge and threaten to kill if my ship doesn't stop firing on them.

Your ship? Where do you come from?

Hesitation. **It's a military ship trying to stop people like them.**

She used his voice as a lifeline to keep herself calm. Now the centaur had hold of the fragile-looking woman with green skin, hauling her up by a punishing grip on her arm. The woman cried out in pain and fear. It was clear that he was hurting her and that she didn't want to go wherever he was taking her.

There are a lot more of us than them. Meri rose to her knees. **If we all attack at once—**

No! She could feel his frustration and dismay. **They have weapons and shields, and you don't! If you make trouble, they could close the doors and pump all the air out of the room, or eject you into space. I know where you are now; at least I have a general idea. Stay there! We're going to get you out.**

The green woman cried out again in pain. The centaur had her frail-looking arm bent double behind her back as he forced her toward the door; it looked as if he might break it.

I'm sorry. I can't just sit here while they do whatever they're going to do to these people.

Dammit! Stop! Silver-Eyes ordered.

Meri ignored him and struggled to her feet. She didn't know what she was going to do, just that she had to do something.

FIVE

"I KNOW WHERE THEY ARE," Lyr declared, scrambling up the access ladder. "And they're about to get themselves killed."

As he and Tamir ran down the hallway, he was still dimly aware of what was going on with the human woman, dividing his attention between her and his actual surroundings. She seemed to be tensing herself to leap onto the Hnee pirate—*Oh, not that guy again,* Lyr thought in disgust.

"Where are we going?" Tamir demanded, and Lyr remembered that Tamir didn't have the same internal map.

"They're on this level, in an interior module of the ship."

"Makes sense. That way if anyone escapes, it'll be harder for them to get to—" Tamir halted in his tracks. "Lyr. Wait."

"What?" Lyr turned back. "What are you doing?"

Tamir pressed a hand to the bulkhead. "The engines. Feel that?"

Lyr took his attention off his connection to the human woman for a moment. The tone of the engines had been changing, but the artificial gravity kept him and Tamir glued to the deck, so they wouldn't have felt it much if the ship was banking and turning in evasive maneuvers. But now the vibration had risen to a level that could mean only one thing.

Tamir was the one who voiced it. "They're preparing to jump. Your collar—" He stopped.

The collar was set to detonate if it lost its connection to the ship it was linked to. That way war-slaves could be trusted to go on raiding parties and even pilot their own jump-capable ships, knowing they couldn't jump to freedom without killing themselves.

If the pirate ship jumped—

Lyr's sudden surge of raw terror surprised him. He hadn't thought he still cared whether he lived or died. Pure animal instinct, he thought; the dragon inside him didn't want to die, even if Lyr himself did.

And maybe that Earth woman, with her courage and her curious, eager mind, had something to do with it too—but he drew away from that thought, not wanting to examine what it implied.

Tamir, meanwhile, didn't hesitate. "Hold still." With no more warning, he moved into Lyr's space and placed a hand at the back of Lyr's neck.

Lyr jerked his head back. Tamir had touched him more today than he'd been touched in the last six months. He hated it.

"Hold *still!*" Tamir snapped. He took something out of a belt pouch; Lyr recognized it, in the glance he got, as the controller to his collar. Loathing flooded him. With that little device, he'd been hurt, abused, punished; with that, he'd been brought to his knees.

Tamir had never used the collar to hurt him, but it still took all his self-control to let Tamir touch the device to his collar. He felt the moment when it went dead, the tiny leads disconnecting from his neck. Abruptly the collar felt looser, sliding freely over his skin.

Tamir's hand, on the back of his neck, gave a spasmodic jerk. It was already illegal, unlocking a collar without authorization. Taking it off would probably get him court-martialed.

But there was only the slightest hesitation. Without speaking, he did something else with the controller. The collar clicked and came apart.

Lyr jerked away from Tamir, wrenching the Galatean's grip off him. As the collar slipped off his neck, he grabbed the hated thing and flung it as far from him as it would go. It clattered somewhere in the darkness of the vents.

They stood for a moment looking at each other, both breathing heavily. Inside Lyr's chest, a spark of heat grew, rising up in rage. He was no longer limited, no longer contained. Every insult that had been done to him during his long captivity among the Galateans could now be avenged. He could rip open the side of the ship with his claws and expose the people inside to raw vacuum. He could shred the engines and the tanks that held water and air. He could leave this ship a derelict husk floating in space.

Hell itself knew nothing so terrible as an enraged dragon.

A soft glimmer flickered across Tamir's body as he powered up his shields. He half-raised one of his hands in what Lyr recognized was a defensive position, preparing to fire if necessary.

Lyr felt his lips curl into something that was not quite a smile. "Afraid?"

"I'm not your enemy," Tamir said softly. "Your enemy is in there."

"Oh, I'll kill them, don't doubt that," Lyr promised. "And after that—"

He stopped and spun around, alerted by movement in the corner of his eye and by Tamir's sudden reaction. A vivid green plasma bolt seared the air in the corridor and splintered on Lyr's shields as he flung them up. A split second later and it would have caught him in the back.

He was a fool, allowing himself to be distracted by emotion. There were two pirates at the end of the corridor, who had just ducked out of sight behind a half-open door. Lyr's grin widened, showing teeth. He felt the tingling rush of the change sweeping over him, a wave of heat and power.

The dragon roared forth from his deceptively human-looking skin, its serpentine mass uncoiling into the corridor as Lyr gloried in the feeling of the two halves of himself clicking into place, making him whole. There were other shifters in the galaxy, including some Galateans, but all of them were constrained by the physical mass of their human body. No others could do *this*. His people theorized that their dragon side represented a fourth-dimensional rotation, bringing the dragon half into the regular universe and taking everything he'd had on him, from clothes to boots to anything in his pockets, into the place it had come from. The only things that couldn't be so easily banished were metal. The implants under his skin hurt sharply and then the pain faded as his body adapted around them. His cuffs stretched to accommodate his much larger wrists, the nanite-enhanced metal designed to be one-size-fits-all. A handful of metal buttons and fasteners clattered to the floor.

He was dimly aware of Tamir dodging backward to get out of the way. The pirates, who had expected to find two human-sized intruders, instead found themselves in a corridor full to the ceiling with a furious dragon.

They fell back in horror as the enraged dragon fell on them, but it was too late. They didn't even have time to get a shot off. He was rage made flesh, tearing them with his claws, ignoring Tamir yelling something at him from behind.

He felt, in some distant part of his mind not consumed with bloodlust, as the Earth woman's fear and anger sharpened to a sudden point of decisiveness. She had chosen to attack the pirates.

MERI KNEW she didn't stand a chance. She also knew that nothing could make her stand here and just watch as the one alien among the captives who had been kind to her was dragged away by these awful people, probably to have something horrible done to her. Silver-Eyes had said they needed hostages, but what if the people on his ship didn't agree to the pirates' demands? Would they simply execute her? Or were they taking her somewhere else to be tortured, raped, murdered?

She got to her feet without being noticed among the milling, anxious prisoners. Meri gripped the heavy clownfish purse by its strap, and she lunged forward, swinging it with all her might at the centaur's arm.

It was surprise, probably, more than anything else, that made him drop his prisoner. The green lady scrambled away on hands and knees, and the centaur lashed out with a hoof, kicking Meri and knocking her to the floor.

She hit hard and tried to roll away. On her hands and knees, she looked up to see the centaur pointing his loosely closed fist at her, with the cuff glittering on his wrist.

This was what came before one of those green energy blasts. There was nowhere to go, Meri realized, and the centaur clearly knew it. His bearded face split in a sadistic grin.

And then everything jerked violently sideways.

A tremendous shockwave bucked the deck just as the entire world seemed to ripple. There was a wrenching instant when there seemed to be no up or down, and then everything snapped back like a rubber band and Meri tumbled bruisingly against the wall, just as the lights went out, plunging her into total darkness. All around her, people were screaming. The air smelled like smoke, and there was noise—a deep groaning in the ship underfoot, as if it was trying to tear itself apart.

THE ENTIRE SHIP JOLTED VIOLENTLY, the deck bucking under Lyr's bloody claws, just as the ship began to jump. The shockwave carried them into the disorienting ripple effect of hyperspace.

A normal jump was a moment of mind-twisting timelessness, in which the ship hung suspended outside the regular universe. But this time, rather than the usual seamless transition, the deck heaved violently underfoot as they snapped back to normal space. A wave of disorientation and dizziness washed through him.

"That was a direct hit right before we went into hyperspace," Tamir gasped, stumbling into the wall. The green light of the shield around him had died. He slapped one of his cuffs with his palm. "I don't think we completed the jump. Are your cuffs working? Some kind of energy pulse—"

The lights went out, leaving them in pitch darkness filled with the hellish screaming of tortured metal. Dropping out in mid-jump was tremendously stressful on a ship. The sudden stresses were ripping the ship's frame apart.

Lyr sank his claws into the metal of the floor. Vacuum wouldn't hurt him in his dragon form, but it would kill Tamir. He focused on his connection to the cuffs. They weren't completely dead; he could feel them trying to come back online, and focused on making a little shield-bubble to trap some air.

The corridor bucked underfoot again, and then it split open, cracking like an egg and exposing them to the cold vacuum of space.

Lyr lost his grip on the floor and tumbled out of the hole in the side of the ship along with anything that wasn't nailed down. His ears popped painfully as he fell into absolute chaos. There was no up and down in space, and the entire world, the entire universe seemed to consist of nothing but pieces of ship, battering him from all sides. He folded his wings around him. Space itself might not hurt him, but being a dragon wouldn't save him if he got himself pulped by a wayward fuel tank.

Tamir, though—

Lyr dived toward Tamir's tumbling ragdoll-shape and caught him in his claws. He extended the small shield-bubble to cover Tamir, who was limp in his claws. At the moment he couldn't even tell if Tamir was alive or if he'd just risked his life to rescue a corpse. Blood drifted in droplets in the vacuum inside the shield that surrounded Tamir, holding the tiny amount of air that Lyr's shields had managed to catch.

But it wouldn't matter how much air Tamir had or how badly he was hurt if they didn't get out of here before they were crushed to pulp. Lyr kicked off a section of the ship's bulkhead, folding his wings to glide through the debris. Momentum wasn't going to get him as far as he needed, but his people had a natural adaptation for flight in deep space: gas sacs in their wings, capable of propelling them in small bursts. When he spread his wings and deployed them, slim jets trailed from his wingtips like smoky contrails as the warm vapor froze in the cold.

He used the gas in small puffs and rebounded from one chunk of debris to the next, gliding silently through the vacuum, out of the death zone. Once he was clear of the drifting junk cloud, he steered in a circle and braked with tightly controlled bursts from his jets to look back at the damaged ship.

From here, the damage was bad, but not quite as devastating as it had seemed from the middle of it. The ship drifted dead in space, surrounded by a floating cloud of its own debris. The outer modules had cracked off and split open, and the engines were a blackened wreck. However, most of the ship's core seemed to be intact, including the passenger module.

He tested his connection to his cuffs. They seemed to be back online, and he used their communications function to scan the local communication frequencies. He could detect no radio chatter in the area. No stations, no ships, no cities. They'd dropped out of hyperspace in a completely uninhabited part of space. He had no idea where they were, except to guess it wasn't wherever they'd been aiming for.

It was peaceful here, outside the debris field. Peaceful and quiet and dark. Lyr hung in the blackness of space and found himself enjoying it. Dragons were creatures of starstuff, dwellers of the void. The depths of space were the natural home of his kind. He would eventually need to seek out food, water, and air, but for now he was reasonably comfortable, the bitter cold sliding off his scales. If he needed to, he could enter the hibernation state of his people and survive out here for as long as necessary. Dragons had traveled between stars in just such a way.

But Tamir couldn't.

Why should I care? he thought furiously. Tamir, who had never helped him. Tamir, who had let his sept die—

Tamir, who had taken off his collar and freed his dragon.

And it wasn't just Tamir. He looked toward the ship again. If the ship's core modules were intact, there might be an entire ship full of prisoners in need of his help, including the human woman with the bright spark of courage that had attracted him.

It was with only the greatest reluctance that he sent a cautious tendril of telepathy questing into the void, seeking the human woman. He didn't want to feel the absence where she had been. And he wasn't even sure if he wanted to feel her living presence; it meant responsibility, it meant going back, it meant thinking about people outside himself again.

But whether he wanted it or not, he felt her immediately, a rush of her fear and elation flooding his head in an odd, confusing mix. His heart lurched and flipped over and seemed to start beating again.

She lived. He broke the contact before trying to speak to her, but the awareness of her survival filled him with feelings he couldn't quite even name. Relief might be part of it, along with a grudging acknowledgment that he had to go back.

And in some deep part of his soul, he admitted that he didn't really *want* to stay out here until he died, however appealing it might be.

There was peace here. Endless frozen peace.

But the ship offered a chance to live, and people who needed him, including Tamir's only chance to survive, if he was even still alive. There couldn't possibly be much oxygen left in the small amount of atmosphere trapped within the shield.

Fine, he thought grimly. It seemed that life wasn't done with him yet. Nor he with it.

Not while people still needed his help.

SIX

FOR THE FIRST moment after the lights went out, Meri could only cling to the metal decking in the grip of the most profound disorientation she'd ever felt in her life. She had never known darkness like this. It seemed to press on her eyes. It had weight and heft.

And then the lights came back, not bright like before, but dim and reddish; she knew emergency lighting when she saw it, even on a spaceship.

In that first instant, pirates and prisoners seemed equally shocked. The centaur struggled back to his hooves and turned Meri's way, pointed his arm at her face—but nothing happened.

There was a startled moment of hesitation as the implications sank in, on both sides, and then the prisoners surged forward.

Meri huddled against the wall and tried to stay out of the way. The centaur lashed out with his hooves and the shock-stick, and used his greater size and mass to struggle to the door, out of the mob, to flee. The other pirate wasn't so lucky. He went down under a wave of attackers. Meri didn't see what happened to him exactly, and she was glad for that. The tormented prisoners had no hesitation about taking revenge for the abuse they'd suffered.

By the time Meri managed to struggle to her shaking legs, it was all over. The pirate was dead and the prisoners were now quarreling over his bracelets and shock-stick. The mood in the room vibrated with tension. Meri wondered despairingly if they'd gone from one powder-keg situation to another. There was no telling where most of these people had come from or how long they'd been prisoners. Some of them looked as hardened and dangerous as the pirates.

But there were also people like the delicate green lady, who was now sitting on the floor with her thin arms wrapped around herself. Darker green bruises blotched her smooth skin. Meri crouched to touch her shoulder. "Are you all right?"

The woman flinched away. "I won't hurt you," Meri told her, wishing desperately she could make herself understood. "I'm a nurse. Nurse. Do you need help?" She touched her chest. "I'm Meri. Meri."

Her calming voice managed, eventually, to penetrate the green woman's panic. "Preet," the woman said, touching her own chest.

"I'm going to touch you now. Is that all right?" She touched Preet's shoulder, waited to give the woman a chance to move away if she wanted to. When Preet offered no objection this time, Meri's well-practiced hands went into the familiar motions of checking for broken bones and gently testing the arm's rotation. *It's just another ER shift. You know how to do this.*

The woman watched her nervously, but didn't try to resist as Meri gently but firmly manipulated her arm. "You're going to be okay," Meri told her, hoping that her smile and confident tone would reassure in the absence of a common language. "Can you help me with the others, please?"

She helped Preet get up and took her over to the little group of Earth refugees, who had stayed out of the mob violence in fear and bafflement. One of the formerly unconscious women was now awake and quietly crying, which meant Frank had two semi-hysterical companions on his hands and looked like he was halfway to turning into a sobbing mess himself.

"What's happening?" he asked Meri anxiously. "Are we being rescued?"

Why the heck do people keep thinking I *know what's going on?* "I'm not sure," she said, and guided the green woman's hand to the shoulder of one of the unconscious women. "Keep an eye on her. Keep her from being trampled. Do you understand me?"

Keep them busy. Give them something to do.

"Should we leave?" Frank was asking. "Should we stay in here? Is someone coming to—"

"I don't know!" It came out sharper than she'd meant it to. The woman weeping on Frank's shoulder collapsed in a fresh round of sobbing. Meri tried not to sigh, got a grip on herself, and put a hand on the woman's shoulder. "I'm sorry. I'm just as much in the dark as the rest of you. Miss, are you hurt? Do you need help?"

"I want to go home!" the girl wailed piteously.

Me too, honey. Me too. Meri's throat ached.

But they were here, and there was no going back. She wished she knew how her friend with the silver eyes was doing; she could really use him here to help. **Are you there?* * she thought as hard as she could, feeling a little silly, but she wasn't sure how else to get in touch with him. **Hi? Can you hear me? Are you okay?**

The response was ... strange. It was him but not-him, a sense of power and heat, the smell of a burning candle and the ghost of something huge and golden just at the edge of her consciousness. But she also picked up some sense of a comprehensible answer. **Here. Okay. Busy.**

LYR DIDN'T REALIZE until after the contact was broken that it was the first time the human woman had intentionally reached out with her own mind and contacted him, and that she'd done it successfully. He was too busy trying to get back into the ship.

Like most spaceships of its size, the pirate ship was composed of a number of separate modules docked together: passenger compartments, cargo bay, engines, etc. In a disaster like this, the modular design of the ship had worked as it was meant to, distributing stress and sealing off damaged areas, allowing the more protected modules to survive intact.

But it had also turned the ship into a twisted maze of off-kilter modules, damaged compartments, and broken seals, surrounded by a minefield of floating debris that included radioactive matter from the engines, the drifting contents of spilled fuel tanks, and other hazards. Finding an open bay wasn't hard; the tricky part was finding somewhere he could get into that would allow him access to the sealed and pressurized modules.

And the clock was running out for Tamir.

Lyr managed, finally, to get into a cargo bay that had what

appeared to be a functional airlock. He fought his way through floating crates and barrels, kicking them aside with Tamir held against his chest with one clawed forepaw. The airlock's automatic controls didn't work without power, but Lyr pried open a panel with a claw-tip and started the emergency cycling procedure. The airlock was too small to fit him as a dragon, so he took a breath and shifted, wrapping his arms around Tamir and extending the shield to cover both of them as he did so.

After once again enjoying the power and strength of his dragon body, he felt all too keenly the shock of the cold and the fragility of this tiny form. Dragging Tamir, he kicked his way into the airlock and hauled the door shut. The airlock cycled; his ears popped, the inner door opened, and the artificial gravity kicked in. Lyr slammed bruisingly to the deck, with Tamir's limp weight on top of him.

He picked himself up and checked the ambient air with his cuffs, then let the shield drop. The air was adequate, though stale, and the corridor was lit with dim emergency lighting. The ship was on backup power. The artificial gravity still worked because it took a while for the grav field to collapse without power, but in a day or two, everything inside would be floating as well as outside.

If they all lived that long.

Lyr checked Tamir's pulse. It was present, though fast and thready, and Tamir was breathing faintly. He looked awful. Even in the dim light, Lyr could tell he'd had a few collisions with floating debris before Lyr got to him, not to mention the vacuum exposure.

"C'mon," Lyr muttered, and hauled Tamir unceremoniously over his shoulder. He missed the weightlessness of space for this. Not that he wasn't strong enough to easily carry him, but Tamir's bulk would put him at a disadvantage if he ran into any pirates.

Which he did, a few minutes later, as he was trying to navigate the section-seal between this module and the one he was pretty sure the human woman and the other prisoners were in. The seal cycled and opened, and there on the other side, looking as startled as Lyr himself probably looked, was—

"Oh, it's *you*," the centaurian Hnee snapped, clattering quickly backward on swift-moving hooves as his shields went up. Lyr raised his own at the same time.

There was no human woman to stop him from killing the bastard this time. But there were two issues. Problem one: Tamir. Problem two: the corridor was too narrow to shift here without tearing it open and decompressing this section.

Dammit.

The centaur started to aim at Lyr, then raised his arm at the last minute and fired above his head. Lyr realized what he was planning too late to stop it. The shot tore through the ship's metal skin, and there was a sudden rush of wind as the corridor began to decompress.

"Oh, so that's how we're going to play it," Lyr growled.

Switching his grip on Tamir, he shifted. His body bulked huge in the corridor, back spikes pressing agonizingly against the ceiling before the weakened metal split along the crack opened by the pirate's weapons. Lyr caught Tamir in his claws and extended the shield forward, covering Tamir and his own forequarters.

The centaur, his eyes huge, fired again and again at the monster that had suddenly appeared in front of him. Lyr closed his jaws around him, prompting a muffled cry and curses. Their shields prevented Lyr from being able to actually bite him. Instead, Lyr dragged him backward down the corridor—the centaur kicked wildly and then tried to brace his hooves, but it didn't help—until Lyr could push him out the hole in the side of the ship. For good measure, as the centaur began to drift free in his shield-bubble, Lyr delivered a powerful smack with the side of his head that sent the little green shield careening off among the debris.

With luck, he'd run out of air or get crushed by some chunk of rubble too massive for his shields to withstand. Even if he managed to find somewhere intact to hole up, it ought to take him awhile to get back."Good riddance," Lyr muttered.

The corridor was still decompressing. He shifted back to his smaller shape, and stumbled against the wind until he could close the section door. A plasma burst from his cuffs heated and warped the metal, sealing it permanently.

"You'd probably approve of all that," he added to Tamir's unconscious form, hefting him over his shoulder again. "I'm not sure if you'd quite call it a diplomatic solution, but he is, regrettably, still alive. You're always telling me I'm too hot-headed and I need to learn to look for nonviolent solutions to my problems. How's that for keeping my head?" No answer, of course.

One surviving pirate meant there could be more. He reached out a cautious question toward the human woman. **How are things where you are?**

He was unprepared for her wave of relief and delight. Since she was still having some trouble controlling her mental voice, he was also treated to an uncontrollable rush of her surface thoughts. **You're okay! Oh, thank God! You're really hot! ... I hope he didn't hear that. What happened? Are we being rescued? Where are you?**

Calm, calm. He found himself automatically sending soothing thoughts through the connection, helping her control her mental outburst, as he had done for his sept-sibs back in the old days. **What's your situation? Are you hurt?**

I'm okay. Her mental voice faltered. **We're* not *being rescued, are we?**

I wish I had better news, but not yet.

He could feel her bracing and steadying herself. He'd meant to send reassurance to her, but instead, unexpectedly, he found her mental strength steadying him. **Okay then. Are there medical supplies on this ship? We have hurt people here.**

There should be some kind of medbay. Where he needed to go anyway. **That place where you were processed when you first got here? It might have what we need.**

Lyr received sharp flashes of memories not his own: rough hands pressing an injector behind her ear; terrified people being pushed around and forcibly subjected to disinfecting procedures. It did seem a likely place for medical supplies, a combination intake facility and infirmary.

I can meet you there, the woman said. **I know right where it is.**

No! It came out more harsh than he intended; the idea of having other people running around the ship, getting into danger—of having her in danger—**No,** he went on more moderately. **There are still pirates on this ship. I'll bring what you need.**

Rather than backing down, he felt her doubling down on stubbornness, like steel walls going up in her mind. **I can help. I'm a nurse. I need to see what's available.**

Through the connection, he understood enough of what she meant by "nurse" to know she had some kind of medical background, even if the details didn't translate.

Fine. Do as you like. Let her get herself killed, if that was her choice.

Is everything all right? the human woman thought anxiously at him. *Are you all right?*

How long had it been since someone had worried about his welfare? *I am unhurt. Go find this medical place. I'll meet you there.*

But she didn't back off. Instead, what came back was a question. *What's your name? Do you have one?*

It doesn't matter. Harsh. He had to be. He didn't *want* that connection. Didn't want to be tied to another person when he'd barely survived those he'd lost.

Don't you want to know mine?

No. He didn't. And he especially didn't want what came with it over the telepathic connection, because a person's name was inextricably bound up with their sense of self.

But she said it anyway. *I'm Meri.*

And with her name came ... light. It was not the bright, cold glare of the electric lights on the Galateans' ships, nor even the harsh light of the midday sun. It was the gentle glow of lamplight, of the golden sun as it sank toward evening. It was a warm light that wanted to creep into every corner of his dark, wounded soul, a light that soothed hurts and left peace in its wake.

She was a warm person, this Meri. She was light and laughter and peace. She was everything he was not. He found himself turning away from her, not wanting her to see the jagged, broken edges of his soul. She couldn't fix him. All he would do was steal the light away from her.

But she hadn't pulled back. She was open, curious. Waiting.

Lyr, he sent back, against his better judgment. *I'm Lyr.*

SEVEN

LYR. As he introduced himself, Meri understood not only the word, but she also caught a sense of something ... bright. Hot. Fierce. Overwhelming. Like the presence she'd touched before, when she had tried to reach out for him with her mind.

Someone shook her shoulder, jolting her out of her concentration. It was the green woman, Preet, who asked her a shy question.

"I'm sorry, I can't understand you." But it was odd; she was almost starting to. It was like there was a whisper at the back of her mind, telling her words she could nearly understand.

So far, Meri had found that confidence, friendliness, and rudimentary medical skills went a long way toward overcoming a language barrier. The other prisoners had quickly realized that she was treating the injured and the sick, and she had a steady stream of patients pressing around her—patients she could do very little to help, without access to better medical supplies. And now she might know a place to get them.

"Preet, will you come with me? I'm going to look for help."

It took a minute, but with pantomime, she was pretty sure she managed to get her point across, at least the basic gist of it. But then she looked at the green woman with her sticklike, bruised arms, and thought, *I need better backup than this. I need to find someone with weapons.*

She looked around for any of the people who had gotten the bracelets or the stun-stick from the pirate they'd killed. The most approachable-looking of these was a young woman with cat fur and ears who was sitting with an older woman. When Meri went over to them, the cat-girl raised her hand threateningly, the bracelet glittering on her wrist.

"Wait, wait! I'm not here to hurt you." Meri pointed to the bracelet. The girl quickly folded her hands under her arms as if she thought Meri was trying to take it away. "No, I don't want to steal it. I just want to know if you can defend us if we meet pirates. I'm going to look for help. Do you understand? Help?"

Preet had followed her over, and began talking to the cat-people. Whatever they said to each other, the cat-girl hugged the older woman and got up. Preet touched Meri's arm and pointed to the cat-girl. "Edrin," she said.

"Hi, Edrin. I'm Meri." Meri touched her chest. "Meri."

The girl smiled shyly, her collar flashing under shaggy lion-tawny hair.

It was very dark and very quiet out in the hall, and Meri was glad she'd decided not to go alone. Lights were few and far between. She was just wondering if she was even going to be able to find her way in the darkness when a sudden bright blue-white light flooded the corridor. It was coming from Edrin's bracelet.

"That's a nice trick," Meri said. "You're going to have to

teach me how to use those." Edrin just gave her a puzzled look and jerked her hand away, like she still thought Meri was going to steal it.

She was so young. Maybe seventeen or eighteen. What kind of life had she had, to cause the wary distrust that Meri saw in her face and body language?

As if you have to ask. The collar glinting on Edrin's neck said it all.

Meri wasn't as confident about her ability to find her way back to the processing room as she'd tried to sound when she was talking to Lyr. But it actually turned out to be very easy; they weren't far away. When they entered the room full of tools and equipment, Preet made a tiny whimpering sound and Edrin shrank back. The bracelet's fierce blue-white glare filled the room with dancing shadows. The only other light came from one of those dull-red emergency lights above each door.

"Shhh," Meri whispered. She put an arm around Edrin, who resisted for a moment and then leaned against her. The girl was trembling. "It's all right." She hoped.

They both stood still for a moment. Meri didn't know what Edrin was doing—reliving past horrors, perhaps—but she herself was straining her eyes and ears for any sign of someone lurking in the dark room. Nothing moved, and there were no sounds ... none at all. Not even a whisper of air.

It was *too* quiet. Like a building during a power outage. Wouldn't a ship like this need some sort of fans to circulate the air? Bad thought—and nothing she could do about it. She had to hope someone, somewhere was trying to get the engines running again.

... well, perhaps not, because "someone" probably meant pirates. Lyr had said they weren't being rescued *yet*. Did that mean someone was coming later? She had a bad feeling the answer might be no.

As she and the women started to look around for things they could use—blankets, bandages—there was a sudden thump from somewhere nearby. Edrin cried out and jerked back, then curled her hands into shaking fists. Preet backed away and hid behind Meri.

Another thump, followed by a metallic clang. Meri thought fiercely in Lyr's direction, **Tell me that noise is you!**

It's me. He sounded distracted.

Her knees wobbled. **Don't do that. I thought you were one of* them.*

Absent-minded apology came through the connection. **Listen, I need you to stand back. This door is sealed and I'm going to open it.**

"It's okay," Meri told Edrin and Preet, pulling them back with her. "It's a friend. Friend, you understand? It's someone who won't hurt us."

In the dimness, she was able to easily make out a glowing reddish spot that appeared on the surface of the door. It traced a slow path sideways, then down.

Edrin gasped and raised her hands. "No!" Meri told her. She put a hand over Edrin's wrist and pulled her hand down. "Friend. Friend!"

The bright red ember traced its way up the other side of the door, and the severed section of the door, still glowing dully at the edges, fell forward with a nerve-rattling clang. Lyr stepped carefully through the glowing edges of the seared doorway, bending his head low and hunching his shoulders to avoid brushing his horns against the top of the opening he'd made. **Help me.**

"With what?" Meri started to ask, before realizing that

he wasn't alone. What she'd taken for some kind of cloak flung over his shoulder was actually a person, a huge block of tiger-striped fur who Lyr now lowered gently to the floor. Meri ran forward to catch the stranger's shoulder, helping Lyr ease him down.

Lyr's bracelets shed a pale moonlight glow, giving Meri a look at the man Lyr had brought in with him. Now that she was starting to get used to the cat-people, she realized how human they actually appeared. This man was even more so than Edrin, because the girl had catlike ears, furry and erect on top of her head, but this man's ears were normal human ones. In fact, the only visible difference from a normal human was the soft tiger-striped fuzz covering his face and lengthening into short fur on his shoulders and chest. If he had a shave, he'd be indistinguishable from anyone on the street. He'd also been through a rough time recently. Blood crusted his nostrils and the side of his head, dark in the glow of Lyr's light. His pulse was weak and rapid.

"What happened to him?" she asked, counting heartbeats against her watch—she'd done this so often she could easily multitask—while Lyr picked up the stranger's limp arm and pressed his silver bracelet to the gold one around the man's lightly furred wrist. Then, remembering he might not be able to understand her, she repeated it mentally.

A number of things. He was recently exposed to deep space without protection, but he also took damage from impacts with debris. She could sense Lyr's distraction; he was focused inward. Concern was visible on his face; this man was important to him, not one of the pirates. **Internal injuries, broken ribs, shattered pelvis, hypothermia—**

"Your bracelet is telling you all that?" she asked in fascination. What she wouldn't have given for a diagnostic tool like that back home! "Who is this? What's his name?"

Tamir.* Along with the name, through the connection came an impression of warmth, admiration, and a startling flood of emotion that was gone before she could catch it. **Can you help him?

"I don't know. We have to get him warm first, get an IV in him." She looked around for the others. "Edrin, Preet, can you bring me some blankets?—oh, I forgot you can't understand. Lyr, can you translate for me, please?"

Lyr spoke aloud in a flowing, musical language, and the pain in her head abruptly spiked. Meri was only vaguely aware of Edrin and Preet hurrying off to search cabinets in the room. She reached up a hand to feel behind her ear, probing at the small hard point under the skin, like an embedded nodule of sand, where most of the pain seemed to be concentrated.

Don't touch it. Dry, warm fingers caught her own. **It's a translation implant. It'll start working once it has a chance to learn your language.**

She looked up at him, his face suddenly so close to her own. Their eyes met, and he pulled his hand quickly away. Meri had to catch her breath; he was very ... intense, at close range.

"A translation implant." She started to reach for it again, but stop herself. "How does that work? They couldn't possibly have injected it into the mastoid process, could they?— no, focus, Meri."

She turned her attention back to her patient. Fishing her little keychain pocketknife out of her purse, she began cutting Tamir's shirt off so she could get a better look at his injuries. The shirt was blue and sleeveless, with gold piping. She'd seen something like this before, and oh, now she remembered—he was one of the space marines from the planet.

"Can those magic bracelets of yours tell me Tamir's blood pressure and his blood oxygenation levels?"

As she would have expected if she'd stopped to think about it for half a second, the numbers that he told her made no sense on any scale she knew, but she was able to get a sense from Lyr's reaction that they were dangerously bad.

There's something I can try. Lyr pried open Tamir's gold bracelet with his fingernails. Though it might only be a trick of the light, Meri thought she saw his nails elongate like needles as he worked at it, only to slide back into blunt human fingertips afterwards. Lyr pulled out a hair-fine wire and connected it to his own silver bracelet.

"What are you doing?" Meri asked.

Syncing our cuffs so I can direct his nanites to help him begin healing.

Meri started to ask what *any* of that meant, then decided to save the questions for later, when she wasn't trying to treat a critically wounded patient. As she cut away Tamir's shirt, she saw signs of severe trauma; his ribs were so badly broken they were noticeably deformed, with bruising visible even through his orange-and-black fur. But there was some good news, at least—his breathing, though fast and shallow, was unimpeded. No punctured lung, no flail chest.

Edrin came back with an armload of silvery blankets. Meri nodded her thanks and began arranging the blankets around the injured man. "Lyr, you said he had a broken pelvis? I need both of you to help me move him carefully —*very* carefully—so I can use one of the blankets to wrap and stabilize his hips."

She hadn't ever done it before herself, but she'd received patient transports from automobile accidents with pelvic wraps during her ER rotations. God, she wished she had a backboard. She wished she had a surgeon. She wished she had a *hospital.* It was going to be a damn miracle if he survived this.

Tamir remained deeply unconscious throughout the process of wrapping and stabilizing his broken pelvis. Meri directed Lyr to start packing blankets around him, while she took off his boots and checked blood flow to his feet. Capillary response in his toes looked good (and she tried not to allow herself to be too fascinated by the fur on top of his feet, or the toenails curved and pointed like claws).

"Lyr, can you and the others look for an IV, or whatever your people use for it? Something to administer liquids intravenously. And any drugs you can find."

Lyr nodded and started to get up—taking her light with him. Her dismayed cry made him stop. He crouched down and clicked his bracelet against Tamir's again. The gold cuff on Tamir's wrist began to glow with its own brilliant light.

"Thank you!" she said.

Lyr nodded again, unsmiling. He hesitated, touched Tamir's arm lightly, and hurried off.

Meri didn't want to get her own hopes up. Tamir needed so much more than she could do for him. Internal bleeding and organ damage were not only likely but, based on what she could see and Lyr's mention of a broken pelvis, a near certainty. With a full surgical suite and a modern ICU, he had a pretty good chance as long as they could get him there fast. He'd be looking at a long, slow recovery, but he could make it.

Without it, he didn't even have a chance. There was no way he could recover with nothing but IV fluids and supportive care.

How could she tell Lyr that his friend was going to die?

We're on a spaceship for crying out loud. There must be advanced medical equipment here somewhere.

Lyr returned and handed her a fat cuff of translucent plastic. Puzzled, Meri turned it over to examine it. There was a multitude of little dots on the inside, protected with a clear sealant strip. She wondered if Lyr had misunderstood.

"This is for fluids?"

Yes, it works like this. Taking it back, he tore off the clear strip and wrapped it around Tamir's upper arm. There was a small snap as it locked into place. Through the translucent plastic, she could see small needles piercing Tamir's skin. **We use these in the field sometimes,** Lyr explained.

"It's very different from the technology I'm used to. How do you get fluids into it?" She squeezed it. There was some liquid inside; she could see it squishing around. "That's not all there is, surely? He's going to need a lot."

There should be saline and plasma pods around here somewhere.

They found them in another cabinet, soft packets of fluids that each seemed to contain about a pint of liquid. Lyr showed Meri how to pull out a short tube to connect a fluid packet to a corresponding port on the plastic IV cuff.

"I guess I'm not really impressing you with my medical skills," she commented ruefully.

You're doing fine, and learning fast. I can tell the difference between lack of competence and unfamiliarity with technology.

She tried not to be flattered by that. "What about drugs? He's going to need painkillers at the very least, and there are a lot of other things I could use, like antibiotics—"

The females were looking in the cabinets. I'll go find them.

Lyr was back in moments with a briefcase-like carrier filled with what Meri took at first glance to be guns and then realized were handheld injectors like the one they'd used to inject the translator into her neck. She picked one up and examined it. Their function looked simple, at least. There was a trigger and a place where an ampoule could be clicked into place, preloaded on some, empty on others. There was no visible needle on the business end, so unless there was a separate needle module—which she saw no sign of—it must retract. The case contained a number of refill ampoules as well.

And every last one of them was labeled in an angular script she couldn't read.

"Are any of these painkillers?" she asked Lyr.

It was playing with fire. On Earth, she would *never* have injected a severely injured patient with an unknown painkiller. It could depress his breathing to the point where he would die, cause an allergic reaction or interact with a drug he was already taking. But if he started to regain consciousness, he'd do more damage thrashing around.

We use this one in the field, Lyr said, handing her an injector.

"Is this the right dose for a person his size?"

It auto-calibrates.

Score a point for super-advanced technology. "You do it; you know how it's done," Meri told him, pressing it into his hands. "Edrin, can you—oh, Lyr, I need you to translate again. Can you please tell her to go back to the prisoners' room and get the injured people down here? There are plenty of medical supplies. It'll be easier to treat them here than to carry it all there."

When Edrin had gotten her orders and hurried off, Meri dispatched Preet to collect more blankets and then began laying out ampoules from the kit. "Lyr, I need you to tell me what these are, any that you know the names of. No —wait—" She rummaged in her purse for the notepad she always kept in there. Everything was topsy-turvy from all the tumbling around, but she found the notepad and a pencil, and began to draw the symbols as best she could, then scribbled notes beside them when Lyr told her what they meant.

This one is a painkiller, weaker than the one you gave Tamir. Better for headaches and minor muscle aches. This one is for infections.

It seemed that, high-tech spaceship or not, they had the same basic kinds of drugs as the hospital where she used to work. Painkillers, stimulants, antibiotics, vitamins. She wanted to give Tamir something to try to get his pulse up—it remained dangerously low, almost nonexistent—but was afraid of triggering some kind of drug interaction with the other shot. Lyr's knowledge was only the most basic, like asking an ordinary layperson to describe the contents of a pharmacy. Two-thirds of the drugs were unfamiliar to him. At least she had a basic selection she could work from.

"Do surgical machines exist here?" she asked. "Like, automatic machines that can do surgery without needing a doctor?"

There's nothing like that in here. Lyr glanced down at Tamir, immobile in his blanket cocoon, chest rising and falling almost imperceptibly. **You think he needs surgery.**

"I know he does."

Can you do it?

"No!" she said, shocked. "I'm not a doctor. I'm not trained for that. I could handle a basic procedure if I had to, like a trachcotomy or removing an embedded object from a non-vital area. But the kind of surgery he needs is way beyond what I can do."

His nanites will help repair his injuries. Through their mental connection, Lyr sounded like he was trying to convince himself.

"You mentioned them earlier. What are they?"

Tiny machines in the bloodstream. He has them as part of his people's standard modifications for soldiers. They help stop bleeding and promote healing. He looked away from her, down at Tamir.

Standard modifications for soldiers. Could something like that have helped Aaron—but no, she shied quickly away from that thought. "Maybe they are helping him," she said, forcing her mind onto business again. "He doesn't seem to be doing as badly as I would have expected for how bad he's hurt." She looked up at Lyr's profile in the soft light of his cuffs. "Oh. There's something on your face."

What? He glanced back at her.

She reached out and touched his face with her fingertips, beside his mouth. She hadn't seen the glistening fluid on his lips, smeared across his cheek, until the light hit it in the right way. It was silver, like mercury, with a hint of pink, and body-warm to the touch.

He looked down at her, lips parted. There were traces of the same silver fluid on his teeth. **It's just blood.**

"Are you hurt?"

Not badly.

In the clear white light, his eyes were molten silver, threaded with gold. She had paused with her hand on his cheek, her fingers touching the quicksilver streaks on his warm skin. There were times when he looked so cold and hard that it seemed touching him would be like touching marble, but he was warm now.

It had been *so* long since she'd had her hand on a man's cheek.

There was a clatter of footsteps in the hallway. What happened next, happened so fast that it left her breathless: Lyr slung an arm around her, swept her behind him, and brought up his hand with the cuff flaring brightly. A tingle spread over her skin, like before in the parking lot. By now she had some idea of what was happening: he'd covered her with some sort of shield.

Edrin came in with her arm around the older woman she'd been with earlier—perhaps her mother or aunt—followed by a ragtag scattering of other prisoners. Lyr dropped his arm and stepped away from Meri, and the tingling sensation vanished.

It had been pure instinct that had made him throw himself between her and danger just now. With no time to even think about it, he'd just done it. What kind of life made a man with a heart like that—a protector's heart, a hero's heart—learn to hide it behind this mile-thick emotional wall?

Stay here, Lyr said suddenly, his gaze going distant and thoughtful. *I'm going to look for something.*

"Wait! Where are you going?"

To look for stasis pods. Many ships like this have them. Stasis will keep Tamir's condition from deteriorating any further until we can get help.

"Where would these, uh ... pods be?"

In a cargo hold, if any survived.

She was filled with sudden fear bordering on desolation at the idea of having him leave, even for a short time. He was safety; he was the only person she could talk to. The strength of the feeling startled her, and she struggled to clamp down on it before he could sense it through their link. It wasn't fair to ask him to stay if it meant his friend would die.

She must not have managed to close the connection in time, because his face softened. He didn't smile, but it was as if he smiled at her in his head—a sense of warmth, like the press of a loved one's hand. **I won't be gone for long. Keep the doors shut and see if you can find something to block the door we had to cut open. That'll help keep you safer.**

"Stay in touch," Meri told him, tapping her forehead meaningfully.

He turned away without answering, and was gone before she could do any of the things she wanted to do—touch him, hug him ...

Kiss him ...

Taking a breath and pushing it away before he could sense *that*, she turned to help the incoming wounded.

EIGHT

GETTING AWAY from all those people, with their helplessness and need, should have cleared Lyr's head. Instead he had to fight the urge to turn around and go back. He could all too easily imagine himself returning to find that the pirates had come back in his absence, leaving nothing but charred bodies—

But someone had to reconnoiter. Leaving aside the matter of Tamir's survival, they needed resources: food, water, air. He had to find out how much of the ship was still intact and whether any of the cargo areas had survived.

And there was no one else to do it, just a bunch of scared, unarmed refugees.

Once he was out of the room, he let the light from his cuffs die. Their charge was getting low and he needed to conserve what power they had left; he could see well enough in the dark. His cuffs would recharge from his own metabolic processes, but it was slow.

It occurred to him that he should have borrowed one of Tamir's cuffs to augment his own. He hadn't even thought of it. For a slave like himself, wearing a citizen's gold cuffs was punishable by death. But that wouldn't matter here. He smiled grimly to himself. At the very least, a disaster like this was a great equalizer. There was no slave and citizen here, just a bunch of people in a lot of trouble.

As he strode through the dark halls of the defunct ship, his mind generated a three-dimensional map of the space around him, adding new levels and corridors as he found them. It was something all his people could do, accustomed as they were to the labyrinthine corridors of their asteroid homes.

Their module appeared to be largely intact, but isolated from the surrounding ship by sealed breach doors. Most of them were icy to the touch, suggesting the bitter cold of space beyond. He also couldn't help noticing the growing chill in the air. They were racing a clock here if they couldn't get the engines back online. The ship had no heat, its life support was down, and it was venting atmosphere from the damaged sections. They had, at most, a couple of days, probably a lot less.

The warm, bright touch of Meri's thoughts tickled the back of his mind. **Lyr? You okay?**

Is there danger? he asked quickly. **Do I need to come back?**

What? No, no. We're fine here. Possibly without meaning to, she sent him a mental image of their makeshift infirmary. It looked like they were in the process of making it almost cozy. Someone had found some emergency lights, and their cool blue glow illuminated people bedded down with blankets and applying first aid to each other.

Your friend is stable, she thought, and he got a mental image of Tamir, still and pale, wrapped in blankets.

His distress must have communicated itself unwittingly

through the link, because he felt her quick concern. **Are you all right?**

I'm fine. He choked off, as best he could, the emotions she was getting through the link.

Her curiosity was bright as a lamp inside his mind. **Who is he to you, anyway?**

Memory assaulted him, decades of memories. He could have said: *Mentor. Father figure. Older brother. The only family I have left.*

But none of that was true. It was all Galatean lies. Tamir's only purpose in training Lyr's sept was to teach them to be good battle slaves. There was no more to it than that.

Nothing, he sent back. **No one. Someone I work with, that's all. Do you want to see what I've explored so far?**

Without waiting for an answer, he let her share the mental map-picture he'd constructed of this part of the ship, as he would have done with one of his own people, or his sept-sibs.

Wow, she said. **It's bigger than I thought.**

He'd actually been thinking it was smaller than expected, as spaceships went. **There's a lot of damage. I think we've lost the entire cargo section. The crew quarters and bridge are either gone or inaccessible.** Most likely for the best, since that's where the rest of the surviving pirates were likely to be.

Have you found any food? Most of these people are malnourished.

Not yet. He thought about telling her that they didn't have enough air for the lack of food to become a problem, but decided it was best not to worry her. Then he stopped as his cuffs began picking up a new hazard.

What's wrong? Meri asked.

I'm detecting radiation. Probably from the damaged engines. He ventured a little farther in that direction, but the readings were getting stronger, fast. At the next breach door, he turned around.

Is it dangerous? Meri asked.

No point in lying. **Eventually it's going to be. Not enough to hurt us short-term, but we need to get away from it.**

And go where?

Yes, that was the question, wasn't it? Lyr called up his mental map-picture and studied it. **I think we might be able to detach this module,** he said.

Module?

For answer, he sent her a mental image of a ship breaking up into detachable parts. **This is a stolen Galatean ship, and every Galatean ship this size is built of smaller modules that detach from each other. The bridge is a module. The cargo bays are modules. We're in a general-purpose module right now; those can be used for living quarters or labs or whatever. The modular nature of the ship is probably what saved us when everything came apart. As long as our module is intact, we still have air, even if we don't have power.**

Like the crumple zones in a car?

I'm not sure what that means, but what I'm thinking is, if we can separate this module from the rest of the ship, it'll drift free and we'll be away from the radiation source and also away from any surviving pirates who might have holed up elsewhere on the ship.

What about other prisoners?

I haven't found any. There might be, but there's nothing we can do for them. We have to save the people we're responsible for.

Fierce anger came through the connection. *We can't just leave them!*

You're a ... 'nurse,' right? You know that you can't heal every patient. If you try to help everyone, you will help no one. You help as many as you can—

And leave the rest to die?

Her anger cut him to the bone. For a moment he was back in deep space, in the middle of battle, feeling his connection to Rook and Rei go suddenly dark.

There hadn't been anything he could do. They had been vastly outnumbered. He'd chosen to help Rook, because Rook was the less-skilled pilot of the two. It was a rational decision, a decision Rei would have supported. But it also meant they were separated, in different units in a vicious deep-space battle. And then Rook's pod had been blown apart, and while he was still reeling from that, he'd lost the connection to Rei too—

He had chosen which brother to help, and in doing so, lost both of them.

Lyr?

Her alarmed voice brought him back to himself. He was shaking like a ship on atmospheric entry as he leaned on the bulkhead. His battle spines were fully extended and his teeth beginning to lengthen as his body prepared itself for a shift. Reacting as if he was under attack, it was defending him the only way it knew how—and he *was* under attack, but from his own mind.

I am fine, he told her, fighting down the emotional reaction until he managed to shove it back into its box.

I'm sorry. I didn't mean to sound like I was accusing you of anything. You're right, we have to help the people we can help.

Her apology shamed him. *No. You weren't wrong. I

_have made too many cold, hard bargains in my life. We cannot abandon people we can save. I may be able to find more survivors._*

Be careful! she answered back immediately. *_If it's too dangerous to search—_*

No, I think I can find them by looking for their minds.

Surprise and awe came down the link. *_You can do that?_ *

He could have, once. He wasn't sure if he could anymore. He clamped down on that thought fiercely before she could sense how deathly terrified he was. *_I'll let you know,_* he told her, and closed the link, leaving only the tiny tickle in the back of his mind that would enable him to easily find her again.

The idea of using his powers this way sent him into a cold panic. He'd worked so hard to shut himself down, feeling nothing, sensing nothing. The deaths of those around him couldn't hurt him if he didn't open himself up to them and acknowledge they were people just like himself, each one a unique spark of mind that could be extinguished like a candle flame.

So you will let others die because you are afraid? You are truly no better than your Galatean masters, then. You are a prince of the Well of Stars. Act like it!

He concentrated and, very cautiously, opened a crack in his mental shields.

The first thing a dragon child learned to do was shield themselves from the psychic presence of people around them. It was part instinct and part training, like learning to walk or talk, a perfectly normal aspect of growing from toddlerhood into early childhood. By the time they reached adulthood, dragons could easily and effortlessly block out the unwanted stray thoughts of other people, and similarly control their own thoughts, letting slip only what they wanted.

He had not realized until coming to live among the Galateans that non-telepaths couldn't do that. His early attempts to mindspeak the people around him had been painful, for him and for them. Their thoughts and emotions were uncontrolled and wild, and he had to struggle to learn how to focus his own mental sending to lightly brush their minds rather than thought-dumping at them as he would have with one of his own kind. It was like playfully wrestling with a child, holding your strength in check so as not to hurt them.

He'd also realized something else, and realized it quickly.

The Galateans had no idea what dragon telepaths were truly capable of—or how vulnerable they were. In his early days with them, they'd tried to use him to interrogate captives. The prisoners' pain and fear had given him incapacitating migraines, and he'd pretended that he could read nothing useful from their minds to make his masters stop using him that way.

Without the ability to control their thoughts as his own people could, these people were uniquely vulnerable to telepaths. He could never have strip-mined their brains for information the way they thought he could, but he could scoop surface thoughts, which was one of the reasons why even the Galateans who liked him were nervous around him, aside from Tamir—the one person who had never viewed him with hate or suspicion.

But he was also incredibly vulnerable to their psychic leakage. He constantly had to deal with unwanted feelings of hunger, anger, pain, or sexual arousal until he learned to strengthen his mental blocks to the point where he wasn't receiving telepathic leakage from the people around him. Since his people rarely associated with non-telepaths and did not have a habit of keeping slaves or allowing outsiders to live in their asteroid ship-cities, he had never been around people other than his own. Most dragons hadn't. Which meant they didn't *know* this.

If the Galateans wanted to conquer his people, all they really had to do was torture some prisoners (any prisoners, it didn't matter) and throw the dying victims into the middle of a dragon city-ship. Every dragon in the vicinity would be paralyzed with pain and fear. Some might collapse into comas; some might even die.

He could never, ever let the Galateans learn this. Which meant he could never let them know how vulnerable he really was, or what he could really do—for his people's sake, and his own. He refused to allow himself to become a tool of conquest aimed at his own people.

So he had locked it all away, setting powerful mental blocks in place, forcing himself to avoid using his powers until even he had halfway forgotten what he could actually do. The only people he allowed himself to mindspeak were his sept-sibs, and once they were gone, he closed himself in an iron-walled prison, allowing no one inside.

For a dragon, it was solitary confinement, the worst kind of torture imaginable. He had lived with it because he had to, trapped in an empty chamber in his own head. It was not only himself he was protecting; it was his entire people.

With Meri, he had allowed a single crack of light to shine inside. Now he cracked the door a little wider and tentatively reached out into the ship around him.

At first there was nothing, only emptiness. No other minds brushed his own. Perhaps he had lost the ability to touch others, and he'd almost rather be trapped in a mental prison cell than know for certain that he'd killed off the part of himself that was even capable of reaching out to others.

But no, he knew that wasn't true. There was one mind he could always find.

Meri?

Her answer came back quick and bright, along with the candleflame warmth and the feeling of being gently wrapped up in a fuzzy blanket that was her mental signature. *Lyr! Are you all right?*

I'm fine. Just checking in. He extended his awareness cautiously beyond her, turning his head blindly in that direction as if it would help.

And—yes, now he felt the others. It was dim, not the same brilliant awareness that he had of Meri's mind, which had become so familiar to him. It was always so with his people; those they knew could be reached from afar, while strangers could be touched only at close proximity.

But the prisoners' place of refuge was well within his range. The telepathic skills he'd learned as a child were coming back to him now, and he began to add to his mental map. There were two concentrations of other minds, one group with Meri and another near them. Those must be the prisoners remaining in what had formerly been their cell. It seemed that most of them had trickled over to join Meri's group by this point, but a few lingered, afraid to leave their prison.

He cast his net wider. A handful of isolated minds, scattered in other modules of the ship, were probably the surviving pirates. He didn't want to make contact with them too closely; the connection was too intimate, and the last thing he wanted was to accidentally forge the kind of bond he now had with Meri with one of those murdering, raping monsters. But he did brush a few stray surface thoughts.

Anger and intensity of purpose were their overriding feelings, where he'd felt mainly fear with Meri's bunch—so yeah, pirates.

His head was starting to ache from the unaccustomed concentration. It felt a little like eyestrain from squinting too long at blurry text trying to make it resolve into something familiar. But he wasn't ready to stop yet, because he'd just picked up another gathering of strangers' minds in the opposite direction from Meri's group.

Lyr allowed his awareness to swoop in on them. He felt panic. They were trapped somewhere. Scared. Uncertain.

Meri was right, damn it. He couldn't just leave them.

*Meri, I've found more survivors. I'm going to go get them out.*

*Do you need help?*

*No. Stay where you are. But stand by in case I need medical advice.*

Probably without meaning to, she sent him an image—it might be a memory or what she was currently doing—of herself kneeling beside Tamir's battered body, feeling his pulse. _*Did you find what you were looking for? Stasis pods? *_

*I don't think there are any. Either this ship doesn't have them, or they were in a cargo section that's too damaged for me to enter. We will not be able to save him that way.*

*You'll find another way,* she thought reassuringly at him.

*False hope brings nothing but sorrow,* he told her.

*As a nurse, I have to disagree. Without hope, people give up. I've seen patients pull through when they should by all rights have died, because they refused to give in. And I've seen people who should have been fine, who went downhill _and died instead, because they decided there was no point in trying.*_

*Are you saying we should all delude ourselves into thinking things are fine when they're not?*

_*No,*_ she said, and the tone of disgruntled, reluctant amusement came through loud and clear. _*I'm saying that if you try to make things work out, and work hard for it, sometimes you get it. If you don't try, you won't ever have a chance at it.*_

He wasn't sure why her certainty annoyed him so much. _*The universe is a cruel place, Meri. You can't get a happy ending just by believing in it.*_

What came through the link next was anger. _*I know how cruel it is. Believe me. But the fact that you're out there trying to help the rest of us makes me think you're lying to yourself as well as to me.*_

*I need to concentrate on what I'm doing,* he said shortly, and cut her off.

He felt a pang of guilt immediately. It wasn't her fault. She was sheltered, he thought. That was her problem. What could she know of cruelty and pain on her nice safe world? The universe was going to kick her in the teeth soon enough, and beat that hopeful attitude out of her, just like it did to everybody.

In the depths of his heart, he found himself wishing he could shield her from that.

You can't protect anybody, he told himself. _Haven't you learned that by now?_

And yet he kept heading toward the bright sparks of those other minds he sensed up ahead.

A sealed emergency door, furred with frost, blocked his way. Lyr touched its bitterly cold surface. From the temperature, he knew one of the decompressed sections lay directly ahead, between him and the survivors. His mental map showed him no way around. And they were so close they must be directly in the decompressed part of the ship.

They shouldn't be alive out there. Yet clearly they were.

Lyr manually cycled the airlock and shifted as he stepped through. Immediately the cold was less severe, the loss of air less worrying. He closed the airlock absently with a claw and looked around. This looked like it had once been the ship's docking bay, or at least one of them; on a ship this size, there was probably more than one.

Their sudden drop out of hyperspace had torn it open. Stars and the blackness of space were visible through huge cracks in the ship's metal skin, and another module had rammed the bay, flattening most of it and crushing whatever other small ships might have made it through the crash ... except for one. There was a transport ship similar to Tamir's chaser-class ship not too far from the door. He was pretty sure the life signs were inside.

The artificial gravity was still working out here, so Lyr walked down the deck to the small ship, with his wings folded and spiky ruff flattened down in the chill. The little ship looked undamaged. He could think of no easy way to convince whoever was in there to let him in, so he tried tapping the airlock release. To his surprise, it disengaged and opened in a cloud of water-vapor-laden air. Huh. They hadn't even locked it. Clearly these people knew nothing of ships.

His dragon's bulk wouldn't fit into the airlock, so he held his breath and shifted, flicking his third eyelids to protect his eyes from the vacuum and cold. He couldn't tolerate this for very long in his human shape, but a minute or two wouldn't hurt without bothering with the shield. He closed the outer airlock and opened the inner one without waiting for it to fully cycle.

A purple-skinned, collared Polaran slave with straggling blue hair confronted him, brandishing a pair of cargo grapples like weapons, one in each hand. "Get back!"

"Oh, stop it," Lyr snapped. He tapped his own neck, touching the ridges of scar tissue where his collar had been for so many years. "I was once a slave like you. I'm here to help you fools."

He surveyed the interior of the ship. Rather than being subdivided into a crew and cargo compartment like Galatean chaser-ships, this one was stripped down for running cargo, probably on the black market. The interior was one large space containing about a dozen ragged people from several different galactic races. Frightened faces in a variety of hues stared back at him.

"Who are you?" someone asked. "Are you with the pirates?"

"Of course not, what do you think 'I'm here to help you' means?" He waved a hand up front, where a bulkhead door sealed off the bridge. "Is someone in there?"

There were headshakes all around. "We don't know how to get into it," one of the prisoners said.

"Or how to fly it," said another.

Useless, Lyr thought. "What are you doing here in the first place?"

"Our group was being taken to this ship to be sold, when the accident happened," a green-skinned man said. "Is that what happened? There was an accident? We crashed?"

"Sort of. And then?" Lyr prompted impatiently.

"You saw what it's like out there," the Polaran man said, his words clipped and angry. "We're the ones who were able to make it to safety. Everyone else was sucked out into space, along with the pirates who were guarding us. We all lost friends." He clenched his fists. "If you're planning to take us back—"

"I don't have time for your paranoia." Lyr held up his hand, displaying his wrist. "Cuffs? Anyone have some?" Headshakes all around. "Well then, you're right, you wouldn't be able to get to the bridge without these, let alone fly the ship. Now move so I can."

The door to the bridge, although sealed to the prisoners, yielded readily to Lyr's cuffs. He was braced to have to fight in case he found pirates sealed inside, but the bridge was empty. Lyr went to the pilot's seat and did a quick systems check.

The ship was a little low on fuel, but otherwise all systems seemed to be functioning normally, set to power standby mode. Despite himself, Lyr felt a glimmer of something that might be called hope. Ships like this were jump-capable. With this, they could get to a nearby star system.

If there were any.

He powered up the small ship's long-range scanners and got the expected dismal results. It detected no radio signals, no power signatures from other ships, no signs of stations or civilization. They were in the dead emptiness between star systems, where no one ever went because there was no reason to.

No one would be coming along to find them out here. They were on their own.

He scanned out to the limit of the sensors' limited sweep, and detected two star systems. One wasn't promising, a red giant star that had probably already obliterated any life that might have existed in its system. The only planets in the system were a gas giant and some asteroids.

The other, though ... He was still getting no readings

indicating civilization in the area, but it had a yellow main-spectrum star and several planets, one of which contained liquid water and an oxygen atmosphere.

We can go there.

They would still be stranded in the middle of nowhere, but it might be a survivable middle of nowhere, as opposed to their present location.

But there were still two problems.

Jump travel was incredibly energy-intensive, and small ships like this one could only manage one or two jumps before recharging their jump drive. He could get them to the star system, but he wouldn't be able to take multiple trips.

And he didn't think all the survivors would fit in here. It might be possible, if they crammed everyone into the ship's hold, but it would be straining the life support to the maximum. It wouldn't be a good idea. They were going to need to take multiple trips. But they couldn't.

Lyr tapped on the control panel, thinking. The practical thing was to leave some of the prisoners behind. Draw lots, maybe. There was always a chance they could come back for the rest ...

Who was he kidding. He knew it wasn't likely; to be left behind was a death sentence.

Maybe we could lie to them and tell them we're coming back even if we're not—

He couldn't believe he'd even had that thought. It was honorless. Cowardly. His skin crawled at the very idea.

No, there had to be another way.

"Hey, is everything okay in here?" a voice asked from the doorway.

Lyr looked up and saw the prisoners crowded in the

door, watching him. "Everything is fine. Don't bother me," he snapped, and they withdrew in haste.

Remind me again why I'm trying so hard to save these useless idiots.

Anyway, even if he could get them all crammed into the smaller ship, it would mean jumping them to an uninhabited system with no food or medical supplies or anything else they might be able to take with them. It would still be a death sentence, just a longer one.

And then he thought of a way.

He turned it over in his head. That would work, wouldn't it? It ought to get them to the star system, at least, with the module and everything it contained. They would have a place to live and whatever supplies might be stored in parts of the module they hadn't explored yet.

Experimentally, Lyr slid his hands into the ship's pilot cradles, engulfing his arms to the elbows, and gripped the handles inside. His cuffs clicked into the control system and connected to the pilot implants in his brain. There was no security system in the computer to keep him out, as there would have been on a Galatean military ship. The pirates had either hacked it to allow them to fly this ship, or picked this up on the consumer market. Most civilian ships had little security since only people with pilot implants could fly them and most people didn't have those.

He fired up the engines and disengaged the ship from its docking clamps, producing a few screams from the back that reminded him he'd forgotten to warn anyone. Well, it wasn't like they couldn't figure it out as the ship started to move. He nudged the ship over to the airlock where he'd come in, carefully maneuvering it until the two airlocks clicked together.

Lyr powered down the ship and pulled his hands out of

the pilot's cradles. "We're leaving," he ordered peremptorily, striding into the back of the ship. After a few nervous looks, the former prisoners fell in line behind him like hatchlings.

Maybe Meri was right about this optimism thing, after all.

NINE

MERI TRIED to rationalize the rush of relief she felt when a commotion at the door let her know that Lyr was back and she glimpsed his tall, horned shape through the crowd. It was only because they were safer with him there. Nothing at all to do with how much better she felt whenever he was around.

Goodness, he was tall. Seeing him among the others made him even more aware of it. Tamir might be about as tall as he was, if she ever found out what Tamir looked like standing up, but Lyr was one of the tallest people she'd ever seen.

And it looked like he'd found more survivors, too. Something was causing excitement in the others, Meri scrambled to her feet, frustrated by her inability to understand them. **Lyr!* she thought at him. **What's going on?**

Lyr glanced around and his silver eyes caught hers. He made his way through the crowd to her. **I found a transport with a jump drive,** he told her. **There is a star system near here. I think I can get us there.**

He sounded dubious for someone delivering good news.

"That's great, right? Should we start moving everyone onto it?"

No. It's not going to be that simple. We won't all fit on the transport. But I have a different plan. Pictures came into her head, illustrating the concept. **I'm going to detach this module and use the jump drive on the smaller ship to jump the entire thing to the star system. That way, we'll also still have any supplies on the module, and the module itself to use for shelter.**

"Way outside my area of expertise," Meri said, "but just tell me what you need me to do."

Lyr glanced around. His gaze came to rest on Tamir in his cocoon of blankets.

I want all the civilians together here, but critically injured patients can ride it out in the ship I found. It'll likely be a smoother ride than inside the module. Can you help me with that?

"I—yes, sure. He's the only one like that we've got." Bruises and broken bones were what she'd mainly had to treat with the others.

Lyr looked around thoughtfully, and then went to a yellow panel on the wall, one of an endless number of things in the room whose purpose she didn't know. He touched it, flipped up a couple of clamps, and it swung down and skidded free, floating a few inches above the floor.

With little visible effort, Lyr lifted Tamir's inert form onto the floating ... well, she supposed it must be the future-spaceship version of a pallet lift for moving goods in a warehouse. Lyr put a hand underneath and lifted, and it slid up to waist height, where it could be easily pushed along.

"How does this work?" Meri asked, peeking under it, where there was nothing but empty air.

Repulsor field. Come, we should do this quickly. Which of these people seems the most trustworthy to you?

"Um ... her, I guess." She pointed to Preet, who was comforting another woman.

Lyr spoke to Preet briefly, while Meri gathered a handful of supplies for Tamir—more painkillers, another bag of saline—and stuffed them into her purse. She almost missed Lyr starting to leave, but then he paused and waited for her while she threw her weight against the floating pallet, pushing it into motion. It was resistant to getting started, but once it began to move, it floated along easily as if on greased wheels.

When she left, Preet was busy organizing the prisoners. "What did you tell her?" Meri asked.

I gave her instructions on getting everyone prepared for the jump, which is likely to be rough. I will deal with separating the connections to the other modules.

It was pitch dark out here, and chilly. She stayed close to him, trying not to get underfoot to the point where he'd run the risk of stepping on her.

"There are still pirates on this ship, right? That centaur guy is still out there."

There are, yes. But not in our module.

"How do you know?"

Lyr tapped his forehead.

"Oh."

Another reason to get out of here, before they have a chance to regroup and mount an organized resistance. Once we separate the module, we will be much safer. He paused by a closed door and touched a panel set in the wall, sliding it aside to reveal a handle. He pulled this, having to drag down on it with considerable strength. There was a clunk that Meri felt through the soles of her feet.

"What did you just do?"

*I'm disconnecting each seal. It'll have to be done manually since the power is down.**

"Can I help?"

Just keep an eye on Tamir.

So she pushed the floating pallet while Lyr threw switches on a series of doors. It was chilly enough that she could see her breath in the cold white glow of Lyr's cuffs. She pulled the silvery blankets more tightly around her patient.

It'll be warmer on the ship, Lyr said.

"Are you reading my mind?"

He glanced over his shoulder at her with a tiny flash of an unexpectedly beautiful smile, a smile that took her breath away. **Just using logical reasoning. Ah, here we are.**

They'd reached another door, and this time, he opened it. The little room inside made her think of an elevator, and she was about to ask if they'd all three even fit in there with the bulk of the pallet when Lyr opened the door on the other side and she realized it was not an elevator, but an airlock, and on the other side was an alien spaceship.

Well, okay, she was *on* a spaceship, but so far all she'd seen were a lot of corridors and rooms. This actually looked like a spaceship on TV. They were standing in an echoing cargo hold, mostly empty except for a few crates and barrels. The doors to the forward cabin were open, showing her a bridge that looked like something out of the kind of show Cora liked to watch, the ones whose names all started with *Star Something*.

"Is there some kind of sickbay on this ship?" she asked, touching the side of Tamir's neck to check his pulse. He seemed to have ridden out the trip okay, not that she could do much if he started to crash.

I'm afraid not. This is strictly a transport ship. Lyr strode toward the bridge. Pushing the floating pallet, Meri followed along behind.

On the bridge, he turned back and touched something on the side of the pallet, lowering it to the floor. Meri barely noticed; she was busy looking around at the dozen or so seats, the forward viewscreen, and the controls, which were surprisingly minimal for a spaceship. There were some panels and buttons and such, as well as a parallel set of holes that she couldn't understand until Lyr dropped into the seat in front of them and thrust his hands inside. Light flared across the panels, and suddenly the screen blinked on, showing a view of a dark, open space lit up with the ship's running lights.

"Oh, wow," she murmured, coming to stand behind Lyr. "Are we doing it right now?"

No reason to wait.

She rested her hands on the back of his seat. The urge to brush her hand down his arm was almost overwhelming. As if he sensed her thought—and maybe he did—he looked back at her, his silver eyes liquid in the lights of the control panel.

You should ride it out in the module, with the others, he told her. **They might need you. It'll be rougher, but if anything goes wrong with the jump, the transport ship will likely take the brunt of it.**

"No." Her tone brooked no argument. "My patient needs me here."

Meri. When I say 'take the brunt of it,' what I mean is 'explode.'

"Then I'll take the risk with you. If we're doing this together, we're doing it together all the way."

STUBBORN WOMAN. The warmth of her loyalty crept through some of the ice in his heart, reaching toward his cold, cold core. He clamped down firmly on that. He *couldn't* care—not for her, not for anyone. Things you cared about could be taken from you, used against you. He could do nothing about the physical effect she had on him, except try to ignore it. But letting her touch his heart ... no. *That* he could prevent. *Would* prevent. He was never getting close to anyone ever again.

Which didn't mean he wanted her rattling around like a loose game piece in a box. **If you're going to be here, you should sit down and put on restraints.**

"Oh. Okay." She dropped into the seat next to him and began to grope around the sides of the seat. "Where's the seat belt?"

Lyr stood so he could kneel by her seat. "What are you doing?" she asked, a catch in her breath. With him kneeling, and her seated, they were on eye level with each other. He was suddenly all too aware of how easy it would be to touch her and find out if her skin was really as soft as it looked.

The memory came back to him of Meri pressed beneath him on the planet as he covered her body with his own, shielding her from the pirates. Such softly rounded curves ...

Pushing that thought aside before she could catch even the edges of it from his mind, he pulled down the restraint spider, a flat disc as wide as his palm, from the seat frame above her shoulder. She turned her head to follow him, her expression curious. If he'd shifted his hand just slightly, he could have brushed her cheek, touched the bow of her parted lips—but instead he pressed the spider to the center of her chest, just above the swell of her breasts under her shirt.

She gave a small cry as the restraint web sprang from the spider and rippled over her body. In less than a second, gossamer threads pinned her torso to the seat from hips to collarbone, leaving her arms free. She held very still, breathing shallowly, before tentatively raising her head to give Lyr a look that was both alarmed and reproachful. "How do I take it off?" she demanded.

Tap the spider. When she only frowned at him in confusion, he clarified with a mental image to accompany the explanation. **That device on your chest. It's called a spider. Tap it.**

She raised a hand slowly, keeping the rest of her body immobile, and gave the spider a nervous tap. Instantly the web sucked back inside, leaving the spider tethered only by a narrow strap that passed over her shoulder to the seat above.

"Oh." She tapped it again, experimentally, and this time when the web covered her, she smiled. "I see why it's called a spider."

Lyr looked away, unwilling to accept how the look of delight on her face warmed him. **That's just its name.**

"No, but it makes a web, right?" She sent him a mental picture, an insect on a netlike support, much like the creature that the Galatean word for the restraint referred to.

Lyr pushed his hands into the control cradle and gripped the handles. The ship connected to his cuffs, and its sensors came online in the back of his mind; he was suddenly there and not-there, sitting in his seat but also part of the ship. **Tell me of it later; we must go now.**

"What about Tamir? Doesn't he need a seat belt too?"

I reversed the thrust on the float-hauler. It'll hold him to the floor, like extra strong gravity.

Meri looked over her shoulder, wide-eyed. "Your technology is really amazing."

It was Galatean technology, technically; she hadn't even seen what *his* people could do. It wasn't worth correcting her, though. He began to maneuver the ship forward, then stopped and hissed softly in frustration as it thunked back to the deck.

Meri had been poking at the spider; now she dropped her hands away. "What's wrong?"

The launch doors need power to open. He flexed his hands on the controls and then muttered a curse in Galatean. What did it matter? The hangar bay was already a wreck, its hull full of holes. He could simply use the ship's weapons to enlarge one of those. **Brace yourself.**

He pressed the firing stud, and light flared on the ship's viewscreens. Meri let out a soft gasp. When the screens cleared, a starfield spread before them, framed by the ragged edges of torn and blackened metal.

Lyr glanced at Meri to make sure she wasn't panicking. Instead her face was a picture of eager delight, unselfconscious and fascinated. It made him think of his own wonder when he had spread his wings outside his home asteroid for the first time.

Have you ever been in space before? he asked, thinking of the state of technology on her planet. She shook her head. **Well then, welcome to space, Meri of Earth.**

Carefully, alert for debris, he nudged the ship out of the hangar bay into velvet darkness pricked with a million stars. Their shields glimmered as small pieces of debris bounced off. Meri gasped as something larger hit them, making his entire ship shudder.

I'm going to pull back to a safer distance. It's a minefield here.

He guided the ship in a long, slow loop around the derelict vessel. Beside him, Meri made a soft, shocked sound when they pulled away enough that the entirety of the pirate ship could be seen—or what was left of it. The central part of the ship was all but obscured by the debris cloud drifting around it.

Meri leaned forward in her seat, straining against the restraint web. "Where were you when the crash happened?"

He pointed to the drifting cloud of wreckage. **There.**

"... Wow," Meri said, her eyes wide. "How did you survive that?"

My people can survive in outer space.

"Really?"

Glancing toward her, he allowed himself to smile just a little. **Aliens. Remember?**

"Okay, good point."

Lyr maneuvered around the badly damaged ship, picking his way with care through the floating debris. **This junk is a problem, and it'll be even more of a problem when we jump, if we drag a bunch of it with us. The last thing we want to do is bombard the planet with asteroids right before landing on it. Hold on.**

He targeted the debris around the ship, systematically blasting one chunk after another until he'd created a clear space where he could get close.

Get ready, he told Meri. **I'm going to see if I can move the module.**

A ship this small didn't have tractor beams, but it did have cargo grapples. Carefully he maneuvered the small ship next to the module, and locked on.

In the vacuum of space, even a small amount of thrust

could move a very large object, if it wasn't resisting. At first he felt the drag of the module getting hung up on other parts of the ship, and then suddenly it was moving with him, gliding through the cleared area.

Lyr let out a breath.

How are you doing? he asked Meri.

"Fine." She was looking around, captivated, as they put some distance between themselves and the debris field. "I wish we had ships like this back on Earth. I would've gone to space on vacation all the time if I knew it was like this."

You like this view?

She turned a beaming smile on him. "I *love* it. It's beautiful."

Some planetbound people's first view of space brought agoraphobia or panic. It pleased him that she was not one of them.

But he was not here to watch Meri admire the view. "Tow ship to main module," he said over comms. "Preet, do you read me?"

"*I read you,*" the soft voice came back after a moment.

"Prepare for jump." Remembering Meri couldn't understand his words, he added, **Are you ready to go?**

Her delight dissolved in nervousness. "What's this going to feel like?"

Nothing like the last time. That had probably been her first time going through a jump. No wonder she looked scared. **It'll be very fast. You'll hardly notice anything. There will be some dizziness and then we'll be there.** If all went well, at least. If something went catastrophically wrong, it was unlikely they'd know about it.

"*Ready,*" Preet said over the comm.

"Jumping on my mark." The thought didn't even occur

to him, until he'd already said it, how strange and yet natural it felt to be giving the orders.

For the first time in years, he was beginning to catch glimpses of a life beyond the Empire. A life as something other than a slave—but he shied away from that thought. It was too much. The air felt strange and cool on his neck, where his collar had rested for so many years.

"Mark," he said, and initiated the jump.

TEN

THE MOMENT of dizziness came as Meri had braced herself to expect. It was still weird, like reality itself slid out from under her, the stars smearing in greasy trails. She tried to turn her head to look at Lyr, but every part of her seemed to weigh a thousand pounds—

And then the stars snapped back to normal, the ship solidified around them, and there was a planet in front of them.

Meri leaned forward, catching a sudden breath at her first sight of another world, a world not her own.

She'd seen pictures of Earth from space, of course: a swirled blue and white marble, streaked with green. Even in a flat photo, hanging against a backdrop of stars, it seemed somehow inviting. The colors were colors she knew, the blue of sky and water, the white of clouds and snow, the deep green of forests and fields.

This planet was shockingly colorful. Once, on TV, she had watched a man dyeing cloth in beautiful swooping patterns by dropping paint onto the surface of a large trough of water and then swirling it with a stick before slowly drawing fabric through the patterned water. This world was like that. Rust and violet, blue and dark green, white and dust-brown, all twirled together—as beautiful as it was indescribably alien.

She glanced at Lyr to see if he shared her wonder, and saw his face set and tense, his shoulders knotted with muscle as he fought with the ship's controls. She became aware of a vibration in the ship that hadn't been there before.

"Is something wrong?" she asked.

We're coming in too low and fast. Lyr's mental voice was tight and strained. *We're about to go down.*

"We were planning on doing that anyway, weren't we?"

Not like this. There's no landing gear on the module. I was hoping to orbit and ferry people down to the planet with the ship. We weren't supposed to jump in this close to the planet, but the gravity well caught us. I don't think I can get out of it.

"Oh," she said faintly.

Make sure your restraints are tight. This is about to get rough.

Meri wasn't sure how to make it tighter, but she touched the restraint web anyway. "Tamir—" she began.

Nothing we can do. He'll survive or he won't. Don't try to get up; I don't need you loose in here as well.

Meri braced herself. The planet filled all the ship's screens, whorls of white and violet and yellow-brown coming up to meet them.

Actually, there is something you can do. Lyr's mental voice was distracted as he focused on flying the ship. *See if you can find me a place to land.*

She started to ask how to get the information he wanted, then closed her mouth. She could figure this out on her own. There was a screen and buttons in front of her. As soon as she touched the buttons, the screen lit up, showing the planet. She pushed buttons until realizing it was actually the movement of her hands that moved the view, like a touchscreen in midair. Rotating her hand turned the planet; spreading her fingers zoomed out, and clenching a fist zoomed in.

I bet Apple wishes they had this technology.

"What kind of place do you need to land?" She tried not to look at the main screen, where the view had become shaky and fragmented as the ship shuddered around them.

Grassland, swamp—try to find me somewhere flat. Someplace near water would be best. There's a lot of desert down there.

"Trying," she murmured. If the screen could find that for her, she hadn't figured out how, and she couldn't read any of the labels. Maybe the colors could tell her? All that brown and rust was probably desert, and Lyr was right, there was a lot of it. The violet and green swirls could be forest or grassland. Some knobbly bits were probably mountain ranges.

I need directions, Meri. Lyr's mental voice was calm, but with a tense thread woven through it.

They broke through a band of high clouds, and suddenly she could see the land below them, not just in a diagram on her console but in the real-world view of the main screen. Mountains seamed the land, topped with white, with vast stretches of desert between. Splashes of purple and green and violent orange wound along the wrinkled coastline. She scanned desperately for something that looked flat enough to land on and wasn't going to put them in the middle of a thousand miles of desert.

"Uh—left, left!"

The ship jolted violently. If not for the restraints, Meri would have been thrown from her seat.

Long ridges of mountains rose to either side, and suddenly there was ocean, vast and glittering. Meri could see the edge of night wrapped around the world ahead of them, turning the water indigo, dark purple, black.

Meri! Lyr's urgent mental voice intruded on her fascination.

"There's a river mouth on the coast we could aim for," she suggested, looking down at the slowly rotating diagram on her screen. "I think it's an estuary of some kind, a big swamp. It sounds like what you told me to look for."

We're too low. We're not going to clear these mountains if I can't get more altitude. Hold on.

Meri clutched at her seat as jagged peaks loomed in front of them. She had never even seen the Rockies in person, let alone anything like these. They were huge, rising so high above the world's floor that the air on their glittering silver peaks must have been too thin to breathe. Surely these were taller than Everest, like a whole range of Everests stacked together.

Surely they were going to flatten themselves on those vast ramparts, they couldn't possibly miss them—

The ship bucked, sudden weight slamming her into her seat. Sky, mountains, ocean danced crazily on the screens. Her heart leaped into her throat and stayed there. From the sudden plunge in the pit of her stomach, it felt like they were going down, not up.

"Lyr—"

I need to concentrate.

The ship shuddered, and again there was the sense of tremendous force pushing her back into her seat. She could see red lights going crazy all over her console, but it wasn't like she could do anything about it. The ship's violent shuddering rattled her teeth. There was a pop and she smelled something burning. She couldn't move; the force compressing her chest made it hard to breathe. Her mouth tasted like blood.

The world filled their screens and hit them like a hammer.

LYR CAME out of a dazed stupor to the smell of smoke and a ringing in his ears. Everything seemed very still after that shuddering hell-ride through the atmosphere.

He had dropped the module on the other side of the mountains. He'd seen a chance and let it go, diving as close to the ground as he dared and then braking hard and cutting the grapples loose. There had been a plateau and a system of lakes, and he thought it was as good a chance at a soft landing as the module was going to get. There was no way he could clear the mountains with the module still attached.

He'd planned to skip over the mountains, circle and come back around to see if the module had come down okay, but he hadn't been able to get enough altitude. The ship had clipped the mountains and they'd had a hard landing somewhere on the other side.

But the ship was steady now, so they were on the ground and not in the ocean or sinking into a swamp. The viewscreen's auxiliary functions had gone down along with the power, so now it was simply acting like a window, letting in natural daylight through a tangle of green and purple leaves.

"Meri?" he asked thickly.

There was no answer. Lyr struggled to extricate his

weak, shaking arms from the pilot's cradle. Next to him, Meri was draped limply in her seat, her head hanging down.

"Meri!"

Unable to reach her physically, he reached out with his mind, probing for both Meri and Tamir.

Two feeble, confused minds answered his anxious sending. Meri was hovering just below the threshold of consciousness after blacking out from the g-forces that had hammered them during their descent. He couldn't tell whether she was hurt from touching her mind alone, but she didn't seem to be sinking deeper; instead she appeared to be coming back. Tamir was harder to read, as deeply out as he was, but Lyr sensed *something* there. It wasn't the emptiness that was all he'd been able to feel when he lost the others.

They were, at least, alive.

Lyr fumbled with his restraints and staggered out of his seat. The tilt of the deck wasn't steep, but it made his uncertain balance even more unstable. He stumbled against Meri's seat and dropped to his knees beside it.

"Meri!"

She was slumped forward. He pushed her gently back in her seat and tilted her head so he could see her face in the light from the window-screen. Her mouth and nose were smeared with blood, the same deep red as Galatean blood, unlike the silver blood of his people.

"Meri," he said again, holding her face in both hands, and reached deep, deep for her mind, throwing her a line that she could use to climb her way back to consciousness.

He used to do this for his sept-brothers and sept-sisters. When they were in danger of passing out during their brutal pilot training, he had used his own mind as a lifeline they could use to hold onto consciousness and therefore avoid losing control of their battle-pods. Lyr, with his more durable dragon's body, had had much less trouble. He was truly worried about Meri right now. Their descent had made *him* pass out, if only for a moment. It could have damaged her lungs, her heart, her mind ...

Meri. Come back to me.

SHE WAS FLOATING SOMEWHERE dark and peaceful. Her body wouldn't move, but it didn't seem to matter. Like sinking into still, dark water ...

Meri!

And into the water came a light.

It was felt more than seen, a great light and warmth that came down all around her. With the light came a deep note like a resonant song, rolling at the edge of her senses and making her think of far-off cathedral music.

She would have had to squint if she'd had eyes to be blinded, but in the place she was, she simply basked in the light and the song that went on and on in a single continuous note. She tried to reach up with the hands she didn't have, because she could sense this presence reaching down for her. It didn't frighten her. She wanted to go to it.

That's right. Rise up. Come back.

Come back. There was nowhere to go back to. Earth, and everything she knew there, lay far behind her.

But *this* was home, this light. Her heart knew it. She could almost glimpse it, a tremendous shape writhing in the darkness of her mind, sinuous curves and many-colored scales, a crown of horns that she wanted to touch.

She reached out.

Reached—

She blinked sticky eyelids and found that she was touching Lyr's face.

He looked awful and beautiful all at once. He was no longer a glorious bronze statue, but a tired man with silvery, opalescent blood glistening on his lips and crusted around his nostrils. His eyes—framed with dark lashes, she noticed for the first time—were soft and warm and full of relief. Emotion, real emotion glistened in those silver depths. He was more lovely than she could have imagined.

"Meri," he said aloud, a musical echo of the voice she'd heard in her mind.

"Hi," she said faintly, and couldn't help it when her lips curved in a smile. He was a nice sight to wake up to.

He seemed to get his breath, and like a curtain coming down on all that vast depth of emotion, his face went cool again. He pulled away, leaving her hand touching empty air. His mental presence withdrew as well. The sense of connection felt so natural that she didn't even notice it until it snipped off at its source, leaving her soul more alone than before.

But he didn't leave her entirely. He helped her undo her restraints, and she tottered to her feet with Lyr's arm around her. The memory of that light was still with her, that warmth and strength, like sunshine raining down on her and pulling her back to the world of the living.

"Can you stand?" Lyr asked her, and she nodded, reaching out a hand to grope for the back of her seat. Lyr's strong arm withdrew; she tried not to yearn embarrassingly after that support. Instead she hung onto the back of her seat until her legs would hold her, and then looked around.

The interior of the ship was dim, though not completely dark. Light filtered in through leaves pressed against the front screen. The instrument panels were dark, the ship's cargo hold cloaked in shadows.

Lyr was bent over Tamir. Meri took a cautious step away from the seat. Her legs wobbled but held.

"How is he?"

"Unchanged as far as I can tell," Lyr said. "I'll see if I can get the instruments up, at least enough to tell if the—what's wrong? Are you all right?"

Meri had been making her way over to them, touching the backs of the seats to keep her balance, but she stopped at a sudden realization. "You're talking out loud. I can understand you now!"

There was the quickest flash of that beautiful smile again, this time slightly embarrassed. "That's right, I didn't even think of it. Your translator implant must have finished syncing. Does your head still hurt?"

"Hard to tell right now with all the bruises." She managed a shaky smile and brushed her hand across her upper lip. It came away sticky. Nosebleed, she thought, looking at the blood on her fingers.

She didn't even realize she'd stayed like that, as if her mental gears had gone out of sync, until Lyr's fingers closed over hers. She looked up at him, struck all over again by how tall he was, how warm and strong his hands were.

"Take care of Tamir," he said gently, and it was backed up by a warm mental undercurrent of support. "I'll check the environment outside and see if I can tell where we landed."

"Okay," she said shakily. He released her hand with a quick squeeze, and it wasn't until he'd brushed past her that she realized he was doing exactly what she'd been trying to do for the others on the ship—giving her something to do, keeping her busy to avoid thinking too much.

She looked over her shoulder at him as he bent over the instrument panels. This was a man who had dealt with people in crisis before.

But he was right; she had a job to do. She knelt beside Tamir and took his vitals. His pulse and breathing weren't better, but as Lyr had said, he hadn't gotten *worse*, and given their rough landing that was close to a miracle, or at least a testament to his profound toughness.

"How does it look out there?" she asked Lyr, who had given up trying to get the instruments working and was standing with one hand pressed against the side of the ship.

"Adequate. At the very least, we aren't underwater or in an active volcano."

"What about the others, in the module? Are they okay?"

"They're not with us," Lyr said. "I dropped the module on the other side of the mountains. I had to. I think they made it down okay, but I can't boost the radio signal enough to reach them without power."

"Can we fix the ship and go look for them?"

"One thing at a time. First let's find out where we landed. I'm not reading anything in the atmosphere that would make it dangerous for your species or mine." To her surprise and pleasure, he gave her another smile, a little wider this time—a conspiratorial smile, an invitation. "Want to see a new world?"

"Yes," she breathed, thrilled.

They left Tamir on the bridge and went through the ship's open cargo hold. The floor just behind the bridge was tilted steeply and then buckled; the rest was mostly flat. They'd run into something, and run into it hard.

Lyr stopped at the airlock and gestured her behind him before raising a glimmering shield with his cuffs.

The airlock opened on a mass of colorful foliage,

broken branches and leaves in many shades of green and violet. After looking around for danger, Lyr dropped the shield.

"Stand back. I'll cut our way out. Be careful of the sap. It might be corrosive or poisonous."

Meri obediently stepped back. Lyr's arm blades folded out; this time she was watching closely and saw that she hadn't been wrong before, they did come right out of his skin, with a faint trickle of silver blood.

"Doesn't that hurt?" she asked.

Lyr paused in the act of slashing at the foliage. "Does what hurt?"

"Never mind." Meri was fascinated by the way the razor-sharp blades cut through branches and twigs. A pungent, spicy smell rose from the cut ends.

"It's not dangerous to you," Lyr said over his shoulder. "Come on out."

"How can you tell?" She ducked as she followed him into the tunnel he'd hacked through the thicket; the sap might not be poisonous, but she still didn't want to get it in her hair. The air was warm and full of strange smells.

"I checked it with the cuffs. I'll be able to test anything we find to eat in the same way."

Okay, she *definitely* had to get herself a pair of those.

They came out of the thicket onto a hillside covered with scrubby light-purple grass. The ship had blazed a raw scar down the hill until its wild slide was arrested in a tangle of trees and brush in the bottom of a small valley. Overhead, the sky was pale blue with a few wisps of high clouds and a faint band of colors crossing it at a steep angle. That vast, arching stripe went from horizon to horizon, like a ribbon across the sky.

"What's that?" Meri asked, pointing up.

"This planet must have rings," Lyr replied with barely a glance, wiping his arm blades on the grass to clean them.

"Oh," she whispered. She hadn't even noticed, coming in; she'd been too distracted by the planet filling the screen.

Rings, like Saturn.

She was standing on an alien planet. She couldn't wrap her mind around it.

Lyr straightened and the blades slid into his arms, leaving only a thin slit visible in the skin. "I'm going to have a look around. Do you want to come?"

Are you kidding? "Of course."

They climbed the hill through knee-high purple grass. Lyr moved with slow, powerful grace, turning his head to look in all directions, alert but unafraid. Meri kept close to him, reminding herself that they were on an alien world full of unknown dangers. And yet she wasn't afraid, which surprised her. Maybe it was just that after dealing with pirates and a spaceship crash, the idea of something jumping out of the bushes and attacking them couldn't really do much to faze her. But there was also a feeling that nothing could touch her, no danger could harm her, with Lyr and his blades and his shields to protect her.

As they climbed out of the brush-choked valley, more of their surroundings came into view. The mountains rose above them, a rampart wall of rock and forested slopes that was no less astonishing up close than it had been from above. She couldn't even imagine how high the mountains must rise; their heads were half-hidden in clouds and frosted with snow and ice despite the warmth of the summer day.

And there was also the sea.

When they reached the top of the hill, a cool breeze ruffled her hair, startling after the stillness of the sun-warmed valley. It smelled of salt and ocean. As a child of the Midwest, Meri had never in her life seen the sea except in pictures. It was as vast and wondrous as she'd imagined, especially with the planet's rings rising from the horizon and arcing overhead.

Their hill, she could now see, was actually a dune. It was more obvious on the ocean side, where grass secured the sand only in patches, with sand-slippage between. More grass-covered dunes rolled down and down, to the ocean far below them, purling with tiny ruffled waves along the shore.

In one direction, the mountains came right down to the sea in towering cliffs with whitewater rolling along their feet, dashed itself on the rocks in miniature towers of spray, shrunk by distance to the size of something from a TV show. When she turned the other way, she saw the estuary, a vast salt marsh marbled in green and purple and gold, bisected with wide loops of river—one sprawling river, or several smaller ones; she couldn't tell, but the marshes went on and on, until they blued with distance to become indistinguishable from the sea.

Meri drew deep lungfuls of the salt wind. It felt like early fall, warm but with a hint of coolness underneath, which made her realize that she had no idea what time of year it was, nor any idea how to tell. Maybe everything turned purple in the fall on this world, or maybe this was the very beginning of spring. Maybe the world was so warm, and they were so far south, that there were no seasons at all.

In all this great emptiness, there was no sign of people, human or otherwise. No cell towers, no contrails, no roads or boats or buildings. Just the two of them.

She glanced at Lyr to see how he was taking it. He was gazing out to sea with a distant expression. She could see the colorful landscape reflected in his silver eyes.

"What is your world like?" she asked.

Lyr gave her a quick, sharp look, coming back from wherever he'd gone in his head. "What's that?"

"What kind of planet do you come from?"

His expression changed little, but something in his face hurt her. "My people are not people of worlds. We may have been, long ago, but not anymore ... or perhaps I should say, our worlds are ships. The great nest-cities of the dragons are hollow asteroids that sail between the stars in the furnace of the nebula where we, as a species, were born."

Glimpses of this spacefaring past came to her through the link: fleeting images of twisting corridors lit with a soft, pastel light that brought out the layered colors in their walls. Nebula space, not empty and dark, but a furnace of heat and light where stars were born.

"It looks beautiful," Meri said. She stopped herself before she said the next part—that she would miss the sky, miss being outside—but the thought was close enough to the surface that he must have picked up some of it anyway.

"Some have skies, inside. They are vast, as big as moons. Each is a little world of its own, made into whatever the clan wants it to be."

His voice made her ache with the longing in it. "What was yours like?" Meri asked softly.

For just an instant, she thought he might open up enough to tell her. It was there in his eyes, a desperate yearning for connection, for companionship. Then his gaze became shuttered, the warmth of his expression cooling toward stone. "It was long ago. There's no sense in bothering with things that are gone."

Meri touched the ridge of callus where she'd worn her wedding ring for all these years. "Lyr—" she began.

He held up a hand. "Wait."

With that he began striding along the top of the dune, only a few steps before he stopped and crouched down, elbows resting on his knees. Meri caught up and looked over his shoulder. In the grass-covered sand of the dune top, there were tracks. Huge tracks. Each was as long as Meri's arm, with three toes and visible claws digging into the sand. There was a drag mark half-obscuring some of the tracks, where a long tail might have rubbed them out.

"Fresh," Lyr said quietly. "It might even have been here when we crashed. The ship must have scared it off."

"Good!" Meri tried to imagine what might have left tracks that big, and decided that she didn't want to. Not if they were sharing the planet with it.

The tracks went down the ocean side of the dune in long strides and were lost, eventually, in the folds of the hills rolling down to the sea.

"Where did it go?" The breeze seemed chillier than it had a moment ago. "Something that huge couldn't just disappear."

"Into the water, maybe. Or it might have a den nearby ..." He stood abruptly. "The water," he said, pointing.

The creature was just sliding into the edge of the sea. From up here it looked small, but she could see by the trail down the dunes how high above it they were. It was colored orange and gray, with a high crest rising from its back.

"That—that's a *dinosaur*!"

Lyr glanced at her. "You have them on your world?"

"We used to." She stared, captivated, as it swam away with a graceful wriggling motion. She couldn't pin it down to a specific kind of dinosaur from the toys she used to play with. It would have been more surprising if she could; it probably wasn't a kind of dinosaur from Earth's past. It was whatever this world had instead.

But, while she might not be the world's biggest science fiction nerd, Meri Rowland had been a pretty big dinosaur geek when she was about eight. She wasn't sure if she could still tell an ankylosaurus from a dimetrodon, but she'd known all of them once upon a time.

That might not be a dinosaur down there, but it sure looked like one.

"There are dinosaurs on this planet," she said, and broke into a huge grin.

Lyr looked like he was trying not to smile. "If you have them back home, is it really that exciting?"

"No, you don't understand! They went extinct a long time ago. It's ... oh, I can't explain. It's just that I never dreamed I'd actually see one, and now I have. Even if it's not really a dinosaur, it's about the closest thing I can imagine. *Thank* you, Lyr, for getting me down safely. Thank you for giving me a chance to see this."

And before she could think, she hugged him.

He had held her once before, as he shielded her when the pirate ship was firing at them back on Earth. But that had been different, a light, precise touch. This time, she threw her arms around him and hugged the stuffing out of him.

Lyr went instantly rigid in her arms. He was *big*; she'd almost stopped noticing that, but being in physical contact brought it back to her full awareness again. Her head barely came up to the middle of his chest. He was basketball star tall, but thicker—and it was all muscle, a frame of pure lean muscle over bone. He was hard everywhere, as if all the softness had been burned out of him long ago.

And yet, when he brought his arms up behind her—very

tentatively, as if he'd forgotten how—it was nothing *but* soft: the brush of his touch against her back, gentle as the touch of kitten paws.

She knew how fierce he could be. She knew his hands could deal death. But she had no fear of him, none at all, not as his arms came slowly around her and he hugged her back with breathtaking gentleness.

ELEVEN

IT HAD BEEN SO LONG, *so* long, since he'd been touched like this.

His people were not, in general, the touching kind. Touch, for dragons, was often a prelude to psychic contact, so they were careful, reserving physical affection for only their most intimate loved ones: family, the closest of friends ... and their lovers.

But he had grown up used to the casual, friendly touches of his septmates. Since their deaths he had ruthlessly shoved away any attempts to breach the wall of personal space around him. His people were reserved, but they were not meant to be alone, forever. It was like being in a prison made of ice.

And now a ray of light shone into the prison, and some of the frost on the walls began to melt.

She was so warm. So small. So fragile in his arms.

And that was what made him snap out of the spell she seemed to have cast over him. He pushed her away with a small shove, not enough to hurt, just enough to make it clear that he needed space.

He had no right to hold something so fragile and precious. Didn't she know how strong he was, what he could do to her with a casual, careless touch? His entire life was about death, destruction, damage.

Meri looked startled and hurt. Lyr tried not to allow that to affect him, pushing his emotions ruthlessly back into their armored box. He took a step back, reestablishing their boundaries, and saw Meri cover her hurt with a smile. (And if there was a part of him that would have done anything to take her back in his arms and soothe that hurt away, hurt *he* had put there, it took all he had not to give in to it.)

"Sorry about that," she said. Her laugh was a little shaky, but not insincere. "I can get a little carried away sometimes. You just tell me if I get up in your personal space too much, okay?"

Lyr only nodded, unable to trust his voice, not while having her "up in his personal space" was all he wanted or could think about. She'd been so warm, so soft ... so ...

... so *female.*

He had not thought about females in a very long time. Everything in his life had been death and war and killing. He'd simply assumed that he would never get back to the Well of Stars, would never see another dragon again, so what was the point in thinking of mates and companionship? No one he'd seen among the Galateans or among his septmates had ever stirred romantic feelings in him. He had not even thought of them as male or female—had not even realized his feelings were capable of being stirred by those outside his own people.

This was new. Unexpected. Standing here, even having re-established physical space between them, he was all too conscious of his new awareness of her physical form and smell.

She was not like the females of his species, but that was part of what charmed him.

"Lyr?" Her voice sounded uncertain now. "If I offended you, I'm sorry."

"It's not you." He drew back when she reached to touch him. He couldn't take the intensity of it; he needed *time* to decide if he was going to stuff his feelings back into their box, to think of her merely as a companion, and not ...

Not as a very desirable woman.

A woman of a different species, who probably had a mate among her own people. He was being a fool.

Meri's hand lingered in the air and then dropped. "I'm sorry," she said helplessly. "We ... we should go back and check on Tamir."

STUPID, Meri berated herself. She hadn't meant to let emotion carry her away. Some people didn't like being touched, and it looked like Lyr was one of those people. She made a mental note to keep her hands off him, even if it was damn hard when she was this close to him, all too aware of the lightly spicy scent of his skin.

Looking down at the ship from up here, it was all the more astonishing to her that they'd survived. It was crumpled and twisted, half-hidden in trees. She wondered if the module had fared better or worse, if Preet and Edrin and the others were even still alive.

"We're going to look for the module, right?" she asked as they retraced their steps down the hill.

"Of course. But our first priority is securing a campsite here."

"Put on your own oxygen mask before helping others, right?"

"I suppose," he said, a slight smile tugging the corner of his mouth.

Approaching the ship nestled in its hollow, with the rampart of the mountains rising above it, brought home to her the true enormity of their isolation. The only sound she could hear was the soft rustling of the grass around their feet and the whisper of the wind through the trees. In this entire world, they might be the only people.

"Lyr, who lives on this planet? Does anyone?"

"I didn't pick up any radio transmissions from space," came his quiet answer. "That doesn't mean it's impossible for this planet to have natives. But they won't be advanced enough to have cities or space travel."

"How are we going to get off it, then?"

"I don't know," he said.

It was oddly comforting to get back to the ship, away from that huge, wide, people-free horizon. Mere hours ago, this ship would have seemed impossibly alien to her. Now it was the only halfway familiar thing in an alien wilderness. Meri picked her way through the pitch-dark cargo hold onto the bridge—where there was at least *some* light, filtered through the branches covering the cracked viewscreen—and checked on Tamir. His IV bag had deflated completely, but she held off on hooking up the only other one she had. The supplies she'd packed before leaving the module would need to be rationed carefully.

Once she'd gotten Tamir settled, Meri went to see what Lyr was up to. She found him clearing a wider space around the airlock.

"I was thinking we could set up a sort of camp out here," he said, wiping his blades with a handful of grass. She was able to get a better look at the blades this time, two gently curved weapons like scimitars, made of metal that gleamed in the sun.

When he noticed her looking at them, the blades shuddered and then folded neatly back into his forearms, like an airplane's landing gear folding up.

"You don't have to hide those," she said. "I was just curious."

Lyr held out his arm. There was only the faintest crease in the skin, like a very old scar running down the outside of his arm, but as Meri watched with interest, the skin rippled and parted, and the blade slid out, shiny and sharp, streaked with silvery-pink blood at the tip.

"Can all your people do that?"

"No. It's a surgical modification. The Galateans did it."

"Did you ask them to?"

"No," he said quietly. "But I didn't particularly mind. My people naturally have defensive spines. This is like a technological version of it."

As he spoke, what she had taken for small dimples or scars in his arms and shoulders suddenly bristled with backward-curving spikes. These appeared to be made of something like tooth or bone, and glistened faintly in the sun.

"Why did they do it?" she asked, to cover up the surprise which he had probably felt from her anyway.

"Why? So I could fight better, of course. At one time they intended to train me as an assassin." His smile curved like his blades. "That didn't work out as they'd planned."

"Why not?"

"Because ... I'm very good at killing things. Just not in the way they hoped." He turned back to cutting down trees with slashes of the blades.

Meri hesitantly reached out for his mind, but he'd closed it off to her.

After a minute or two of watching him, she wandered a little ways away—far enough not to have to worry about flying branches and sap, near enough to feel safe—and sat in the sun-warmed grass on the hillside. After smoothing out a patch of grass with her hands, she opened up her purse and took a careful, systematic inventory.

Her coworkers might joke about her over-stuffed handbag, but she had never been so glad of her long-standing habit of carrying anything and everything in the succession of oversized bags she'd owned over the years. She pulled out items and laid them down systematically, row after row. The medical supplies she'd brought for Tamir were followed by a veritable catalog of the last couple years of her life.

Tylenol and aspirin and allergy medication and baby wipes and a mini flashlight. Phone, of course—she picked it up to check for a signal automatically, only to find that the battery was dead. Tissues and a memo pad and no less than four pencil stubs plus two ballpoint pens with business logos on them. One glove, with no mate to be found. A hairbrush from when her hair used to be longer. A spray bottle of cheap perfume she'd gotten as a book club giveaway. A handful of coupons. Some redeemable point stickers she'd been collecting from a gas station chain. Her keychain multitool with a can opener, screwdriver, and scissors—she stowed *that* in a pocket where it would be easily accessible. A pair of reading glasses, which she didn't use much but had started carrying around with her in reluctant acknowledgement of the fact that she no longer had twenty-year-old eyes. A couple of fun-sized bars of last year's stale

Halloween chocolate, which she put aside, mouth watering as she began to realize how hungry she was.

The inventory went on: A paperback romance novel she kept on hand for reading while standing in line. A wad of yarn, six rubber bands, three lipsticks, an old wristwatch with a plastic band and a dead battery, an Ohio library card, a pumpkin-spice-scented tealight candle, a takeout menu for a Chinese restaurant, $2.37 in loose change ...

And her wedding ring, of course.

She became aware that Lyr had stopped cutting down trees and was standing over her, looking down curiously at the items spread out in the grass. "What is all of this?" he asked.

"The consequences of not cleaning out a handbag for years." She covered the ring with her hand, suddenly embarrassed for reasons she couldn't explain.

He's an alien. He doesn't even know what a wedding ring is.

Still, she scooped it up first and put it back in its pocket, then began to restow everything else, one item at a time.

"What a very useful thing to carry around with you," Lyr remarked. "Did you pack in the expectation you might encounter an emergency?"

"Not this kind of emergency," she admitted with a soft laugh. "Being abducted by aliens and taken to outer space definitely wasn't on my to-do list for this week. But I guess I'm just this way by nature. I like to be prepared."

"A useful trait, when one is stranded on an unfamiliar planet."

"I guess I can't argue with that. But I wish I'd thought to bring a backpack filled with camping gear and a tent." She held up a mini Snickers bar. "Do you want to split this with me?"

"What is it?"

"Candy. Uh, a snack food, from my planet."

Lyr held out his hand. Meri started to put the chocolate bar into his hand, but he only brushed the cuff against it. "Hmm. I don't think I can eat that. But you should. You need energy, and there may be more supplies on the ship."

WITH HER MOUTH full of chocolate, she helped Lyr begin a systematic search of the ship's cargo area and various compartments. It was an odd assortment of things that they found. There were several barrels containing what Lyr told her was a chemical cleaning solvent. Much more usefully, he located some blankets and a bale of flat packets, each about the size of a package of freeze-dried camp food, that he said were food packets, "with enough nutrients to sustain most human-derived life forms." Meri hoped they tasted better than Lyr made them sound.

Even with the ship's power off, the taps in the bathroom still worked, producing potable water that Meri sucked down eagerly from cupped hands.

"I can try to find a way to refill the tanks later," Lyr said. "For now, with just the two of us, the supply on the ship should last us for weeks as long as we're careful about our consumption."

There were more odds and ends scattered throughout the ship, mostly tools. Meri found a handheld device shaped like a wand that turned out to spray out a mist of plastic that hardened on contact with air; it produced thin sheets of plastic that they draped over and around the open airlock door to create an outdoor tentlike shelter where they could make a fire.

Darkness was falling by the time Lyr had a fire burning, crackling just outside the cargo door. The plastic sheeting was angled to direct smoke away from the ship, though Meri still got smoke in her eyes when the wind changed to blow just the wrong way. It made her think of camping out when she was in college.

They couldn't afford nice vacations, of course, not a bunch of cash-strapped college students. But back in the days when she was dating Aaron and Cora was dating Dave, they used to occasionally go on couples camping trips to local campgrounds or state parks. They'd build a fire and roast weenies and marshmallows, before crawling into the big old canvas Army-surplus tent that Dave had found somewhere. It was a heavy monstrosity that smelled like mold and took an hour to set up, with a lot of pinched fingers and jury-rigged rope tying up the sagging places.

She wondered whatever happened to that tent. Surely Cora and Dave hadn't dragged it all the way to Kansas City.

It was very hard not to think about Cora and Toni, last seen huddled in the car. They'd be okay, she thought. Those bastards hadn't gotten them. Cora was probably home in Kansas City right now, with an awful story to tell Dave but not otherwise the worse for wear.

I wonder if she thinks I'm dead.

But she couldn't worry about Cora; there was nothing she could do about it, any more than she could help the other passengers on the crashed module. Secure your own oxygen mask, then help others—it was good advice.

"So how do you open these?" she asked, squeezing one of the ration pouches. It was firm but slightly yielding. She couldn't see any sign of a place to tear it, but there was a button on the side that made her think of the pull-out inflation tube on an air mattress. She tried to work her fingernails under it to see if it pulled out.

"Not yet," Lyr said. He put his hands over hers. "May I?" When she nodded, he flipped the pack over and ripped off a strip of metallic silver stuff that she hadn't even noticed.

But it still didn't open the package. "What's—" she began, and then nearly dropped it as it warmed in her hands. "Sweet! It's like an MRE."

"A what?"

"Military camp food on my planet. They have a chemical heater in the package, too." In her hands, it was now almost too warm to hold comfortably. "Time to open it now?"

"Now you do what you were doing before." He popped out the tube she'd been pulling on. "And you suck on it." He demonstrated, taking a mouthful before handing it to her and reaching for one of his own.

Meri hesitated before putting her lips on it. It was intimate and strange, a kiss one degree removed.

"Blargh," was her reaction when she'd found out what the stuff in the pouch tasted like. It was a bland, slightly salty paste. "You'd *have* to be hungry to eat this stuff. I think even MREs are better than this."

"It's healthy," Lyr said, heating his own.

"Yeah, it tastes like it."

She sipped at the tube, trying not to gag. The night outside their plastic lean-to seemed very dark and very large, filled with strange rustling sounds.

"Do you think the others made it?" Meri asked quietly, when the vast darkness away from the fire became too much; she had to fill it with some kind of sound. "Preet and Edrin and the rest of the prisoners?"

Lyr didn't answer immediately. At last he said, "If we

did, the odds are pretty good for them too. I'll scout when it gets light."

"It'll take days to get over the mountains."

"Not for me," Lyr said. "I'll just fly up and get an overview of the landscape."

Meri turned to give him a deeply startled look. "You can *fly?*"

"Didn't I mention that?"

"No!"

"I keep forgetting you don't know of dragons."

"Dragons?" she repeated. Surely he couldn't mean—*that*. She got the sense sometimes that the translator was struggling to find a rough equivalent for something that had no similar word in the target language. But she also remembered the huge hot presence she'd touched with her mind, after their crash—the way it was him, and not-him at the same time—

"Dragon?" she asked, and sent him a mental image, which happened to be the CGI dragon from the *Hobbit* movies; it was the first thing she could think of.

A quick flash of surprise lit his eyes. "Your world knows of us?"

"Yes—but—they're not real. They're imaginary."

But aliens weren't supposed to be real either. And she was sitting beside a campfire on a planet with actual dinosaurs. Why not dragons too? In the firelight, with those iridescent ripples of color across his bronze skin whenever he moved, he did look like a dragon made flesh, a dragon in a man's skin.

"I am very real," he assured her, and brushed her hand with the side of his own.

"Do you actually change shape, or what? You don't have wings."

"I do change shape. I'll show you tomorrow, when it isn't dark. I'll also see how the hunting is. We may be able to eat those—what did you call them?" He sent her a mental picture of the swimming creature.

"Dinosaurs. I mean, obviously they aren't, since we're on another planet and all, but they kind of look like them."

"In any case, it's possible we can eat them. I'll have to catch one and scan it with the cuffs to find out."

Meri touched the silver band bisecting his wrist. He didn't seem to object. "I need to get some of these. Can you teach me how to use them?"

Lyr shook his head. "They won't work for you unless you have the mods to use them. Do you?"

"Mods?"

"I expect that's a no." Lyr touched one of his cuffs and it sprang open, leaving his wrist bare. He turned his arm to show her his naked wrist in the firelight. Hair-fine silver threads glimmered on his skin. "There are implanted contacts to connect to the cuffs, and nanites in my bloodstream to power them and allow them to receive mental commands. This is one of the ways that Galateans keep other races from stealing and using their technology."

"But the pirates had them, didn't they?"

"Most of the pirates were Galateans. And it's not impossible for other people to use them. They just need to have had the necessary surgical modifications." He touched the underside of her wrist lightly with his fingertips, a soft touch shivering across her skin. "Most people who live within the Empire have the mods. You need cuffs to do things as basic as open doors and make financial transactions. Of course, most people don't have the military-grade ones that Tamir and I do."

His fingertips still moved across her unmarked, unmodified skin, tracing the lines of tendons and veins. It was a feather-light touch, a reminder of the incredible delicacy of which he was capable. Just as the ferocity with which he'd hacked up the trees had reminded her of the other side of him, the killer and warrior.

"I am sorry if I offended you earlier," Lyr said quietly.

"When?"

He was looking not at her, but at her hand, lying open and relaxed in her lap. His gentle tracing of the lines of her wrist moved on to her palm. "On the hill. When you hugged me."

"You didn't offend me." Her voice came out on a breath, the words mostly unspoken, carried on the link between them.

"I don't want you to think that your touch was ... unwelcome."

"I didn't think that," she breathed.

The link between them was alive and thrumming with energy, with anticipation. She hadn't been aware of it strengthening until it was there, shivering at the edge of her awareness.

"Lyr ... do your people kiss?"

His fingertips paused in their sweeping motion across her skin. "Kiss?"

"Kiss. Yes." She could feel her cheeks growing warm. "You know ... touching mouths?"

"I know what kissing is." He seemed amused, and perhaps a little wistful. "But as for your question, I do not know."

"You don't know?" She'd anticipated a number of reactions, from a confident "Of course" to disgust or dismay. But this wasn't any of those.

"I was young when I left my asteroid. My people are

reticent about public displays of sexual interest. I am not sure what our courting behavior is like."

"You do have sex, though?" she asked anxiously. If she was going to have to stop fantasizing about that firm, copper-colored body flexing against her own, she wanted to know *right now*.

"Oh, yes," he murmured. "We do."

"Do you want me to ... show you? How to kiss?"

"I ... I'm not sure."

His hand still rested in her palm. She covered it with her own, and was shocked to realize he was trembling.

"Lyr ... what are you afraid of?"

I don't know. Through the link, this time, and with it came an abrupt glimpse of a starfield, something exploding, a raw flood of grief and pain—

A sob caught in her throat. Meri realized there were tears in her eyes. Lyr tried to jerk his hand away, but she held onto it, wrapping her fingers tight around his. He'd cut off the rush of emotions as soon as he'd realized she was feeling them, but that raw ache lingered, tightening her throat and sinking claws of grief into her chest. She knew that pain; it was what she'd felt after Aaron died.

"Lyr ..." Her voice came out strangled, still fighting her way through a grief and loss that was not her own. "What *was* that?"

"Nothing." It was spoken aloud with no mental component at all; he had pulled back, putting up walls. But she didn't *want* him to, not now, not when she was finally starting to feel as if there was something real between them and not just the desperation of two people in danger together. She groped for him mentally, not sure what she was doing, but wanting desperately to know what emotions underlay that single flat word, reaching for another look at that star-laced ... metaphor? memory? that she'd seen earlier.

*Don't.*

It came down the link, carrying the force of a rebuke, with the weight of his anger behind it. Startled, she jerked back, and he pulled his hand free.

*Don't,* he repeated. _*To seek after another's private thoughts is unforgivably rude. It is the first thing we teach our children. Don't ever do it again.*_

"I'm sorry."

"You didn't know." But the link between them was closed, and she had the sense of a barrier in the way, something he'd erected to keep her out.

"I'm _really_ sorry. I won't do it again."

"I'm not angry. You simply don't have the mental control my people do. I keep forgetting that."

"Where are you going?" she asked as he got up.

"To gather more firewood. I'll be back soon."

"I did offend you, didn't I? Lyr—"

"Hush." He touched her shoulder, a light brush of his fingertips. "I'm not angry at you. I just need a few minutes alone."

Meri put up her hand to cover his, and he let her for a few seconds before sliding his fingers out from under hers. "Okay. Just come back soon."

*I will.* The words lingered on the link between them as he vanished into the darkness outside the circle of firelight.

IT WAS NOT as dark as it had seemed at first. There were two moons in the sky, one high and crescent-shaped, the other lower and fuller. The planet's rings had a faint luminescence as well, like a band of pale chalk drawn on the night sky.

Lyr had to work on keeping his mental barriers in place. Underneath was a roiling, seething mass of emotions, as if everything he'd been trying not to feel was boiling up, on the verge of erupting.

He thought he'd trained himself to feel nothing; instead it seemed he'd only managed to bottle it up.

He wanted to shift and fly, but he didn't dare in his current state. Everything was closer to the surface when he was a dragon. What he needed now wasn't catharsis, but calm.

He emptied his mind and simply let himself exist, listening to the small rustles of night creatures going about their business around him. It had been a long time since he'd been on a planet at night. When he let himself think about it, he felt overwhelmed by the knowledge that he was at the bottom of a planetary gravity well, with space immeasurably far away. It was almost as if he could feel the weight of all that atmosphere pressing him down.

He still found planets indescribably alien. Home was the darkness between stars. Home was the curving tunnels of a hollow asteroid, twisting around in organic shapes and opening into huge caverns big enough to fly in, softly lit in gentle colors that were soothing to dragon eyes.

And home, or a home of sorts, was the sterile corridors of a spaceship, ringing with the echoing sounds of voices and footsteps and clanging machinery.

But home had never been *this*, a place so full of life and smells and growing things that every breath he took was a brand new sensory experience. Even the crushed grass beneath his boots was fragrant.

It was serene and beautiful in its alien way. And slowly the pain and rage began to ease out of him, soothed by the calm of the night—and by Meri's presence back at the fire. He could feel her at the back of his mind, humming softly to herself as she went about her business at the campsite. Every once in a while, her thoughts turned his way, and she sent a tentative question in his direction, a little tickle of his name and a wordless, half-formed *Are you okay?*

As he stood there in the dark, it seemed to Lyr that he was balanced between two worlds. One was the great, dark, empty night, the whole wild planet out there. As a dragon, he could vanish into that wilderness. He could live here for the rest of his life, hunting to survive, needing nothing and no one. The Galateans would never find him; he could make sure of it. No one would ever find him.

Freedom—not the sort he wanted, but freedom nonetheless. He would never go home, but as he'd told Tamir, it wasn't as if they would take him back anyway. His people had sold him into slavery, and anyone who had ever loved him had probably forgotten him by now.

Honor held him prisoner, but he hadn't even been trying to escape when freedom had fallen into his lap anyway. And now an empty world, a world that might be completely unknown to the Galatean Empire, had been laid in front of him. Fate had handed it to him like a gift.

But ... then there was the *other* world, that pool of warmth and light back there. When he looked down the hill, he could see the tiny flicker of their campfire, like a candle flame holding back the darkness.

Meri and Tamir needed him to survive. One was badly injured; the other had never been off her world before and could not possibly defend herself against this world's wild creatures.

Meri was still singing softly. Her mind was wide open. He wasn't prying ... not exactly ... but he listened to the words she was singing in her own language, translated through the implant. It was a sweetly sad song about lost love. Freedom was an illusion, Meri was singing in the words of her people; it meant only that you'd lost so much you had nothing else to lose.

Aimed at him? No, he thought; all he sensed from her was the slow easing of her worry and anxiety as the song calmed her. To her, it was only a song.

But she wasn't wrong, he thought, looking out into the dark. The trade-off for escaping his responsibilities would be a lifetime of loneliness. There was a big wide world out there, where he could live forever as a dragon, with no one to care about, no one to mourn.

A great, wide, utterly empty world.

Meri's soft, husky voice sank into low, wordless humming. He looked toward the firelight again. He could see her shadow cast across the side of the ship, dancing in the flickering firelight with each graceful move she made.

He didn't have to walk away now, he told himself. He could always make sure everyone else got safely offworld and *then* make his own way in the wilderness.

And for tonight, perhaps he could catch them some fresh meat.

It only took a few minutes. The night was full of small, skittering creatures. He strode back toward the fire down the hill with a small blue-and-orange lizard dangling from his hand, dispatched with a quick stroke of his arm blades. It was good to know he could still hunt.

While he was gone, Meri had moved Tamir's float-hauler from the bridge down to the cargo bay and parked it on the floor just inside the airlock. She had also begun to set up a little camp inside the open airlock, spreading blankets near enough to the fire for its light and comfort, but inside the door so they could close it if anything dangerous came along. She'd even washed out their empty ration packs and filled them with water so they didn't have to keep going back to the taps in the ship's head.

Lyr sent a feather-light touch across her mind so that she knew he was there before she looked up from arranging the blankets and saw him in the firelight.

"Just doing a little housekeeping," she said with a quick smile, and then her smile turned teasing. "No firewood?"

"I ... forgot," he admitted sheepishly.

Meri's playful smile turned to a full grin. "It's a relief to know you can forget things like a normal person. What's that?"

He held up the lizard. "A better dinner than the ration packs."

Meri didn't look as pleased as he'd hoped. "Uh ... I think I'd like it better with barbecue sauce and a nice gas-powered grill."

Lyr squatted to give the lizard a quick scan with the cuffs, finding it perfectly compatible with both their metabolic processes, and spitted it on a stick. "What is that song you were singing?"

"Oh? It's called 'Me and Bobby McGee.' It's by a famous blues singer on my world." Meri smiled crookedly in the firelight. "Not that you know what blues is. But I can see you know music."

"Yes. My people have music." He looked down at his work, rather than at her. "I must apologize to you for walking off like that. I behaved dishonorably—"

"Oh, don't start. I know you weren't mad, and if you

were, you had a right. I wanted to know more about you, but that's no excuse for snooping."

"And I should have taught you properly." He looked up, with effort managing to put on a smile. "It's been a very long time since I've taught someone else."

"Did you teach people before? —No, never mind." She shook her head. "That's up to you to tell me. I won't pry."

"I did." With the lizard speared on a stick and propped over the fire, there was little else to do except wait for it to cook. He rose from his crouch and came around to her side of the fire. "They were my sept."

"What's that?" Meri asked quietly. In response to a polite mental request that he sent without even thinking about it, she held out the container of water she'd brought down, tilting it so he could wash his hands under the flow. His people liked to be clean.

"They were my brothers and sisters. The Galateans took them from their homes as children and trained them to fight. Such child-slaves are divided into septs and put under the supervision of an older child. That child was me."

"Oh," she whispered. He risked a glance at her, and found that her eyes were deep and dark in the firelight. "I didn't know ... How old were you?"

"Nineteen standard." Realizing that he didn't know how Earth years compared to Galatean years, he sent her a mental image of himself at that age, lanky and gangling, still growing into his height.

"You were a teenager," she murmured, reaching out a hand as if to touch the image of his younger self. "Put in charge of children."

"Tamir was responsible for all of us." He looked over at Tamir, just visible inside the inner airlock door—a bundle of silver blankets and tufts of striped fur, sunk deep in a coma that might heal or kill him. "He was the one who taught us to fight, while I handled the day-to-day care of the sept."

For so long, he had refused to think about those days. Now it came rushing back to him. They had been so small when he had first met them, a diverse group of children from different worlds, each with his or her own unique skills and abilities.

"Where are they now?" Meri asked.

"Dead," he whispered. "All dead."

The warmth of her hand on his own made him flinch, but when she started to pull away, he turned his hand up and she settled hers in his, and held on.

"Do you want to talk about them?"

Someday, he sent through the link, not trusting his voice. **Not tonight.**

He sensed wordless acknowledgment, and finally brought himself to look at her. She was beautiful in the fire-light, her skin a gorgeous warm brown, with the fire's glow bringing out a thousand shades of amber and green in her dark eyes.

"But tonight," he said quietly, aloud. "... Tonight I would like you to remind me that I am still alive, even if they are not. Tonight I want you to show me how to kiss."

TWELVE

HIS WORDS STARTLED HER, but not as much as his face, turned toward her in the firelight with his lips parted. His eyes were molten silver in the flames' flickering light.

She leaned forward, drawn to that silver fire. His lips were as soft as they looked. Their first touch was the gentlest brush of his mouth on hers, but she was the one who surged back toward him, opening her mouth, letting him taste her.

He tasted *good*. His mouth was wet heat and restrained eagerness, and desire coursed through her in a sudden, shocking rush. It had been so long since she'd been touched that way, so very long, not since Aaron—

She clamped down fast on the thought of Aaron, not wanting Lyr to know that his kiss had made her think of another man. But it was too late; even if he didn't understand the reason for it, he'd already noticed that she'd gone still against him. He pulled back immediately.

"Did I hurt you?" he asked, fast and worried. "Was I doing something wrong?"

"Oh, no, no." She brushed her hand across the side of his

face. His skin was so warm; how could she have ever thought it would be cold? "It wasn't you. What hurt me was ... something else. Something that happened to me years ago."

"Do you want to tell me?"

"Lyr, I ..." How could she share her grief with him, her small and personal grief, when he'd lost so much? She hesitated, and as she did, she felt him start to pull back. He must think she wanted him to. "No, wait. It's just ... this is hard for me to talk about. I haven't really talked to anyone about it yet. Just my grief counselor—" She stopped, sensing his puzzlement. "Surely you must have something like that? Someone who was there to talk to you after your friends died? Someone who was assigned to do it, perhaps?"

She got a quick flash of Tamir before it was suppressed. "No, no one."

"They didn't do *anything*?"

"Why would they? I'm hardly a person to them. I'm a tool."

Meri took a breath and ran her hand across her face before taking his hand in both of hers. "I think that's reprehensible. But I guess I'm not one to talk, because even with all the resources in the world, I went through the motions of going to therapy, but I never really opened up. Not to the therapist. Not to my best friend." The pang that she felt at the thought of Cora was already more distant than it had been earlier in the evening. Earth seemed so far away it was hard to imagine now.

Lyr was still waiting, listening—not just with his body language, but with his mind as well. She couldn't even say how she knew, but she could sense that his mind was open for whatever she wanted to show him or share with him.

"Aaron," she said softly. It had been a very long time

since she's spoken her dead husband's name aloud. "Aaron was his name."

Now that she'd said it, the words came easier.

"We were high school sweethearts. I guess I always knew I was going to marry him, but life happened first. I went to nursing school, and he went into the Army—the military. He was a soldier." As she spoke, she felt the pride well up in her, still as fresh as it had been all those years ago when she had first seen him in his uniform. She'd been scared, she would be lying if she said she hadn't been, but also so excited. And *he'd* been excited. He had wanted to travel and see the world, and neither of them had the money for it.

"We got married after I graduated. Our lives were so good then. But I was also so afraid for him. He did two deployments to a place called ... well, it doesn't matter what it was called. A far-away place on my world. We had decided when we married that we were going to wait to start a family until he got a stateside placement or got out. I didn't want to be like some of the other military wives I knew, struggling to raise small children with their husbands so far away." She swallowed hard, pushing down the bitter lump in her throat. If they had made different choices back then—would it have made it easier to bear, if she'd had a little piece of Aaron to keep with her after he was gone? Or would it have only given her more grief to raise a son or daughter who had never known their father?

"Was he killed?" Lyr's voice was so soft she heard it mainly through her mind. He must be sensing the grief that had come flooding back, crushing her heart.

"Yes," she whispered. "But not in war. Not in war. And that was the most unfair thing. He came back *safe*. He wasn't planning to re-up after the second time—that is, he wasn't going to stay in the Army after he finished the years he signed up for. We had it all planned. We were going to buy a house and raise a family and ..."

She had to stop as her words faltered and died. Instead she opened up her mind and pushed the thought at Lyr, the memory of the worst night of her life, when she'd gotten a call from a fellow nurse at the ER to warn her before the police could talk to her. On the way home, on a rainy night, her husband had stopped to help a stranded motorist change a tire, because that was Aaron: always doing things to help people. In the dark and the rain, he'd been struck and killed by a speeding car.

Lyr's arms were around her. She couldn't even remember how that had happened. She held back for only an instant before resting her head against his shoulder.

"I always used to love the rain before that," she whispered. Was she speaking aloud, or only inside her head? Either way, she could tell Lyr heard her; she sensed him listening quietly, sending support down the link. "I loved listening to the rain on the roof, soothing me to sleep. After that, though ... for a long time I couldn't sleep on rainy nights at all. I would sit up with a cup of coffee, trying to read or watch TV or whatever it took to keep me from thinking about—"

The tears came without warning in a sudden flood.

She couldn't even remember the last time she'd cried on someone's shoulder. She tensed up in his arms, but Lyr pulled her against him, rubbing a soothing hand up and down her back, and Meri gave in to a tide of grief she'd been fighting for years. She had cried a lot in the immediate wake of Aaron's death—but in private, trying her best to hold it together at work. Eventually she'd pushed it down completely, convincing herself somehow that, against all odds, she had to get on with her life.

Except she hadn't, had she? Cora had been right, those times they'd argued on the phone as Cora tried to talk her into moving out of Columbus, getting out and seeing a little of the world, living a little. She'd been spinning her wheels, going through the motions, losing herself in her daily routines because she didn't want to think about a future without Aaron in it.

But the future kept coming, whether you wanted it to or not. All she had managed to do was get ten years older without ever really getting anywhere else at all.

As awful as the last couple of days had been, she hadn't felt this alive, this present in the world, since that night when she'd gotten that awful phone call. For a long time she'd felt as if some part of her had died with Aaron, but she now realized it was more like she'd ... *stopped*. She'd gotten stuck that night, and she had been living in that endless, terrible moment for the last ten years.

But now, sobbing on Lyr's shoulder, even as grief cut through her like a knife, she realized that she was *feeling* it. She wasn't dead inside anymore. She was aware of everything: the warmth of his arms around her, the crackling of the fire and the smell of smoke, the unaccustomed aches and pains where she'd been wrenched around and thrown to the deck on the ship.

And that made her cry even harder. She didn't *want* to go on without Aaron. They were supposed to be forever.

But it dawned on her slowly, as she sobbed and Lyr petted her back and sent wordless reassurance through the link, that she *had* gone on. It was ten years later now. She'd survived a grief that she had thought would destroy her, and now that she was letting it in again, she found that it wasn't as devastating as she remembered. In fact ...

She was sad, but she didn't feel broken. Those days right after Aaron's death when she'd laid in bed for days and never wanted to get up again were over. It hurt, but it hurt like the pain of a twisted ankle or a torn muscle that was starting to heal. Even broken hearts could recover. There would always be a scar, but as a nurse, she knew that sometimes things healed stronger than they were before. A broken bone deposited new bone around the break, and muscles had to be hurt a little bit in order to get stronger.

"Thanks," she mumbled. She pulled away and sniffled, wiping uselessly at her face and trying not to think about how messy and swollen it must be. "I'm sorry—" But she stopped herself. She wasn't going to apologize for grieving. Not to him. "I mean, thank you. Thanks for being there for—"

She broke off, because she had looked up to his face, and was startled to see something glistening there.

Tears.

Lyr looked equally puzzled when she gazed at his face in open surprise. "Are you all right?" he asked.

"Yes ... I mean, no, but I will be. It's just ..." She touched his face lightly, felt the dampness on her fingertips. "I didn't know your people could cry."

"I'm not ..." He broke off and raised a hand to his cheek. Wonder dawned on his face. "Oh."

"Are *you* all right?" She wasn't sure how to read his stunned expression. He was staring at his damp fingertips as if he'd never seen them before.

"I didn't know I could do that anymore," he murmured. He raised his wet eyes to her face. "I thought I had lost my ability to weep, as I've lost my ability to love."

Her heart broke anew, and not for herself this time. She took his hands in hers. "Lyr," she said quietly, "if there is one thing I've learned about you by now, it's that you definitely haven't lost the ability to love."

She leaned forward and kissed him again, and this time there was only the faintest, most fleeting thought of Aaron—mainly, that she didn't think Aaron would want her to be alone; he would have been the first to encourage her to move on and find someone new—and then she lost herself in the heat of Lyr's mouth, the touch of his hands.

They kissed and kissed in the firelight. Her body thrummed with desire, and she felt something answering across the link, an intensity of emotion that quivered like a plucked guitar string. And yet ...

"Lyr," she said at last, breathless from kissing him. "I don't want you to think—I mean, I'm really enjoying this, a *lot*, but I think ... maybe I'm not quite ready for anything else. Not tonight. Is that all right?"

"It is fine." He caressed her hair lightly. "I don't think I am, as you say ... ready for anything else tonight either. And you are very tired."

"You can tell that, huh?"

"It's been an extremely long day for both of us."

"No kidding." Now that he'd mentioned it, weariness came crashing down on her. She could hardly keep her eyes open.

Lyr gave a sudden, short laugh, and lunged to rescue the lizard-on-a-stick from the fire. "Also, I am afraid that dinner might be slightly burnt."

It was charred black on the outside, but still pinkish on the inside. They both picked at the pale meat, which tasted a lot like chicken to Meri. (It's true, she thought; everything tastes like chicken.) Half-burned lizard washed down with plain water wasn't exactly a gourmet meal, but it was better than the ration pouches ... slightly.

While Lyr heaped ashes on the coals of the fire, Meri checked on Tamir again and hooked the last saline pack to his IV. If he didn't wake up soon, she was going to need to figure out something else to prevent dangerous dehydration. Distilled water, perhaps? She wished she knew more about field medicine. Everything she knew relied on having an entire hospital full of equipment, drugs, and specialized surgeons to back her up.

But he'd hung in there so far. She found no sign of infection or fever. "Keep it up," she murmured, patting his shoulder.

Lyr was spreading blankets on the floor, making up beds for them. Meri took off her shoes and decided to keep everything else on; it was getting chilly in the cargo bay now that she was no longer getting her face toasted by the fire. And there was another reason, as well.

"Lyr," she said, sitting on a blanket with her arms around her knees. "Could I ask you to do me a favor?"

He looked up. "Of course."

"Will you hold me while I sleep?"

"Yes," he said quietly. "Yes, I would be very happy to do that."

He closed the airlock door most of the way, leaving only a thin sliver open to the night, not big enough for anything dangerous to get in but wide enough to give them some fresh air. Then they arranged themselves in a nest of blankets.

Meri had slept alone for ten years, and it felt strange, relearning how to fit herself together with someone in her bed. There was some fidgeting and rearranging as they both worked out where all their limbs should go. But eventually they were curled together, with her head pillowed on his arm.

"You tell me if this gets uncomfortable, okay? I don't want you to end up with your arm falling asleep or something."

"I am not uncomfortable," he said quietly, and moved slightly, tucking one of his feet under hers.

"Try telling me that in a few hours," she murmured.

"Go to sleep, Meri."

She expected to have trouble falling asleep; she always had difficulty sleeping in a strange place, and this time she was sleeping on a bare floor on an alien planet. But sleep washed over her like a tide. Wrapped in his arms, she sank into darkness before she even had time for the day's memories to haunt her.

THIRTEEN

LYR WOKE with Meri's head pillowed on his arm.

He had awakened frequently throughout the night, alerting every time something small rustled in the brush. Each time, he found Meri sleeping deeply against him, as if she hadn't a fear in the world with him nearby. Her sleeping contentment was a warm, lazy hum in the back of his mind, soothing him back down into sleep every time he woke.

It was light now, a shaft of thin morning sun slanting through the crack in the door. Lyr lay for a time and looked down at Meri's sleeping face, struck anew by her beauty in the soft dawn light. Her skin was perfection, a warm soft brown, endlessly touchable, infinitely beautiful.

He succumbed to temptation enough to brush the backs of his fingers across the corner of her mouth. She stirred slightly and then sank back into sleep.

Lyr sat up and carefully untangled his limbs from hers. He left her tucked under a blanket, and stepped out in the clean air of morning. The sky was a vivid blue overhead, with only a few trailing wisps of clouds. He walked a quick circuit around the perimeter of the campsite, checking for tracks and scenting the wind, but there was no sign that anything larger than the tiny forest-dwelling lizards had approached them last night. No predators or obvious dangers, no reason why he couldn't leave his companions alone for a few minutes while he took a quick look around from the air.

He climbed the hill that he and Meri had walked up last night. At the top of the hill, he shifted and sprang off the edge, spreading his wings as he fell and then flew.

It had been a long, long time since he'd flown with wind rather than vacuum beneath his wings. Flying in atmosphere was always a feast for the senses, in a way that flying in space wasn't. The air was pleasantly cool, carrying the sharp salt tang of the sea. It rushed over his wings as he circled higher, basking in the sensation of cool breezes and the sun on his back.

It was his first opportunity to get a good overview of the area around their campsite. The little valley in which they'd landed was one of many such valleys where the ramparts of the mountains rolled down to the sea. The entire coastline was rumpled like an unmade bed. It made him despair of being able to find the fallen passenger module. Even if it had survived their crash landing, it could be anywhere.

He flew lower, sweeping along the white sand of the beach. A small cluster of medium-sized lizardlike creatures with long legs bolted at his approach, bounding across the sand in long leaps. His claws twitched with the urge to pick off one of them for breakfast, but instead he soared higher and watched them take shelter in a brush-choked ravine where one of the many streams flowed from the mountains down to the ocean.

He could hunt later. Right now, he didn't want to get distracted, give in to his instincts, and leave Meri alone and unprotected. Anything could attack while he was gone. Once they had the campsite better secured, he could start making longer excursions and begin a systematic search for the module.

For now he contented himself with a single quick survey flight. Rising on thermals, higher and higher, he scanned the landscape and particularly the mountains. He was confident could fly over them without difficulty, but it would take him out of range of Meri's ability to contact him. He wasn't prepared to leave her and Tamir alone on a world filled with unknown hazards, not quite yet.

After one last long circle over the sea, he touched down on the hilltop, shifting as he landed, with a moment's regret for the loss of his wings. He'd almost forgotten what it was like to be able to shift and fly whenever he wanted. Already he yearned for the sky again.

But not yet.

He could still feel the warm, dreaming presence of Meri's sleeping mind. She wasn't awake yet. He'd work while she slept, he thought, to make the campsite safer and nicer for her.

He tried not to think of it as making a beautiful nest for his mate. But some part of him was thinking it anyway.

MERI WOKE to the sound of strange birds singing. She had been dreaming a flying dream. She'd had them before, but never so vivid. It was like she was really there, hanging between sky and earth with her own wings keeping her aloft.

For a little while she lay wrapped up in blankets, drifting between sleep and waking, listening to the unfamiliar whistling songs and the rustling of wind in the trees. It was light outside, the clear gold light of early morning, with an unseen sun shafting into the cargo bay to paint the opposite wall in shades of amber and rose-peach and other paint-chip colors.

She wasn't afraid, nor did she feel lonely. Lyr was no longer under the blankets with her, but she could feel him nearby. He was sending out a little trickle of reassurance to her along the link, letting her know that he wasn't far.

I'm on an alien planet, she thought, and tried to work her mind around that thought. It was too huge, too hard to believe.

I'm on an alien planet with dinosaurs.

That worked a little better; at least it made her laugh to herself.

You're awake! Lyr said in her mind.

Good morning, she said back, as she sat up and stretched. Her arms and shoulders were stiff from sleeping on the floor, and she felt rumpled and sticky, now regretting the choice to sleep in her clothes. Her eyes were puffy and dry; she'd forgotten how unpleasant it was in the morning when you'd had a good cry before bed. And she *really* wished that she'd stuck a toothbrush in her purse along with all the other things.

If you need hygiene items, there are a few in the ship's head. I can show you.

A little later, maybe. What are you doing?

Rather than answering in words, Lyr showed her. He was knee-deep in water, wrestling a large rock into a half-built dam.

You found a spring! Is it close?

A 3D mental map showed her his approximate location, a little deeper in the thicket, not too far from the ship. The images rotated and changed to show her what he was up to, piling rocks to pen up the rushing water. He'd already made a fairly respectable pool.

What's that for?

Bathing, for one thing. I was also thinking we might be able to divert some of the water to the ship's tanks, once we start running low.

Strong muscles rippled under his gleaming bronze skin as he picked up another rock. With her mind in contact with his, she could feel the satisfying stretch and pull of muscles that wanted to be worked, even as she was also seeing it from the outside in the images he sent her. Sweat glistened distractingly on his bare arms.

I can feel you watching me, he added in a teasing mental tone.

You're* showing *me, so it's not like you have anything to complain about. Meri ran her fingers through her hair, tucking in a few twists that had started to come undone. **Is that pool ready for its inaugural test yet? Because a bath sounds great.**

Amusement came back to her through the link. **The water's cold.**

Yeah, but it's cold on the ship too, and I think I'd rather bathe in a sunlit pool than sponge-bathe in the dark.

More amusement. Agreement. Assent.

She got up and went through the by-now-familiar routine of checking on Tamir. He showed no signs of waking up, though breath still whispered through his dry lips. Meri peeled off the IV cuff and wondered if it would be possible to rouse him with a stimulant enough to get him rehydrated by mouth. It probably wouldn't be good for him, but there were no good choices here. The longer he stayed comatose, the weaker he'd get and the less likely he'd come out of it at all.

But she wasn't giving up on him yet, and she hated to ruin the morning with dark thoughts. She cleaned him up, changed his blankets, and bundled the soiled ones to wash.

She found the supplies Lyr had mentioned in the bathroom, an alien toothbrush that was recognizable as such, and a couple packets that smelled like soap. She couldn't quite bring herself to find out if the soap was also meant as toothpaste, so she brushed her teeth with water, standing just outside the cargo door. The morning was fresh and bright and smelled like clean growing things.

The birdsong actually turned out to be coming from tiny lizards, sitting on tree branches and warbling their tiny, piping cries. Meri tried whistling one of their songs back at them, and was utterly charmed when they whistled it back to her.

The thought of taking a photo occurred to her, and she crept back into the cargo bay to get her phone, only to remember that the battery was dead.

Lyr, do you think your cuffs can charge my phone?

Your what?

It's ... well, kind of what your cuffs are to you, I guess. I wanted to take some pictures.

Bring it with you. I can try.

She tucked the phone into her pocket and gathered up the bundle of soiled blankets. When she ducked out from under the plastic shelter, the whistling lizards scattered, only to reconvene on a higher branch.

Do any of these animals have names? she asked Lyr.

Not that I know of. I've never seen most of them before.

Can we name them?

Amusement. *What do you want to name?*

She tried to send him a mental image of the whistling lizards. *We could call them whistlers. Or song-geckos.*

What would you call last night's dinner, then?

Better than those ration things, she sent, and felt his silent laughter in her head.

She expected to have to fight her way through the thicket, but discovered that Lyr had cleared a path down to the spring. Meri picked her way around hacked-off, finger-thick stumps oozing sap and ducked under low-hanging branches with strange, vivid leaves. Something dashed out from under her feet, making her jump.

Meri! Is something wrong?

No, I just got surprised by some kind of animal.

Dangerous?

I don't think so.

She caught sight of it again, a rabbit-sized creature, bright green and red, running on its back legs. It stopped at the base of a tree and looked back at her with sharp, beady eyes. It looked like a lizard, except—was that _fur_?

*Lyr, that lizard you killed last night wasn't furry, was it? *

No.

This one was covered in green fur, or maybe hairlike feathers. It had a bright red throat, standing out like the jeweled throat of a hummingbird and pulsing as it breathed. She sent a picture of it in Lyr's direction.

I'm going to call this one a hummingbird gecko. Please don't eat it; it's too cute.

Amusement came down the link. *There are plenty of other options. But you can't be too picky when you're in a survival situation. I take it your people aren't hunters.*

I've certainly never hunted.

I can teach you. He seemed to like that idea.

Someone woke up in a good mood today, she thought, and the tangible sense of Lyr's good mood lifted her spirits even further. She started walking onward, and the lizard whisked about and vanished into the bushes.

Her practical nature told her sternly that she shouldn't be this cheerful while trapped on an alien planet with no idea how they were going to survive. But somehow she felt like things were going to work out. Lyr could take care of her. He'd hunted the lizard last night; he could do more of that. And someday they would find a way back to civilization. She knew before too long, she'd be missing things like Netflix and Starbucks and proper indoor plumbing.

But right now, she had no particular desire to go back at all, not to Columbus or Kansas City or anywhere else.

I'd rather be here than living in Cora and Dave's guest bedroom, that's for sure.

Seeing the spring in person gave her an odd sense of déjà vu after seeing it in Lyr's thoughts. It looked like something from a calendar picture, a twisting ribbon of fast-flowing water between rocky banks. Lyr stood knee-deep in the slowly expanding pool he was building, adding more rocks to his dam. As she'd seen in his mental image, he was naked to the waist and barefoot, with his pants rolled up above the knees.

"It's not very deep yet," he said over his shoulder.

Meri dropped the bundle of sheets and dipped her hands into the springwater to wash them. "You weren't kidding when you said it's cold!" she exclaimed. "How can you stand it?"

"I prefer 'refreshing.'" He hesitated, but she could sense the question he wasn't asking, hovering just below the surface.

"Tamir's the same," she said. "Not worse, but not better."

"Ah." He didn't ask more. She had a feeling her own pessimism about Tamir's prognosis came through the link.

But they were alive. And on this brilliant morning, for the first time in ten years, she had absolutely no regrets about that. She *wanted* to be alive. She was ...

She was ... happy?

Meri grinned. Yes. She was happy. She had almost forgotten what it felt like.

Lyr waded ashore to wrestle another rock out of the muddy bank. "I could give you privacy if you'd like to bathe."

"In a minute. First, can you see if you can charge my phone?"

"Oh, yes. Of course." He washed the mud off his hands and crouched beside her on the bank. "Show it to me."

"This is where the power cord normally plugs in." She showed him the plug. "But I don't have it with me. I left it on and it drained the battery."

Lyr stroked a thumb across his cuff and extruded a thin wire. Holding her phone in his palm, he slipped it into the power plug.

Surely that couldn't work, Meri thought. It would be like plugging a laptop charger into her phone only vastly more so. But like the auto-calibrating dosage on the injectors, the advanced tech of the cuffs seemed to be able to deal with it. When she powered on her phone, the screen brightened.

"What does your device do?"

"You use it to talk to people, or to look up things on the internet." Not that he'd know what the internet was, but maybe they had something similar. "Not that I can do any of that here, I bet." Indeed, there were no service bars, not that she'd expected any. "You can also take pictures. May I take a picture of you? If it's not against your culture or anything."

"No, go ahead."

With the phone still attached to his wrist by the wire, she took a picture and then turned the phone to show it to him: Lyr, bronze and gorgeous, his dark blue hair gleaming in the morning sun and the alien forest behind him. It occurred to her that perhaps having photographic evidence of aliens wasn't the best idea if they ever got back to Earth, but if it did happen, it would be nice to have something to remember him by. It wasn't like she could take him back with her.

"You're sad," Lyr said. "What's wrong? You were happy a moment ago."

"It's nothing." How could she say she was thinking about the future for the first time, and already regretting their parting when they hadn't even got off this planet yet?

Besides, who says we have to say goodbye? We could be intergalactic pen pals. Or more ...

"If you have a picture of me, may I take a picture of you?"

"I'm probably a mess," she demurred.

"I can assure you, you are definitely not a 'mess.'" Lyr raised his arm and rotated his palm. "You are beautiful. And now I have your lovely smile frozen in time."

"Oh, you did it just now? I didn't know your cuffs could take pictures too."

"Certainly. I'll show you."

An image manifested above his wrist, floating in midair. It was her, all right, caught in the act of nervously half-smiling and looking like a total dork.

"Oh, Lyr, *please* take a better one. Give me a chance to smile properly, at least."

A smile tilted his mouth and crinkled his silver eyes. "You tell me when."

"Now," she said, through her best weddings-and-graduations smile.

"Hmm." Lyr manifested a new image beside the other. "I like the first better." His eyes sparkled.

"They're both terrible," she protested, swiping a hand through them. The images wavered and stabilized. "Here, I'll do it. Do your people take selfies?"

"What's a selfie?"

"How can you have wrist cameras and not take selfies?" She held up her phone at arm's length, brushed back her twists and smiled at the camera. "Selfie," she said, showing him. "Here, let's do a proper one with both of us."

Before she could let herself get shy about it, she put her arm around him and pressed her cheek to his. Being this close was very nice indeed. "Smile," she told him, and snapped a couple pictures of them.

The result, when she paged back to the gallery, was startlingly weird: Meri with her arm around a silver-eyed, blue-haired alien wearing the nervous grin of a senior on prom night. Meri laughed out loud. "What do you think?"

"I think I am not terribly fond of how I look in pictures." But his voice was playful.

"Oh hush, you're gorgeous." Lyr still had his arm around her; she snuggled against him and paged back. "Do you want to see my world? What it looks like when it's not being attacked by aliens, I mean."

"I would love to."

What exactly *did* she have pictures of in here, anyway? Hopefully nothing embarrassing. "Uh, this first part is touristy stuff, it looks like. I did some sightseeing with my friend Cora. So this is the world's largest basket, and this is the famous Dublin, Ohio field of giant cement corn cobs, which I'm sure you care a lot about. And here's me with Cora and her baby at my apartment, former apartment, I mean. Cora is the friend I was going to live with, if I hadn't gotten, well, you know."

"Is that who you were protecting on your planet? In the vehicle?"

She turned against his shoulder to give him a surprised look. "I didn't know you saw that much."

"I saw you used your chemical weapon against the Hnee pirate. I was very impressed with your courage."

"My—oh, the pepper spray? Yeah, for all the good *that* did." But his praise made her glow. She looked back at the picture, the baby in Cora's arms and Meri with her arm snugged around her friend. Was the dissatisfaction and unhappiness on her face always that obvious to other people? She looked, in the picture, like she didn't want to be there—like she didn't want to be much of anywhere.

It made her uncomfortable to look at. She paged back.

"Oh, this is my going-away party at the hospital." Balloons, a cake, presents. No selfies here, thankfully. She didn't want to look at that miserable attempt at a smile anymore. "And this is ... why the heck did I take a picture of a *hamburger*? I guess I must have been posting it to Facebook." She wished she had a hamburger right now. She paged past that one quickly.

"What is F—"

"Oh no. I am not explaining Facebook to an alien. Anyway, I bet you have your own version. I bet there's something like Facebook anywhere people have the technology for it, complete with an alien Mark Zuckerberg and everything." She had to laugh at herself, then. "I'm probably confusing the heck out of you. Sorry."

"I might not understand everything you say, but I like to listen to you talk about your world." He reached a fingertip to flick past a few pictures of autumn leaves and a neighbor's cat and then— "Who is this?"

"Oh," she said softly. "That's Aaron. My, uh. My late husband."

It was a photo of Aaron in his dress uniform. She was going to speed past it, flip on to something else, *anything* else. But she hesitated, her fingertip resting just below the smile she missed so badly.

"There is no shame in loving one who is gone," Lyr said quietly. "Your love does you credit. I know he was dear to you. He will always be dear to you. He looks like he was a fine man."

"He was," she whispered. Tears threatened again, but didn't fall. She was so goddamn *tired* of crying, and that made her angry—angry at herself, angry at Aaron for leaving her, angry at the world. She brushed her finger across the screen to banish the photo gallery. "Maybe that's enough pictures for now."

Lyr played gently with her hair, light strokes of his fingers that helped to ground her. "What else can your phone do?"

"Well, it can't make laser shields, that's for sure." She dashed at her eyes and was a little surprised to find them dry. "Let's see. You can play games on it." She brought up a chess game to demonstrate, noting in passing that the battery, in defiance of everything she knew about phone battery chargers, was nearly at full charge already. "You can play music. Oh, do you want to hear the original recording of the song I was singing last night?"

She put on "Me and Bobby McGee," and Janis Joplin's husky voice rolled out of the phone's small speaker.

At first Meri wished she'd picked another song; the wistful tale of lost love and regrets hit a little too close to home. But the song's regretful tone suited her mood. She leaned against Lyr and listened to the music of another world, here in an alien glade with lizard-songs for accompaniment in the background.

And gradually she became aware that Lyr was humming along, a low vibration that thrummed through his chest, picking up the harmonics of the music and carrying them to her, skin to skin.

When the song ended, she tapped the phone to pause it and looked up at Lyr. "I didn't know you could sing."

"The city-ships of my people are filled with music. The corridors are designed for their acoustics as well as their aesthetic beauty." He sounded wistful.

"Will you sing one of your people's songs for me?"

"Most of our songs don't have words. Will that bother you?"

"Of course not," she said, snuggling against him. "We have music without words, too."

After a moment, he began to hum. The sound developed subtle resonances, high and low tones. Meri didn't think a human throat could have reproduced it. The melody was utterly alien, but its beauty entranced her. When the final notes shivered into stillness, she found tears in her eyes for a new reason.

"Lyr, that's lovely. You're incredibly talented."

"Me?" he said, surprised. "I was never more than ordinary. Those of my people who are trained for music are truly sublime. It's like hearing the music of the stars themselves."

"I would love to hear it someday. I used to sing in choir when I was a girl, but I haven't sung in a long time."

"But you were just singing last night. Your voice was very pleasing."

"... oh," she said musingly. "I ... I didn't really think about it. I always used to sing when I'd do housework or go on drives, back when—back when Aaron was alive. I stopped, after."

Had last night really been the first time she'd sung anything in ten years? It seemed impossible. And yet she couldn't remember another time.

"Will you teach me how to sing one of your songs? I would like to learn it."

"After hearing what your music is like, I don't see how ours can possibly compare."

"But I would like to sing with you," he said. "Among my people, to sing with another is an expression of ... emotion, and partnership, and unity. One sings with one's family, and one courts a lover by singing with her. I would like to sing with you, Meri."

She had been aware of what was growing between them, but hearing it voiced was still—almost too much. Music was better than words. She reset the song to the beginning. Lyr hummed along with the acoustic guitar intro. Meri was expecting him to sing the lyrics as she began to sing, but instead he continued to hum. The deep resonance of his voice, the harmonic overtones, made it seem like the accompaniment of a whole orchestra, or the youth choir she used to sing with. She had almost forgotten the soaring delight of singing along with other voices, feeling the vibration of meshing harmonies through her entire soul.

The music segued into a different song, one that was outside her comfortable vocal range, but Lyr kept humming. The music was like a balm, soothing the wounded places in her soul.

She could have stayed here forever ... except she was itchy in the clothes she'd been wearing for days, and starting to get hungry.

"Lyr," she murmured, nudging him. He was still humming, now in melodious (if slightly incongruous) accompaniment to Madonna. "How about we get clean?"

Lyr sat up and detached her phone from his cuff to hand it back to her. She set it on a rock and left it playing. It was probably a little inappropriate to be listening to Prince and David Bowie and Lenny Kravitz instead of the rustling of wind in the trees and the rushing spring, but the little taste of something familiar among all the strangeness was making her happy.

"Do you want privacy?" Lyr asked. "I can go back to the ship if you'd like to bathe alone."

"No." She smiled at him. "I don't mind if you stay."

I don't mind at all.

She wasn't sure if she thought the last part strongly enough for him to "hear" it through the link, but he shot her a quick glance. "You don't mind?"

"Not at all."

She still had to admit to a certain amount of nervousness as she peeled off the clothes she'd been wearing for—wow, how long now? Days? She'd completely lost track of how long it had been since she'd left Earth. She didn't even know how long day and night were on this planet, compared to what she was used to.

But that didn't matter, not really, not right now; what mattered was that the last man to see her naked had been Aaron, ten years ago. And a decade left tracks on a woman's body. She was only in her mid-30s, but as she peeled off her shirt and pulled down her jeans, she still feel acutely self-conscious of every sag and blemish. Lyr was so gorgeous and smooth and toned, like a bronze statue, gleaming in the sun. She was—

Beautiful.

The thought came into her head so strongly that it staggered her.

She looked shyly away from folding her jeans to see Lyr gazing at her in unconcealed wonder. The link between them was as open as it got, and he was sending *Beautiful, lovely, wonderful* at her—not in words, but in a steady flow of inarticulate appreciation.

Girding herself a bit, she undid her bra. Lyr's fascination and *wanting-to-touch* surged at her through the link, along with a strong feeling of restraint—she could sense him holding back. She couldn't help tickling the link back with *want-you-to-touch-me* and she both felt and heard him take in a quick breath.

Beautiful, beautiful, beautiful.

His appreciation tingled through her, a shared circuit of desire, rolling back and forth between them and growing stronger every time.

"You know," she said, as she folded her clothes and put them on a rock away from the risk of getting wet, "I don't think it's fair that I'm not wearing any clothes, and you still have your pants on."

"You know, I think you're right." He stripped off his trousers, making her aware that first of all he wasn't wearing any underwear, and second, if there were any anatomical differences between his people and hers, they weren't visible on the outside. He was gorgeous, wearing nothing but his cuffs. Which of course led to thoughts like—

"Why *do* your people look so much like humans, Lyr?"

"I love that that's what you're thinking about right now," he said, smiling as he waded barefoot into the water's edge.

"I can't help it! I've been medically trained and I keep wondering about it."

"We *are* shapeshifters," he pointed out. "Adjusting our shifted form to resemble our primary trading partners makes sense for us."

"Well, okay, but does all the equipment ... er ... work?"

The smile broadened and became teasing. "Come here and find out."

"Just a minute." She dug through her pockets. "I found these soap thingies in the bathroom. At least I think that's what this is."

"Yes, that's what it is," Lyr said as she held up the packets. "It's a powder. A little goes a long way." He held out a hand. "Come here and enjoy your first bath on this world."

Meri put her foot in the water and instantly jerked it out again. "Oh!"

"It's cold," Lyr said, looking playful.

"I know, I know." She stuck her foot back into the water, curling her toes on the sandy bottom.

"It'll be easier if you just get in. You'll warm up."

"Hypothermia is a thing, you know."

But he was in the water and she wanted to be where he was, so she waded in to her knees, gasping with every step. He was right, though: the icy chill became less noticeable the longer she stayed in.

Or it could just mean that I'm going numb.

She tore open a packet and poured out some of the powder into her palm. It was pale blue and made her think of the pink delousing stuff, which she was still finding traces of in the folds of her clothes. She sniffed at it. There was no smell.

"Do I need to do anything special, or ...?"

"No, it foams on contact with water. One packet should be enough for both of us."

She passed him the rest of the open packet and tried scooping up some water. He was right; it frothed instantly when it got wet, tingling in her palm and looking a lot like shaving foam. She spread it over her skin, and she wasn't sure if there was actually some analgesic property or if it was just psychological, but it seemed to soothe her bruises and smooth away the itching. Splashing cold water on her skin to wash it off was startling but invigorating.

She decided to leave her hair alone; the twists were good for at least a few more days yet, and aside from having to dust off delousing powder occasionally, she really wasn't to the point where her hair needed washing.

Lyr scrubbed himself briskly and efficiently, scooping up handfuls of sand for additional exfoliation. Meri decided she wasn't quite *that* ready to commit to Daniel Boone wilderness survival tactics. Mainly she was just enjoying watching him, the flex of his wet body in the sun, the smooth ripple of his muscles. He was nearly hairless, but his oddly spiky blue hair grew all the way down his neck to the top of his spine, almost like a short mane.

And yet, he seemed physically human in so many ways. She watched, fascinated, the interplay of muscles and bones in a body that could almost *be* human, but for the gleaming soap-bubble colors of his iridescent skin. She wanted to run her hands over his ribs and collarbone, tracing the anatomy that she'd seen in textbooks to tease out the subtle differences.

Lyr had closed his eyes as he poured water over his head from his cupped palms, but when he opened them, he was smiling. "You can touch, if you want. You don't have to stand over there."

She waded to him. Her hands were still slippery with soap. She laid a hesitant palm on his chest, and he put his hand over hers, strong wet fingers guiding the glide of her hand across his pecs.

The hairlessness was both fascinating and strange. Aaron hadn't been a particularly hairy guy, but he'd had chest hair, a scattering of tight dark curls tracing a treasure trail downward. Lyr's chest was—

—was Lyr's, she thought, and he deserved to be taken on his own, not compared to another man. Lyr was himself, utterly unique and utterly beautiful.

Her soapy hands glided over his pecs and shoulders, traced gentle circles over the little dimples in his skin where the spikes came out: a scattering on his shoulders, a line running down each arm to the thin seam of his arm blades. He was a sheathed knife, dangerous, she knew, but not to her. Never to her.

His hands, when they came to rest on her hips, were exquisitely gentle.

She mapped his skin with her hands and then her lips, pressing kisses to his chest. He leaned down to kiss her—the height difference was more noticeable like this—and she finally had a chance to run her hands through his hair, feeling its odd spiky texture, almost more like fine feathers than hair. She stroked her hands through it at the base of his neck, where it grew short and bristling, and felt him shiver against her when she ran her fingernails across his skin.

He kissed her deeply and then made her gasp as he lifted her, bearing her weight seemingly without effort. She wrapped her legs around his waist and her arms around his shoulders and found his mouth again with her own.

The music played on, but it seemed to fade in and out beneath the rushing of wind and water. A soundtrack from another world, blending seamlessly with the sounds of this place, as their bodies melded together until she could hardly remember where he ended and she began.

With telepathy, there was no need for questions. He knew what she wanted, and after years of marriage—even if it was a lifetime ago—she had no hesitation about going for what she wanted. Without breaking the kiss, she reached down to guide him into her.

If she'd had any lingering doubts about whether aliens could have sex the way humans did, it was dispelled in moments. He thrust into her and she cried out in incoherent ecstasy. The link thrummed with their shared pleasure.

"I'm not—on any kind of birth control," she gasped between his thrusts.

"I cannot make your kind pregnant," he murmured against her hair. "We are not compatible that way."

"Oh—carry on, then ..."

After ten years of enforced celibacy, her body had absolutely no doubt that it knew what it wanted and it was headed there at breakneck speed. "Lyr," she gasped, struggling to hold back, but she'd forgotten that he would be able to feel her approaching orgasm through the link. He sped up; she cried out, unable to contain herself any longer, and as the tingling rush became a flood, she felt him start to tip over the edge too. Their shared pleasure washed through her like a tidal wave, and she gasped through the surges with her mouth open against his shoulder, tasting soap and salt on his stream-washed skin.

His shuddering eased, and he let her down carefully into the water, sliding out of her.

"Holy shit," she muttered, clinging to him. She raised her face and Lyr, after a moment's confusion that she felt through the link, realized what she wanted and carefully sampled her mouth.

Good, he sent to her, with his mouth fully occupied with hers. Once again, it wasn't words, just an overall feeling of pleasure and satisfaction.

Good, she sent back. **But my feet are getting cold.**

I think we both need another bath now.

The mental link gave her a hint of what he was about to do. "Lyr!" she gasped as he swept her up in his arms. "Lyr, no! If you dunk me, I'll scream and attract every predator in a twenty-mile radius, I'm not kidding!"

"I'll keep you safe," he murmured, and bent his knees gracefully, taking them both down into the cold pool.

She managed not to scream, but it was a close call as the cold water engulfed her body. The feeling was shocking but not unpleasant—far from it, in fact. With her body already tingling and sensitive, the chill of the water over her whole body brought a flood of new sensation that rushed through her and left her shivering not with cold but with reaction and something bordering on sensory overload.

The water closed over her head. She could very easily have splashed her way to the surface—the water wasn't deep—but instead she let Lyr bear her down to the bottom of the pool. She opened her eyes, something she'd never done underwater before, and found him looking at her through the clear water. He smiled, and she grinned back; then cold water flooded her mouth and she sat up quickly, spitting and choking.

"I'm sorry," Lyr said, supporting her with an arm around her back. "Are you all right?"

"Fine, just thinking I might need more practice at playing in pools." She shook her head, flinging drops of water from her saturated hair, and scooped up a handful to splash on her face. Sitting on the bottom of the pool, the water was up to the tops of her breasts. She was getting used to the chill. The current tugged on her gently, like a slow-motion Jacuzzi as it eddied behind the rock dam. Her entire body was full of a sense of well-being and general deliciously good feeling, despite the goosebumps stood out on her arms.

"I haven't been swimming in a really long time. Can you swim, Lyr?"

"I suppose so," he said thoughtfully. "I haven't ever tried it. I expect it would be much like flying, except underwater—"

He broke off and put a wet hand on her arm.

Meri was silent, responding to the sense of warning coming to her through their link. It wasn't fear that she sensed from him, more like a wary alertness.

You need to get back to the ship, he told her through the link, his sharp gaze scanning the dense brush and trees around the pool.

"Why?" she whispered. "What is it?"

There is something in the woods.

FOURTEEN

LYR WISHED he could be more specific, sensing that he was alarming her even more with his vagueness, but he wasn't sure himself; he wasn't even sure, at first, what had alerted him. It was the sounds of the small animals of the forest, he thought ... or rather, the lack of them.

There was always background noise on a planet. It had made him jumpy at first, but he was starting to think of it as something like the noise of engines and life support equipment on a ship. The background noise meant everything was working as it should. It was when things got hushed that you knew something was wrong.

And right now, things were hushed. The cheerful music seemed extraordinarily out of place.

"Could you turn off your music?" he asked her quietly.

They waded ashore together. Meri was starting to shiver now, with the breeze caressing her wet skin. She shook water off her hand and tapped her device. The music cut out, making him all the more aware of how quiet it was. Ominously so.

Staying close to Meri, Lyr looked around, seeking a hint

of what might have alerted him. He even looked up at the clear sky above, bisected with the colorful band of the planet's rings. It wasn't weather. There was something down here on the ground with them, in the thicket surrounding the pool.

As he had done on the ship while looking for survivors, he tentatively opened his mind to the world around him.

On the ship, it had been overwhelming enough. Here, the thriving ecosystem around him slammed into his mind like a bolt of lightning. He staggered against Meri, sensing her alarm, and managed to stabilize himself only by shutting his mind like the airlock of a ship, with all that life and all those tiny minds on the other side.

He was going to have to practice back at their camp. Until he relearned some control, it was simply too much. He couldn't rely on telepathy to tell him what might be coming for them.

"What should I do?" Meri asked quietly.

We should dress and get back to the ship. Necessities only, he added as she reached for her underwear, and she dropped it and started pulling on her trousers instead.

"Is it that urgent?"

I'd rather not find out.

He was sealing the snap-strips on his trousers and Meri was hastily pulling on her shirt when branches snapped in the thicket. Lyr moved to interpose his body between Meri and whatever might be coming out of the woods. Movement flashed among the sun-dappled shadows.

"Lyr—" she began.

"Stay behind me," he told her softly.

The creature that slunk out of the thicket's edge, across the pool from them, was like a huge version of the smaller lizards Lyr had seen darting in and out of the woods. It was long and lean and *big*, with its pebbly hide mottled green, yellow, and brown in a camouflage pattern that made it nearly vanish in the sun-and-shade dappling of the forest.

"It's a velociraptor," Meri murmured, her voice shaking with the effort it was taking her to remain calm. "A huge one. More like a T-rex-sized—"

Lyr clamped a hand on her wrist. **Don't speak aloud. There are more of them.**

She opened her mouth and then closed it as another creature slunk out of the woods, abreast of the first one.

"Lyr!" Meri had forgotten to be silent, but he didn't blame her, because her alarmed thoughts warned him even before he glanced over his shoulder that two more of the creatures had stepped out onto the path leading back to the ship.

They were surrounded.

Lyr cursed himself for a fool. He had checked for signs of predators or spoor around the stream this morning, but he'd never expected anything to come upon them so quickly, let alone predators that were clearly intelligent pack hunters. He had allowed himself to be distracted by Meri's beauty in the sunny glade, and had forgotten they were stranded on a planet filled with unknown dangers.

"Can you fight them?" Meri asked quietly, struggling into the other sleeve of her shirt without taking her eyes off the creatures.

"Hopefully I won't have to." He aimed at the nearest, fingers curled into a loose fist, and unleashed a low-power stun burst from the cuff.

The green light flickered across its scales, and nothing happened.

"What the—" He raised the power and shot it on the lethal setting. This time there was some effect—it flinched violently and jumped back, then growled low in its throat. Smoke curled up from a shallow, scorched place on its scales.

"What's wrong?" Meri asked.

"My weapons can't penetrate their scales." He'd heard of it, but had never seen it. A few kinds of creatures were naturally immune to Galatean energy weapons. Something about their scales was acting like natural armor, deflecting attacks as shields did.

The whole pack now had their attention focused intently on the two people by the spring. Heads went down, tails swished. That was hunting behavior.

Meri pressed closer to Lyr.

The scales couldn't possibly cover them everywhere. He ought to be able to shoot them in the eyes, but it was going to take some very precise targeting. If he poured enough power into it, a single shot should be able to penetrate their natural shielding, the same way a high-powered energy weapon could punch through a shield. But he only had enough power for one or two shots like that. Not enough to take out the entire pack.

Well ... let them deal with a dragon, then. He could already feel his draconic instincts climbing up inside him, eager for a fight. Letting go against the pirates had been so one-sided that it hardly felt satisfying. It had been a very long time since he'd been able to fight an enemy that gave his dragon a good workout. He curled his hands as the claws began to lengthen. His fangs extended sharp in his mouth, his fighting spines slid out of his arms—

—and Meri flinched away with a gasp as the spines pricked her.

Meri.

He couldn't just let go of his rational side and fight.

Meri would be hurt. That awareness was like a bucket of ice water thrown over his growing bloodlust. He battled it back and got rational control of himself again.

Another of the lizard-creatures had appeared upstream. That made five of them, and possibly more hidden in the woods. It would be a challenging battle even without Meri to worry about.

Getting her to safety was his first priority.

"Stay where you are," he told Meri quietly, and getting a firm grip on his dragon side, he released it slowly, and flowed from his smaller shape to his larger.

The world around him eddied into a new configuration. Everything was much smaller from this vantage. The enemies that had seemed so huge were now rather small, each of them about half the size of his dragon. With his sharper senses, the world was rich in sounds and smells.

Through the barrage of new sensory input, he became slowly aware of Meri's awe and astonishment coming to him through the link.

Which was the point at which he remembered that she had never seen him shift before.

HE REALLY WAS A DRAGON.

His vast flank rose and fell against her as he breathed, as unexpectedly warm as his skin had been, pebbled with tiny scales and the same iridescent bronze color as his human skin. Although her first thought was that he looked like a storybook dragon, there was also something indefinably alien about him. He bristled with spikes, and when he turned his head, long jaws half parted, a row of serrated fangs glistened. His tail twitched like a cat's, dragging in the edge of the water. His dark blue hair, which she had thought of as a mane in his human form, really *was* a mane now, bristling all the way along his neck to the top of his shoulders.

Meri caught herself wondering if he could breathe fire.

The huge dinosaur-like things—velocirexes?—were clearly startled, but not enough to run away. They had stopped their approach when Lyr transformed; now they began to creep forward again, cautiously, with their heads lowered and tails stretched out behind to counterbalance.

Enormous wings unfurled from Lyr's back. They were translucent enough to let the sunlight through, surprisingly fragile-looking with their complex arrangement of delicate bones and a row of tiny spines on the leading edge.

I don't know if I can fly and carry your weight, Lyr told her, answering the question she hadn't asked aloud. **My wings are meant for flying in vacuum, not atmosphere. Anyway, there's not enough room here between the trees to take off. Stay with me.**

He lowered his half-furled wings like shields, blocking her from the dinosaurs. She could still see dimly through the translucent membranes, but not enough to make out exactly what was happening on the other side. The tiny hairs rose on her arms, like a static electric charge, as the green glimmer of Lyr's shield covered them.

A moment later, beneath the leading edge of Lyr's wing, she glimpsed one of the dinosaurs charge. Meri drew back against his side with an involuntary cry. Its claws raked down Lyr's shield and slid off—but Lyr jerked back.

"Are you okay?" she asked.

Yes, but I don't have enough power to shield against too many attacks like that. Blunt-force blows will drain my* *shields quickly, and the cuffs haven't had a chance to recharge fully since yesterday.

"So you're saying you can't shield us for very long."

Unfortunately, no.

Keeping his wings around her, he started forward, toward the path leading back to the ship. Meri hung back. "Wait, my phone—"

You can get it later.

He was right. Better that than her life. "Should I get on your back?" she asked. The idea seemed ludicrous, but he was as tall as a horse; she *could* ride him. In theory. "Or am I too heavy?"

You aren't too heavy, but if I have to fight, you'd be in less danger if you stay on the ground than if you go into battle with me.

Meri wasn't too sure about that. At least she had her blouse on, but she hadn't had a chance to get her shoes, and being barefoot made her feel terribly vulnerable. The path was a minefield of sharp sticks, though she realized as soon as she stepped on one that the shield blunted their sharp edges and kept them from hurting her.

Another dinosaur lunged at them, slamming into them from the side with snapping teeth. The impact made Lyr stagger sideways, curling a protective wing to keep Meri from falling over. She was starting to realize that even with the shield in place, there were still plenty of ways the dinosaurs could hurt them. They could make Lyr fall on her, for example. Or just pile onto him and batter him. It was clear that the shield wasn't able to absorb all the force of a body-check attack.

At any other time, she'd be fascinated. This was better than the Dinosaur Pavilion at the state fair. But alien dinosaurs were a lot less fun when they were trying to kill you.

New plan, Lyr said suddenly. His great clawed forepaws closed around her, and without warning she was whisked off the ground.

"Lyr!" she yelped as he reared onto his back legs. She had a dizzying glimpse of dinosaurs and trees and a flash of the sun on the silver surface of the crashed ship some ways off among the trees. She thought for an instant that he was going to fly after all, but then scratchy branches poked at her bare skin and she was deposited in the upper branches of one of the biggest of the smallish trees around the pool.

"Lyr!" she yelled, this time in a mix of fear and fury as he twisted away from her and fell back to all fours.

She hadn't been much of a tree climber even as a kid, and certainly hadn't done it since, let alone with dinosaurs after her. He had deposited her about twenty feet off the ground, as high up as he could reach. It felt simultaneously *way* too high and (given the size of the dinosaurs) not nearly high enough. She didn't think any of them could reach her even if they stood on their hind legs, but what if they could climb?

Lyr backed away from the tree and spun around with a snarl to face the dinosaurs.

As if they had been waiting for a signal, or simply waiting until he was distracted, the whole pack charged.

Meri wrapped an arm around the tree trunk and stuffed her fist in her mouth to keep from screaming his name. The last thing he needed right now was a distraction.

She'd seen a couple of dog fights growing up, and this made her think of a much larger-scale version of those. It was a snarling, spinning mess, except in this case the combatants were big enough to knock over small trees. She glimpsed occasional flickers of green light, but how much of this could Lyr's shields take? She couldn't even tell who was winning. The edge of the pool was churned to mud, the dam half destroyed. Water fountained up from the dinosaurs' clawed feet as they stumbled into it when Lyr's blows drove them back. Her phone, her shoes, Lyr's boots—she knew it was stupid to worry about that kind of thing at a time like this, but she wished she'd at least managed to grab her shoes; she didn't have any others.

One of the velocirexes slammed into the trunk of her tree, making the entire tree shudder. She let out an involuntary yelp, and it looked up, its hairless snout wrinkling back from jagged teeth. Then it set its claws into the bark of the tree and began to climb.

"Lyr!" Meri screamed. "No! Go away!" She hurled handfuls of twigs and leaves into its face, which did nothing to deter it from its focus on her. It seemed impossible to her that something so huge could climb so well. It was bigger than a bear, its claws raking curls of bark from the tree. The trunk swayed under its weight. It was close enough that she could see threads of saliva trailing from the corners of its jaws. Its eyes looked like catseye marbles, vivid green and gold, and just as cold and hard. She could even smell it, a harsh animal musk.

"I don't want to die half-naked in a tree!" she shrieked, and finally remembered to use the link. Lyr was too occupied in his fight to hear her, but he should be able to pick up her distress. **Lyr! Help!**

The result this time was instant. Lyr whipped around from the scrimmage with the other dinosaurs, raised both heavily clawed forepaws, and a bolt of green light stabbed out from his paired wrists and speared the dinosaur through the skull. It was already dead as it fell. It hit the ground with a shuddering impact and lay twitching, with a wisp of smoke curling up.

She was about to ask why he hadn't done that sooner when the green glimmer of the shield died, and she realized he'd drained his cuffs saving her.

He was now entirely vulnerable to the dinosaurs' claws.

At the moment, none of them were attacking; they seemed to have learned caution from their packmate's death, and had withdrawn to snarl at him from a distance. Meri wondered why more of them weren't injured—one had a dangling, broken leg, but otherwise they didn't seem to be hurt any worse than Lyr—until she remembered how the stick under her foot had felt blunt instead of sharp. The shield worked both ways, dulling the dinosaurs' claws so they slid off, but also preventing Lyr from hurting them with anything other than blunt force trauma.

Lyr began to back toward her tree. The dinosaurs seemed to take this as retreat, because they plunged after him.

This time, without the shield in the way, the scrimmage went somewhat differently. The first dino to collide with Lyr was sent into panicked retreat, shrieking, after Lyr's claws raked across its face and left it bloody and blinded. Its smaller, faster packmate managed to viciously savage Lyr's shoulder; Meri cried out in sympathy. It didn't seem to slow him down. There was a brief flurry of brutal fighting, a good deal bloodier this time—she couldn't follow it with her eyes; it was nothing but flying claws and screams of pain and rage—and then the remaining dinos fled into the woods, blood streaming down their pebbly hides.

Lyr stood over the dead dinosaur, his bloody sides heaving, staring into the woods. The spikes on his head were flat, like a dog's lowered ears, but slowly they raised as the dinos didn't come back.

"Lyr?" Meri called down hesitantly. "Could I get, uh ... a hand here?"

Right. Sorry.

Lyr reared up on his back legs and closed his forepaws carefully around her. Meri had to pry her aching hands from the tree; its bark had left creases in her skin. Lyr lifted her off the branch and settled gently to the ground. Now that she was no longer completely panicked, she was able to appreciate the strangeness of being cradled in a dragon's hands. The skin of his palms was warm and leathery and a little bit rough, like a dog's pads.

Meri wobbled when her feet touched the ground and caught herself by clutching at Lyr's massive claws. They were sticky, and she tried not to think about what they were sticky with.

Are you all right?

"I'm fine." She looked in worry at the torn flesh on his shoulder. His pale, silvery blood was mixed with the red blood of the velocirexes. "Are you?"

I've had worse. She sensed pain but also amusement through the link, as he looked down at her from luminous silver eyes that were both like and unlike his eyes in human form. *I'm sorry. I didn't mean to spring this on you quite so abruptly.*

"Well, I wanted to see it." She reached out a hesitant hand. "May I touch you?"

By all means.

She brushed her hand along the warm, soft skin of the tip of his snout. The scales were so fine and close together here that it was indistinguishable from normal skin. As she ran her hand from his snout-tip along his jaw, she felt the scales becoming harder and larger until they overlapped like armor on his throat. When he moved, his scales rippling like liquid metal.

"You're amazing," she whispered.

Amusement fluttered gently against her mind. **I'm going to shift back now. Are you prepared?**

"Yes." She stared at him, wide-eyed, wanting to fix every second in her mind. There wasn't much to see, and yet it was the most amazing thing she'd ever seen. His body rippled and flowed smoothly, collapsing down to his familiar human shape.

"How can you change size like that? Where does the extra go?"

"Believe me, my people have spent a lot of time arguing about it." He grimaced and touched his shoulder.

At that, her nurse side took over. "We need to apply pressure to that, and clean the wound. Animal bites are filthy."

"It should stop bleeding soon. My nanites will seal the cut, and my people heal fast anyway ..." He hesitated, and an odd look crossed his face.

"Lyr?"

"Dizzy," Lyr murmured as he slumped against her. Meri, shocked, tried to catch him, but he was heavier and his weight bore both of them down to the ground.

"Lyr? What's going on?"

"It burns," he muttered, pressing his hand against his bleeding shoulder. "*Curse* it. They're poisonous."

"Lyr!"

True panic washed over her. Even the dinosaurs hadn't scared her like this, because Lyr had been there, tall and strong and ready to deal with them. Now Lyr trembled in her arms, barely able to sit up. His fingers, clutched over the wound on his shoulder, were covered with silvery blood, and it traced pinkish-silver streaks down his skin, visibly trickling even as she watched. He was bleeding a *lot*. Some kinds of venomous snakes had anti-coagulants in their venom, preventing their victims' blood from clotting. This might be similar.

First aid for snakebite, she thought. Keep the victim calm and still: easier said than done, when he was covered with blood in a wilderness full of dangerous predators. Give antivenom: well, *that* wasn't going to happen. No Earth hospital had ever seen this particular poison before, even if there was a hospital closer than a dozen light-years away.

"Stay with me," she told him, forcing her voice to remain steady. Lyr's eyelids fluttered; his eyes were starting to roll back in his head. "Lyr, we have to get you back to the ship." She hated to move him in this condition, but there was no other choice. She couldn't even apply a tourniquet to slow the spread of the venom because the wound was on his shoulder, not far enough down a limb to be isolated—and dangerously close to his heart.

"Come on. You have to stand up."

She got an arm under his shoulders and struggled to help him to his feet. She'd never appreciated just how much bigger he was, or how heavy. He fought to get his legs under him, but they were spastic and uncoordinated. His jaw was locked tight, and though he was trying to keep it from her through the link, she could tell how much pain he was in.

The speed with which the venom was taking effect terrified her. Most snake and spider bites on Earth took much longer; it was one reason why the fatality rate from even a very poisonous snake was usually low, because there was time to apply first aid and get the victim to a hospital. This was more like a jellyfish sting. If it kept advancing at this pace, all she was going to be able to do was watch him die.

No! I won't think like that. I can help him back at the ship. There must be something that will help.

But that depended on getting him *to* the ship. His legs wobbled at every step, swaying and threatening to take them both to the ground. Only his iron self-control was keeping him on his feet.

And that control was faltering as his grip on consciousness slipped. To her horror, she could feel him slipping away from her through the link. He was fading, growing more distant, spiraling down into a place she couldn't follow.

"Lyr! Fight it!" she told him desperately.

His knees buckled. She fought to hold him up, but ended up being dragged to her knees by his weight.

You have to go. It came to her faintly through the link, although his eyes were closed, only a slit of the whites showing. **Not safe here. They didn't go far ...**

"I'm not leaving you!"

Go ... And the tenuous thread snapped; she couldn't feel him in her head anymore.

"Lyr!" She took his face in her hands and kissed his slack lips. She wasn't sure why she thought it would help. There was no response. He was still breathing, she found as she took his vitals with quick, practiced motions. His pulse was faint and incredibly fast, 200 beats per minute at least.

The venom? His body trying to handle the venom?

"Come on, Lyr, hang in there," she muttered. She struggled to her feet and gripped him under the arms. She knew she couldn't carry him, so dragging it was going to have to be. This wouldn't be fun, but splinters would heal. Getting torn apart by dinosaurs wouldn't.

The dinosaurs ...

A low growl made her look up.

"Oh no," she whispered.

Covered with blood, its catseye-marble eyes glinting, a dino stood on the path between her and the ship. Its head was down, its murderous intent clear. Meri didn't need to be able to read its mind to know what it was thinking. As far as it was concerned, the huge winged monster that had attacked it earlier was gone, leaving only crippled and bloody prey.

"Go away!" Meri shouted.

She pulled at the cuff on Lyr's wrist, but it wasn't like she could do anything with it anyway. It was drained of power and wouldn't work for her even if it was at full strength.

She had no weapons. No gun. Nothing.

Not that it looked like anything short of a rocket launcher would work on this thing.

Muscles bunched under the dino's pebbled hide. It took a step forward, its gory claws crackling on the dead sticks and leaves of the path.

This might even be the one who'd bitten Lyr. Strings of bloody drool trailed from its jaws.

And Meri was suddenly, viciously furious. She seized a stick and leaped to her feet. The dino jerked back, startled.

"Go away!" she screamed, swinging the stick at it.

For an instant she thought it almost might work, from the element of surprise if nothing else. But then the dino seemed to process enough of the situation to understand that one small human with a stick posed no threat to it. A growl burbled up from its throat, and it tensed to spring.

Meri stood between Lyr and the dino, and she thought clearly, *I'm going to die.*

Then a blast of green light flickered across its hindquarters. The creature looked baffled, and turned to look over its shoulder.

There was a stranger on the path between them and the ship. A stranger—no—

Tiger-striped fur, ragged blue uniform pants ... it was Tamir.

FIFTEEN

"YOU HAVE TO HIT IT HARDER!" Meri shouted, as the dino growled, swinging its head as if trying to decide which of them to attack first. "Lyr's attacks just bounced off."

The creature finally seemed to make up its mind. It leaped toward Meri and Lyr, only to jerk in mid-leap, all its limbs flailing. It crashed to the path in an enormous heap, with its tongue lolling out of its mouth.

"Emperor's Firstborn," Tamir said. It sounded like a curse. "That took nearly all the power I had. What are these things made out of?"

Meri dropped her stick, got her hands under Lyr's armpits, and dragged him around the crumpled bulk of the dino. "Is it dead?" she panted.

"Not sure. Let's hope so." Tamir's voice was ragged, torn out through clenched teeth. He was leaning on a stick like a crutch, and she could see he was in bad shape, his fur dull and matted, eyes crusted and lips pale. Still, he reached for one of Lyr's arms, Meri got the other, and between the two of them they got Lyr up, supporting his deadweight between them.

"How are you even *up*?" she asked as they began a wobbling, awkward sort of three-legged race back toward the ship. "How are you awake? And how the *hell* are you walking on a broken pelvis? You shouldn't be doing this! You shouldn't be *able* to do this!"

"My nanites are holding me together," Tamir said through gritted teeth. "Can we move before we find out if that thing is going to wake up or not? What *is* that?"

"Your guess is as good as mine. I've never seen one before today."

Tamir glanced at Lyr, whose head was lolling on Meri's shoulder. "What happened to him? How badly is he hurt?"

"They're venomous. One of them bit him."

"Damn," Tamir muttered. "Must be a hell of a venom, to take him down like this."

"He just collapsed. I don't know what to do for him. I'm a nurse, but there's nothing here I know how to use. We had to leave almost all our medical supplies behind on the pirate ship anyway, wherever the rest of *that* is."

"I'm getting the impression I missed a lot while I was out."

"You weren't *out*, you were *dying*," Meri panted. Focusing on Tamir was better than thinking about her desperate worry for Lyr, or the pain in her bare feet, which she kept bruising on sticks and rocks. "I still don't understand how you can be walking around like this. Back on Ear—uh—on my planet, you'd be in intensive care for weeks and in the hospital for months longer. And that's with surgery and other supportive care that we just don't have here."

"Can we figure out the mysteries of our respective medical technology later? Ah, we're here."

They stumbled into the ship and Tamir turned back to

slam the airlock door. The cargo hold was plunged into darkness, but Tamir's cuffs lit up an instant later, illuminating the space with pale, cool light. Meri let out a breath; it was the first time she'd felt halfway safe since that pack of *things* showed up.

Between them, she and Tamir lowered Lyr onto the rumpled blanket nest where Tamir had been lying. Tamir followed him down in a sort of controlled fall.

"You really need to lie down," Meri told him. She pulled back Lyr's eyelid. His pupils were responsive, and he continued to breathe, though it was rapid and shallow.

"I'll be fine. Just give me a minute."

"As the closest thing we have to a doctor around here, you are *not* fine. Stay down." She stroked Lyr's pale face. "At least he seems to have stabilized. He's not deteriorating any further."

"You're a doctor?"

Meri looked at him over Lyr's unconscious body. Sitting on the edge of the blanket, he regarded her calmly in the soft moonglow of his cuff. It seemed very odd to her, suddenly, to be able to talk to him like a person, rather than having him simply as an inert patient that she was responsible for.

Also, she'd just remembered that she had never buttoned her blouse, and her bra was still back there at the spring with her shoes. Feeling her cheeks heat, she hastily buttoned herself up.

"I'm a nurse," she said. "Not a doctor, but someone who cares for ill patients on my world." She managed to smile, wan though it was. "We do all the work, the doctors get all the credit."

Tamir gave a hoarse laugh. "As a field soldier, I can

relate. You do all the work and take all the risk, and the brass walks in like they were the ones who won the fight."

"*Exactly* like that. And I can relate; my husband—my late husband—was a soldier on my world."

"I'm sorry," Tamir said sincerely.

It was odd to speak of Aaron in this almost matter-of-fact way. *Is this what healing feels like?* "Me too," she murmured, and started to get up to get something to clean Lyr's wound, then sat down again when pain knifed through her foot. Some of the splinters that had jammed into her poor soles felt more like toothpicks. "*Damn* it, my shoes are still down at the spring. I'm going to need those."

"Tell me what you need and I can get it."

"You are staying right there," she told him. He started to get up anyway. "Did you not hear me?"

"I was going to look for food."

"I'll get it! Stay there."

Limping, she brought him a ration pouch, along with a cup of water from the bathroom. He didn't even bother pulling the heat-tab, just popped out the tube and started sucking on it.

Meri sat with Lyr's head in her lap and pulled a blanket over him, then began to carefully clean around the wound on his shoulder with a wet piece of blanket. There wasn't anything else she could think to do at the moment. He was warm to the touch and restless, twitching in his sleep. She sent mental reassurance to him and wondered if he could hear it. With Lyr as settled as she could get him, she turned to picking the splinters out of her feet and cleaning the scrapes.

Tamir had finished the ration pack and gotten himself another one. "You might want to slow down," Meri told him. "You've been sick. I wouldn't recommend anyone eat like that, especially if they just started to recover from what you've been through."

"I need the energy," he said, but he laid the second, mostly-empty pack on his knee and took a slow breath. "Though you're right. Won't help if it makes me sick. My body's been repairing itself and the energy has to come from somewhere." He blew out another slow breath, scratched at his head, and looked ruefully at the loose fur that had come out in his hand.

"You really shouldn't be sitting up on a broken pelvis. Actually, you shouldn't be doing any of the things you were doing out there. You shouldn't be able to."

"My nanites—"

"Yes, you said that, but there's no medical technology on my world that could get you up and moving this quickly, not in the shape you were in."

"My world is more advanced than yours." He said it matter-of-factly, and scratched at his fur again, grimacing as more of it came out.

"Yes, well, just looking at you is making my hips hurt, so do you think you could do me a favor and lay your highly-advanced self down for a while and give your little micro machines time to fix you more?"

Tamir grinned, giving her a startling flash of fang-like canines, and settled back on the blanket with a grunt of poorly concealed pain.

"Yeah, that's what I thought." She leaned out as far as she could without disturbing Lyr and dragged another blanket close enough to flip it over Tamir's legs. "How worried should we both be about your fur falling out like that?"

"Not worried. It's normal when we're healing. Itchy and

unpleasant, but normal." He took another sip from the half-empty ration pack. "Where are we?"

"I don't know. I'd never even been off my home planet 'til a couple of days ago."

"Well, the last thing I remember was shooting at pirates and then the ship falling apart, so you've got to know more than I do."

"Oh, right." She took another look at him. "You were unconscious for all of it."

"All of what?"

"Hoo boy. Where to start. So we got caught by pirates—you were one of the people trying to help, right? Space marines or whatever you guys are." Tamir nodded, though she got the impression that he was encouraging her to continue more than he'd actually understood most of what she was asking. "After we got stranded in space, Lyr rescued a bunch of prisoners and he found a ship and got us to this planet. We got separated from the—uh, he called it the module? Where most of the other prisoners were. So we crashed on this planet and that was like a day or so ago, and, uh? Here we are, in the middle of nowhere," she finished, feeling somewhat as if her explanation had not been the best.

Tamir looked amused, which made her realize that he actually reminded her of Lyr in some ways; he had the same quiet sense of humor. It was no surprise they liked each other. "Do you know the planet's name?"

"I don't think it has one. Lyr says it's uninhabited, at least he thinks so."

"And you said something about a module? Of the pirate ship?"

She nodded. "We lost track of them when we crashed. We're pretty sure they survived, but they're on the other side of the mountains, so we haven't found them yet." She got a sharp twinge at that, thinking of the people she'd helped. Surely they were just on the other side of the mountains. When Lyr was better, he could fly and look for them.

He was going to get better.

"What about the pirates? Are any of them still out there?"

"There are a few still alive on the ship, but we left them behind." She tried not to think about that, either. Stranded to die in the darkness of space ... did even pirates deserve that?

Then she thought of the haunted looks on the prisoners' faces, the way the pirates had casually jabbed their shock-sticks into their captives and used those awful torture collars on them. Perhaps they *did* deserve it.

Also, the alternative was that the pirates had managed to make it to the planet and were here with them, which wasn't a comforting thought.

"There's no one else on this ship?" Tamir asked. "Just us?"

"Yes, it's just us, and it's been just me and Lyr while you were unconscious. You know, it's weird that I know nothing about you," she told him. "I've been taking care of you for days. But all I know is what I've gotten from Lyr."

"Yes, about that ..." Tamir's curious gaze drifted to Lyr's head in her lap, where—absently, without really thinking about it—she'd been stroking his hair. "I can see that I've missed a few things."

"It's not ... we're not ..." Her face felt hot; she was suddenly hyper-aware of the satisfied tingle between her legs, and she had to remind herself (it was surprisingly difficult to remember, after all this time alone with Lyr) that

Tamir couldn't read her mind. At least, she didn't think so. She hoped not.

Anyway, she was an adult. She could have a relationship if she wanted one; there was nothing to be ashamed of.

"Okay, maybe we are." She dropped her eyes to Lyr's face. He hadn't precisely gone pale—with such light-colored blood, it might not be possible to get paler than he already was, under the bronze tone of his skin—but he looked grayish, washed out, as if some of the vitality had been drained out of him. "And then he got hurt protecting me. Without me, he could have gotten away easily."

"He wouldn't have left you," Tamir said, and she looked back at him. His eyes were cat's eyes, green and gold, catching the light in reflective glimmers. "Lyr is a protector. It's what he does. I don't know if it's something inherent to his people or if it's simply him, but he's always been that way, ever since I've known him. He might try to deny it, but it's as much a part of him as his claws and wings."

"You've known him a long time," she said. "He said you were in charge of his—sept?"

"That's right." His face was surprisingly expressive, given the tiger-striped fur on his cheeks and jawline. But it didn't seem to conceal expression so much as it enhanced it. Right now he looked wistful and distant, as if he was looking back into the past. "I met him when he was a teenager—a very proud, very angry teenager."

His tone was fond, but the words made her own protective instincts flare. "From what he's told me, he was a slave, so I think he had every right to be angry."

"It's not precisely ... hmmm." Tamir looked thoughtful. "How much has he told you about his past, about how he came to be among my people?"

"Not much." She ran her hand gently along Lyr's hairline. Even in the depths of unconsciousness, he didn't look relaxed, as if his demons had chased him down into his dreams. She hoped he wasn't in pain.

"Sounds like him," Tamir muttered. "He's not wrong, but it's also more complicated than that. His people and mine have had an uneasy truce for a number of years. One of the conditions of the truce is an ... an exchange of hostages, I guess you'd say. Lyr is a prince among his people."

"A prince?" She looked back at Lyr's slack face, startled.

"From what I can tell, it sounds more impressive than it is." Tamir's tone was wry. "Much like we didn't send *them* anyone important, they seem to have sent us a random assortment of distant relatives of their queen, who apparently is related to half their clans through some kind of complicated alliance system you have to be a dragon to understand. Still, I gather that Lyr's family was fairly high-ranking within their local power structure. When I met him, he had never been away from his home city-ship. He was arrogant and incredibly naive, and completely convinced that his people were powerful enough to protect him from anything that *my* people might want to do to him. Convinced that we would see how important and powerful he was, that his queen would always protect him." The look that crossed his face was profoundly sad. "He learned differently, over time."

Tamir might not be sending her telepathic imagery the way Lyr did, but she could picture it anyway, that slender golden-skinned teenager with his face set in sullen lines, beautiful and cool, trying to put on a brave face while surrounded by his enemies.

"Poor boy," Tamir added softly. "Poor, lonely kid."

Unexpectedly, this made her smile, though tears had

gathered at the corners of her eyes. "I don't think he'd appreciate you calling him that."

Tamir flashed a quick grin, showing glimpses of canine teeth pointed enough that they might be called fangs. "I know he wouldn't. But I remember that was my first thought when I saw him. *You poor, poor kid.* He could be an incredible pain to deal with, you know. Nobody really liked him all that much. By everyone else's standards, he was pampered. Spoiled. He didn't know how to deal with military life, let alone having to take orders from people he considered beneath him. He was used to people taking orders from *him.* Now he was in a place where he was at the very bottom of the social ladder, wearing a face that most of the people who met him distrusted on sight—we've been at war with his people, off and on, ever since our expanding territory butted up against theirs. And I don't think anyone else really saw him as a kid at all. He was as tall as an adult, capable of shifting into a creature who could kill a dozen of us at a go without breaking a sweat. The only thing that made them willing to deal with him at all was that he was collared."

"Collared," she repeated.

"I took it off," Tamir said simply.

He leaned over—Meri had to suppress an instinctive urge to cover Lyr with her body, to protect him, though she knew Tamir meant no harm—and brushed the vulnerable skin of Lyr's exposed throat with his fingertips. Meri looked where he indicated.

There were scars on Lyr's throat, tiny round ones, and a faint ridge of scar tissue that girdled his neck. It was very slight. She had never noticed it before. And now that she thought about it ... she *did* remember the silver slash across his throat, the first time she'd met him. Everything about him had been so alien, then. She hadn't even realized what it meant.

It took Meri a moment to notice that her hands were shaking from anger. She had to wait out a surge of rage so powerful that her ears rang with it, her vision darkened with it.

Oh yes, she remembered the collars on the prisoners on the pirate ship, the way the blue-skinned man had collapsed and writhed on the ground at the touch of a button.

"You put a *collar* on him, like a *dog*, and you wonder why he's angry at you."

"I never had to wonder," Tamir said, a trace of a wry smile touching his mouth.

She wasn't about to soften toward him, not an inch. "I don't care if you had second thoughts. I don't care if you didn't like it. That makes it even worse, in a way, if you knew it was wrong and went along with it anyway. *Look* at this." Her hand quivered above the marks on Lyr's neck. Marks of abuse; she hadn't been a nurse for all those years without knowing what she was looking at. "Your people took a prince of a proud warrior people and did *this*."

She expected Tamir to avoid her gaze in shame. Instead he raised his green-gold eyes to meet hers, facing her anger head-on. The shame was still there, and something else as well, something she hadn't expected: an anger that nearly matched her own.

"I *know*," Tamir said. "I'm not going to excuse it. I could even tell you, if I wanted to, that there was nothing I could have done, and it wouldn't even be untrue ... not entirely. His people can't be free in the Empire, they're not *allowed* to be, because none of us trust them within a dozen light years of us without some kind of power limiter. And he couldn't go home because his people wouldn't take him back. He is here to ensure peace and cooperation between our peoples. If he ran from that responsibility, they would consider him without honor and cast him out."

"He was a child." Her voice trembled. "He was a *child*. No one gave him a choice. They sent him to live in a foreign land and made a slave out of him and no one ever gave him a *choice*."

"Some would say," Tamir murmured, in a voice that hitched slightly in the middle, "that it was for the good of both our peoples."

Meri looked down at Lyr's face, and now the tears came, blurring her vision until all she could see was a rainbow web of light and dark. "If that's how it is, I think both your peoples should wipe each other out. The galaxy would be a better place for it."

Tamir didn't answer. After a moment, he touched one of his cuffs, took it off, and laid it on the floor, leaving it glowing, illuminating the cargo bay. Then he got up stiffly and carefully with the aid of his walking stick, and went outside.

HE DIDN'T COME BACK.

Meri wet a scrap of blanket and bathed Lyr's forehead and wrists. The wound on his shoulder was hot and puffy, livid with oddly pale bruises, but it seemed to her that it had healed noticeably since she'd been sitting with him; the torn edges of flesh were knit together, the pinkish-silver blood no longer seeping.

"You'd want me to go after him, I expect," she said, tracing his closed eyelids, the bruiselike shadows under his eyes, with the gentlest brush of her hand. She missed the touch of his mind already; it was like a mental coldness, that dark place she'd so quickly learned to expect him to fill with light and warmth.

She kissed his cheek and rolled him very carefully into the recovery position on his side, then picked up the glowing cuff and two more ration packs. Gathering the blanket around herself, she went to the airlock door.

Tamir turned out to be right outside. He'd stirred up the fire and was sitting next to it, legs stretched out, looking scruffy and uncomfortable.

"Here." Meri shoved the cuff at him; he took it back and clasped it around his wrist. "I didn't go to all that trouble of taking care of you just so you can get yourself eaten by a velocirex."

"By a what?"

"Dinosaur ... thing. I guess you wouldn't understand." She glanced around with a shiver. The thicket around the ship seemed suddenly much too close and dense, and she was all too conscious of her current undressed state and the ground prickling her bruised, bare feet.

"They don't seem to be around," Tamir said, stroking his fingertips across the cuff on his wrist to seal it. "I brought your shoes, by the way." He gestured across the fire. "And your, er, other garments. They were a little ... muddy. I washed them in the spring."

Meri looked in surprised gratitude at the items spread out to dry by the fire. "Thank you," she said grudgingly. "Uh ... I don't suppose you saw any sign of my phone when you were down at the spring?" She held up her hands to demonstrate its shape. "About yea big, square electronic thing."

"Sorry, no."

Great. Probably stepped on by a dinosaur or buried in the mud. RIP, phone.

"I could go look for it," Tamir began, but Meri shook her head.

"I'll survive without it. It's not important enough to run around unarmed and hurt, looking for it."

"I'm never unarmed, any more than Lyr is." Tamir glanced up and smiled. "I guess there are a few things he hasn't told you about Galateans."

"Oh, let me guess," she said, testy. "You turn into a dragon too."

"Not a dragon ..."

"Seriously?!"

He shrugged, then a spasm of pain crossed his face as the movement tugged his healing injuries. "I'll show you later. Not right now. Shifting took more out of me than I expected."

Wordlessly, she handed him one of the ration packs, and then sat with her back against the airlock door to eat; she didn't quite trust Tamir's assertion that the dinos were gone. She'd almost forgotten how awful the ration packs were. She would prefer charred lizard.

"I feel like we got off to a bad start back there," Tamir said suddenly. "I've also realized that I never asked your name. I'm very sorry. I'm Lieutenant Tamir *adn* Kynn. You can call me Tamir."

She heard his name with an odd overlay from the translation implant, giving her a sense of the meanings. Lieutenant was his rank, of course, though a different word that the implant translated to something vaguely familiar to her. *Adn* meant something like *son of*, with the implication of belonging to a family or group. Kynn was his clan.

"Meri Rowland. Call me Meri." She held out a hand without thinking; Tamir looked at it in confusion. "This is something that my people do. We shake hands when we meet someone."

He clasped her hand carefully in his big, callused one. Meri gave it a shake, at which, startled, he let go.

"And this makes us friends by your people's customs?" he asked cautiously.

She had to suppress a smile at his earnest desire to get along with her. "No, that part comes later, if it comes at all. But at least now we know each other a little better. Look, I'm not going to apologize for getting angry at you. It's just ... the more I find out about what he's been through, the angrier I am about it. You were *there* for all those years, Tamir. And you didn't do anything."

"I know," he said quietly. "I *do* know that. I raised those kids. And I sent them off to die. Can you imagine what that was like?"

"My husband was a soldier. Of course I can. But he *wanted* to. Where I come from, we have an all-volunteer army. He was proud to be part of it. And I was proud of him. This ... this is different. Those kids that he told me about—they didn't have a choice."

"Most of our army is there by choice as well," Tamir said. "It's a proud profession. My clan always sends a certain number of warriors to serve the Empire, firstborn sons especially, like me."

"So what about Lyr and his sept? Child slaves, he told me. Did they choose *that*?"

"They're conscripted from our subject worlds." Tamir held up his hands when she gathered for an angry retort. "I *know*. I don't like it either. It's more like indenture than slavery, for whatever that's worth. They serve a term of twenty years and then they can go home."

"Unless they're dead."

"I know."

"Or hostages like Lyr. How many of those are there? How many of them get to go home?"

"I don't know that," Tamir said softly. "I'm sorry. I don't have answers for you. I don't even have my own answers."

They sat in silence and she choked down the rest of her ration pack. Tamir had already finished his. Maybe they were less terrible when you'd been eating them for years. She was going to have to ask Lyr to hunt more lizards, when he was back on his feet—she refused to imagine Lyr *not* getting better before they needed to replenish their food supply.

Could they eat the dead dino by the creek, maybe? There was plenty of meat on it, if they got to it soon, before it started spoiling. But they didn't have a refrigerator, or any way to keep it fresh. It seemed pointless to risk their lives to retrieve it when they still had plenty of food, even if it was kind of disgusting.

She went inside to check on Lyr. He was just as she'd left him, feverish to the touch, lying very still. Meri wet down the scraps of blanket she was using to bath his face and wrists, and then knelt beside him with her hand on his forehead and thought good thoughts at him. She felt a little silly, but maybe he could hear her.

When she looked up, Tamir was in the doorway. Meri got up quickly and gathered their trash together, the remains of the ration packs and scraps of the blanket she'd been dissecting for bandages.

"You are very close to him," Tamir said thoughtfully as she cleaned up.

"Going through a crisis makes people closer; it's a documented fact." She didn't meet his eyes.

"Lyr doesn't get close to anyone. Not anymore."

"Maybe I'm just special."

She meant it to come out flippant, but Tamir said, "Yes. I think you are."

MERI SPENT most of the day sitting with Lyr, who continued to drift in a feverish state of unconsciousness. Sometimes she thought she could sense him around the corners of her mind, like someone saying her name just on the edge of hearing, but when she closed her eyes and listened, there was only silence.

Feeling self-conscious at first, she sang to him quietly, a mix of half-remembered pop song lyrics, lullabies from childhood, and hymns from her youth choir days, even Christmas carols. Tamir listened quietly, and after awhile, worn out from his morning's explorations and still healing, he fell asleep.

So she was the only one awake when there was a sudden pattering on the ship's metal skin. She stared up at the ceiling, clutching Lyr's limp hand and wondering if they were under attack from something else. Were those the footsteps of a whole herd of tiny dinosaurs? Then a breath of damp, cool air washed over her from the airlock door—left open a few inches for ventilation and light—and she laughed quietly at herself. It was only rain.

She got up, laying aside the cloth she'd been using to bathe Lyr's temples, and went to look outside. The light filtering down through the thicket had turned gray and dim, and rain beaded on the plastic sheeting and ran off in streams. Under the edge of the plastic, the low, banked fire was still burning, although occasional raindrops hissed on the coals when the wind blew it sideways. Water dripped off the overhanging trees.

Meri took a deep breath, inhaling the smell of the rain, overlaid with woodsmoke and the sharp scents of plant sap and unfamiliar flowers. She waited for the bitter, aching grief of Aaron's death to rise up and overwhelm her, but it never came. It was more like the old ache of a broken limb, long healed but still giving twinges of pain in the damp.

And then, she looked over her shoulder into the dark interior of the ship, where Lyr was just visible in the dimness, and tears sprang to her eyes. A bone could heal the first break, or the second, but how many times could a shattered heart put itself back together?

She went back inside and, for the fortieth time, checked on the bite wound on Lyr's shoulder. Was it just her imagination that the swelling had gone down slightly? It still felt hot to the touch.

"Lyr, please," she whispered. She pulled back the blanket and crawled underneath, and stretched out against him, skin to skin. Pulling his head against her shoulder, she whispered into his hair. "Lyr ... I think I might love you. Please don't go. Please come back to me."

SIXTEEN

IT WAS PEACEFUL HERE, wherever he was. Dark, quiet ... like the still cold space between the stars. No one else but him. No one to fail, no one to betray, no one to watch die. Just him, alone.

But it was lonely.

Terribly, terribly lonely.

How had he never noticed the crushing weight of that loneliness before? It was a pain he'd learned to live with, pushing it down until he no longer felt it. But the pain was still there, and now it threatened to smother him.

It was so dark, and he was so alone. It seemed the cold would overwhelm him, and he fought as hard as he could to hold onto the spark of warmth inside him—but he didn't know the way back, there was only darkness and cold ...

**Lyr.*

Until there was, in that darkness, a faint tendril of answering warmth, like a hand reaching out to clasp his. There was a song curled around it, a song half-heard, unfurling down to him in the void.

**Lyr. Please come back to me.*

All he had to do was reach back. Yet he hesitated, because to answer that call was to open his heart once again to loving and hurting. It would mean acknowledging that he cared.

But really, he'd known all along, hadn't he?

He reached out, not with his hands in this bodiless place, but with his mind, stretching and straining for the offered lifeline.

Lyr!

Her sudden warm delight blazed up like a flame. It felt like her arms coming around him, holding him, guiding him back.

No ... her arms really *were* around him, and he was clinging to her as he shivered in her grasp. Alternating waves of hot and cold washed through him. He felt terrible. He felt ...

Alive.

"Lyr," she whispered, stroking his hair. "Lyr, Lyr. Don't *do* that. You scared me so much."

"I think I scared myself," he whispered. He couldn't stop shivering in her arms, haunted by the memory of that cold, dark place—that prison in his heart, where he'd spent too much time.

Now all he could do was hold her ... feel her. Feel her in his arms. Feel her in his heart.

A feeling too tentative and new to give a name to, but real nonetheless, sang inside him like the resonant song of his people.

He wasn't sure what she felt through the link, but she clung to him just as fiercely, and then her lips were on his, and he fell into the heated eagerness of her mouth. His body responded to the fierce urgency of her kisses, rising against her—

"Lyr," she mumbled, and then she was the one to pull away, though her hands were still tangled in his hair. "Lyr, um ... we're not alone."

"Huh?" he said intelligently. In the dim light of the ship's cargo hold, he could see her looking over his shoulder. Lyr rolled over, wincing at the pain from his injured shoulder, to find out what kind of threat she needed to be protected from.

Tamir, in his own tangle of blankets, was propped up on his elbow, looking both embarrassed and amused.

"I didn't want to spoil the moment by saying something," he said.

"Aargh," Lyr groaned. He rolled over and turned his back to Tamir, clasping Meri tightly. "Trust you to ruin everything."

"How are you feeling?" Tamir asked. Lyr, still obstinately not looking at him, heard little rustles as he sat up.

"Shouldn't that be my line?" Lyr demanded. "Last time I saw you, you were—" *Half dead and not likely to live.* A confusing mix of pain and relief stole his breath at that thought.

"He saved us," Meri said. "On the path to the spring. Do you remember?"

"No," he said with automatic stubbornness, but come to think of it, he *did* remember something: a voice shouting at them, a confusing whirl of sky and trees and ground as darkness swallowed the world ...

"I should check your wounds." Meri untangled herself enough to sit up. Lyr ended up with his head in her lap, which he was fine with. "Tamir, could you give us some light?"

The cargo hold lit up with the glow of Tamir's cuffs. Lyr submitted to Meri's painful poking and prodding at his shoulder. He kept his eyes half closed; he didn't particularly feel like he needed to know. He didn't feel like he was dying and that was the important part.

"This is amazing. The swelling is almost completely down." Her cool hand touched his forehead. "And I think your fever is down too. I wish I had a thermometer—oh wait, your cuffs can do that, can't they?"

Tamir's cuff clinked against his own. "His temperature is half a standard degree off from normal for his species, but not enough to worry about."

"How are you feeling?" Meri asked. Her face above him was a study in light and shadow, sharply drawn in the cool silver-white light. In any light, she was the most beautiful thing he'd ever seen.

"Better," he said, stirring himself out of contemplation of her features. It wasn't even untrue. The shivering had mostly stopped, though an occasional tremor still ran through him. He recognized it as his body's attempt to burn the poison out of him. Mainly, he was ragingly hungry.

Which Tamir, who had been dealing with him for a long time and had many of the same needs, would know. Lyr was not about to ask, but small rustles nearby, followed by footsteps, indicated that Tamir had been thinking along similar lines, and a moment later, a ration pack landed on his hand.

"You should eat," Tamir said. "I could use another one, too. I'm still replenishing the reserves my body used up while it was healing. Would you like one as well, Meri?"

They were on a first-name basis? Apparently a lot had gone on while he was unconscious.

"Not quite hungry enough for another of those," Meri said ruefully. "Not yet. Give me a little while."

Tamir sat on his blankets with a pained grunt and pulled the heating tab on his. "They're vile, aren't they?"

"They taste fine to me," Lyr said, mostly to be contrary. He tried to sit up and flopped back down ungracefully in Meri's lap.

"So stubborn," she murmured, and her soft, strong hands were there under his shoulders, helping him sit up. She propped him with a warm shoulder as he popped the tab to eat.

It was very peaceful here, with Meri leaning against him and the rain drumming outside. He managed to finish about half the ration pack, but found his eyes drifting shut, and forced himself awake again. He needed to keep watch—

"Sleep," Tamir said. "Other people can keep an eye on things for a time. You don't have to do everything." His voice was fond.

Lyr wanted to argue, but sleep was pulling him down. **Meri?** he said, not wanting Tamir to overhear.

I'm here.

Would you sing to me again?

Embarrassment-pleasure-surprise raced through her thoughts. **I'd love to. Anything in particular?**

Whatever you like. I enjoy all your music.

After a silence, she began to sing him a song about something blowing in the wind. He didn't understand what half of the words were talking about, but that wasn't important. What mattered was the warm lilt of her voice, and the way the song's words and melody were laced through with emotions. Someone in her family used to sing this song to her when she was a little girl. The sound of her voice and the gentle tide of nostalgia carried him away to sleep.

THE RAIN SLACKENED to a light drizzle later in the afternoon, leaving the world damp and dripping. Meri sang herself hoarse and then fell asleep. She woke from her nap some unknown time later to find a cool, empty spot in the blankets next to her. Lyr was up and about in the dim gray light of the ship's interior.

"Where are you going?" she asked sleepily.

"Hunting," Lyr said. Meri got a vague sense from him (she wasn't sure if he meant to send it) of "bring food back for mate" that she found adorable, flattering, and ever so slightly weird. However, her nurse instincts reared up immediately.

"Oh no you don't. You almost died earlier today. You're going to sit here and rest."

"I'll go," Tamir offered, rising stiffly. "I could use the exercise. I'll see if there's anything salvageable on the carcass by the stream, and scout for small game."

Meri sighed. "It's useless to point out that you should be resting too, isn't it?"

"Yes," he said, with an amused glint in his cat's eyes. "Besides, I don't think you two would mind the alone time."

Lyr looked like he wanted to say something but stopped himself.

"I am about to shift," Tamir added, hooking his fingers in the waistband of his trousers, "and for that I need to be naked. I suggest anyone with nudity taboos look away."

Meri averted her eyes, mostly for Lyr's sake, but she couldn't help sneaking a glance back, just in time to see Tamir lean forward as his muscular fur-covered body rippled and flowed into the four-legged shape of a tiger, still wearing the gold cuffs on the ankles of his front paws. He was smaller than an Earth tiger, with a lean, long-legged physique.

He gave Meri a sideward look, as if to say, *Impressive, isn't it?* and then limped to the door, with a pronounced hitch in his step from his healing pelvis. Meri couldn't help thinking of a cat waiting to be let out, which made her grin. She got up and pushed the door farther open for him. Tamir lashed his tail and slipped through the opening. Meri watched as he vanished into the forest.

"You don't need to look so impressed," Lyr said in a grouchy tone. He'd joined her in the doorway, looking out after Tamir.

She laughed. "It's not a competition. Anyway, your dragon is *much* bigger than his tiger."

He was still staring after Tamir. Meri nudged at him until he let her steer him to sit down on the blankets.

"He's not well," Lyr grumbled while she checked his healing wound again.

"Ah, you *do* care."

"I care about having an extra set of hands to help around the campsite, rather than having our hunter get himself killed by going out before he's ready."

"Like you were about to do?" she couldn't resist pointing out.

"I can *fly*."

"Mm-hmm." She manipulated his arm, checking range of motion. "I can't believe how fast this is healing."

"My people heal quickly."

"So do Tamir's, apparently. Right now I feel like humans are the only people in the galaxy who have to crawl through our healing process one painful step at a time."

"Tamir *is* human," Lyr said.

Meri snuck a peek at him to see if he was joking. He seemed serious. "Tamir's from *Earth*? Lyr, I don't know how unfamiliar you are with humans, but I've never seen one that looked like that."

"I didn't say he was from Earth, I said he was human. His people were originally taken from Earth by highly advanced aliens, a very long time ago, and made to look the way they do now."

Meri plunked down on the blanket beside him, staring at him. "You're kidding."

"Not about this. Out in the wider galaxy, Earth is known as Birthworld. Your planet was lost for a very long time and only recently rediscovered. It's why you were abducted for the black-market trafficking trade, because your people's DNA is incredibly valuable on the galactic market as a source of mutation-free genetic material. I was part of a Galatean garrison trying to enforce a blockade on the planet to keep raiders out." He turned to look at her with a faint smile. "This is all coming as news to you, isn't it?"

"Yes," she said. "Yes, it is." She shook herself. "You know what, I really want to hear about this, but maybe not right now. I feel like we shouldn't waste all this lovely, lovely alone time talking about pirates and Galateans and Tamir when, for a change, he's not even around."

"Mmm." It was an agreeing sound; she could tell through the link, especially when he leaned in to open his mouth over hers. "Perhaps," he murmured against her lips, "you could teach me more about kissing."

AFTERWARDS, they lay tangled together in the blankets, loose-limbed and relaxed. Lyr's healing injury hadn't interfered with his ability to please her; now, through the link, he could feel her happiness and contentment as she lay pooled against him in a happy puddle. Her fingers brushed through his hair and along the side of his neck.

"You don't have any body hair," she murmured. "Just your head hair and eyebrows. It's so interesting."

"Your people aren't *that* hairy. It's not such a huge difference." He found her light body hair delightful. It was soft to touch. He liked it.

"You haven't seen some of our men. They're almost as hairy as Tamir. Well, okay, maybe not quite that hairy. They don't have *pelts*."

The mention of Tamir reminded Lyr that he wasn't back yet. Cautious, questing, Lyr reached out with his mind, as tentative as a blindfolded man feeling his way along a ledge. The abundance of life outside the ship roared like a waterfall in his senses, but it was easier when he was using a familiar mind as an anchor. He used to reach out for Tamir's mind all the time, and he still knew the feel of it, like a bright beacon guiding him in. Tamir was not far off, and still tiger-shaped as far as Lyr could tell. Touching Tamir's mind, as always, was like sinking his hands into warm fur, with hints of woodsmoke and echoes of the adrenaline-laced thrill of the chase.

He wasn't expecting to be discovered, but he was out of practice and didn't jerk away soon enough. **Well, hello there!** came Tamir's response, surprise and pleasure flickering around the words. **I thought you weren't doing this anymore.**

Don't get used to it, Lyr grumbled at him.

She's a good influence on you.

Shut up.

Wordless, teasing amusement came to him, with undertones of affection. He pulled away reluctantly, like trailing his fingers through someone's hand when neither person wanted to let go. It was *good* not to be alone in his own head anymore.

Meanwhile, Meri's wandering fingers had found their way to the sensitive skin at the base of his horns. When she rubbed at the ridge of skin where horn met flesh, Lyr's whole body quivered, his extended senses snapping back into his skin with a sudden jolt of pleasure.

Meri pulled her hand back quickly. "Sorry! Is it tender?"

"No, don't stop. Yes, it is, but ..." Lyr touched her wrist and guided her hand back. "... not the way you mean. I was just startled, that's all."

"Well, in that case ..." She went back to idly rubbing around the base of his horns. Lyr curled into her, contentment flowing through the link.

"It's so quiet here," she murmured, her voice a breath against his neck. "I used to go camping, but it was never like this. I never camped far enough from the highway not to be able to hear cars and other campers."

It didn't seem quiet to him. To his sharp senses, physical and telepathic, the world was so full of life that it seemed to vibrate. But compared to a city or a starship, he could see what she meant. It was certainly lacking in the kinds of noises that people made.

"I mean, eventually I'm going to want, like ... showers," she went on. "And Starbucks. And I can't say I wouldn't mind not having to look both ways for killer dinosaurs before leaving the house. But I do kinda like this place."

"I find it pleasant as well."

"Mmm." She nuzzled against his neck and kissed him, languid and slow.

His chest felt warm and full, not hollow and empty. He just wanted to lie here, holding Meri, kissing her occasionally—never wanting to let go.

He had to, eventually; his injured shoulder was starting to cramp up. And he was hungry again. He got up and got another ration pack. Meri shook her head when he offered her one.

"So you said earlier you can't get me pregnant." She was sitting with her arms slung loosely over her knees, a gorgeous study in light and shadow. "What about STDs?"

"STDs?" he asked, genuinely confused.

"You know ... diseases that I might catch from you, when we have sex."

"No, our species are too different. Germs that affect humans don't affect me, and vice versa. As for pregnancy, I'm quite sure we aren't cross-fertile." He sat down beside her and she leaned against him, warm and soft. "It is a well-established scientific fact about our two species. We reproduce quite differently."

"How differently?"

"You give birth to live young. We do not. We aren't mammals."

Meri looked up at him with a skeptical frown, as if she suspected him of having her on. "What are you, then?"

"We reproduce only in our dragon shape; we are not fertile at all in the bipedal form. It might be possible for the two of us to have a child in a test tube, if you wanted to, but not to produce an egg as my people do."

"Wait, *what*. You ... hatch out of *eggs*?"

"And I'm glad of it," he said, amused. "I've seen how the human peoples of the galaxy reproduce. Your women must carry babies in their own bodies until you are enormous and uncomfortable. Then your baby is born more helpless than the newest hatchling. *We* have nurseries, warm and quiet, with soft lighting and soft music. Eggs are carefully tended and parents come to check on them and talk to them until they hatch. It's believed that the young can hear their parents' voices in the shell ..."

His voice drifted off, and instead of trying to tell her, he opened his mind to her and showed her the nursery caves, all graceful curving lines and hollows in the rock filled with opalescent colors, each hollow lit by its own gentle glow with the egg backlit against it. The attendants wore soft, flowing robes. Nothing was harsh or loud. There were no sharp corners. Everything was soft, gentle, beautiful. Music hummed through the corridors, piling echoes on echoes until the entire world sang with it.

"What's that sound?" Meri asked quietly, squeezing his hand.

"It is the music of the nursery. The attendants sing for the children. Music fills our lives, from the earliest days in the shell."

Parents coming to visit their unborn children walked softly and spoke in quiet voices. They led their young children by the hand, bringing them to meet their new baby brothers and sisters. It was through the eyes of such a child that Lyr shared the nursery with Meri, because that was how *he* had seen it, when his parents had taken him to meet ...

"You have a sister?" Meri's voice was startled and soft.

He hadn't thought about her in years, had tried desperately not to. Now it felt strange to say her name, hearing the soft liquid sounds spoken aloud for the first time in decades. "Cerivel."

Memories drifted into their connection at her name. He remembered touching her egg, feeling how warm the pearly shell felt beneath his fingers. Baby dragons were in their dragon forms in their egg, so all each baby needed was the warmth and light of its hollow to grow and grow. When

Cerivel crawled from the egg as an awkward baby hatchling, tottering along on her little legs with her wings wet and crumpled on her back, she had toddled to him first.

"Where is she now?"

"I don't know." He'd last seen her when they were both teenagers, Lyr just on the cusp of young adulthood, Cerivel still all awkward elbows and gawky knees, her mane short and bristling in a low-on-top, high-in-back cut that was popular with adolescents their age.

He showed Meri how Cerivel had learned to shift, ending up in all kinds of goofy-looking halfway steps between a plump-bodied dragon hatchling and an equally plump-bodied little girl with tiny nubs of horns on her forehead.

"She'll be grown now," he said softly, wonderingly. "She might be visiting the caves herself now to sing lullabies to her own children."

"Tamir told me that you—"

She broke off quickly, but she didn't have the control to hide a swirl of thoughts. *You're a hostage. You can't go home again. Your people wouldn't take you back. Sorrysorrysorry—*

He wasn't able to hide the pain that stabbed through him, and he felt her flinch, both mentally and physically.

"I'm sorry," he said, at the same time she said, "I'm sorry," and then she gave a small laugh and Lyr even managed to smile. He turned to wrap her in his arms and ran his hand down her bare back.

"I should have told you."

"We shouldn't have been talking about you behind your back."

"I don't blame you for being curious." He didn't even feel angry at Tamir for telling her. It was odd ... all that anger he'd been carrying around with him wasn't *gone*, exactly, but it was no longer simmering just under the surface, making him lash out at everyone. Instead it had faded and mellowed, like a healing bruise. "I suppose it's easier if you already know."

"I can't believe they would blame you for trying to escape from the people who made a *hostage* out of you."

"It was my duty to my people."

"What about your duty to yourself?"

"That doesn't matter."

"Doesn't it?" Her voice was so quiet he heard the words as much through the link as through his ears. "You know ... I told myself for years that I didn't deserve to be happy now that Aaron was gone. As if I could honor his memory by making myself miserable for the rest of my life. But I was *wrong*, Lyr. I *do* deserve to be happy. And so do you."

Guilt twisted inside him and he turned his face away.

He couldn't see her, but he felt her move against him, slip an arm around him. "Lyr, what's wrong?"

"What's wrong," he said harshly, "is that I'm the last person to deserve joy, or peace, or forgiveness. Every faith that has ever been placed in me, I've broken; every person I've meant to protect, I've failed."

"I know that's not true," she murmured, running her hand down his arm. "You protected me. You saved Tamir."

"I failed my siblings," he gritted out. "Every last one of them."

"What happened?" she asked gently.

"They died." He took a breath. "No ... that's too gentle a word for what happened. They were killed."

He didn't mean to let the memory slip through, but it did.

The chaos of battle between the stars. The swift darting battlepods of the Galatean advance guard, the dark knife-like Kk'rek ships, the glittering arc of interstellar dust against the distant pinpoint of the sun in the system they were defending.

He had often fought in these battles as a dragon, his collar reconfigured each time to allow him to shift unimpeded. For the first time Meri was able to see, through his mind, how his people were meant to be. He couldn't reach his full size in a planet's atmosphere, with the atmospheric pressure itself interfering with his ability to shift to his fully mature shape. In space he was huge, his bronze wings spreading wide against the stars, his spikes and blades glistening.

He had worn two plasma cannons, one under each wing, and a high-powered shield that glittered down the length of his body, giving him a greenish sheen in the starlight. He was more maneuverable than any ship, all but unbeatable close up. He let the shield drop so he could use his claws to rip the enemy's small fighters open, exposing their pilots to space; he twisted and darted around their comparatively sluggish ships, firing ship-slaying plasma bursts from his cannons.

His mere presence was a major part of his effectiveness in battle. Dragons were rarely seen outside the Well of Stars, but tales were told of them throughout the galaxy, blown up in the telling until dragons became fearsome monsters the size of interstellar cruisers, taking on whole fleets singlehandedly. He couldn't do that, of course, but merely having a lone dragon wreaking havoc among their fighters was enough to damage the enemy's morale.

All the while, he had divided his attention to help his sept-siblings—lending them support, alerting them to incoming fighters they might have missed. He connected the entire sept into a whole that was greater than the sum of its parts, a network of eyes and ears and weapons.

But they had died. One by one, they'd died. Until it was only Lyr and Rook and Rei, and then *that* battle happened, a little more than half a standard year ago.

He still remembered with stark clarity the sudden winking out of Rook and Rei's minds, the slip of the last two tethers that held him to the family he'd gained and then lost.

"Oh, Lyr," Meri whispered.

"There weren't even bodies," he murmured. In the depths of space, there wasn't much left of a battlepod after the enemy's cannons hit it.

He became dimly aware that he'd partially extended his spines, and pulled them back in with a force of will. But he was rigid and trembling in Meri's arms.

And now he couldn't stop thinking of Rook and Rei's last moments. That instant when he'd felt Rook's mental presence leap in surprise and then wink out. And then Rei flickering off their mental network moments later, leaving him alone, alone ...

He had tried to die, then. Dragons could flame but a few times in their life; each time they tried it, they burned up part of their life force, shortening their lifespan and risking self-immolation. The rumors about dragons being able to take out whole fleets were wrong, but a dragon's white-hot plasma flame *could* actually take out a cruiser-sized ship, or a significant portion of a smaller fleet. He'd tried to do that, and he still remembered the searing pain of the flame burning him up from within—

—only to wake days later in the medbay, covered in the sticky net of a life-support web, with an exhausted-looking, grief-worn Tamir looking down at him, and nothing but cold darkness in the corner of his mind where his sept used to be.

From that day forward, he had done nothing but hope for his own death.

And now ...

... now, he felt the grief and guilt pressing down on him, but it was different, somehow. When Rei and Rook had died, he hadn't been able to see beyond the instant of their deaths. There was no future for him without them.

But now ... now, he could see an "after." He could see a future for him without Rook and Rei and the others, a future with Meri.

He could see that future and it terrified him. He didn't deserve it. If he stayed here, frozen in this moment of grief, of guilt, of loss ...

"It wasn't your fault." Meri's voice came to him, murmuring into his ear, while her mind put out a steady flow of warmth and love and calm ... and her own guilt and grief, as well. "It's not your fault, any more than Aaron's death was mine. We can't live in the moment of their deaths forever. They wouldn't want us to."

She was right, and yet, he found himself wanting to stay there, because it hurt, it *hurt*, but at least he wouldn't have to acknowledge that he—

—that he had a future.

That he deserved a future.

In her arms, he trembled in the grip of a grief so vast it had no name, a grief he had not allowed himself to feel until now.

Meri's grief blended with his, and he felt her tears wet his neck. And he realized slowly that not all the grief he felt was for himself; in fact, not even the largest part of it. He felt for *her*, and in that realization he began to see his own despair cast in a larger context. He was not the only person who had ever lost someone; he was not the only one who'd ever felt that emptiness or that lack of future.

He hurt for Meri as much as he hurt for himself.

There was a selfishness to grief, he thought. An understandable selfishness, the mind's instinctive urge to protect itself. But a selfishness still. It made a person turn away from the world, turn inward, wall themselves off from all that was good and kind and worth living for.

Meri was right. Rei and Rook and the others would never have wanted this for him.

He couldn't save them, any of them. But there was one last person he could save: himself.

He could do it for them. And for Meri. And maybe, someday ... for himself.

ALL MERI COULD DO WAS HOLD him, cradling him against her.

And she cried: she cried for Aaron and for herself, she cried for the children they never got to have, and she cried, too, for this family of Lyr's that she never got to meet, and for Lyr himself, who had deserved so, so much more from life than he'd gotten.

She wept herself to weary stillness, and after that, they just held each other and rocked slowly together. When she looked up at last, opening wet-lashed eyes, she saw Lyr looking down at her with eyes that reflected her emotions like damp silver mirrors.

"Thank you," he whispered, and kissed her gently, kissing her tears away.

"For what?" she asked shakily, wiping at her face.

"I don't know," he said, and gave a laugh that sounded

close to a sob. But the smile that followed was genuine, if tired. "For ... giving me a reason to get out of my head, I guess. For telling me the truth. For giving me something to live for."

Meri felt her own smile breaking through her tears. "If I hadn't met you, I'd still be back on Earth, living in my former best friend's spare bedroom and stuck in an endless loop of reliving Aaron's death." Grief caught in her throat, saying it aloud, but it wasn't the consuming, smothering grief that she'd been living with for the last ten years. It still hurt, would probably always hurt, but it was less like a raw and gaping wound, and more like the itch and ache of something that was beginning to heal.

Lyr brushed at her tears, and his voice, when he spoke again, was almost shy. "Would you like to meet my brothers and sisters, Meri?"

"I'd love to."

She was expecting pictures from his cuffs, but instead, slowly and gently, an image began to unfold in her head.

"The first of them I met," Lyr murmured, "were the twins, Rook and Kite. They were Tyborians, from a mountainous world of cliffs and spires and trees that reach as high as outer space itself."

The shadowy shapes in her head resolved into two children. They looked much more human than she was expecting, a little boy and girl with reddish-purple skin and hair that was barred brown and white, like the feathers of a hawk. At first their coloring was the oddest thing she noticed about them—until they spread their wings, fledgling wings with tufts of fluff, still growing their flight feathers.

She saw them pounce on a bronze-skinned teenager, who she recognized with a start as a young Lyr. He was so ...

open, so happy-looking; he laughed when the children jumped on him and began wrestling with him.

"Then Rei came to us," Lyr said, his voice bringing her back to reality. "He was a wolf shifter from the planet Polara. I remember him as a shy child, fond of art and quiet things."

Rei was a little boy with dark blue skin and bright, startling golden eyes. In the images playing out in her head, she saw Rei curled up crying in a corner. The little winged boy and girl went to him and hugged him, wrapping their wings around him.

"And then there was Haiva, who was of Galatean parentage. She was taken as a child to pay off a clan debt."

Haiva was slightly older than the others, an active girl with the ears of a cat and tawny, spotted leopard fur. She seemed to be a perky, cheerful child, eagerly reaching out to the others to make friends.

"Thorn was the most unusual among us. He was a chimera, created in a lab, part of a Galatean experiment to create a new kind of warrior."

This child had skin of a patchwork silver and blue, and eyes that flashed red in the dark. He didn't want to look at anyone, hiding, keeping to himself. But when Haiva crouched and took his hands, he looked up at her and smiled shyly, and then he hugged her. It was plain that they were especially close.

"Selinn was our teleporter. She was of a people called the Rhuadhi, and her people are unique among all the peoples of the galaxy because they are bonded to symbiotes that enable them to teleport from place to place. As you might expect, Rhuadhi are hard to imprison, though very sought after by those who wish to exploit their unique talents."

The new girl had skin as smooth and brown as Meri's, and green hair hanging to her waist. She reached a hand above her head and drew it down like she was unzipping an invisible coat hanging in the air in front of her. And the air did unzip, parting in a shimmer of eye-searing blue and purple to expose a view of an orange sky and distant mountains.

"A symbiote?" Meri asked. "What's that?"

"It's a lab-engineered creature that lives inside their bodies. I don't know how it works, but I know what she could do. The Galateans wanted to use her power to send her to conduct secret assassinations."

In Lyr's memory, Selinn drew a deep breath and squared her shoulders. She looked scared but determined as she stepped through the hole in the air. It closed up behind her.

"And then there was Skara, the Iustran. Skara was our troublemaker, and our finder. He worked as a team with Selinn."

The new child had purple skin and vivid red hair. In Lyr's memories, he was a whirlwind of constant motion: climbing on top of things, picking locks, stealing small items and hiding them, playing pranks on the other children and on their keepers.

"What do you mean, your finder?" Meri asked.

"It's something his people can do. They can imprint on people and find them again. It's how they recognize each other, since their people can change shape."

His memories shifted. Now the children were playing a game that seemed to be a cross between hide-and-seek and paintball. They didn't carry toy guns; instead they shot beams of colored light from their cuffs. It was clear that they were having fun, but it was also serious. If these were child soldiers in training, this was how they were trained.

And it was clear that Skara had no trouble finding the other children. The purple-skinned boy, now a lean and muscular teenager, had an unerring ability to locate any of the others. Meri watched a dizzying montage of memories (different games, different years). Skara scuttled up a sheer brick wall using an extra set of limbs that he grew for the occasion and then jumped down onto a well-hidden Rei; he extended a set of wings and leaped onto Lyr's back, throwing his arms around Lyr's neck for playful roughhousing and nearly scaring Lyr out of his skin.

"He was your favorite," she realized, feeling the emotions underlying that memory.

"I didn't have favorites," Lyr answered quickly, but she gave him a look, and he broke into a tentative smile. "Okay, maybe I had a *slight* favorite. I don't know why. He was just such a *problem* all the time. But it was sort of like ... he could be so charming that you couldn't hate him for it, even when his pranks got us all punishment detail. The thing about Skara ..."

He trailed off, and she thought he might not have intended to show her the next memory—his own hands, helping a shaken and trembling Skara out of some kind of dark box. It was a punishment; Skara had been shut up in there.

"They couldn't break him," Lyr said, his voice low and fierce. "All the rest of us gave in, sooner or later. We might be only pretending to go along with them, but we *did* go along with them. Skara, though ... they could beat him, starve him, threaten him with any kind of punishment. He just didn't care. Nothing they did to him made him less defiant, and I think through him, we all managed to hold onto a little bit of freedom."

"He sounds like someone I wish I could have met."

She regretted the words almost immediately, but Lyr's smile was wistful instead of sad. "I wish you could have, too. I'm not sure if you would've liked each other; he drove most people crazy—"

He broke off at the sound of footsteps outside, crunching on the foliage. But it was Tamir's tall, broad-shouldered shape that appeared in the half-open doorway. Meri grabbed for a blanket and pulled it over her chest.

"Fresh fish for supper tonight," Tamir declared. He paused to shake rainwater off his fur before holding up a string of fat silvery fish. "I went back to see if I could salvage something from the carcass down by the spring, but it'd already been scavenged pretty thoroughly; there's not much left—" He stopped mid-sentence, taking in what he was seeing. "Er ... I could go back outside again."

"Maybe long enough for us to get dressed?" Meri asked.

"Right." His fur hid his ability to blush, but she recognized his embarrassment by the hunch of his shoulders as he ducked quickly out the door. Meri looked at Lyr, who met her gaze with humor chasing the shadows of grief from his eyes.

"I guess we're one of *those* couples now," she said, laughing, as she reached for her blouse.

"Those couples?"

"The kind who embarrass everyone around them with PDAs." Lyr looked politely blank. "Public displays of affection."

"Hmm. Well." He caught her hand and nipped lightly at her fingers before letting it go and groping around for his pants. "I can live with that."

MERI HADN'T EXPECTED that fish without seasonings or butter or even salt, seared over a campfire, could taste so good. It was probably the relief of eating something other than those awful ration packs. She decided to celebrate by breaking out the rest of her chocolate stash. Lyr couldn't eat it and Tamir declined, so she ate a slightly stale, more than slightly squashed, fun-sized Mars bar by herself. It tasted amazing.

A renewed rain squall drummed on the plastic sheeting overhead as darkness settled slowly around them. Lyr stirred up the fire. Meri would have thought she'd feel a lot more nervous sitting out here, but with Lyr beside her and the fire sparking golden, and the possibility of retreat into the ship at her back, she was starting to enjoy the campout feeling again.

Tamir turned in early, still healing and exhausted from the day's activities, leaving the two of them alone. Lyr sat with his arms around her, occasionally leaning forward to add a stick to the fire. Rain ran off the plastic in a steady cascade.

Meri relaxed in his arms. The things he'd told her and showed her ran around and around in her head. Her life seemed so sheltered, compared to his.

But who would ever have thought that she'd end up having adventures like this? Stranded on an alien planet, fighting dinosaurs, making love to a dragon prince ...

Cora would never believe this, she thought. That life seemed so far behind her now. She sent another hopeful thought toward Cora and Toni, hoping her friend had made it out okay—and then let it go.

"You told me once that you didn't like the rain," Lyr said quietly. "Is this hard for you? We can go inside if you wish."

"No. I'm okay." It surprised her to realize that it was true. "On Earth, yes. But here ... it's like a fresh start. All those bad memories are a million miles away." She looked up to see that Lyr was smiling. "What?"

"The image you just shared with me. I saw you dancing in the rain."

"Oh," she said, embarrassed. She'd accidentally flashed back to a memory from college, when she and some of the girls from her dorm had run outside in a rainstorm to dance on the campus quad. She hadn't realized he had seen it.

But when had she forgotten how much she used to love the rain? As a small child, she liked to play out in it. During thunderstorms, she used to stand on the porch and watch the lightning. And then there were those wild nights on campus: taking off her shoes to walk barefoot on the wet grass, spinning around in the rain with her arms spread wide to the sky.

"Lyr ... do you want—"

Her mind shared the image before she could ask the question: Meri with rain coursing down her face and shoulders, dancing barefoot on an alien hillside with Lyr's hands in hers.

She sensed his anxiety, not fear so much as wary tension. "Are you sure? You know what's out there."

"You'll protect me."

"Are you two going somewhere?" came Tamir's sleepy voice from inside the cargo hold as they got up.

"We're going for a walk in the rain," Meri told him.

"Hmm. Don't let anything eat you." But he sounded more amused than worried.

Lyr took her hand as they left the shelter. Rain soaked

her immediately. As her blouse dampened and clung, she realized there might be a flaw in her plan.

"I forgot we don't have anything to change into."

"Clothes will dry. We have blankets."

Well, her clothes needed to be washed anyway, she reasoned. Tilting her head back, she closed her eyes and let the rain run down her face. The wet grass was soft under her bare feet.

Opening her eyes, she saw the flash of Lyr's teeth as he grinned at her. He was staying very close, almost clinging—not that she minded, with the possibility of large predators around.

It seemed unlikely that anything would be out in this kind of weather. Still ... now that she'd thought of it, nervousness stripped some of the joy out of the experience.

"Aren't you enjoying yourself?" Lyr asked.

"I'm thinking that dancing in the rain was more fun when I was twenty-two."

"Perhaps your dance needs more ... dancing."

And to her surprise, he took her hands and twirled her on the hillside.

After the first breathless instant, when she came very near to being literally swept off her feet, she caught herself and began to skip along with him. It was not a formal dance so much as the kind of thing she used to do when she was younger, an improvised skip-jump, like kids playing.

Lyr's hands were strong on hers. Rain ran down her hair and her feet were splattered with mud. It was stupid and ridiculous and completely, in all ways, *not* how you were supposed to act when you were stranded in a wilderness filled with man-eating dinosaurs. (Not that there was an instruction booklet for that, exactly.) But it was also the most fun she could remember having in years. It was reckless and crazy. She found herself laughing, her mouth open with rainwater running in. She heard Lyr laugh, and tried to remember if she'd ever heard his laughter before.

They spun to a stop, breathless, on top of the hill. Meri leaned into Lyr and he caught her as she giggled helplessly.

"That was amazing," she gasped as she got her breath back. "That's one of those things I'm going to remember all my life."

"I'm glad you liked—" Lyr broke off suddenly, and surprise rippled through their link.

For an instant Meri thought they were being attacked, but he wasn't angry or afraid, just curious. He was looking up at the sky, so she looked too, just in time to see a bright flash of light streak through the clouds. It didn't flicker and branch like lightning; instead it was a straight line that suddenly changed direction at near right angles to its first trajectory and vanished behind darker clouds, leaving only an afterimage blazoned across her retinas.

"What was that?" she asked, startled. "Does this planet have weird lightning, or what? How did it *move* like that?"

"That was a ship."

"Wait, what? Really? Does that mean we're saved?"

"Unlikely." He stared into the rainy darkness, shielding his eyes with his hand. The wind lashed the trees, and Meri moved closer to him. "Think about the possibilities. The only other people anywhere near here, as far as we know, are pirates. They may well have found another functional escape vessel in the wreckage, like the one we took. And if it's not them, then the Galateans have found us."

She couldn't understand, at first, why he didn't sound happier about it, but then the penny dropped. "And you're an escaped hostage."

He looked down at her, rain running down his face and

dripping off the ends of his hair. "I will not let anyone hurt you."

"I know." She moved into his arms; he wrapped them around her. "Just don't let them hurt *you*, either. What are we going to do?"

"If it is the Galateans, they will not pose a threat to either you or Tamir. Tamir is a respected soldier, and as for you, they will simply return you to your world."

"Not without you!"

"Just listen. If I disappear into the forest and leave you and Tamir to contact them, you'll both be safe. You can go home—"

"Lyr. Listen to me." She gripped his arms and tried to project her thoughts at him so he would recognize her sincerity. "There *is* no home for me without you, don't you understand? What's waiting for me back on Earth, anyway? A spare bedroom in the house of an old friend I don't even really feel close to anymore, and a new job in a new city that I don't really want to live in. What am I supposed to do, go on Tinder looking for a date when I could have *you*?"

In the darkness, she wished she could see his face better.

"Let me make this clear to you," she said, squeezing his forearms. She felt the hard lines of the blades under his skin, but she wasn't afraid of being cut; she knew he'd never hurt her. "If you're going to vanish into the wilderness, I'm coming with you—do you understand? I'd rather be stuck on this planet with you forever than go back to Earth alone, knowing all of this was out here, that *you* were out here, and never able to do anything about it. Got it?"

"Yes," he whispered, staring at her.

"Good." She realized she was shivering, in her wet clothes and her bare feet. "Let's go back to the fire."

Tamir was awake and up when they got back to the ship, feeding the fire underneath the plastic shelter. He looked up and grinned at their bedraggled appearance. "I expect you two are going to be regretting this when you have to put on your wet clothes in the—" He stopped as their solemnity registered on him, the smile dropping off his face. "What's wrong?"

"We saw a ship," Meri said.

"Most likely a ship," Lyr corrected. "Although I can't think what else it could have been. It was no meteor, not moving like that."

Tamir rose to his feet. "Pirates? Did it land?"

"If it came down anywhere, it's not close to us." Lyr wrung out the dripping tails of his hair and crouched by the fire. "I don't think we've been found, not yet. It's possible that it's your people."

"Hmm." Tamir studied the two of them, then disappeared into the cargo bay. Meri was trying uselessly to wring out the sleeves of her blouse when he came back with two blankets. "Here. Get out of your wet clothes."

"We need to make a decision," Lyr said. "Should we seek to contact them, or hide and prepare to fight?"

"Why does it have to be one or the other?" Tamir countered, shoving a blanket at him. "Perhaps we could play it both ways. We don't want them to stumble upon us unawares, but let's face it, we're not getting off this planet without a working ship. This one's beyond repair."

"So ... what are you suggesting?"

"Hide the campsite," Tamir said immediately. "Have an escape plan if we need it. But go ahead and contact them. We don't really have a choice."

"I can reconnoiter as a dragon," Lyr argued. "We need to

know more before we go charging into anything. You're the one who's always telling *me* I jump into things."

"I'm not suggesting jumping into anything blind, I'm just saying if there's a working ship on this planet, we need to talk to the people in control of it."

With the blanket draped around her, Meri wriggled out of her jeans underneath it. She was starting to get almost blasé about casual nudity; there simply wasn't much opportunity for privacy, living in close quarters like this.

She let Lyr and Tamir go ahead and argue over their plans. This was way out of her depth. But one thing she did know. Anyone who tried to separate her from Lyr was going to have a problem on their hands.

SEVENTEEN

MERI WOKE at dawn with Lyr sleeping warm and heavy against her, roused by the sound of Tamir rustling around in the cargo hold. She waited until he was gone, then wrapped a blanket around herself and tiptoed outside. The rain had rolled onward during the night, leaving the world fresh and clean.

Her clothes were still damp, as well as mildly smoked from the campfire, but it wasn't like she had any other options except wearing a blanket all day. Teeth clenched against the chill, she squirmed into her clammy jeans.

"Morning," Tamir said, appearing out of the edge of the forest with an armload of firewood.

Meri buttoned her blouse and stamped into her damp but mud-free shoes. "Good morning to you too. Any sign of, um, pirates? Or anything?"

He dropped the firewood and shook his head. "No. If it wasn't for Lyr having spotted the other ship last night, I wouldn't know anyone was around. Still, I think hiding our tracks would be a good idea."

"Can I do anything to help?"

"You could give me a hand with this." He picked up a branch, and when he leaned it against the side of the ship, she realized it wasn't firewood—it was camouflage to conceal the ship in the thicket.

"So we *are* trying to hide."

"We're being cautious," he corrected her.

They worked in silence for a little while. Tamir seemed better today, still limping but moving more easily. He paused occasionally to scratch with irritation at his fur.

"I see that you're still shedding."

He grinned at her. "If this keeps up, I'm going to end up bald as the rest of you."

"Your fur looks too itchy anyway," she teased back, then sobered. "Tamir ..." She didn't really want to ask it, but after what she'd seen of their technology and ships, she had to. "Are your people planning to try to conquer my world?"

Tamir was silent for long enough to worry her. "Not right now," he said at last. "My ship was part of a garrison keeping people like those pirates away from your planet."

"*Not right now* doesn't sound as reassuring as I'd hoped for."

"I know that. According to rumor, my people want to open diplomatic negotiations with your people, like we have with the dragons; they're just still working out the details. But ... I don't *know*, Meri. I'm a soldier, not a politician."

Meri blew out a breath. It wasn't his fault. As a former military wife, she knew all too well the feeling of having the brass and politicos make decisions that moved the ordinary grunts around like pieces on a chessboard. But he was still one of them; the fact that she liked him didn't change that. "And if that ship we saw last night was your people, come to take you and Lyr back ... what will you do then?"

"I don't know," Tamir said quietly, and went to gather more branches.

Meri was still working on piling branches to hide the ship's silver gleam when Lyr stepped, yawning, out of the open cargo door. He gave her a quick kiss. "I could get used to this kissing thing," he remarked.

"I'm not sure if I believe that your people don't do it. Are you sure that's not a line?"

Lyr smiled. He looked at what she was doing, then lifted an entire small tree and casually tossed it onto the top of the ship.

"You're not supposed to be exerting yourself!" she protested.

"I feel much better today." He grinned at her. He did look better. She still wasn't sure what constituted a good color for people of that particular iridescent-metallic-bronze shade, but there was a bright energy to him today that suffused him from the inside out.

It made her heart sing, too. It was almost enough to make her not care about the fact that she was wearing clothes she'd been wearing for three days and hadn't had a proper bath in that long, either.

... okay, she still cared about that. "We're all going to need changes of clothes before too long," she remarked, plucking at her damp sleeve. "Just getting rained on is not going to do it. I can probably make some ponchos or something out of our spare blankets that'll do for a little while, but it's not going to be comfortable."

Lyr hefted another small tree, one of many severed in their crash landing and by his later clearing efforts around the ship, and leaned it against the hull. "If we can't resupply soon, we're going to need a lot of supplies we don't have."

"I know," she sighed. "But there's no point in wearing our

clothes until they're rags while we're waiting." She watched him fling another tree on top of the ship. "You know, I'm feeling mildly outclassed here. Why don't I start breakfast?"

There were still a few fish left from last night, cleaned and packed in layers of leaves. Meri had stirred up the fire and was practicing her fish-spitting skills when Tamir appeared out of the woods again, his fur damp from the rain-soaked foliage.

"You know," he remarked, "for the record, you're both at the top of my list of people I'd like to be stranded on a savage planet with."

"That's good, since you don't have any other options." Meri stood back to survey her handiwork with the fish, and tried not to wish *too* desperately for coffee.

"Well, as my contribution, I found these." Tamir held out a handful of dimpled purple-blue fruits, the color of a ripe blueberry but each as large as a grape. "I checked them out with the cuffs. They won't hurt us."

"Which isn't exactly the same thing as being tasty," Meri murmured. She sniffed cautiously at the one he handed her. It smelled mildly citrusy. "Also, it's still possible to be allergic."

"I'll be your test case. I've already eaten a few and I haven't dropped dead yet."

"I'm going to remind you of that when we have to do CPR on you later."

LYR FOUND it baffling how well Meri and Tamir were getting along. It was sibling-like bickering, almost, that carried to him from the campfire as he worked on hiding the ship. He was definitely not jealous. That would be ridiculous.

"Lyr!" Meri called. "Breakfast!"

"And fruit for dessert," Tamir added as Lyr joined them at the campfire, wiping sap off his hands with a handful of wet leaves.

Meri made a face. "Those are awful. You talked me into eating one, but I'm not having another."

"What about you?" Tamir asked Lyr, offering him a dark blue berry. "This one has no adventure in her soul."

"This one doesn't want to poison herself, thanks."

"Analysis says they're harmless."

"Do you even know how many people I treated in the ER for eating something weird they thought was harmless?"

Lyr tried a berry and had to agree with Meri's assessment; it didn't taste particularly edible to him. The fish was much more satisfying.

"After this I'm going up for awhile," he said, pointing skyward. "Now that you're awake to keep an eye on Meri—"

"Wait, what's this?" Meri said indignantly.

"—that is to say, now that you can watch out for each other, I can do some more long-range scouting. I'll look for the module and the ship from last night."

Meri wanted to see him off, so they left Tamir hauling more branches and walked up the hill hand in hand. Around them in the grass, tiny alien lizards sang high, piping songs.

"I think with a nice little house with indoor plumbing, this would be a lovely place to live," Meri said. "Er ... and perhaps a high, electrified fence around the yard."

Lyr smiled. "Is a house in the forest what you want?"

"I don't know what I want," she said simply. "I haven't

thought about the future since Aaron died ... not like that." After a pause, she asked, "What about you?"

Strange to think about having a future—a future he got to choose, rather than having all decisions made for him. It was a pressure like a gravity well, like the weight of all that air above him. "I don't know either. Perhaps it is best not to make plans; so many things are uncertain still."

"That doesn't mean we can't have dreams." She looked up at him, her fingers twined in his. "Do you want to go back to your city-ship, Lyr?"

"They would not have me."

"But if you could?"

His heart cried out for it. And yet ... "The Galateans say you can never go back to your childhood home. You will always see it through an adult's eyes. I think I've seen too much and been too many places to be truly happy there anymore."

"So tell me about your dream house."

What *did* he want? He had never thought in those terms before. But when he thought about it, an image came to him slowly. He opened up his mind and shared it with her.

A house on a cliff. Somewhere high, somewhere with sky all around. A big house, rambling and full of rooms. Room for ...

... for what, he didn't know. Once, it would have needed to be big enough for his sept-sibs. But they were gone. Room for anyone who needed a place to go. Escaped slaves. Refugees.

He shared it with her tentatively, shyly. Maybe she wouldn't want such a thing. Maybe her people craved privacy and distance from others. But he liked the idea of having others around, even if he didn't know exactly who, yet. He liked thinking that he might be able to create a place where the lost and the abandoned could feel safe, the way he hadn't been able to. Maybe someday, he could feel safe there too.

Meri's hand tightened on his, and he realized he'd let that last thought slip, as clumsy as an untrained hatchling. The answer she sent him through the link was not in words. Instead it was a picture of the two of them together on a balcony outside just such a house, drinking cups of some bitter drink that he gathered was a traditional drink of her people. Just sitting together, looking down at the view together.

I would live in a house like that with you, her images said.

With the link between them singing with warmth and her fingers tangled in his, they climbed to the crest of the hill. Below them, the land dropped away steeply toward the beach. A fresh breeze off the ocean rippled the grass around their feet.

"And you're absolutely sure you're feeling up to it?" Meri asked.

"I'll be careful. Stretching my wing will be good for its healing. I was worried about leaving you alone before, but now that Tamir's up and about, you'll be fine with him as long as the two of you stay close to the ship."

She kissed him quickly and then stepped back with an eager look on her face. "Go on. I want to see you as a dragon again."

Lyr tried not to preen *too* obviously, and relaxed into the satisfying feeling of the shift. As always, the world altered around him, becoming smaller and simultaneously richer in sounds and smells. He blinked draconic eyes and looked down at Meri, who was gazing up at him in rapture.

"You're so beautiful," she said, and reached out her hands. Her open wonder was charming, and before he realized he was doing it, he'd dipped his head so she could stroke the softer scales on the underside of his neck. "Are you sure I can't come with you?"

Maybe we'll experiment sometime soon. I might be able to carry a passenger, but I've never tried, and I don't think it would be a good idea to try it with a healing wing.

"Oh no, of course not." She stepped back to look at him critically. "How do you feel? Does your wing feel all right?"

He stretched out his wings, giving them a cautious, experimental flap. **Only one way to find out for sure. Can you move back? I don't want to risk hurting you.**

"You would never hurt me," she said decisively, but she moved back to the edge of the nearest thicket.

Lyr ran toward the crest of the dune, wings spread. Meri's alarm flickered at the back of his mind, but he felt nothing but elation as he leaped off. There was an instant of pain and unexpected strain when his wings caught his weight, and then he was aloft, soaring higher and higher in great sweeping circles beneath the sun.

Meri's fear had turned to joy, tickling his mind like effervescent bubbles and blending with his own delight, until he couldn't tell where his happiness left off and hers began.

Soon I'll be too far away to easily talk to you, he sent to her. **So don't worry if I'm out of touch for a bit.**

Have fun and be careful! Don't go too far. Come back to me.

I will.

He didn't add "I promise," but it was there, a gentle

underlying assurance. He had something to come back to now. He wasn't going to leave her behind.

Be well, she told him.

You too.

He flew in a wide, sweeping circle over the crash site. They'd done a decent job of hiding the crashed ship under foliage, but there was nothing to be done about the huge scar where the ship had torn a furrow down the hillside until it came to rest at the bottom of the valley. At least it wasn't immediately obvious that there was anyone living there.

Meri, walking down the hill back to the campsite, looked up and waved. Lyr tilted to dip his wings to her, and then soared higher, looking down until even his sharp eyes could no longer pick out her tiny figure.

From up here, the trees blurred together into a patchwork carpet of green and purple and gold following the natural rise and fall of the land. The beach was a white ribbon clinging to the shore of the wide, sparkling sea. Far out over the ocean, a few large, dark-winged shapes wheeled against the sky, too far away for him to make out anything about them except that they were very large, possibly even close to dragon-sized. He made a mental note to try to get a better look later ... but maybe not from too close.

In the meantime, he was an object of curiosity for other flying creatures. A flock of small, bright-colored winged lizards fluttered around him for a moment, straining their little wings to keep pace and then falling back to dive and vanish under the forest canopy.

So far, he saw no sign of any other ship. But this country would be all too easy to hide in, with all of its many hills and valleys like the one their ship had crashed into. This boded well for their ability to avoid detection, but it also meant there could be any number of other ships here, and he'd never find them.

He flew higher, and yet higher, through thin ribbons of clouds draping the mountains' peaks. There was snow on the highest peaks, and he thought of diving into it, sliding and swimming in the frozen waves.

He needed to bring Meri up here. He wanted to share it with her.

And then he realized that he could.

Love? he asked, only realizing after he'd already opened the connection that he had called her thus. **Can you hear me?**

I'm here, her answer came back, thready and distant, but strengthening as the connection grew firmer between them. **Is something wrong?**

Not at all. I wanted you to be able to enjoy this view with me.

And he opened up to her. He still kept careful control, as he always did with non-telepaths, sending images in a trickle rather than a flood. But he could feel her joy and awe coming back down the link as he shared with her not just the glorious view but also the sensations he felt: the crisp chill of the air around him, the damp cool feeling of soaring through clouds, the thin warmth of the sunlight on his wings.

I had a dream, the first morning I woke on this planet, she sent back to him. **It was just like this. Were you flying that morning?**

I took a short flight to look around. I didn't realize you sensed it.

Neither did I. Her mental voice was filled with wonder. **Until now.**

Lyr circled in wide spirals above the high peaks,

enjoying the shared experience almost as if she was here with him. He flew through a pass between two high, rocky peaks, and got a look at the other side of the mountains for the first time since their crash. It was less steep than the ocean side, the mountains rolling down in a series of smaller peaks to a plateau.

Are you still there? Meri's mental voice was faint now, distance-attenuated.

I may be out of range for a little while. I won't be gone long.

He flew lower, skimming the mountainside. The landscape was drier here than on the ocean side of the mountains, the forest sparser and made up of tall, spiky trees rather than the dense, leafy thickets on the other side. The open forest would be easier for hunting, he couldn't help thinking, as a small herd of dinos scattered under the shadow of his wings. It also made it harder for predators to hide and sneak up on unwary prey, such as what had happened to him and Meri at the spring.

His wings were starting to burn from the unaccustomed strain. He'd better turn around soon, or else he'd need a rest before he tried to fly back over the mountains—

Wait. Was that a glimmer up ahead, as of the sun glinting on metal?

Yes. There it was. The module had come to rest at the edge of a lake on the plateau. Like their own crashing ship, it had plowed up a great furrow in the earth, now half full of water, like a long canal pointing toward the bulk of the crashed module resting in the marshy lake-edge.

The presence of survivors was clearly evident from the air. In the few days since the crash, they had begun to build a little village on the sightly higher ground just above the module. Lyr circled to get a better look. He was impressed despite himself. They'd built a circle of crude huts, little more than branch lean-tos at this point, but he saw signs that a larger structure was starting to go up nearby. Smudges of smoke indicated the presence of campfires. A party of hunters or foragers were headed back from the woods, carrying bundles. They looked up as his shadow fell across them, and ducked under the trees with evident alarm.

His wide-winged presence was causing general panic in the village as well. As he banked over them, they scattered for shelter, making him think they might have had some experience with the large flying creatures he'd spotted earlier. Or perhaps they were merely being cautious of large lizards on a strange planet ... something he probably should have taken to heart himself.

The ache in his injured shoulder was growing more acute, like the point of a dull blade digging into the joint. He needed to land soon or he was going to make a spectacularly undignified entrance by belly-flopping in the lake.

The wide space at the center of the circle of huts looked big enough to land in. Lyr folded his wings and dropped the last couple of body-lengths to the ground, shifting as he went and bending his knees to take the impact.

Just in time, too. A crude homemade spear sailed through the space his larger dragon body had just occupied, swishing over his head.

"Really?" Lyr said. He put up a shield, although the handful of visible onlookers peeking out from doorways and from behind trees now looked more startled than hostile. "That's the thanks I get for saving you people?"

"It's you!" A young green-skinned Kvarian woman ran out of one of the huts. Lyr recognized her as the one Meri had seemed close to on the ship, though he couldn't recall her name. "You're all right!"

"It's me," he acknowledged, taking a quick step back just in case she was thinking about hugging him. Reluctantly he let the shield drop, as there seemed to be no danger at the moment.

... except from spontaneous hugs, because now a small crowd of the escaped prisoners were gathering around him with tearful thanks. Lyr fended them off, resisting the urge to stun anyone.

"We all made it through the landing just fine, just a few injuries, nobody badly hurt," the Kvarian woman exclaimed. "What about the rest of you? Meri—is she okay?"

"She's fine. We came down on the other side of the mountains."

"You're a dragon!" someone else said.

"Yes, I'm a dragon, thank you for pointing that out. How did you *think* I managed to take on an entire ship full of pirates almost singlehandedly?"

The mention of the pirates was like a bucket of cold water dumped on the party atmosphere around him.

"We saw a ship enter the atmosphere last night," one of the men said. "We hoped it was you."

"No. It was not." He glanced around the now much more sober group. "Have any of you seen signs of other people around?"

"No, but it's got to be either pirates or the Galateans," another of the men said. He touched his throat, where the silver slave collar gleamed. *Either way it's bad news for us*—he didn't have to say it.

"My friend has a collar controller," Lyr said. "He can take them off."

This caused a stir to ripple through the escaped slaves.

"If your *friend* is a Galatean citizen, very likely he won't *want* to take them off."

"You are underestimating him." Lyr held up his hands, displaying the silver cuffs, not gold like a citizen would wear. "I was once a slave like you. He took mine off."

A dark-skinned woman with her throat unmarked by a collar pushed to the front of the group. "We don't all belong here," she protested. "Not all of us were slaves before the pirates took us. I just want to go home."

"I'll try to arrange that," Lyr promised. "If I can."

"And why should we believe you?" someone else asked.

"I swear it on my honor."

"And what's that worth?"

"Everything," Lyr said grimly. "If you know anything of my people, you wouldn't ask that question. Once I've given my word, I *will* keep it. I will see you safely back to the worlds you wish to go to, or protect you here, should you wish it."

He could almost have laughed at himself. He'd never meant to get tangled up like this again. Now here he was, not just with Meri to worry about, but an entire village of people that he'd suddenly gone and made himself responsible for.

They still seemed unsure, but after some hesitation, one of the men asked, "Would you like to stay and eat with us? We can't offer you much, but there's fish in the lake and we're learning to find edible plants in the woods."

Lyr shook his head. "Your hospitality is appreciated, but I can hunt for myself. And I need to get back. I promised I wouldn't be gone long. I'll return soon and remove your collars."

With that, he shifted back to his dragon form and spread his wings. The assembled group fell back, but there was more wonder than fear this time in the way they looked at him.

He couldn't help thinking, as he rose into the air with a powerful downbeat, how beautiful it was here with the lake glittering in the sun and the snow-capped mountains rising beyond it. They could have come down in much worse places. There was the lake for water and for fishing; there was fertile soil and timber. It would be entirely possible to establish a village here. A permanent one, perhaps ... a haven for escaped slaves from across the galaxy, like the vision he'd shown Meri but on a grander scale.

It wasn't a plan. It was barely even an idea yet. There were so many variables, not the least being that an entire fleet of Galatean ships could already be in orbit around the planet.

But ... as he circled above the collection of crude huts, and a few people waved to him, he thought it was something he'd like to try to make happen.

He ought to head straight for the mountains; his wings ached and he was already tired. But rather than flying back immediately, he flew in a wide sweeping arc across the forest. The idea of checking for pirates lurked in the back of his mind, but there was something else he wanted to find first.

—and, aha, there it was: a small herd of medium-sized lizards, about the size of Tamir in his tiger-shifted form, browsing on grass at the water's edge. He'd figured a lake like this would attract wildlife.

They never saw him coming. He swooped in and broke his target's neck, then picked it up in his claws and flew with heavy wingbeats across the lake to the village. Moments later, having dropped off his offering, he made for the mountains without staying to hear their thanks.

After all, it was easy for him to hunt, and much harder for them.

He was starting to regret going quite this far on his first flight since being injured, in atmosphere no less. His wings ached and his shoulder hurt. When he got back to the campsite, he was going to eat two of those ration packs, or maybe a nice fat lizard if he still had the energy to catch one, and collapse into sleep for a while.

But still, it was glorious flying under these brilliant blue skies, with the arch of the planet's rings spanning the horizon. And he was looking forward to getting ...

... home?

Yes. Yes, it *did* feel like home. It was a crude campsite in the middle of nowhere, but it was the first place he'd wanted to go back to in longer than he could remember.

Because Meri was there.

He smiled, in his dragon form, at the thought of Meri by the campfire, her skin glowing in the firelight, her eyes soft and warm with her affection for him. Maybe he wouldn't fall asleep immediately. Maybe he would undress her there by the fire, take her apart gently again and again, with the sounds of the forest around them, and hum lullabies until she fell asleep ...

Mind occupied with pleasant thoughts, he swept through the pass between the mountain peaks and came out the other side. He had no expectation of danger. The only creatures nearby that could harm him in the air were those huge fliers he'd seen out over the ocean, and they were easily visible from a long way off.

So the attack came out of nowhere, without warning.

There was a stab of searing pain, and suddenly his wings weren't working. He went into a tailspin, sky and mountains and ground all whirling around each other in a jumble of confused images.

Meri! he cried, reaching out with his mind in an instinctive cry for help as he went tumbling down into darkness.

EIGHTEEN

"LYR!"

Until Lyr's distress blazed through her mind, Meri had been sitting by the firepit, cutting up a blanket with the scissors from her keychain utility knife in the hopes of making clothing out of it. She was no seamstress; her experience with a sewing machine was limited to a high school home-ec class and a few attempts to save money by repairing her own socks and hemming too-long jeans, which hadn't gone so well. Still, she figured that even if her attempts came out looking like potato sacks, it would be better than going around naked while they washed their regular clothes.

Tamir was working on what he'd told her was a fish trap, made from supple tree branches woven together. As far as she could tell, he was about as good at making fish traps from branches as she was at making clothing out of blankets. They seemed to have arrived at a mutual, unspoken agreement not to point out the numerous flaws in the item taking shape in the other person's lap.

Meri was just realizing that she hadn't thought ahead to

sewing without a needle and thread (could she tie the pieces together, maybe?) when Lyr's sudden alarm went off like a bomb inside her head.

She doubled over, crying out and clutching her temples. Dimly she was aware of Tamir saying her name in surprise and worry, but she had no thoughts for anything but Lyr.

There was pain, an awful sensation of falling, and then —nothing.

"Lyr!"

"What's wrong? What is it?" Tamir was kneeling beside her now, his hands on her shoulders.

"I ... I don't know. Lyr!" She looked up at the treetops, as if crying out his name would bring the welcome appearance of his long-winged shape skimming over their campsite. But he was too far away for that. She didn't know how far he was, only that it was far enough his mind could barely brush her own.

And now he was gone. When she tried to reach for him, in that strange mental way she was only gradually learning to use, she could find nothing—no sense of Lyr's mind reaching back for hers. It was like he'd vanished.

Or died ... but no, *no*, she wouldn't even think it.

"What happened?" Tamir's voice was steady, the pressure of his hands secure but gentle as he knelt next to her, a solid and calming presence. She had often calmed a skittish patient in the same way.

"I felt him in my mind, as if he called out to me. Something was wrong. I think he fell. He might have been hurt." She looked up at the sky again. "And then there was nothing. Tamir, do you think he could have strained himself, lost his ability to stay in the air ..."

She trailed off, because she'd remembered something

else. The feeling of falling hadn't been the only thing that had come into her head with Lyr's jumbled sensory impressions. He'd been *angry*.

And there was more pain than just the strain of overstressed wings.

"Tamir, he was shot! That's why he fell. Someone shot him."

Tamir's catlike eyes widened. "Are you sure?"

"I—I think so." It was so hard to be sure. The impressions she'd gotten from Lyr's mind were already fading.

"Where is he? Could you tell?"

"In the mountains somewhere, I think." She squeezed her eyes shut, trying to bring back those brief memory-flashes before they faded into haziness, like a dream upon waking. "I saw the ocean. I think he was on our side of the mountains." Her eyes snapped open. "I saw something green, I think. A green flash. Like those weapons you and Lyr use."

Tamir rose swiftly to his feet. He stood looking up at what could be seen of the tops of the peaks through the trees—which wasn't much, down in the valley as they were. Then he turned and began kicking dirt over the fire and scattering the tidy pile of firewood.

"I suggest we move everything we've been using to the bridge. It's more defensible, and it gives us a second line of defense in case they get inside the cargo hold. Also, it means if anyone gets inside, it won't be immediately obvious that someone's been living here."

"What about Lyr?" Meri protested as she bundled up blankets and ration packs, helping him carry them through the derelict ship.

"I haven't forgotten him. I'll be leaving shortly. But I'm

going to have to leave you unguarded. I need you barricaded on the bridge—"

"Okay, no," Meri said flatly. "If you're going after Lyr, I'm coming with you."

Tamir dropped an armload of blankets between the seats on the bridge. "Meri, I hate to be blunt, but you are not a trained fighter. And I can move faster without—"

"*Can* you?" she interrupted, with a sharply critical look at the way he was still limping. "And what if you get hurt even worse up there? What if Lyr's hurt?"

"Your skills would be useful, but Lyr tasked me with keeping you safe. I gave him my word."

"What about keeping *him* safe? What if you need a second person for a two-person rescue plan, and don't have me?"

"I cannot put you in danger—"

"Okay, fine, so what's your brilliant plan for finding him? Are you going to search the entire mountain? I might be able to get in touch with him mentally and lead you there."

Tamir rubbed at his temple. "Meri—"

"And anyway," she forged onward, "if you leave me behind, I'll just follow. I am *not* sitting here all day in this stupid ship, waiting for pirates to show up, while you go running off on a rescue mission."

"I am starting to see," Tamir said with a slight grin, "how it is that you're able to handle our stubborn dragon prince. Very well. We will go on a rescue mission together. We will need supplies in case we're not back by tonight."

He worked quickly, making two piles of blankets and ration packs. They had no canteens, so Tamir filled some of the empty ration packs with water. As he handed her each item, she stuffed it into her purse until it was full to bursting.

"I don't suppose you have any weapons in there," Tamir said.

"Just this." She showed him the multitool with the scissors attachment. She flicked out the tiny knife blade. It was maybe two inches long, already dull from how much she'd used it on this trip.

"I think," Tamir said, looking at it, "that you'd best leave the fighting to me."

"Can't you give me any weapons at all?"

"Hmm." With his own blanket-wrapped bundle slung over his shoulder, he shoved open the airlock door and took a quick look around the remains of their campsite. "Do you have any fighting experience at all? Staffs? Unarmed combat?"

"Aaron once showed me how to break a grapple hold."

Tamir looked politely baffled at this.

"Aaron is my late husband," she explained, and felt only a slight stab, not the heartbreak she'd automatically braced herself for. Her mind was too caught in up *Find Lyr, find Lyr, find Lyr!* "He showed me a few self-defense tricks." In the interests of honesty, she admitted, "I don't know if I can remember any of them now."

"How about a club?" he asked, hefting a solid-looking stick from their scattered firewood.

Meri gripped it and felt its weight, giving it an experimental swing. She thought about slamming it into the face of whoever had hurt Lyr. "I think a club sounds great."

Tamir smiled and turned to haul the door shut. He used his foot to scatter the fire's cooling ashes and kicked some more dirt over them. There was no disguising the stumps of the trees Lyr had cut, but those might be mistaken for damage from the ship's crash landing. It was amazing, Meri thought, how their tidy little campsite had been made to look as if no one had been here, as if no one at all had survived the crash.

"Are you ready?" Tamir asked, shouldering his bundle.

Meri slung the purse across her body and gripped her club. "Ready."

LYR CAME GRADUALLY AWAKE with a splitting headache to go with a whole assortment of other aches and pains.

This is a stun headache, he thought muzzily as his brain began to struggle back to consciousness. Someone had stunned him. Which meant ...

Which meant he had been attacked with Galatean-style weapons.

And that meant either pirates or Galateans. There had been no warning or attempted contact, so probably pirates.

He kept his eyes closed with an effort. He could hear movement nearby and smelled traces of woodsmoke. His cheek was resting on dirt, and when he gave a slight, experimental twitch, he felt the tug of bonds. His hands were tied behind his back.

Hands ...? Ah, so he'd shifted back. His people sometimes did that instinctively when injured or unconscious, because it took much less energy to maintain and heal their smaller forms.

Lyr fought down a smile. *Let's see how you people like dealing with an angry dragon when I shift again. You're certainly in for a surprise.*

He reached out tentatively for the energy of his shift, and found it coming to him with odd sluggishness. That was strange. It was almost as if—

Shock, horror and outrage rushed through him with the force of a whirlwind, and his eyes came open, his lips drawing back from his teeth. He had not felt, at first, the cool weight of the collar against his neck; he had worn one for so long that he'd stopped noticing it. But now that he struggled to reach for the shifted shape he'd once more come to take for granted, he was all too cruelly aware of it.

And they had taken his cuffs. His wrists felt naked. That was a small indignity, however, next to the greater one.

"Ah, so you're awake," a harsh voice said. "Welcome back."

Lyr blinked. He was lying on his side. Brilliant sun filtered down through foliage, so he hadn't been out for long, unless a full day and night had passed, but a stun didn't usually last that long. Through blurred vision—the stun hangover was hitting him hard—he glimpsed hazy figures moving around a campfire. At least a half dozen pirates, he thought. Not good.

A shadow fell across him and rough hands pulled him into a sitting position. Lyr bit back his outrage (and, underneath it, icy fear) with a lifetime's practice and tried to look woozy and hurt. It wasn't hard. He now recognized the way that the collar was damping down his body's natural energy, making him slow to heal and even interfering with his ability to think clearly.

The human-derived Galateans, who had developed the collars, didn't have that problem. But Lyr, a creature made partly of the raw energy of stars, had always felt like the collar did more than just suppress his ability to shift. It crushed his dragon half, turning him to a shadow of what he normally was.

How had he lived like this for so many years? Panic rose into his throat, threatening to choke him. He fought to keep his expression flat. He would get the collar off. If they'd put it on him, they must have at least one controller in this campsite; all he had to do was get his hands on it. If not, Tamir had one.

Anyway, even collared, he was far from helpless. Lyr flexed his hands, and felt, as he did so, that he wasn't tied with rope but with some kind of wire. If he struggled too hard, he might cut his own hands off. But even so, he had weapons—the blades in his arms, the spines, his natural size and strength.

"Oh, you're not getting those off anytime soon," declared the pirate standing over him, a cruel edge to his voice.

Lyr looked up at him with a resigned sigh. It was the centaurian Hnee. *I wish I'd cut his throat while I had the chance.* "You again. You're like that story about the cursed coin, always turning up in every—oof!"

A vicious, powerful fist drove into his stomach, followed by a backhand blow to the face. "You can call me Zef," the centaur said. "Or *sir*, if you're so inclined." He bent the knees of his horse half so he could look Lyr in the face, while Lyr gasped for breath. "You'll pay for destroying our ship. But first you'll help us recover our cargo, before we sell *you*, of course."

"You have not yet ..." Lyr panted. "... given me any reason ... to help you."

"Oh, it's a reason you need, is it?" Zef straightened and stepped back with a quick skipping motion of his incongruously graceful horse half. "Let's see if this is motivation enough." He took a small device from a pouch at his belt.

Despite his attempt to control his reaction, Lyr flinched violently at the sight of it, as if he was already feeling the pain it could inflict.

Zef grinned, showing crooked teeth, some gold-capped

and others broken. "Oh yes, you know what this is, don't you? I've always liked using these." And he touched a thick, dirty finger to the collar controller.

Pain exploded in Lyr's spine, in his skull, behind his eyes. He couldn't think, couldn't breathe. The entire world was pain. He wasn't even aware of crashing to the ground until the pain stopped and he realized his face was pressed into the leaf-mold of the forest floor. There was dirt in his mouth and a taste of blood where he'd bitten his tongue.

Cruel laughter came from the other pirates. "Is that enough of a reason for you?" Zef asked from somewhere above him.

Lyr flexed his hands cautiously as feeling returned to his tingling limbs. He felt blood trickling down his wrists where convulsions had torn his skin against the wire, but nothing seemed to be too badly damaged.

I am going to kill you, he thought with enforced calm. *I am going to kill you, and then I am going to find whoever designed this horrible thing, and kill them too.*

But first, he had to get through the next few hours. The collar could kill, at a high enough setting. He didn't think the pirates would kill him on purpose—the price they could get for a collared dragon had to be worth their entire cargo of ordinary slaves. But killing him by accident, because they enjoyed torturing him ... he could entirely believe them capable of it.

It startled him to find out just how much he wanted to live. He *had* to live; he had to get back to Meri.

"Get him up," Zef said, but Lyr struggled to get up on his own before they could put their hands on him again, and managed to stand on legs still quivering from the aftereffects of the collar.

Their camp was small and crude, offering no shelter

and no comforts except a small campfire which one of them was even now putting out; apparently they planned to move on. He wasn't exactly sure where he was. All he could do was hope they weren't too close to the site of the camp where he'd left Meri and Tamir.

Zef idly examined the collar controller, and Lyr's stomach turned over. "So," Zef said in a casual way, "when we last saw you, you'd just gotten away with an entire shipment of *our* slaves. Where are they now?"

"Killed on landing," Lyr said. "I'm the only survivor."

Zef tapped the button lightly. This time Lyr was braced for it, but it was also shorter duration, a single sharp burst of pain.

"What purpose would I have in lying?" Lyr demanded. "I'm alone on this world."

"I don't know why you're helping them, but I *know* you're lying. We've smelled smoke since we've been here. We're not the only people here."

This time the shock was of longer duration. Lyr went down to his knees.

There was no possibility of helping them find the escaped prisoners' village, no matter what they did to him. Even if he hadn't given the villagers his word, he would rather die than help these honorless bastards. He braced himself for more pain, but instead Zef said to one of the other pirates, "Can he shift while he's wearing this thing?"

"No," Lyr answered for him. "You have to take the collar off." It wasn't the whole truth—it was possible to deactivate the function that stopped him from shifting—but since they didn't seem to know how it worked, he wasn't about to give them that much power over him.

Zef stroked his thumb over the button that controlled the pain function, but didn't touch it. "You sure about that?"

Lyr braced himself for more pain and drew his lips back in a humorless grin, tasting his own blood on his teeth. "If I could shift, don't you think I already would have?"

"Damn," Zef muttered. "I was hoping we could use you for aerial recon."

"Why do you need me? You have a ship, don't you?"

A couple of the other pirates barked laughter. Zef said, "We barely made reentry in one piece. We aren't going anywhere."

"So why are you worried about picking up slaves here? You can't get them off the planet anyway."

Zef grinned. "Distress beacon, my lad. We have our own frequencies. If there's one of ours nearby, they'll be here soon enough."

Wonderful. Lyr remembered Tamir talking about pirates having a fairly well-established network of communication frequencies and hideouts, but he hadn't been paying a whole lot of attention. He really hadn't cared about his officially assigned duty much at all in those days.

Now he wished he'd paid more attention so he'd have a better idea of how big their network was and who was likely to be in the vicinity. Back then, it was just a duty, an assignment. Everything was duty. Nothing mattered.

I'm going to get out of this, he thought as they hauled him roughly to his feet. He didn't offer resistance this time, saving that for later. Let them think he was but the docile slave they wanted; let them think they'd broken him. They would learn soon enough, to their despair, the wrath of an angered dragon.

"You planning to cooperate now?" Zef asked him.

Lyr smiled again, grim and sharp. "As you command."

"Hmm." The pirate leader looked down his broken nose at Lyr. Not stupid, this one. It would've been easier if he was nothing but the hotheaded brute he appeared. "Still sticking to your story that there's no one else but you on this planet?"

"That's all I've seen," Lyr said, and then, taking a slow breath, "But I was separated from the others in our crash landing. It's possible some of them might have lived."

Let's see how you like wandering around on a stray asteroid chase, asshole.

"Now we're getting somewhere, eh?" Zef fingered his controller pointedly. "See how much easier it is when you play our game?"

And playing you is exactly what I'm doing. "I've already searched the other side of these mountains and found no one," Lyr said. He tried to orient himself along the slope of the hillside. The last thing he wanted to do was inadvertently lead them to Meri and Tamir. As he spoke, he tried reaching out very gently, very cautiously with his mind—he didn't want them to sense it—and mentally massage their credulity, make himself sound more plausible. "I was going to search along the shore. I thought I might've seen smoke when I was up there, before one of *you* shot me down."

"Think he's lying, boss?" a leopard-spotted Galatean pirate asked.

"Oh, probably," Zef said, stroking the controller lightly as he looked down at Lyr. Lyr prepared himself for an explosion of pain, but none came. "If he wants us to go down, we'll go up. Let's move."

They marched Lyr out of the clearing, keeping hold of him by a rope tied to his wire-bound hands. Up, Lyr thought, which would slow them down and offer him more opportunities, on the high slopes, to spring an ambush on his captors.

Once, long ago, his Galatean masters had wanted to use

him as an assassin, a mind-killer. He had learned the hard way that he couldn't do it without hurting himself and potentially killing himself. But if it came down to that, it might be possible to take one or two of them with him.

I've got my eye on you in particular, he mused grimly, glancing at Zef.

On a more subtle level, he thought he might be able to use his telepathy to confuse their minds somewhat, keep them wandering in circles, as long as he could.

At the very least it would help keep them away from Meri.

He didn't want Meri and Tamir to know how much trouble he was in—the last thing he wanted was those two mounting a rescue—but he needed to warn them. Cautiously, hesitantly, he reached out.

To his surprise, he found Meri almost immediately. She was reaching out for him too, and it felt like she'd been doing it for a while.

Lyr. Lyr. Lyr!

Clumsy at mental speech, unaccustomed to it, but trying her hardest.

Meri?

Her wordless delight and relief flooded over him. He had to struggle to keep it off his face. His carefully schooled calm, practiced over the years, seemed to have fallen apart.

It helped that he tripped over a root just then, distracted by Meri in his head.

Lyr! Are you hurt?

No! It was basically true ... and it had also dawned on him that she was much closer than she ought to be, even if he was lower on the mountain and closer to the camp than he thought he was. He could also tell, from the general sense of her surroundings bleeding through the connection, that she was outside the camp on the hillside somewhere. The conclusion was inescapable: they were looking for him. At least he hoped Tamir was with her. **You have to stay away. I'm not alone. The pirates are here.**

I know! We're going to rescue you.

NINETEEN

"LY'RS ALIVE! And I think he's close!"

Tamir looked up at her delighted exclamation and touched a finger to his lips. Meri nodded and hushed.

They had been climbing for a while now, making their way up the mountain following animal trails through thick, colorful brush. They'd stopped to rest in a small clearing with a staggering view down the mountainside, making her realize how high they'd already climbed, and were sharing a ration pack when Meri's attempts to contact Lyr finally paid off.

"How close?" Tamir asked quietly.

Lyr, where are you?

She got nothing back but stubborn stonewalling.

Lyr! Knock it off! She tried to wedge her mental fingertips into the cracks in his walls. **Lyr, I know you want me safe, but if the pirates are here, none of us are safe. Where* are *you?**

A reluctant answer came in the form of a mental picture. She couldn't see Lyr himself, just the woods around him as she looked out through his eyes. All the forest looked pretty much the same to her, so that was no help. She could tell that he was climbing and probably had his hands tied.

What truly alarmed her was the sight of the pirates around him. There was that centaur jerk *again*, and about a half-dozen rough-looking individuals, mostly Galatean, though there was also a shorter man with green skin and a hooked blade in each hand. No—the blades were part of him, like Lyr's arm blades, but thornier-looking, like the edges of a crab's claws. This guy looked almost insectile, with strangely large eyes and short, spiky hair.

Lyr, can you show this to Tamir too?

There was reluctance, but then she could feel him acquiesce. What happened next was a slightly unnerving experience. She could still feel Lyr, but now she could sense Tamir as well; it was as if Lyr was connecting them in a psychic party line. She saw the surprise on Tamir's face and felt it in his mind as well.

It's been a long time since we did this. She had never heard Tamir's mental voice before, but recognized it immediately, a warm strong voice with a tiger's growl underneath. It seemed somehow deeper than Lyr's, despite the fact that neither of them was speaking out loud. **Lyr used to connect us like this when we were training his sept,** Tamir added for her benefit.

Can we focus? Lyr inquired grumpily. **Show me where you two are, because I'm getting the sense you're not in camp.**

Meri concentrated on showing him their surroundings and was aware of Tamir doing the same. **We're going to rescue you,** she told him.

No! Stay away.

Why? Meri asked.

Before Lyr could answer, she felt a rush of anger from Tamir. *You're collared again, aren't you?*

Lyr's response was a nonverbal surge of tangled emotions, mostly shame and anger and resentment. Meri felt Tamir trying to soothe him, sending out a blanket of calm that also helped damp down her own urge to spring to her feet and dash off into the woods to get him free right then and there.

Lyr. Easy. I can get it off you, like I did before.

*They can't use it to force you to do evil things, can they? * Meri asked. *Can they make you attack us?*

Not directly. But listen, there's more. They have reinforcements coming. They've sent out a distress call and they seem to think there are more pirates on the way.

Tamir cursed quietly under his breath.

Which is why you two need to do something more important than coming after me, Lyr went on. *I found the rest of the escaped slaves, your green friend and the others. They're on the other side of the mountains. You need to get over there ahead of us and warn them. I'll do everything I can to slow this bunch down.*

A mental map of the village's location followed, but Meri wasn't paying attention. She leaped to her feet, gripping her club. *We're not leaving you!*

Tamir struggled to his feet with a wince and put a hand on her arm. *Meri, hold on. Lyr, listen. It's not an either-or situation, either you or them ... understand? It's going to take us days to get across these mountains on foot. It makes more sense for us to rescue you first and then you can fly over and warn them.*

You're rationalizing this.

I'm making a sensible decision as your commanding officer. You're a valuable asset and we need you. And, Tamir added, with warm affection underlying his mental voice, **you need to stop trying to throw yourself on every bomb that comes along. Think about Meri and what leaving you behind would do to her.**

Listen to him, Lyr! We're going to get you out.

Stubborn silence followed. She sensed that Lyr was done with the conversation for now.

"We're not going to leave him, are we?" she demanded of Tamir, who was getting his gear together.

"Of course not, but there's no reason we can't do both," Tamir pointed out. "If they're climbing, and Lyr wants us on the other side of the mountains as well, then our paths lie in the same direction. We'll try to get ahead of them and set up an ambush."

"You can get that awful collar off him, right?"

Tamir nodded. "I just have to get close enough. But in case I can't, let me show you how to use this." He took a small, square object out of his belt pouch and pressed it into her hand. It was made of rugged gray plastic, or something plastic-like. There were two buttons (one blue, one red), what looked like a weird-shaped power prong, and a colorful strip that changed from blue on one end to red on the other.

Meri's skin crawled, looking at it. This was what had been in the hand of the pirate who had made the blue-skinned captive writhe at his feet, back on the ship.

"You first need to sync it to Lyr's collar," Tamir explained. "It won't affect it until you do that. This—" He touched the power prong. "—needs to make physical contact with the collar. There's a small dimple at the back; you just need to tap it. This controller was synced to Lyr's old collar but it won't be on the same wavelength as his new one. Then—"

"I don't need to know all this," Meri protested. She pushed it at him. "I don't *want* to know all this. You can—"

"I can't be the only person who can take it off him. You need to know. Anyway," Tamir said, "you can use it to take the collars off the others when we find them, too. Don't you want to know how to do that?"

Meri nodded. She swallowed her revulsion along with her desire to throw the thing to the ground and crush it. "What do the buttons do?"

"This one turns it off." Tamir touched the blue button lightly. "But you have to turn the correction level all the way down first. That's this." He stroked his thumb across the red-to-blue strip, from the red end to the blue end. Blue, Meri thought, must be like green was on Earth. "Otherwise it'll give them a surge of pain when it turns off."

"This is horrible. Your people make these?"

She didn't need telepathy to sense Tamir's discomfort. "Pay attention," he said gruffly. "This is the correction button." He touched the red one. "Once the controller is synced to Lyr's collar, do *not* press this button. It'll hurt him. At high levels, it can kill him." He used his thumb to slide a small, transparent panel across the buttons. "This locks it so they can't be pressed by accident. Got it?"

"This thing is vile." She thrust it back at him. "Yes, I've got it. And once we take the collars off everyone, we are destroying them, and this, and everything to do with them."

"Deal." He gave her a small smile, that she didn't return.

THEIR NEED TO get ahead of Lyr and the pirates turned the next part of the climb into an exhausting ordeal. Meri had thought she'd been pushing herself before, but now she discovered reserves of strength that she hadn't known she had.

Tamir guided their path, finding animal trails through the brush and open spaces between the trees. In spite of her renewed dislike of the Galateans and all the misery they'd caused, Meri couldn't help being impressed by his wilderness orienteering skills. She would have been quickly lost on her own.

But it was a miserable, exhausting trek. She was covered in sweat and harassed by bugs, which had rarely been around at the lower elevations but rose from the underbrush in choking clouds as they climbed higher. The insects didn't seem to bite, just swarmed around their heads and crawled on their skin and made an already tiring and unpleasant hike even harder to endure. Meri could tell she was rubbing blisters, and she was so tired that the muscles of her calves and thighs quivered and twitched whenever they collapsed for a rest. Her only consolation (and it wasn't much of one) was that the climb was wearing Tamir down even more severely. He looked gray under the fur, and when they stopped to rest, he sank down where he stood and had to lie there for a few minutes before gathering the strength to get out one of their makeshift canteens.

"Are you sure we're not going to run right into them?" Meri asked on one of these breaks.

Tamir shook his head. "They're over that way," he said, jerking his thumb in a vague direction into the trees.

"You can tell that?" They'd been in occasional communication with Lyr, but mostly it was just a little mental tickle, letting them know he was still there. She didn't think he'd been talking to Tamir without also talking to her.

Tamir nodded. He was still short of breath enough that

it took him a moment to go ahead and say, "Practice. You can learn to do it."

She tried not to be jealous that Tamir and Lyr had known each other so much longer, as well as resentful that he hadn't told her he could do that. "Can you teach me?"

"I don't know." Tamir propped himself on his elbows. His already scruffy fur was plastered with leaves and dirt, caked on with sweat; he looked like he'd been living in the woods for months rather than hiking through it for half a day. Meri had a feeling she looked just as bad. "I'm not a telepath myself. I can't do a thing without Lyr to facilitate it. I guess I'd say he just *feels* stronger in one direction than another. It's like when you close your eyes, you can tell which direction a sound comes from." He paused for breath, then said, "Actually, closing your eyes might help."

She did that, shutting herself into the darkness behind her eyelids. The afternoon was quiet, the absolute silence of a planet without highways or airplanes or cities. And yet, as she had learned over the last few days, it wasn't really silent at all. Leaves rustled, insects droned, small creatures skittered in the grass. So far they had seen no large wildlife, but from the size and well-beaten state of the animal trails they'd been following, it was pure luck that they hadn't run into anything so far, and they already knew Tamir's cuffs wouldn't be much help against this planet's wildlife ...

Not helping!

"I can't," she said, opening her eyes.

Tamir gave her an encouraging smile. "Well, you can practice the next time he says something to us. Try closing your eyes and focusing on it, and see if you can feel which direction he is." He grunted in pain as he struggled back to his feet. "We better move."

Dusk found them high enough on the mountainside

that the trees were starting to give way to low, shrubby brush and boulders. There was little cover here, and Meri was reluctantly grateful for the darkness; it made her feel less horrendously exposed, although it also covered the approach of anything that might creep up on them in the night.

"Are we going to stop?" she panted as darkness settled around them. Tamir lit their way with a cuff glowing ever so faintly, just enough to make sure the next few feet of the path didn't suddenly vanish into a crevasse (as their paths occasionally had done before).

Tamir shook his head. Teeth gritted, he lurched onward, one dogged step at a time, clinging with a white-knuckled grip to his walking stick. "I want to get to the pass before we stop," he explained finally.

"Pass?" Meri looked ahead. The sky was still faintly luminous above the peaks, allowing her to see how the jagged line of the mountains cleaved sharply downward. It was impossible to tell how far it was; she'd already discovered how deceptive the steep angle of the mountainside could be, making her think they were mere minutes from boulders and other landmarks that could take an hour or more to reach. The darkness made it worse.

"We're ahead of them now," Tamir managed, between short, sucking breaths. "They will almost certainly angle for the pass in the morning. It's the place with the best chance of setting a trap."

She almost said something like, *We're going to attack them?* but managed to close her mouth before the words came out. It helped that she was so out of breath she could barely talk anyway, her feet and legs in agony. She had no idea how Tamir hadn't fallen over by now.

A feather-light touch of worry brushed her mind. **How goes it, my love? Where are you?*

My love. Pleasure rippled through her, despite her exhaustion. **Above you, according to Tamir.*

**They've stopped for the night. I helped them along by subliminally pointing out how tired they were, until it finally sank in.* He sent her an image of a flickering fire with the pirates squatting around it, roasting small lizards on sticks. Stupid space pirates got to sit down and eat, Meri thought resentfully.

**Tamir says he's planning on setting up a trap,* she told Lyr. **I hope he knows what he's doing.*

**He generally does,* Lyr said. **But you should rest. I can tell you're ready to drop. They're going to be fresh in the morning. You don't want to be exhausted.*

She hadn't realized he was talking to both of them until Tamir muttered, "I know what I'm doing, kid."

**My mate's life is in your hands, old man. I'd rather have you protect her than risk some ill-planned venture for rescuing me.*

"I can do both."

**Not going to argue about the poor planning?*

"It's not like there are a lot of options here."

Lyr was giving them something to focus on other than the misery of the climb, Meri realized. She guessed that he used to do this kind of thing for his sept-siblings too. Lyr had been the glue holding them together.

**What* are *you planning, anyway?* Lyr asked.

"We're going to try to beat you to the pass and set up some kind of trap," Tamir said.

**Can you be more specific?*

"I don't know yet. I need to see the lay of the land first." He panted for breath for a minute, then added something mentally that Meri only caught the edges of. It was nonverbal encouragement, a general sense that Lyr just needed to hold on, that they were coming for him.

Lyr didn't answer in words, but Meri continued to be able to sense him as they climbed higher. He sent a steady feeling of encouragement, supporting their stumbling steps, lending them some of his strength. His mental voice was a resonant hum in the back of her mind, a familiar song without words.

Still, by the time Tamir finally stopped and sank to the ground, Meri was so exhausted that she felt like she'd been physically beaten. For the last half hour or so, they'd been picking their way up an incredibly steep slope covered with rocks that threatened to twist underfoot and send her sliding all the way down the mountain. She couldn't tell how Tamir was choosing which way to go; there were no paths, just a steady, endless climb. It was fully dark now, although their way was lit by the faint luminosity of the sky and a moon low on the horizon, at least enough to tell if they were about to step over a precipice. Most of the light, she realized, came from the luminous band of the planet's rings arching overhead, as bright as if the planet had another moon.

When Tamir collapsed, her first thought was that his strength had given out. She managed to struggle the last few steps to him and bent over to put her hand on his shoulder. "Are you okay?"

"We're here," he rasped out, raising his head with an effort.

But where was *here*? To her, this part of the mountain looked the same as any other. "We're in the pass?" she asked.

"We're above it." He waved a hand, the faintly glowing cuff darting like a firefly.

Meri took a few cautious steps in that direction. He was right: in darkness lit only by the dim luminosity of the sky, the ground fell away suddenly and sharply in front of her. She couldn't tell how far down it went; all she had was an impression of depth and space. In her current exhausted state, unable to see her footing clearly, she didn't dare go closer. She tottered back to Tamir and sank down next to him.

"Drink some water," Tamir said hoarsely. "We're both probably dehydrated."

Meri took a few swallows. "I don't have much left."

"We need to look for a spring." He sighed and let his head flop back down. "Soon."

Meri eased the strap of her purse off her aching shoulder. She had been switching it back and forth between sides, with the strap across her chest to help spread the weight, but all she'd managed to do was bruise her shoulder on both sides instead of just one. She fingered the welts with a hiss of pain and then opened the purse. "Do you need painkillers? I have some with me."

It took him a moment to answer; then he struggled weakly to an awkward, half-reclined sitting position. "Let me see what you have."

Meri dug in her purse, initially searching for the aspirin, but then she found the handful of injectors she'd brought with her from the infirmary on the pirate ship; it seemed like a million years ago now. Tamir picked out two, a painkiller and one of the ones that Lyr had identified for her as—

"That one's a stimulant," she said.

"I know." He pressed the painkiller to his arm and squeezed the trigger. There was no hesitation; he'd clearly done this before. "I suggest you take one as well. Once we've rested a bit, we need to start rigging our little surprise for the pirates."

Meri tried to muster an argument, but he was right. She was exhausted and now that she was sitting down, the ache of her strained muscles was making itself known in a major way. *If I do this, I'll be in a world of hurt tomorrow.* But she *had* to. There was no time, and this might be their only chance to get the jump on the pirates and rescue Lyr. If they didn't, he might die.

Tamir, on the other hand ...

"I have to tell you, as a medical professional, I really don't recommend doing that," she told him as he unwrapped the second injector. "The combination of painkillers and stimulants is dangerous, especially for someone recovering from a major injury. You could rebreak your pelvis or worse. There are a lot of major blood vessels in that area. I don't think Lyr's going to be happy with you if you bleed out on this mountainside."

"Lyr's not here to have a vote," Tamir said as he injected himself.

Meri stared down at the stimulant. They had one more left after this. She blinked, her eyelids growing heavy as her exhausted body tried to drag her down into sleep.

There was no choice, not really. At least, no choice that would save Lyr.

She pushed it against her forearm as Tamir had done, and felt the sting of the needle sliding home.

THEY SPENT the night in small bursts of activity, moving rocks and wedging logs under boulders. Tamir explained he was setting up a sequence of avalanche traps. Meri decided to leave the details to him. Her brain felt like it was stuffed with cotton wool, vibrating unpleasantly as the stimulant poured artificial energy into limbs that still trembled with exhaustion. She'd worked long hours as a nurse, including shifts that went on for upwards of 24 hours, but she couldn't ever remember experiencing this particularly unpleasant combination of physical exhaustion and inability to give in to it.

Lyr's mind prodded her gently awake in a gray dawn, after she and Tamir finished their preparations and collapsed to catch an hour or two of exhausted sleep. Even the stimulant couldn't keep her from sleeping at this point, and Lyr had to coax her gently and carefully back to wakefulness.

They're breaking camp to move out, he said into her mind. **Are you all right?**

**I'll be fine. Are* you?*

As well as I can be. Listen, if fighting starts, just stay out of the way, okay? You don't have any weapons that can get through their shields, or any shields of your own.

Trust me, I'm not planning to wade into a fight against people with high-tech alien weapons.

Lyr's response was a dry mental image of Meri back on Earth, attacking pirates with pepper spray.

Hey! I didn't have a choice, buddy!

You were fierce and beautiful. I had never seen anything so magnificent.

Her cheeks grew hot. **Well, you should see me now. I'm the exact opposite of magnificent, unless you find filthy women with sore muscles and sticks in their hair sexy.**

I would find you sexy with any number of sticks in your hair.

The thing about telepathy was that she could feel his

sincerity, turning what would otherwise be a hopelessly cheesy statement into a heartfelt compliment.

You too. We're going to get you out of there.

Lyr didn't answer, and a moment later Tamir groaned and rolled over, so she wasn't the only one being prodded by their very own dragon alarm clock.

It was time to get moving.

Meri tried to sit up and sank back down with a faint moan. Everything hurt: arms, legs, back, feet. She didn't know she *had* muscles in some of these places. Even her fingers hurt, bruised and scraped and hot to the touch from yesterday's work.

Somehow she got herself on her feet. She'd fallen asleep with all her clothes on, shoes included, so at least she didn't have to try to pull shoes onto her aching, swollen feet.

After all this is over, I deserve a week at a spa. Or, if one isn't handy, a nice long soak in the ocean.

Her mouth was dry and crusty. She drained the last of one of their makeshift canteens down her dry throat and limped behind a boulder to relieve herself. Crouching down to do her business was a new circle of hell for her abused legs and calves. She had to hold onto the boulder to keep from falling over.

Did I say a week at a spa? How about a month. With daily massages and skin treatments.

She emerged to find Tamir poking around in her purse. "Sorry," he said, jerking his hand back guiltily. "I was seeing if you had any injectors left."

"One painkiller, one stimulant." She knelt stiffly to get them out of the pocket she'd zipped them into. "You're going to take them, aren't you?"

"No choice. I need to be able to fight."

"Well, you're an adult. I can give you medical advice, but I can't tell you what to do."

Meri watched him inject himself. She thought about asking if she could have some of the stimulant, but remembered the fuzzy-headed, jittery feeling from last night and decided she'd rather not.

Instead she took a few aspirin and opened one of their last ration packs. Tamir tried to wave it off, but Meri shoved it into his hands. "I don't care if you're not hungry with that drug cocktail you're on. You have to eat something."

She opened another for herself and limped on sore, blistered feet over to the edge of what turned out to be, by daylight, quite an impressive cliff. They were high up on the side of a steep-sided, saddle-shaped pass. She wondered if Tamir expected the two of them to somehow climb down there, picking their way down the loose rock slides, past terrifying cliffs and patches of gravel that looked like it would start sliding at the slightest touch.

She could see why he'd picked this place for an ambush. She just wasn't sure how they were actually going to help Lyr from up here. At most, they could give him a distraction to get himself free. Maybe it would be enough.

The view was certainly beautiful. She could see both sides of the mountains from here, the sea stretching off endlessly in one direction, and when she turned the other way, a hazy patchwork landscape of forest, swamp, and lake on a high plateau.

Despite the warmth of the newly risen sun on her face, the mountain's cap of snow was very close here. She could have easily climbed to the nearest patches of snow if she'd had the time. Snow-fed waterfalls threaded between the rocks, reminding her achingly of her thirst. Some of them were pretty close. She and Tamir could refill their canteens here, maybe boil the water over a campfire to make sure it was safe—

Sudden movement in the pass, along with a clatter of rocks, caught her attention. At first she thought the pirates and Lyr were already here. But this was higher on the hillside. Something had set the loose gravel on the far side of the pass to sliding. She followed it back up with her eyes, to a dark cleft among the rocks where something was moving.

Crawling.

Spreading wings ...

Meri crouched down among the boulders and watched in shocked amazement as something straight out of her old dinosaur books—pterodactyl? pteranodon?—spread leathery wings and shook out its dull, scaly body. It wasn't graceful and beautiful like Lyr, but it was impressive in its own right, especially when it launched itself into the thin air over the pass. It dropped like a rock until the wind caught its wings, and then it rose in a slow, gliding circle.

"Tamir!" she whispered urgently over her shoulder. "Tamir! Come here!"

He joined her a moment later, leaning heavily on his stick. "Is something wrong?"

"Look," she said, pointing.

By now two more of the flying dinos had joined the first one, all of them gliding slowly upward on thermals. They weren't exactly pteranodons, but certainly made her think of them, with their heavy, oversized heads and wide membranous wings.

"Watch out," Tamir murmured. He placed a hand on her shoulder, and there was the by-now-familiar tingling sensation as his shield covered them both. One of the pteranodons swooped overhead so low that Meri could hear its wings creaking and see the glitter of its small reptilian eye turned down to look at them.

Tamir lifted his hand and the tingling stopped as the pteranodon banked and vanished behind the peak.

"What do we do?" Meri asked.

"Hope that they're more dangerous to the pirates than to us, I guess." He beckoned her. "I found a spring. Come here."

The spring was little more than a thin trickle of water behind a boulder, but it was deep enough to dip her hands in. Meri washed some of the dust off her face, while Tamir began filling their canteens from a little waterfall upstream.

"Is it safe?" she began, and then, "Wait, you can test that with your cuffs."

"Correct. This high in the mountains and fed with snowmelt, it's not contaminated."

It still felt like a leap of faith, but she slaked her thirst from the refilled pouch of water and then from cupped hands. The water was cold and good.

Heads up, Lyr said suddenly into her mind. **We're just below the pass.**

Tamir gave Meri a tight smile and set the canteen aside. "You know what you need to do?"

"I'm ready."

"Good." He reached out and touched the skin on the inside of her wrist. "You can't wear cuffs at all, can you?"

"No. I don't have the—" What had Lyr called them? "The right mods."

"Damn. I'd give you one of mine for protection if I could."

"I'll be safe enough up here. You and Lyr will protect me."

"Just stay out of the way if you can." He took the collar

controller from his pocket and touched it to his right cuff, where it adhered in some way Meri couldn't figure out. "Let's go."

Unselfconsciously he shucked off his ragged pants. Meri jerked her eyes away, and when she looked back he was a tiger, scruffy and lean, naked but for the gold slashes of the cuffs on his front ankles.

Meri followed him to the edge of the cliff. Looking downhill, she could see a small group of figures toiling up the mountainside. Even from here, she recognized the electric blue of Lyr's hair, and her heart leaped.

Tamir had already vanished among the boulders, his tawny fur fading into the rocks; she couldn't even tell where he'd gone. Her throat felt dry again, this time with tension. Swallowing, she crouched in position and set her hands on the length of deadwood that Tamir had used to set up their first avalanche trap.

She couldn't help being amazed at how far she'd come from where she had started out. That lost, grieving woman in the car with Cora, driving to Kansas City to start a new life she didn't even care about, seemed so far away now that Meri could barely relate to her. Now she was about to fight a bunch of space pirates for the sake of the man she loved. Her hands trembled with nerves, but she felt strangely unafraid, adrenaline keying her body to a state of intense readiness verging on eagerness.

Cora, if you could only see me now.

TWENTY

THE PASS HAD SEEMED much gentler when Lyr had flown through it yesterday, blissfully oblivious to the steep terrain beneath his wings. On foot, he was all too aware of how steep and rough the approach was. And Tamir and Meri had done this yesterday, in the dark? Their tenacity amazed him. He already knew Galateans were tough, but he was never underestimating Earth humans again.

He'd been working hard to slow the pirates. All through yesterday afternoon he'd done his best to lead them in circles, not only guiding them astray but reaching out with small telepathic nudges to make them think they were choosing the right path when actually they were heading away from the pass instead. It was difficult to lead them in the wrong direction now that the pass loomed just above them, a target even the stupidest pirate couldn't hope to miss. Still, he did his best, sending out tendrils of sleepiness. He couldn't cloud their minds, not really, but he could make them lethargic and inattentive to their surroundings, the same way he had once eased his frightened and anxious sept-sibs into sleep.

When all else failed, he twisted his feet to kick loose rocks that the cursing men behind him had to dodge.

Through it all, he had been keeping his eyes open for a chance to escape. The wire around his wrists and the rope trailing to a guard's hand were only temporary setbacks; the collar was the true limiting factor. If he could only get the controller ...! But he would have to overpower Zef, and the centaur kept the controller safely anchored to his left-hand cuff, within easy reach at all times. Easy to use. Easy to defend.

He rehearsed his own actions over and over in his head. When Tamir and Meri sprang their ambush, he needed to get the controller from Zef. As long as the pirates could reduce him to helpless incoherence at the touch of a button, he couldn't effectively fight. All he needed was a few seconds with the controller, just long enough to deactivate his collar.

After *that* ... oh yes. After that, they would regret the day they decided to capture a dragon.

A sharp spasm of pain erupted from the collar and raced down his spine. Lyr jerked, but managed not to fall. He'd already fallen a number of times on this climb. Without his hands to catch him, he had acquired some new scrapes and bruises to go with the other half-healed ones.

"Just a little reminder," Zef said, hooves clattering alongside him. The centaur was limping; he'd picked up a stone in his hoof yesterday. Another of the small collection of advantages Lyr had mentally catalogued was that the terrain up here was much better suited to running bipeds with hands to help them climb, as opposed to a horse-bodied creature. Zef could easily have run him down on flat ground, but Lyr could just as easily outclimb him.

Not that any of it would matter if he couldn't get the

controller. And if he could get the collar off, climbing wouldn't matter anymore; he'd have wings.

"A reminder of what? That you're an asshole? Already figured it out, thanks."

He was braced for the surge of pain this time, but it still drove him to his knees. He spat out a mouthful of blood, having bitten the inside of his cheek, and got up wordlessly.

If only I could shift!

His dragon still felt muted and strange, as if layers of cotton batting kept it apart from him. Reaching out telepathically to Meri and Tamir took a concerted effort of will, especially since he was already tired from the little mental tickles he'd been sending at the pirates.

How did I manage to live so long like this?

He could tell he was getting closer to Meri. Her nearness lifted his heart, but also worried him.

We're ready, Meri thought at him.

They were entering the pass now, the high rocky walls closing around them. **Where are you?** he asked.

Look up.

He did, unable to help himself, and glimpsed a flash of movement high above—an arm, waving briefly.

Stay out of sight, love!

Sorry. You're right. Meri's arm vanished.

Lyr glanced at Zef and the others. It didn't look like they'd seen her, but all of them were alert and wary despite Lyr's best efforts to keep them complacent. Even if they didn't suspect a trap, the pass had an ominous feeling after the open mountainside. Those looming rock faces felt like the walls of a prison cell closing in.

Tamir? Lyr reached for his friend's mind. **Are you here?**

I am. Closer even than Meri. He couldn't pinpoint

Tamir's location exactly—he was out of practice, and it wasn't a precision art when talking to non-telepaths anyway—but he could tell that Tamir was somewhere among the boulders in the pass, probably tiger-shifted.

Lyr glanced around at the pirates. All of them besides Zef and the insectile Mantid were Galateans, but not all Galateans could shift; in fact, most couldn't. The trait had been lost for the most part among families that hadn't specifically arranged their marriages to keep it—the royal family, for one, and some of the old warrior clans like Tamir's. Otherwise, it still came up as a rare trait in some families, but not often. He had no way of knowing if any of them could do it until they did it.

One of the pirates pointed at the sky with an exclamation. A few of the flying beasts Lyr had noticed on his flight were visible against the clear blue bowl of the sky, wheeling lazily like great birds. Dangerous? he wondered. He hadn't been concerned as a dragon; now he began to wonder if they would attack human-sized prey. He doubted they'd go after a group of this size. Still, it wouldn't hurt to warn Meri and Tamir, especially if those creatures were as impervious to energy weapons as the pack of hunters he'd fought by the spring.

We saw them, Meri said in response to his mental tap.

He became aware, then, that Tamir was trying to get his attention telepathically. **I hear you,** Lyr said, strengthening the connection and opening it to Meri as well.

You're in position for our trap. Ready?

I am ready. Go.

Tell Meri do it now, Tamir said.

Meri heard that, Meri said. **I'm on it.**

Lyr couldn't tell what she did—he got a brief impression of exertion and the straining of sore muscles—but a moment later, he heard rumbling and the pirates around him burst out in cries of alarm.

It was difficult at first to tell where the rumbling was coming from, though he could feel it through the soles of his feet. Then he glimpsed movement on the mountainside. It looked like part of the cliff face was crawling, accelerating and gathering speed as the avalanche spread.

*That's a hell of a trap, Tamir.*

*Custom avalanches aren't a precision art, you know!*

Panic spread among the pirates as tiny pebbles began clattering around them. The bulk of the avalanche was behind them, with no time to go back, so they bolted forward as the slide gained momentum—only to have a second avalanche begin its slide in front of them, trapping them between the two.

As the pass filled with rubble and a choking cloud of dust rolled across them, a plasma bolt speared through the group, taking advantage of their moment of distraction. One of the Galatean pirates dropped without a sound.

Lyr immediately flung out all the mental confusion he could manage. The mental images he sent were unlikely to be mistaken for anything real under normal circumstances, but in the haze of dust he gave the panicking pirates images of attackers, an entire army of guerrilla ambushers. The pirates whirled around, shooting blindly, even shooting each other in the fray, ignoring Zef bellowing at them to stop. This would never have worked on a disciplined company of Galatean soldiers, but the pirates were little more than a rabble at the best of times.

*Take out the Hnee centaur; he's their leader!* he sent to Tamir. _*And he's got their only collar controller.*_

*I can't get a clear shot at him,* Tamir said, his mental voice tight.

As shields started going up all around him, Lyr threw all his strength into breaking the wire around his wrists. It bit deep into his flesh—he was going to have scars from that—but it was no match for draconic strength. The wire snapped and he spun around and flung himself at Zef's horse legs. Zef was already shielded, so it wasn't like Lyr could break his legs or do any serious damage, but he collided with the centaur's front legs and they both went down in a tangle.

His fingers slid on Zef's shield, glistening with a soap-bubble sheen and covering Zef's wrists and cuffs like a second skin. He couldn't reach the controller with the shield in the way, or get the cuffs either. All he could do was desperately try to stop Zef from being able to have a moment of leisure to use it.

As Lyr and Zef thrashed together in the gravel and the dirt, there was chaos all around them—shouting men drawing knives or raising their wrists to shoot at nothing. Tamir came out of nowhere, a lean tiger bursting out of the dust cloud to bear one of the men silently to the ground. Lyr couldn't see what happened next; he had his hands full with Zef. He managed to get first one of Zef's arms and then the other pinned against the ground, while Zef thrashed and kicked, but Lyr was at a severe disadvantage grappling with an opponent who had more body mass as well as four legs to Lyr's two. A flailing hoof caught Lyr in the side, knocking the breath out of him.

The controller was manually operated, but the cuffs were mind-controlled, and a sharp bolt of tingling pain shot up both Lyr's arms as Zef belatedly realized he could get Lyr off him by shocking him. Lyr flung himself away before he could be stunned into insensibility.

Zef got to his feet, his dusty horse flanks heaving. Lyr

started to lunge again, but agony caught him mid-stride and sent him crashing to the ground. Instinctively he tore with his hands at the collar, but all he did was cause himself more pain. He tasted blood; he'd bitten his tongue again.

It's only pain, he thought, gathering the shreds of his self-control. *It's not actually damaging you. You can push through this.*

Slowly, with great effort, he got to his knees. Panting, he stared through the sweaty hair hanging in his eyes, his body rigid with the effort of fighting against the agony burning him up from the inside.

"What the hell? You can't do this!" Zef fumbled with the controller, cranking it to a higher setting.

Lyr gritted his teeth until his jaw popped. Fists clenched so the nails bit into his palms, he struggled to his feet.

And then suddenly he was aware of Meri in his mind, supporting him, lending him her strength. **Fight it, Lyr! You can do it!**

He didn't want her to feel this pain too. For an instant, as he tried to block her out, he lost his ability to fight back against the agony of the collar. Dimly he was aware of his knees hitting the rocks with a bruising impact, then his hands.

But Meri pursued him mentally. **We're in this together. You can do it. Fight him!**

He pushed himself up to his knees again, and then to his feet. As Zef stared at him in shock, Lyr lurched toward him, one step at a time. Meri braced him, holding onto him in his mind.

"You can't do this," Zef said in disbelief. Fear broke across his face, and Lyr took a vicious satisfaction from it.

The slave master, the one with the controller and all the weapons, was afraid of him.

*Lyr!* Tamir's mental voice came to him. _*I can't get to you in time; there are too many of them in the way.*_

*Throw it to me,* Lyr managed to send back.

*Are you sure? If we lose it—*

*Do it! Now!*

Tamir came into view as he leaped to the top of a boulder behind Zef, as a tiger, and shifted to a naked man in mid-stride, streaked with blood and dirt. He plucked the controller from one of his cuffs, where it had been nano-glued on, and hurled it toward Lyr.

It almost worked.

The controller arced through the air, glinting in the sun. Lyr threw every bit of concentration he could spare into not letting Zef know it was there. _Don't look up. Don't look up. Don't look up._

Tamir's aim was good. The controller tumbled toward Lyr and he raised his hand to intercept it, his rigid muscles fighting against the spasms of pain wracking his body.

Slow. Too slow.

He reached, he almost had it—and the controller bounced off his fingertips and went tumbling on a different trajectory.

Zef's eyes widened in surprise, and the centaur flung out his arm. A plasma bolt stabbed from his cuff and melted the controller to slag in an instant. It dropped out of the air and landed in the sand, blackened and useless.

Damn it! Damn it!

Now the only controller they had—his only chance of getting the collar off—was Zef's.

With an effort, Lyr extended his fighting spines and the

blades in his forearms. He might lack cuffs and shields, but he had weapons of his own.

"You're more trouble than you're worth, you know that?" Zef growled. "I don't care how much cash you'd bring in."

With his other hand still holding down on the pain button, he brought his wrist to bear on Lyr.

He was going to shoot.

Lyr's muscles were locked rigid with the effort of fighting the collar. He needed to dodge, but he couldn't move. Without shields, a single shot from the cuffs would kill him.

A shadow flickered over him. The flying dinosaurs were still up there, and it gave him an idea—the only thing he could think of to do.

He'd never tried to manipulate an animal's mind before. These were simple minds full of simple needs, hunger and the urge to defend their territory and the thrill of the hunt. With a silent apology for what he was about to do, Lyr pushed on those minds hard. *Danger down below. Danger to the nest.*

Sweat ran into his eyes. Everything seemed to slow down; his awareness narrowed to his mental focus and the gleam of Zef's cuff pointed at him.

And then great wings broke through the dust cloud as the flock of flying beasts dived on them from above.

THE RELEASE of Lyr's pain was like the snap of a tether, sending Meri sprawling to the ground at the top of the cliff as her knees gave out. After taking a minute to collect herself, she sat up. Her head throbbed as if from a sinus headache, and she felt shaky and weak. And this was just from the secondhand pain.

Those collars were *evil.*

Lyr? Are you okay?

Busy, came the distracted answer.

The battle between the pirates, Lyr, and Tamir had now turned into an all-out brawl with the dinosaurs. Reptilian shrieks of pain and hoarse yells echoed up the cliff to her. She couldn't tell what was going on down there; it was all fast-paced confusion and dust. Lyr and Tamir had both told her to stay out of the fray, up here where it was safe. But ...

But she'd already triggered the avalanche traps. There was nothing more she could do up here. Down there, she might be able to help.

Meri took a bracing breath, and gripping her club firmly in one hand, she began scouting for a place to climb down.

She was no Tamir, to spring from boulder to boulder on feline paws. But the rockslide, if nothing else, provided a way down. It was still steep and difficult, and she ended up in something that was more like a controlled fall than a climb, her feet slithering in loose rocks. If she stopped moving for even an instant, she was going to fall on her face.

But that was her entire life on this planet so far, wasn't it? Just keep moving, don't take time to think, just take one step and then another and another—

Her wild ride down the rockslide eventually dumped her off in a patch of boulders near the bottom. If things had been confusing from up top, it was a thousand times worse down here. The fighting had stirred up a new cloud of rock dust, from which green flashes of light and occasional combatants appeared, locked in battle. She saw Tamir slashing and snarling at another big cat, some kind of leopard, with a tool belt around its waist and gold cuffs on its ankles. A dino burst out of the dust cloud, beating its heavy leather wings as it tried to gain altitude with a pirate clutched in its claws. He wasn't hurt; the soap-bubble gleam of his shield protected him, but also blunted the edge of the knife he was using to batter at the beast's legs. In all this chaos, she couldn't even see Lyr.

Lyr, where are you?

What are you doing here? Stay away!

Lyr, I'm here to help! I can get the collar controller and get that thing off you! Where's Tamir?

He doesn't have it anymore. It was destroyed.

Which only left—damn it. The centaur was fighting one of the dinos. Screeching and flapping, it battered him with his wings as his attempts to shoot it splintered off its scales.

It's always that stupid centaur guy. I hate that guy.

She wished she still had her pepper spray.

Meri, stay away from him! He'll kill you!

But I have to help you!

Meri! A new mental voice—Tamir's—intruded on their link. **If I throw you something, can you get it to Lyr?**

Yes! she said, though in truth she was far from confident. Catching and throwing things had never been her strong suit. She dropped her club and got ready. **Go!**

Tamir scrambled backward, putting some distance between himself and his opponent. Shifting back to human, he unclasped one of the gold cuffs around his wrist, leaped and threw it at her.

His aim was excellent. She held up her cupped hands and it dropped right into them. It was warm to the touch; she'd never handled one of these things before. **Lyr!** she called. **Catch!**

She hurled it with everything in her. It was probably the

very definition of throwing like a girl, a clumsy and untrained throw, but at least she got some distance to it.

It was still going to fall short. Lyr dived for it, hitting the ground with a painful-looking impact, and his hand closed over the cuff's golden gleam.

Yes! Meri fist-pumped and picked up her club again, looking for somewhere she could be useful.

LYR SLID the cuff over his wrist and snapped it into place. Summoning a shield, he felt it spread tingling across his body, and with it, a renewed feeling of strength and power.

All right, bastards. I'm not as vulnerable as you think I am.

The most important thing was to get the collar controller. Until he did that, Zef could still reduce him to a helpless, pain-wracked heap at the touch of a button.

Lyr took a moment to focus his mind like an arrow and aimed it at Zef. He really didn't *want* to do this. In the early days of his captivity, when the Galateans were trying to train him to use his mental powers as an assassin, he'd learned that any damage he tried to visit on his targets rebounded onto him. But at least *he* would be expecting it. Zef wouldn't.

Holding onto that, he punched Zef's mind as hard as he could.

Rebounding pain made him stagger, but it also drove the centaur to his knees. Lyr leaped forward. The dino Zef had been fighting took advantage of his distraction to beat its wings and clear the battlefield, and Lyr sprang onto Zef. He grabbed the wrist of the hand holding the collar controller, and focused all the energy in Tamir's cuff into hitting Zef's shield with everything he had and breaking just that part of it open.

For an instant, he almost had it, but then Zef shook off the lingering confusion from the mental stun, and squeezed the controller viciously.

No—damn it—

Lyr crashed heavily to the ground. This time Zef wasn't messing around; he'd cranked the pain setting on the controller to its maximum extent, the lethal setting, and Lyr's back arched as white-hot pain blotted out his world.

MERI RAN up from behind and bashed the centaur with her club.

It glanced off his shield, sending a shock through her arm and all the way down her body. The centaur turned to stare at her, as if he genuinely couldn't believe that this tiny, annoying creature had attacked him.

She could no longer feel Lyr's agony, but she couldn't tell if that was because he was no longer being tortured, or because he'd passed out. He lay on the ground at Zef's feet, twitching occasionally.

Zef backhanded her across the face with casual strength. She hit the ground with a bruising impact and lay half-stunned; the club flew from her hand.

A shadow fell across her. She blinked up at the sky and the blurred shape of Zef looming above her. One of his hands hovered over her and, with a weird sense of déjà vu, she saw the green gleam around the cuff. He was going to kill her, and there was nothing she could do, no jump accident to save her now. She couldn't even move. All she could do was stare up at the clear blue sky, knowing her last sight was going to be the cool, distant beauty of the planet's rings arching overhead.

Well, she thought, finding herself oddly clearheaded, *I can definitely say I had an interesting life, at the end anyway.*

At first she thought the sudden flash across the sky was the flash of Zef's cuff, ending her life. But ... she didn't die. She was still breathing, the sky was still an inverted blue bowl overhead, and now Zef was looking up too.

Out of the blinding brilliance of the sky came a shape. Something flying.

Another dinosaur? she thought fuzzily, but no, it was too big, and it didn't have wings. It was another ship, a truly extraordinary ship.

The ships she'd seen so far were sleek and silver and very sci-fi-looking. This one, as its unknown pilot guided it into the mountain pass and its shadow fell over them, looked like someone had taken one of those ships and gone nuts decorating it. Swirls of purple, orange, yellow, and electric blue turned it into a crazyquilt of color, and it was also decked out with lights—rows of colorful running lights along its fuselage and wings and the stubby vanes projecting outward around its engine end.

It looked like a giant Christmas tree ornament.

Apparently she wasn't the only one who had never seen anything like it before, because she heard Zef mutter, "What the hell is that?"

The ship stopped and hovered completely stationary in the air, about fifty feet above them. A door opened in the side.

Meri caught only a glimpse of the creature standing inside before it sprang out of the opening and dropped to land in the midst of the pirates. Meri sat up in time to see it land directly on top of a pirate, smashing him to the ground.

It scrambled to its feet, aimed both hands at the pirate's head, and blasted him with a bolt of green light.

The newcomer was at least seven feet tall and built like a brick wall. The only clothing it wore were a pair of dark pants and boots on an oddly small lower half; its bare, over-muscled torso burst upward from these like the Incredible Hulk, bristling with warts and spikes. The only good thing she could say about the face was that it had the usual human number of eyes, nose, and ears, but the eyes all but vanished beneath an overhanging brow ridge, and its huge lantern jaw had a pair of tusks twisting upward from a half-open mouth. It had no hair, just a bunch of spines like a cactus. Its entire body looked prickly in the same way.

It laid into the remaining pirates around it. Meri boggled for a minute and then, since Zef was distracted, crawled across the rocks to Lyr.

"Lyr!"

She reached for him mentally through the link; there was no response. With shaking hands she checked his vitals. There was a pulse, weak and thready, and he was breathing, but his eyes were closed and she couldn't rouse him. Silver blood glistened at the corner of his mouth and trickled from his nose and ears.

Meri fumbled with the hated collar. Her fingers slid off it. If only she could get her hands on a controller!

"Please be safe," she whispered, kissing Lyr's forehead. "Please wait for me." Then she staggered to her feet.

The huge alien might have waded into the fight for reasons known only to it, but it seemed to be getting the better of the pirates. At least it was distracting them. Meri managed to locate a blood-covered heap of tiger fur and stumbled rubbery-legged across the battlefield to Tamir.

"Tamir!" She thought at first, for a terrible moment, that

he was dead, but his side was rising and falling with quick, panting breaths. She shook his shoulder until he shifted back to a panting, blood-covered naked man.

He lifted his head, swiped sweaty hair out of his face, and stared at the enormous alien as it picked up a pirate and flung him into a pile of boulders. "Who the hell is that?"

"I don't know, and right now I don't care! Can we get the collar controller? Lyr said you lost yours. Please tell me you have another one!"

Tamir shook his head. He tried to get up and then sank back down, his legs trailing limply.

"You rebroke something," Meri guessed.

Tamir grimaced and nodded.

"Stay there, then. You're probably bleeding internally." His skin was ashy under the fur; he must be in extreme pain and mostly likely shock.

"Be careful," Tamir panted. "We don't know if that creature is helping us or—dammit!"

He flung out a hand and grabbed Meri's wrist. A shield blossomed around her just as green energy splintered off it.

Zef reared above them, furious. Meri had a split second to realize he was about to trample them before his hooves crashed down and met Tamir's shield with a green flash.

Zef reared and stamped again. He'd lowered his own shields, and Meri remembered how Lyr had to drop his shields in order to use handheld weapons properly. Zef's own shields would sap the energy out of his attacks if he kept them up while trying to stomp them. There had to be a way to use that to their advantage, she thought—but just then Tamir's eyes rolled back in his head and he collapsed, and the shield around both of them died. His hand slid limply off her wrist.

"Tamir! No!" She shook him desperately, and then cried

out in pain as Zef caught hold of her hair, yanking her toward him.

It was horribly like the way all of this had started out. Once again she was terribly aware of the centaur's strength; it was like being caught in a vice. She screamed and clawed at his hand, tears springing to her eyes from the pain.

His other hand clamped down on her shoulder, and she realized in a moment of breathtaking horror that he was strong enough to break her neck, and it seemed that was what he had in mind.

—until he stumbled back, dropping her. Meri fell to the ground and looked up, shocked, to see Lyr swaying on his feet, with his arm blades buried in the centaur's glossy flank.

"Get away from her," Lyr croaked.

Grimacing with blood-stained lips, Zef twisted his human torso to wrap an arm around Lyr's neck. The two of them grappled in grim silence, punctuated only by grunts and wheezes. Zef steadily bore Lyr down to the ground, but Lyr's blades were buried in Zef's body. Lyr wrenched them out and stabbed him again, this time in his human torso.

Meri averted her eyes. This time, she did not intend to ask Lyr to show mercy.

When she looked up again, it was over. Lyr stood above Zef's body, staring down at his dead enemy with a blank look on his face.

"Lyr?" she said.

Give me a minute.

Meri busied herself checking Tamir's pulse. It was weak, but steady, and he was breathing evenly. With her hand on his arm, she looked around.

It was almost over. The only fighting still going on was at the far side of the battlefield, where the huge alien was putting down the last of the pirates. Lyr looked that way too, and then tottered over to collapse near her, leaving a space between them.

Meri edged over to lean against him, heedless of the blood. He hesitated before putting an arm around her.

"You should be lying down," she managed at last.

"I'd rather sit up." He looked down at her, and smiled briefly, a silver-edged smile. "If I lie down I'm not sure if I can get up. But before I do either, my mate, would you help me with a small task?"

His blood-sticky fingers unfolded from a small gray box.

Meri took it very carefully. Her very skin wanted to shrink from contact with the horrid thing. "How do I use this?"

"Flick that switch—" Lyr indicated it. "—as you touch it to the back of my collar."

After all of that, it was somehow anticlimactic. The controller clicked against the back of Lyr's collar, and the collar visibly loosened on his neck and split along a fine seam. Lyr yanked it off and threw it away from himself with a shudder.

Meri started to drop the controller as well, then tucked it into her pocket. They would need it later to help the villagers.

Lyr was fingering his neck. There were visible burn marks where the collar had contacted his skin. Meri laid a gentle hand beside the injuries. "This is horrible. Those things—" She felt Lyr tense under her hand. "What's wrong?"

"Company," he murmured. "Stay here."

Meri looked where he was looking. The huge alien, having bested his last enemy, turned and strode toward toward them. He was surprisingly quick and light for someone so huge.

Lyr shuddered, and with a visible effort he got to his feet. The blades deployed from his arms as he stepped between Meri and the newcomer.

The alien stopped about ten feet away from them, and smiled, which was a horrifying effect on its twisted, hideous face.

"Oh, don't be like that," it said in a voice that was disconcertingly light and youthful.

With that, its entire body seemed to melt and collapse. As Meri stared, the huge, monstrous shape collapsed into a much smaller and more human-looking form: a man of about average height, well-built and handsome, with waves of dark red hair flung back over his muscular shoulders and purple skin marked with swirling white tattoos. Impossibly, though she had never seen anything like him before, Meri felt a sense of familiarity, as if she knew him from somewhere.

Lyr huffed out a breath like he'd been punched in the stomach.

"Well, now you've met my battle shape," the stranger said in that same light, laughing voice. "I call him Tank."

"Skara," Lyr breathed.

Now she knew where she'd seen him: in Lyr's memories.

"You've led me a merry chase, brother," Skara declared. "First to some backwater end of the galaxy, then you vanish off to the middle of fuck-all nowhere and then when I finally intercept a signal on the pirate 'net and figure out what planet you're on, you end up gallivanting all over that too. Are you trying to avoid me?"

"... what?" Lyr said. He looked dazed.

Before she could stop herself, Meri exclaimed, "Aren't you supposed to be dead?"

Skara's eyes sparkled, vivid green against his violet skin. "There was a plan to that effect, yes." He swept a deep bow. "Who is this lovely lady? Brother, aren't you going to introduce us?"

"What do you mean, that was the plan?" Lyr demanded. Sudden anger flared on the telepathic wavelength. Meri could feel it like the heaviness in the air before a thunderstorm. She'd never seen him this angry at anyone who wasn't actively trying to kill them.

"How *else* does one escape from slavery? Faking my death seemed like a perfectly sensible plan to me." Skara took a second look at Lyr, and the manic humor dancing in his eyes died. "You look terrible."

"And *you* are an asshole," Lyr gritted out. "You died. You *vanished*! I couldn't feel you anywhere."

Guilt flashed across Skara's face, so quickly that Meri almost thought she might've imagined it, before Skara's expression locked down into belligerent stubbornness. "It was necessary. Or would you prefer that we stayed in captivity until we died?"

Lyr looked like he was gearing up for a counterattack. Meri stepped in quickly. "Listen, before we argue about this any more, do you have medical facilities on your ship? Lyr is hurt, and we have another friend who's badly hurt as well."

"Yeah, of course." Skara tore his gaze off Lyr and prodded Lyr's inert collar with his boot, with a look of revulsion on his face. "And this abomination, of course. May I do the honors, brother?"

"Do as you like," Lyr said tightly.

Skara aimed his wrist at it and melted it to slag with a blast from his cuffs. "Ah," he exclaimed, brushing his hands together. He was smiling again, but this time Meri was aware of just how much of his manic cheerfulness was a facade, now that she'd seen under the cracks for a moment. "*That* felt good. And now, shall we get out of here?"

Meri looked up at the ship hovering overhead, but Skara didn't even look in its direction. Instead he made a flamboyant gesture in the air and flicked his hand down as if he was unzipping something invisible. And the air itself unzipped behind his hand, peeling open. Beyond the slowly widening gap, edged with a vibrating border of violet-blue too intense to look at, was a white room full of equipment that looked like some kind of medical bay.

"What the—!" Meri exclaimed. Lyr was now giving Skara a very puzzled look.

"The only person I ever met who could do that was Selinn."

"Yeah, I've got my very own teleporting symbiote too," Skara said cheerfully. "Long story. Very long story. There's been a *lot* happened to me since you last saw me. C'mon, let's get you lot on the *Discordia* before any more little friends show up."

He picked up Tamir, staggering a bit, as Tamir was considerably bulkier than Skara's slim but muscular frame. "Go on, quick," he added, gesturing with his head. "It won't last for long."

Meri took Lyr's hand, and ducked as she stepped through the portal, trying not to touch the edges. There was no sense of transition. It was like walking through a doorway. One minute she was standing with rocks underfoot and the mountain breeze teasing her hair; the next she was in the sterile environment of the ship.

Skara followed closely, nearly stepping on their heels as he stepped out of the portal; there wasn't much room. The portal collapsed, natural daylight winking out and leaving only the bright white lights of the medbay. Skara deposited Tamir on the room's one small bed.

"I'm going to go set the ship down somewhere," he remarked, leaning over the bed to draw something gossamer and weblike across Tamir. "I saw a nice beach, flying in."

"Trust you to scope out the beach while the rest of us are getting our asses kicked," Lyr muttered.

"You really *are* siblings," Meri couldn't help saying as Skara left the room.

"What?"

"Never mind. What is this?" She lightly touched the filmy web covering Tamir. It seemed to consist of a large number of hair-fine tubes crisscrossing each other. When she looked closer, they had extruded slender filaments that burrowed beneath Tamir's skin. It was eerie, like watching him taken over with a fungus.

"It's a life support web. It'll keep him stable and help his body heal itself."

Wow, that'd sure be a nice thing to have back on Earth. She turned to look at Lyr, taking in his exhausted and bloody condition. "Do you need one of those?" she asked, reaching out cautiously to brush his arm with her fingertips.

"I'll be fine. I could use a sealant for the worst of these cuts."

He dug into drawers in the medbay and came up with wipes and something that looked like a hand-held perfume spritzer. "What's that?" Meri asked as he started to apply it to himself. It sprayed something like purplish plastic onto his wounds.

"It's a synth-skin sprayer. A sealant and disinfectant. It'll keep me from losing more blood until my body can deal with the injuries."

"May I help?"

He didn't put up a fight, just pulled out a stool from under the medbay's small counter and slumped on it. Meri set to work, cleaning around his wounds with the wipes and then spraying the plastic-like stuff. *This would be awfully nice to have back home too,* she thought. Maybe when all this was over, it would be possible to arrange some kind of trading between Earth and the Galateans for medical supplies.

Skara popped back into the medbay. "I found us a nice piece of beachfront property where we can hang out for a little while," he declared, and then took a look at both of them. Lyr was blotched with patches of purple synth-skin and covered in dirt and blood, and Meri could only guess what she looked like. "Not to be rude," Skara added, "but have either of you considered a shower?"

"You have showers?" Meri said eagerly. "Do you have clean clothes too?"

"If it means getting you two out of those rags, I think I could dig something up." Skara waved a hand. "Come this way."

Lyr swayed as he got up; Meri put her shoulder under his arm and ignored his attempts to shrug her off. Skara took them down the hall and touched a control panel to open the door to a small cabin with a bed and an open door showing what was recognizably a bathroom.

To Meri, it looked like heaven.

"I'll bring some clothing for you two," Skara said. "I suggest making an intimate acquaintance with the shower. Soon."

As soon as they had stepped inside, the door slid shut behind them. Meri couldn't help grinning. "I think he's saying we stink."

"And not subtly, either." Lyr sank onto the bed. He

started to pull his boots off; then his hand dropped away as if he didn't even have the energy to do that. "I can't believe he's alive. And he's still a complete ass."

"I can't believe *we're* alive." Meri unlooped the purse strap from across her chest and dropped it on the floor, feeling weird and light without the weight that she'd almost stopped noticing.

She was beginning to tremble with reaction. She'd seen violence in the ER, even had to deal with it herself—people off their heads with drugs, domestic-violence abusers, even one time a bunch of teenagers had gotten into a gang fight with knives right in the middle of the waiting room. She'd seen people die so many times she'd become ... well ... not hardened to it, never that, but she'd been able to keep her head and comfort the younger nurses.

But this was on a level beyond all that.

Is this what Aaron had to deal with, over there ...?

She leaned a hand against the wall, her knees suddenly wobbly.

"Meri?" Lyr said, and then asked into her mind, **Are you all right?**

She nodded, not quite trusting her voice, but when he held out an arm, she collapsed next to him and leaned into him and shivered for a little while.

"How do you deal with it?" she asked, pressing her cheek against his chest.

He didn't have to ask what she meant. "I don't know. It gets easier, I guess. You did great out there."

She screwed her eyes shut, but that was worse; she kept seeing the fight in a dizzying replay. "I thought you were dead."

"I'm not," he whispered into her hair. "You're not.

Tamir's not. *Skara's* not ... somehow. We're okay. We're all going to be okay."

"I know." She clung to him and slowly, slowly her heart rate calmed; slowly she began to feel less like she was going to shake herself apart. And finally, she grinned. "You know, Skara's right. We *do* stink."

"You can have the first turn in the shower."

She pulled back to look up at him. "Are you sure?" Then, with a cheeky smile: "Are you saying *I* stink?"

Lyr brushed a hand across her cheek. "Never. But I can tell you'd be more comfortable that way."

"Mmmm." She got up reluctantly, tottering on sore calves and even more painful feet, and got herself some ibuprofen out of her purse. "You want some of this? It's a mild painkiller. Though I'm not entirely sure it's safe for your species."

"Don't worry about it. If I need anything, I'll call Skara."

"Okay." She waved a hand vaguely in the direction of the shower. "I'm going to, uh ..." It seemed stupid to ask him if he'd be there when she got out. But after all this time in such close proximity, she couldn't bear the idea of being separated. "You could join me, you know."

"I think I'll rest, and imagine it. There will be time for that later." He lay down on his side atop the bedcovering, turned to face her, his eyes soft. "I'll be here when you get out, my love. Right here."

TWENTY-ONE

THE SHOWER, at least, was basically a normal shower. The controls were easy enough to figure out, and a recessed alcove in the plastic wall dispensed a sweet-smelling substance that foamed like the soap powder when she rubbed it between her hands. Meri wasn't sure if it was meant to be shampoo or shower gel, but she used it for both.

It felt unbelievably good to get really, truly clean. She washed and washed, sluicing dirt and blood down the drain, wincing as the hot water stung her scrapes and trying to be gentle with her bruises. Carefully, with her fingertips, she picked out her unraveling twists and plucked leaves and twigs and bugs from her hair.

She had never thought it *could* feel this good to get clean.

And some of the stress and tension seemed to wash down the drain along with the dirt and leaves. By the time she finally shut off the water with wrinkling fingertips, she felt ... not okay, exactly, but maybe like she was getting there.

When she turned off the water, the shower switched to

a drying cycle that blew hot air all around her. After a moment of surprise, she just relaxed and enjoyed it, stepping out finally on wobbly legs.

Lyr was still on the bed, lying on top of the covers just as she'd left him, and looked fast asleep. Meri thought about dropping into bed next to him, but she was too hungry, and she wanted to check on Tamir. Instead, she got dressed in the clothing that Skara had left in a neat pile just inside the door—a clinging strip that she eventually decided to wrap around herself in lieu of underwear, loose brown pants, and a dark red shirt. There were slippers, much too big, but it was better than trying to squeeze her sore, swollen feet into her shoes. She was in for a surprise, though, when she put them on; they shrank to fit her feet. Something about the way they adapted to the exact size and shape of her feet made them feel almost like they weren't there, even soothing her blisters a little.

She figured out how to open the door after poking at the controls, and poked her head out into the corridor. The lights were dim inside the room, but bright out here, and it fascinated her to see that the walls of the corridor, like the outside of the ship, were painted with bright, swirling patterns. The hallways on the pirate ship had been a dull industrial-looking gray.

Cautiously, looking around, she padded down the corridor. The sound of rattling and clinking drew her to a small kitchen where she found Skara. He'd taken a shower too, and put on a loose white shirt, open to the waist, that made him look even more piratical but also somehow softer.

"You're human, right?" he said. "Some kind of human. So you should be able to drink tea." Without waiting for an answer, he pushed a cup into her hands.

The liquid within was light blue and looked like no tea

she'd ever seen, but when she sniffed it, the smell was something like tea with a coffee-ish undertone. She took a cautious sip. It was intensely bitter, and Meri made a face. "Is there sugar?"

"But of course." Skara took a small stick out of a canister and swirled the end in her blue coffee-tea. "How's that?"

Meri sipped again. "Better."

"It's a bit of an acquired taste. How's tall and grouchy?"

"Asleep. He has every right to be angry at you, you know."

"I know," Skara said, sobering enough to give her another glimpse of someone much more serious and thoughtful beneath his light, devil-may-care facade. "Tamir is still out too, by the way—another person who'll be quite angry at me when he wakes up, I'm sure." He flashed her a grin, the cheery facade sliding back into place. It made her think of the way Lyr had been when she'd first met him, except in Lyr's case, his defense mechanism was a wall of ice covering his warm heart. Skara covered up with a careless playboy demeanor, but she was starting to think it was just as fake.

"How did you find us, anyway?" she asked, sipping cautiously at her weird blue space tea. "Not that I don't really appreciate the save."

"Couldn't have planned the timing better myself," Skara said cheerfully. "Well ... maybe a few minutes earlier would've been a little better. But yeah, I'm on the pirate-net —don't look at me that way, I never claimed to be a saint— and I picked up their distress beacon, then I found out that Lyr and Tamir were *both* here, which was enough to get me intrigued."

"How did you know that?" Meri asked, but checked herself, remembering what Lyr had said about Skara when he was telling her about his siblings. "Wait a minute, Lyr said you can find people."

"Yep. It's an Iustran thing."

"A what?"

"Iustran? My people?" He waved a hand at himself. "We're shapeshifters, and there aren't that many of us, so we'd never have lasted as a species if we didn't have the ability to recognize our own kind. We always know a fellow Iustran, and we can also imprint on individuals and then recognize them again. Contrary to what *some people* think, it's not an unerring ability to home in on people from anywhere in the galaxy, but I could definitely tell Lyr was on the planet once I got here. Actually ..." He held out a hand. "May I imprint on you? It might come in handy."

"Uh ... it won't do anything weird to me, will it?"

"No, you won't feel a thing."

Hesitantly, she held out her arm. He closed his hand lightly over her wrist and shut his eyes. Meri was pretty sure that she *did* feel something, a slight tingling like the feeling of Lyr putting his shields up, but it passed as Skara withdrew his hand and opened his eyes.

"That's it?" she asked. "You can find me anywhere?"

"No, I can find you from relatively nearby, on this planet, say. Otherwise it's more of a gamble, usually just a vague sense of 'thataway,' if I even get that much. And a light contact like that will fade quickly; it won't last very long unless I renew it." Skara leaned a hip against the counter and gave her an appraising look. "But now I'm even more curious about you. Where *are* you from? You don't know about Iustrans, you don't even have Galatean cuff mods, and I've never seen anyone quite like you. If I didn't know better, I'd say you were pure unmodified Birthworld human."

"I ... think I might be, from what people tell me," she said slowly. "I come from a planet that we call Earth. Lyr says it might be what you people call Birthworld."

Skara's scruffy red brows went up, and his gaze fixed on her in fascination. "I've heard rumors in some of my circles that Birthworld had been rediscovered and unmodified Birthworld DNA was starting to show up on the black market. Never figured there was much to it. Someone's always passing off a shaved Galatean or a dyed Rhuadhi as 'pure, unmodified human' and trying to walk off with a profit before the buyer realizes they've been conned."

"Not in this case. At least, they seem to think so." Curiously, she added, "People don't really pay that much for human DNA, do they? Lyr said something about that, but it seems so hard to believe."

Skara laughed. "Ah, sweetheart, it's just about the most valuable thing there is. You know, all humans in the galaxy were descended from Birthworld stock, originally." He swept a hand down his body, with its violet skin and swirling tattoos—or at least what she assumed were tattoos, though she suddenly wondered if they were a natural part of his body. "We've all been modified heavily from the originals, and there was never that much diversity to start with, so over the years, some of the disadvantages of inbreeding are starting to show up. A drop in fertility, for one."

She couldn't help bursting out with an abrupt, incredulous laugh. "You mean aliens are really trying to kidnap our women to breed with them? Are you telling me that's a thing that actually happens? I always thought it was just a silly thing in some of the books that my co-workers used to read."

"At the very least, an influx of fresh blood is sorely needed." He shook his head, looking at her. "Birthworld. I can't believe it. I have to see it someday."

"Can't you just use your ... teleporter thing and go there anytime you like?"

Skara smiled and shook his head. "I can only portal to somewhere I've seen or, preferably, been. And I can't do it over that kind of distance. To different parts of a planet, yes. Across light years, sadly, no."

"How does it work? How can you *do* that?"

"Magic," Skara said, tapping the side of his nose. "But you have magic all your own, Birthworlder. That magic genetic material of yours. I don't suppose you'd mind me collecting a sample as a gesture of goodwill for helping you ...?"

"Skara!" Lyr arrived behind Meri in the small kitchen and put his arm around her. He smelled of the soap from the shower, and wearing a pair of clean but too-short pants and nothing else. The purple patches of synth-skin stood out vividly on his freshly washed torso and bare feet. "You may not sell my mate's DNA, Skara. Do not even ask."

"It wouldn't hurt her," Skara said.

"Don't I get a say in this?" Meri protested. "And I refuse to think about this until I eat something. I'd even eat one of those terrible ration packs at this point."

Skara's eyes lit up. "Oh, I can feed you *much* better than that."

He dug in cabinets, and began squeezing pouches into a large pot, rebuffing all their offers to help. Meri's skepticism turned to interest when the pot turned out to provide its own heat and the contents began to bubble. "How does that work?" she asked, reaching for it and then pulling her hand back.

"It's not hot." Lyr touched the outside to demonstrate. "It's just an ordinary cooking pot."

"We have those too, but they don't do their own cooking."

"You know what, it's getting crowded in here," Skara said, glaring over his shoulder while briskly unwrapping what looked like uncooked flatbreads. "Why don't you two go outside and I'll bring the food out to you when it's done, if you haven't gotten yourself eaten by anything in the meantime."

"Wait," Meri said, "are we still on the same planet?"

"Of course we are. How long do you think it takes to get to *another* planet?" Skara waved a floury hand at them. "Go go."

Lyr grabbed a couple of something that looked like foil-covered granola bars from a rack on the counter. Skara growled and swatted at him, and Meri was caught off guard by Lyr's quick, mischievous grin.

"I forgot he used to cook," Lyr said thoughtfully as they left the galley, handing her one of the bar-things before unwrapping his own. "He was actually pretty good at it."

Meri was still stunned by that glimpse of a playful, boyish Lyr. This was the person he'd been with his siblings, she thought—before the Empire was done with him. But that person was still inside him, and Meri hoped he'd get a chance to come out more often.

"Is something wrong?" Lyr asked her.

"Nothing," she said. "I think ... things are right, actually."

They stopped by the infirmary to check on Tamir. He was still deeply unconscious, but his vitals seemed strong. After watching him recover once from injuries that should have killed him, Meri was a little less worried that he wouldn't make it this time. Still, she tucked the blanket around him, and Lyr brushed the back of his hand across Tamir's fingers before they left the infirmary.

This ship was bigger and more complex than the one they'd crashed in, but they made their way through its colorful corridors to a cargo hold that closely resembled the one in which they'd been sleeping for the last few days, aside from having a lot more crates and barrels in it. Lyr opened the airlock and raised a hand to keep her back.

It was late afternoon outside, the light warm and golden. Skara had landed the ship on top of a dune. She could feel heat shimmering off the sand.

Lyr looked around, then jumped to the sand a couple of feet below the door and turned to give her a hand down.

Meri wondered how close they were to their original campsite. It was impossible to tell; the beach and ocean looked just the same to her, and when she turned to look up at the towering ramparts of the mountains, she couldn't figure out which cleft in those jagged peaks was the one where they'd nearly died.

"This must make you feel at home," Lyr said. Her puzzlement must have come through. "The oceans, I mean. Your world has vast oceans."

"Yes, technically, but I've never been to one."

"Never?" he asked in surprise.

"No. Never. I went to the beaches along the Great Lakes—which I guess means nothing to you, but I used to live near there. The actual ocean, though ... not at all." She laughed. "I can't believe we've been this close to a real ocean for days and I never even dipped my toes in the water."

"Well, then." Lyr took her hand. "Let's do that."

They started down the dunes, although as it grew steeper, Meri slowed and began to stumble, her sore calves protesting.

"I've got you," Lyr said. He shifted in midstride, and Meri, startled, found herself swept off her feet by a flood of rising bronze scales. She clutched wildly at the spikes on Lyr's neck before finding equilibrium astride his back.

Comfortable? Lyr asked, twisting his head around on his supple neck.

"I—I guess so." Lyr's stride was smooth and swift, like riding a fast-moving horse. His flanks rippled between her thighs with the rhythmic movements of his legs. By the time they reached the edge of the water, she was breathing hard for reasons that had nothing to do with climbing.

Lyr shifted in mid-motion again, this time twisting around to catch her deftly as he changed back. "How was the ride?" he asked, steadying her, with a spark of joy in his silver eyes.

"I'll ride you anytime," she said, and laughed. "Okay, I don't think I'm cut out for dirty talk if I can't even get through it with a straight face."

"Join me in the water instead."

"I don't have anything to wear. And Skara could show up anytime."

Lyr shifted again, and suddenly she had her arms around his serpentine neck. His eyes danced just the same in his dragon form as he lifted his head and arched his wings above them.

"Yes yes, thanks for the reminder that some of us don't need bathing suits."

Come and swim with me, Meri.

"You're persuasive, I have to admit."

She pulled off the loose shirt and pants, stripping down to the wraparound garment that functioned as alien underwear. Lyr, meanwhile, waded into the ocean's edge. He ducked his head to meet the oncoming waves and snapped at them like a puppy playing in the water.

"Oh, it's cold!" Meri gasped as the edge of the waves washed over her bare toes.

It's not that _cold. Within human tolerances. You'll get used to it if you get deeper._

"Easy for you to say! I think I'll just stay on the beach here."

Lyr twisted his head around. *_I don't want to leave you alone._*

"I'll be fine." She wrapped her arms around his enormous muzzle and kissed him on the tip of his snout, where the skin was surprisingly soft. "I'll be right here where you can keep an eye on me, and I can call you if I need you."

I think I might try to catch a fish. I need protein and Skara is taking forever with lunch.

Meri's stomach grumbled. "I'm hungry, but not that hungry. Have fun."

She climbed up to the sun-warmed sand out of reach of the waves. Sitting with her knees under her chin, she watched Lyr playing in the waves.

It was really extraordinary to see him so expressive and playful. He dived under the water, folding his wings, then surfaced farther out with a tremendous splash, water streaming down his scales. A silver fish glistened in his jaws. He flipped it up into the air and snapped his jaws on it. The fish vanished down his throat in a single bite.

"Ewww!" she yelled across the waves.

It's excellent. You don't know what you're missing. Also very good for you. Grows healthy bones and scales.

"I prefer no scales, and I think you're going to have to brush your teeth if you expect a kiss later, buddy."

Germs can't survive the shifting process.

"It's not germs I'm worried about—well, okay, it partly is, but mostly it's just the ick factor."

Lyr dived beneath the surface again, and splashed out closer to shore. **Are you sure you wouldn't like to come in? If the water is too cold, I could shield you.**

"Would that work?"

Come here and I'll show you.

Intrigued now, she came down to the ocean's edge, until waves purled around her toes. Lyr rose out of the water in front of her, glistening in the sun, and held out a clawed forepaw. The cuff glistened on his wrist. **Take my hand.**

She laid her hand on his scaled arm, noticing as she did so that the cuff was considerably larger than it had been when he was human-sized. Or, no—it had simply grown thinner and longer. "How does that work?" she asked, touching it. "It can change size?"

Nanometal. It's meant to accommodate itself to users of any size, because there is such a wide variety of different shaped people in the Empire.

"One size fits all," she murmured. "Where *do* your clothes go when you shift, anyway?"

I don't know. It's just how my people work. There is a theory that we obtain the energy for shifting from some other dimension, a different plane of reality, and our clothes and anything we're carrying go there while we're shifted and come back when we change back.

"But the cuffs don't?"

He shrugged, a ripple passing across his scales. **Metal can't cross the barrier, so it stays in this reality. Jewelry, say, or my metal implants, or—**

He stopped before saying *collar*, but she could still read the thought in his mind, along with the memory of despair. Meri squeezed his wrist. "That's over now," she told him firmly. "And my feet are getting cold, so go ahead and show me what you had in mind."

Yes. Of course.

Her skin tingled as the faint green glimmer flowed over her body, and suddenly her feet were no longer in the water. She could still feel its coolness and a slight tickling sensation as the waves flowed around her feet, but it was oddly distant, almost like her feet were numb.

Now get on my back. Lyr obligingly lowered his belly to the sand to make it easier for her; waves rolled around his sides. **Stay in contact with me or the shield will drop.**

"Um ... okay." She climbed on. "What are you going to do—oh!"

Lyr began to wade deeper. Water surged around her thighs and then around her waist, the sensations still weirdly dulled, as if she felt them through a layer of cotton.

It's all right. She felt reassurance coming to her through the link. **With the shield around you, you'll be able to breathe underwater just fine.**

"Wait, we're going und—"

She broke off and clamped her mouth shut instinctively as Lyr ducked downward and water closed over her head. She also squeezed her eyes shut. But her face didn't feel wet, and after a few seconds she opened her eyes, squinting.

A submarine world stretched around her in both directions, filled with an ambient blue-green glow as sunlight filtered down through the water. The ground beneath Lyr's feet was the same pale sand as the beach, with patches of seaweed waving lazily and little schools of fish flitting about.

You can breathe. There's plenty of air inside the shield. Trust me.

She did trust him, so she took a cautious breath. The air seemed perfectly normal.

There is still some oxygen/carbon dioxide exchange through the shield, so you shouldn't run out of air, but let me know if you begin to feel lightheaded. Would you like to go deeper?

"I ... I'm not sure." It felt strange, speaking out loud underwater. Her voice echoed oddly. She could feel the buoyancy of the water tugging on her, trying to lift her, and she clutched with both hands at Lyr's spiky mane and clamped her thighs firmly around the barrel of his body.

We can surface if you become uncomfortable. Just let me know.

"Okay," she said, speaking to herself as much as him. "Okay. Let's go."

Lyr kicked off from the bottom in a swirl of sand, startling her. For some reason she'd been expecting him to walk. But of course there was no reason to; he hadn't been standing so much as drifting below the surface with his feet in light contact with the sand.

He swam with a twisting motion, kicking occasionally and using his wings to steer. His body undulated beneath her in a way that was odd at first, but she adjusted quickly; it felt almost like the water was carrying her along, except for the steadying pressure of his body against her.

**Are you enjoying this?* Lyr asked.

"Oh, yes," she breathed.

The water was very clear around them, fading to deeper aqua in all directions. Tiny creatures darted about their business, not just fish but a variety of other things, including some she was pretty sure were jellyfish (or something similar) and things she couldn't identify at all, like an undulating square that resembled nothing she'd ever heard of on Earth.

Are you cold?

"Not at all."

He circled back around to the shore at last, and his back surfaced out of the water while his feet settled on the sand. Meri blinked; it hadn't been that dim under the water, but now the sun seemed very bright. The shield winked out around her, and suddenly she could feel the warmth of the sun on her head and shoulders, and the water rushing past her legs as the waves rolled in and out. Her toes were brushing the sand.

Lyr twisted under her, and then she was holding Lyr the man, standing waist-deep in the water with his clothes billowing around him. He kissed her; his lips were salty.

"I tried so hard not to love you," he whispered. "But now I think I loved you from the first time I saw you."

"You mean when I was running and being chased by pirates?" It seemed so long ago now.

"When you were fighting back bravely and impressing me with your courage and spirit? Yes." He brushed his hand across the side of her face and stroked his fingers through her hair, untwisted now into a fluffy cloud floating around her face. "Yes, I loved you then and I love you now."

"I love you too." Her soul seemed to lift with each word. "I love you. I love you."

Lyr's face melted into a soft-edged smile, and he leaned down to kiss her again.

"Hope I'm not interrupting anything!" Skara's clear voice carried across the dunes. Meri broke the kiss and looked up just in time to see a violet-edged portal winking out, leaving Skara behind with a picnic basket and a blanket thrown over his arm. "I see you two have found ways to entertain yourselves," he added.

"While you were taking days preparing our meal?" Lyr called ashore, his tone very dry. "What a surprise."

Skara spread the blanket on the beach, out of reach of the rolling waves. "Fine, if you don't want to eat ..."

They splashed ashore and Meri grabbed for her shirt, all too aware that the clinging material of the undergarment had become semitransparent in the water. She wasn't that crazy about getting dressed over wet underwear, but there were dry clothes back on the ship, and the sun was warm.

They sat on the blanket and used warm flatbreads to dip from bowls containing different things—some were like oddly spiced curry, others had beans or rice in them. Skara spread out little pots of various condiments and Meri watched carefully to see how they were supposed to be used and combined, then cautiously tried them herself. Once she got used to the unusual flavors, she stuffed herself; there was plenty of everything.

"I can't believe this is the first time I've had actual alien food since leaving Earth. Your actual, traditional food, I mean. Except for those awful ration packs."

"Aren't they terrible?" Skara said, making a face. "Supposedly they have every nutrient you need to survive. You can live on them for years—indefinitely, even, according to the packaging."

"I think I'd almost rather starve."

"They're not that bad," Lyr said.

Meri poked him with a flatbread. "You ate a raw fish. I don't think your opinions count here."

"Ah yes, the hunting peoples of the galaxy," Skara remarked with a small shudder. "The Galateans are like that as well, and Rei's folk. *My* people are more civilized. I like my food cooked."

"*Thank* you," Meri said, holding out a fist. Skara looked puzzled, and she explained, "You bump it with yours. Earth custom. It means 'right on,' or 'me too.'"

"Ah." He bumped fists. "Where did you find her, brother? She's wonderful. Is she *really* unmodified, completely and totally?"

"Yes," Lyr said with weary patience, "but you may *not* have her genetic material, now or at any other time. It is not for sale."

"Oh, I don't know," Meri remarked thoughtfully, reaching for another flatbread. "I might want to sell my DNA to inbred Galateans someday, but if I'm going to do it, I'll sell it myself, got it?"

"I could act as your middleman," Skara suggested. "A cut for me, most of the profit to you. I know the black market, I have the contacts ... you *need* me."

"Don't make me turn into a dragon and bite you in half," Lyr growled.

Skara laughed. "It's so good to see you, brother. I missed being threatened on a daily basis. Now we can have a regular reunion, if I can just figure out where Selinn's gotten off to these days—"

"Wait." Lyr's face was a picture of shock. "Selinn's alive too?"

"Of course she is." Skara looked genuinely astounded. "I didn't realize you wouldn't realize—Who do you think got *me* out?" He raised a hand in the unzipping gesture that he used to make portals. "I didn't have my little friend here yet. No, Selinn and Kite did it for me, once Selinn figured out how to portal without setting off her collar—"

"Kite's alive? Are they all alive?" Lyr looked dazed. Meri put her hand on his arm. "*All* of them? No," he corrected himself. "Not Haiva. I watched her die. She was shot in front of me."

"Haiva is really dead," Skara said. He leaned forward, his sharp, guarded face softening. "Lyr, I really am sorry. I know it couldn't have been easy. We just didn't have any safe way to get in touch with you."

"You've all been alive. All these years. Where *were* you?"

"Around," Skara said. "Hiding out, while we made plans for Selinn to portal in and grab the others. She finally got her shot at Rook, but we—that's me and Kite—think something went wrong. We haven't heard from her since. Kite's worried as hell."

Lyr shook his head. "Wait, wait. Back up. Rook and Selinn—"

"She portalled into his pod and grabbed him right before the pod blew up. At least, that was the plan."

"I felt him die," Lyr said, his face blank. "No ... I felt him *vanish*. Rei as well—was she going to grab Rei too?"

"I don't know what happened. Kite and I have been trying to find them."

"You let me think you were *dead*."

"We had to," Skara said, his face serious. "There simply was no other way. We had to fake each death as completely as possible, because if the Galateans ever got the slightest idea we might be alive, they'd never stop looking. The only way we'll all be free and safe is if they never think to look for us."

Lyr made a hissing noise like steam escaping a teakettle.

"We would have told you if we could have," Skara added gently.

Lyr looked away, staring out to sea, and then glanced back at him. "So your brilliant plan was just to have Selinn portal away each of us, one at a time?"

"It worked, didn't it? At least up until Rook and Rei. We still don't know what went wrong there. I don't think they're dead, they're just *gone*, but it means we've lost our teleporter." He wiggled his fingers. "And that's why I have my portally little friend now."

"Yes, where *did* you get that? I thought Selinn's people were the only ones in the galaxy who had them, and it's a very closely guarded secret. They never give them to outsiders. In fact, they don't even talk to outsiders, ever." To Meri, he said, "Selinn's the only one of her kind I've ever met, in fact one of the only ones I've ever heard of outside the Rhuadhi homeworld."

"I stole it," Skara said casually.

Lyr stared at him. "You ... *stole* a symbiote that allows you to teleport, from a planet of xenophobic teleporters who never leave their homeworld."

"Pretty much, yeah."

Lyr blew out a breath. "Only you, brother. Only you."

Skara grinned, a bright sharp-edged grin, and then he rose to his knees and leaned forward to clasp Lyr in a quick hug. Lyr looked utterly flummoxed, and was still looking stunned when Skara released him and sank back into a cross-legged seat at the edge of their picnic blanket.

"I did miss you, you know," Skara remarked, picking up a flatbread. His voice was casually playful as usual, but Meri was close enough to see his hand tremble and then steady. "For one thing, I'd forgotten how much fun it was to watch you get that look, yes, *that* one, when I tell you about things like—ooh, do you want to hear about how I had to scale a thousand-foot cliff in a hurricane to break into the—"

"No," Lyr said flatly. He raised a hand to surreptitiously dash at his eyes.

BY MORNING TAMIR WAS AWAKE, but Meri refused to let him out of bed.

"It's your own fault for fighting pirates and dinosaurs with a broken pelvis," she told him when she brought him breakfast. The life-support web had been disconnected, but he was still bundled in blankets and weak enough he could barely sit up. "And that's a sentence I never thought I'd hear myself say, believe me, but I mean it."

Tamir smiled at her in between wolfing down the food she'd brought him. Breakfast was a sort of wrap-type thing involving fresh fish from the sea and frozen vegetables that Skara provided from the ship's stores, crunchy red and purple carrot-like things. Meri had had her doubts about serving fish tacos to a recovering patient, but she'd forgotten how hungry both Lyr and Tamir got when they'd been healing.

"You want more?" she asked when the food had been reduced to crumbs.

"This will do for now. I'll want meat later, if we have any."

"I'm sure we could get that for you."

Tamir nodded his thanks, but then he turned hesitant. "Skara is here, correct? That wasn't a dream?"

"He's here." She hadn't thought until that moment, seeing the tentative hope on Tamir's face, that Tamir must have been as close to the rest of Lyr's sept as he was to Lyr. "You know the others are alive, right? Someone must have told you. I *hope* someone told you."

"Lyr did. It's still hard to believe." Tamir plucked at the crumbs of his meal with claw-tipped fingers. "Next time you see Skara, if you could ... send him up, perhaps, I'd appreciate it."

"There's an easier way. He's been with Lyr all morning."

With that, she sent a mental question to Lyr, and got a visual answer back. The two of them had their heads together over an open engine access panel. It looked like Skara was showing Lyr how the ship worked.

Lyr, can you tell Skara that Tamir wants to see him?

Just a second, Lyr said. **I'll send him over to the medbay.** Meri sensed a fierce satisfaction behind the words, and Lyr left the link open so she was able to see Skara blanch when Lyr said, "Tamir wants to see you, brother. Pity I won't be there to see you get the chewing out you deserve."

Tamir's not calling him up here to yell at him, Lyr. Don't be cruel.

He deserves it.

Meri rolled her eyes and broke the connection. She noticed Tamir watching her curiously. "Lyr says he's on his way." He was still gazing at her, until she asked, "What's wrong?"

Tamir shook his head. "Nothing's wrong. Things are right, maybe, for the first time in a long time."

Meri hesitated, and then sat on the end of his bed. "What about you? What are you planning to do next?"

It took him awhile to answer. "I ... don't know. I have a duty, to my people and to my clan."

Meri's heart clutched. "To turn us in? To turn *Lyr* in?"

"No!" The answer was quick and vehement. "No," he added again, more quietly, looking at the white wall of the medbay rather than at her. "I just haven't figured out how I'm going to explain any of this. And as for Skara—"

"Taking my name in vain?" Skara asked lightly from the doorway, where he was lounging casually against the door-frame. Meri hadn't even noticed when he got there; she had the feeling he'd taken the time to arrange himself for maximum casual-draping effect and then awaited his moment before he said anything.

"It *is* you," Tamir said, staring at him. "Lyr told me, but actually seeing you—"

"I know, I'm quite a sight to behold."

"You are an idiot," Tamir said. His voice cracked in the middle.

Meri went off and left them alone.

SHE DIDN'T REALLY WANT to bother Lyr if he was busy, and she could tell by casual brushes at his mind that he was still working on the engines, so she wandered up to the ship's bridge. She was sitting on one of the padded seats with her feet tucked under her, looking out at the ocean, when footsteps came in and Lyr's arms went around her neck from behind. Meri sighed and leaned into his embrace.

"Are you fixing the ship?" she asked as he crouched down beside her seat.

"It's more that I'm getting a feel for all the modifications Skara's made to it. This is quite a ship, even if it is ..." He glanced around at the brightly painted walls of the bridge. "... also quite the aesthetic eyesore."

Meri laughed. "I like it." She played with his hair and petted the base of his horns, feeling him relax against her. "So where do we go from here?"

"It depends on what you want to do, but our first stop should be the refugee village. We need to take the collars off the escaped prisoners and pick up any who need transport back to their homes, including those from your world."

"Oh," Meri said blankly. It had already occurred to her that having a spaceship meant she could go home to Earth, but it hadn't really hit her that it might be soon. That it might be *today*.

"It's up to you," Lyr added, his voice gentle, "whether you want to go back or not."

I could, she thought, dazed. *I could go back and ...*

And what? Live in Cora and Dave's spare bedroom? Introduce her seven-foot-tall dragon boyfriend around at the neighborhood block party?

Get an ordinary job and live an ordinary life, after she'd flown on spaceships and been chased by dinosaurs and fallen in love with an alien?

The hell with an ordinary life.

"C'mon," she told Lyr, tugging at his hand. "Show me how the kitchen works on this ship. I'd rather not be dependent on other people to feed myself, if I'm going to be here awhile."

Lyr's silver eyes brightened, and he smiled.

TWENTY-TWO

THEY LIFTED off from the shore in a brilliant afternoon with the planet's rings arching overhead. As the ship circled above the beach, Meri—strapped into a seat on the bridge—saw that thunderheads were building up over the ocean. It would rain again later today.

She tried to think if there was any reason to go back to their crashed ship, but she couldn't think of any. She had her purse with her and everything she wanted to bring was in it. Still, she found herself feeling oddly nostalgic for that place, as uncomfortable as it had been. The rock pool where she and Lyr had made love for the first time (and then almost died), the hill they'd climbed, the campsite where they'd talked and gotten to know each other and fallen in love.

Maybe we could go back someday, she thought, as the beach fell away beneath them and the mountains loomed large in the ship's forward screen. There was a whole crashed spaceship, after all, even if it didn't fly. They might be able to salvage some things that would be useful.

Useful for whom, though? We're not staying on this world for long.

She tried not to feel regret for that.

Rather than skimming high above the mountains, Skara flew slowly through the pass. Meri didn't understand why at first, until she noticed Lyr examining the slope and Skara paying close attention to the ship's instruments, and she realized they were probably checking for survivors. She didn't want to look too closely at the debris of the avalanche for fear of what she might see, and she was relieved when they soared on through the pass and down the other side.

"No survivors," Lyr told her quietly, and she nodded.

She felt strange about her part in it, but couldn't quite find it in her to feel too sorry for them. They'd deserved everything they'd gotten.

And now she got her first good look at the lake-dotted plateau that she'd seen through Lyr's eyes, spreading to the horizon and lightly furred with colorful green and violet forests. Meri leaned forward, fascinated, and then was startled by a light touch on her hand. Looking down, she found that Lyr had reached between their seats to hold her hand.

"So where's this village you mentioned?" Skara asked. He was flying the ship as Lyr had the other one, with his arms buried up to the elbows in a projecting console in front of his seat. Meri had yet to see anything like what she considered normal controls—a steering wheel, a joystick. She wondered if it would even be possible for her to learn to operate it. If she was going to be living among these people, though—and increasingly she knew she wanted to—she hoped Lyr would be willing to show her. If it meant she had to get the implants Lyr had talked about, she didn't really mind. She'd spent her adult life working with medical technology, after all. To her it didn't seem that different from getting an IUD or a pacemaker, and she'd worked with plenty of patients who had those things.

"It's on the shore of that lake," Lyr said, pointing.

Their ship circled wide above the lake, and Meri glimpsed a circle of crude huts and people running for their shelter. "Skara, they're going to think you're a pirate," she said.

"I *am* a pirate. Technically."

"You know what I mean. The bad, prisoner-taking kind of pirate."

"They'll figure it out as soon as they see you," Skara said, but he set down the ship a little ways back in the woods.

Lyr led the way to the village; Meri and Skara followed behind. By the time Meri broke out of the woods, Lyr was already in the center of the circle of huts, surrounded by eager villagers as he took their collars off, one by one.

Meri and Skara were ignored for a few minutes in the excitement. Then someone broke away from the cluster of people around Lyr. "Meri!" cried a voice she recognized.

"Preet!" Meri hugged her. "You're all right!"

"And so are you!" the green woman said, and Meri realized with a shock that she could understand her. But of course she could; the translator had long since kicked in.

"We're going to call this world Haven," Preet said in excitement. "We've already named this place Lake City."

"You're staying here?"

"Most of us are. We have nowhere else to go."

This wasn't true of all of them, of course. There were the humans from Earth, and other prisoners who'd come from other far-flung worlds. But that was business that could be attended to later, sorting out those who wanted to leave from those who wanted to stay. The first priority was seeing to the injured and handing out food and medical supplies from the ship's stores. (Skara grumbled about this, but didn't seem particularly bothered by it.)

After the excitement died down, Meri and Lyr found time to walk on the lakeshore. It seemed strange to have leisure time on this planet with no one trying to kill them and no need to struggle for survival.

"An entire habitable planet," Lyr mused, "technically within the Empire but unknown to the Galateans. There must be many such. Space is enormous, and worlds are many, and the Empire is large. Who knows what else is out there?"

"Preet—that's the green lady—told me they plan to call this world Haven."

"A haven for escaped slaves," Lyr murmured. "It could be that." He looked down at her. "Your people will want to go home."

"Yes. And we'll take them there, if Skara will help us."

"At this point, I think you'd have to *pay* him to stop him from going to your planet, and even that might not work."

Meri laughed, but then she sobered. She didn't want to break the warm mood, but she knew it was time for the other thing she'd been putting off. "Lyr ... can we talk about something?"

"Of course. Anything."

"You asked me awhile back about this." She took Aaron's ring out of her pocket and held it out, a simple gold band resting in her palm. Such a tiny thing to contain all her hopes and dreams, once upon a time.

Now she had other hopes, other dreams, and it was a golden link in a chain holding her to the past. It was time to let it go.

"I remember it," Lyr said quietly. "What is it?"

"My people have a custom. When a couple commits to

each other for life, they exchange rings to symbolize their bond. Not everyone does it, but a lot of people do." She turned the gold circlet over, flashing the inscription: the date of their wedding. "This was the ring Aaron gave me."

"It must be very special to you."

"It was ... once. A long time ago."

She held the ring for a moment longer, pressed it to her lips and kissed it. "Goodbye," she whispered, and then she dropped it into the water. It sank out of sight into the depths of the lake.

"Are you sure ...?"

"I'm sure. His ashes are scattered on Earth. I think it's appropriate that I bury the last of him here, where my new life began. He always liked to travel. He would have loved knowing that a little part of him went to another planet."

She'd been afraid that she would burst into tears, but the heart-rending grief didn't come. Instead there was a gentle, wistful sorrow, and the warm, supportive pressure of Lyr's arm around her.

After a little while, they began to walk again. She looked back, trying to find a distinctive landmark to pick out that patch of lakeshore, and then she made herself stop. It all looked the same anyway, with water grasses and overhanging trees, and that was how she wanted it.

It was time to move on.

"Are you all right?" Lyr asked.

"Yes," she said, and realized that it was true. She *was* all right, for the first time in a long time. With her heart full, she leaned against him. "You know, this really *is* a nice planet, aside from the lethal wildlife. What this place needs is a lakeside resort, maybe a nice restaurant or two, with a dinosaur-proof electrified chain-link fence ..."

"That's what you and Lyr can do with your blissfully

happy future together," Skara declared, dropping down the bank out of nowhere to join them. "You can run your very own lakeside resort."

Lyr rolled his eyes, and Meri said, "I think taking care of a village of escaped prisoners is going to keep us busy enough for a while, don't you think?"

Skara grinned and plucked a flower from the lakeshore that he tried to tuck into her hair and, when she resisted, tucked into Lyr's instead, which got him a glare. "No desire at all to go back to your homeworld, lovely unmodified human lady?"

"Well, *eventually*, sure. I want to pick up some clean clothes, for one thing, and a few, um, other things." She hadn't yet had to figure out what the Galatean Empire had in lieu of tampons, and wasn't sure she wanted to know; plus, she planned to buy a lifetime supply of coffee. "But in the long term? No. There's nothing for me back there. Not anymore." She put her arm around Lyr's waist and enjoyed his warmth against her, and the gentle touch of his mind at the back of her own. "Everything I want, everything I *could* want, is here."

EPILOGUE: KANSAS CITY, MISSOURI

Cora came downstairs quietly to make herself a cup of tea. Toni was down for her nap, Renee wouldn't be home from school for a couple of hours yet, and today was a day off in the part-time work schedule that she'd kept since Toni was born. Time to have a cup of tea, sort the bills, get a load of laundry in the washing machine, and have a leisurely afternoon to herself for a change.

But she found herself at the table, tea cooling by her elbow and paperwork spread out on the table, drifting away into thoughts of that night in Illinois that had occupied her mind ever since Meri went missing.

The official story was that a gas leak had caused an explosion and produced mass hallucinations that had sent people running into the cornfields, convinced aliens were chasing them. Cora kept telling herself that hallucinations were all she'd seen, too. But it had seemed so *real*, all those smells and sights and sounds. It horrified her to think that she might have been under the influence of some sort of hallucinogenic gas with a small child to care for.

Of course, the alternative was to believe that her best

friend had been abducted by aliens—that she herself had been attacked by aliens who looked like cats and horse/human hybrids. It was insane!

In the months since Meri vanished, she had poked around on the internet, trying to understand what had happened to her, and had unearthed an entire secret world of message boards talking about alien abductions and other weirdness. Most of it was too bizarre to believe—hidden civilizations inside a hollow Earth, the government manipulating people's minds by putting things in the water, and that kind of thing.

But then there was stuff like photos of UFOs over the Midwest cornfields that looked so real it was hard to believe they were CGI (though she knew they could do amazing things with computers these days). There were people talking about a meteor strike in Wisconsin last fall that had actually been a spaceship, and eyewitness accounts of alien sightings in downtown Eau Claire that sounded an awful lot like those cat-aliens from the freeway rest stop.

She found others looking for missing people, too. There was a man who had posted on all the boards looking for his missing wife. There was a woman who claimed her sister had talked about aliens right before going missing in Boston.

And sometimes Cora would go out in the backyard and look up at the stars at night, washed out though they were by light pollution from the Kansas City urban center, and wonder what she really *had* seen that night, and where Meri was ...

She shook her head and picked up a utility bill. This was ridiculous. Dave kept telling her what happened to Meri wasn't her fault, that she had to stop dwelling on the past. But it wasn't guilt, not really; it was a desperate need to know, to understand.

I just want to know what happened to me, and where my friend is.

A sudden knock at the kitchen door made her jump and almost spill her tea.

It must be a neighbor; a salesman would be at the front door. Cora blew out a breath, and tried not to look like a bundle of nerves when she went to answer it.

"You'll need to keep your voice down, because my daughter's asleep—" she started to say as she opened it, and then all she could do was stand in shock.

Meri was standing there, hand upraised to knock again.

Cora stared at her. Meri looked whole and healthy and not at all alien-abducted. Actually, she looked ... good. She'd lost the grayish, worn-down look she'd had ever since Aaron's death. Her hair was growing out of that red dye job, but she'd done something different to it—now she had little sparkly threads woven through it, glittering in the sunshine in the same colorful way as fiber optic cables. She was wearing a loose white blouse very different from her usual style, and wide gold bracelets gleamed at both wrists. The absurd clownfish purse was hanging over her shoulder, although it looked considerably the worse for wear since Cora had last seen it, like it had been dragged through the dirt and beaten with a hammer.

"Cora?" Meri said with a cautious smile, and Cora let out a laugh and threw her arms around her friend and hugged her.

"Meri! What are you doing here? Where have you been? No, really," Cora said, holding her out at arm's length to stare at her some more. "Where have you *been*?"

"I'm sorry. I guess I've been ... finding myself."

Cora was caught between collapsing in relieved laughter and shaking Meri until her teeth rattled. So it really *had* been hallucinations, not aliens. And Meri had let them spend all this time thinking she was dead or worse ...! "I want to slap you silly and hug you at the same time, girl. Okay, no, I'll hug you." And she did. "What's wrong with you? Why didn't you call? Where *have* you been?"

"It's a long story. Such a long story. It's just been hard getting in touch with people. I've been ..." Meri cleared her throat. "Out of the country."

"Out of the—*where*? Have you spent all this time in *Canada*?" She hadn't even known Meri had a passport. And what had she done, hitchhiked to the border without so much as a toothbrush?

"Something like that. Are *you* okay?" Now Meri was looking at her with concern. "And Toni?"

"Toni's fine, she's napping upstairs. Renee's at school and Dave's at work. But really, Meri—Canada?"

Meri choked on a laugh. "I always wanted to see Canada," she said, her eyes bright with humor, and as much as Cora wanted to yell at her for worrying her like that, oh, it was so *good* to see her looking like she used to, with the bright eagerness of spirit that Cora remembered from when they were college students together. "Anyway, I'm sorry for not calling ahead, but I wanted to let you know I was all right and also pick up some of my stuff, if you still have it. I understand if you don't—"

"Of course we do. It's in the garage. Come on in, let me make you some tea, or would you rather coffee?"

"Coffee," Meri said eagerly, "*please.*"

They took their cups of coffee to the garage—Meri already having gulped down half of hers; she drank it like she hadn't had coffee in months—where the boxes of Meri's things from Columbus were stacked by the water heater and labeled neatly in black laundry marker. Meri sorted through the boxes and Cora helped her carry them out to her little rental car at the curb. They had to put most of them in the backseat, because the trunk was full of cases of coffee.

"What in the world are you doing with that much coffee?" Cora wanted to know.

"Stocking up," Meri said vaguely. "It's hard to get coffee in ... Canada."

"Canada doesn't have *coffee*?"

"Not the kind I like," Meri said, and hastily changed the subject. "So how are the girls? How's Renee liking school? What grade is she in now?"

So they chatted about that until they finished loading the car. "Where are you staying, anyway?" Cora asked her. "Do you have a hotel? We can clean out a bedroom for you."

"Oh, no, I have a place," Meri said, although the direction she looked was not towards the city; it was out in the direction of what Cora knew was nothing but suburban sprawl and then cornfields.

"Well, you should at least stay for dinner. I know Dave and the kids would love to see you."

"I'd love to, but I'm afraid I can't. I'm in kind of a hurry." Meri hugged her again. "Thanks so much for keeping my stuff for me. I wish I could stay to chat. I'll stop by the next time I'm in town and we'll have a good long visit, okay?"

"I still want to smack you silly for worrying me like that. And, Meri ..." Cora hesitated, but she felt like she had to ask; she got a feeling it might be a long time before she saw her friend again. "Meri, I wanted to ask if you—if that night, if ..."

But she hesitated, while Meri looked at her with a hard-to-read expression. She didn't even know what she wanted to ask. She wanted to know what Meri remembered about that night; she wanted to know if Meri, too, had had nightmares for months about something that couldn't possibly have been real. She wanted to know how in the world her best friend had managed to disappear for months, only to resurface looking like she'd been getting happily laid every night, grab her things, and disappear again.

She wanted the answers to all of these questions, but she had a feeling that Meri wasn't going to tell her the truth (*Canada, right; as if I really believe you've been in Canada*) and she didn't want what might be their last conversation for a long time to end up in half-truths and lies.

Instead she said, "Meri, are you okay? Is anyone making you do anything you don't want to do?"

Meri broke into a wide smile. "Oh, no. Not at all. My life is really good. Honestly, it is."

"You're happy?" But she could see the answer in Meri's beaming face.

"Oh yes," Meri said. "I'm *so* happy. I wish I could tell you about it. I'll come back soon and we'll talk, okay?"

"Call me," Cora told her, and they hugged. It was only as Cora waved to the receding car that she realized Meri hadn't mentioned if she had a different phone now. Cora had left message after message, only to get Meri's voicemail every time, and eventually a disconnect message.

Where are *you these days, Meri?*

But wherever it was, she obviously *was* happy. And she pretty clearly had not been abducted by aliens, so at least Cora knew she could let go of that fanciful notion, no matter what the message boards on the internet said.

Aliens. She couldn't believe she'd thought it was true for a minute.

Warriors of Galatea will continue in *Metal Pirate*!

Not a typical one-night stand ...

Claudia was just looking for some fun, a one-night stand with a hot stranger to celebrate her birthday and knock an item off her to-do list. (Item: lose virginity.) Except now she seems to have acquired a bad case of sexually transmitted teleportation, and there are alien bounty hunters after her. As soon as she figures out how to control her new what-the-actual-hell superpower, she's going to find Mr. Hottie and give him an enormous piece of her mind ... and maybe some of the rest of her. If he apologizes enough. (It was a *really good* night.)

Skara has spent his life trying not to get attached, but one night with a beautiful Earth girl changes his world forever. Not the least reason being that she now has his ability to teleport, she's in danger because of him, and he has to get back the alien teleportation symbiote that she somehow stole from him because he'll die without it.

Falling in love wasn't supposed to be part of the plan ...

Coming soon!

ABOUT LAUREN

Hi, and thank you for reading! I'm a writer, artist, and lifelong Alaskan, and I write my books in a cabin on the highway, surrounded by fireweed and birch trees. I also write as Layla Lawlor (urban fantasy and science fiction) and as Zoe Chant (a shared romance pen name with several other authors; my books as Zoe are the Bears of Pinerock County and Bodyguard Shifters series).

Join my mailing list for new releases, free stories, and sneak preview chapters! Get a free story just for signing up. https://www.subscribepage.com/LaurensList

Email: laureneskerwriter@gmail.com

Facebook page (*news and updates*)
https://www.facebook.com/laureneskerwriter/

Website: laurenesker.com

ALSO BY LAUREN ESKER

Shifter Agents

Handcuffed to the Bear

Guard Wolf

Dragon's Luck

Tiger in the Hot Zone

Shifter Agents Boxed Set #1

(Collecting *Handcuffed to the Bear, Guard Wolf,* and *Dragon's Luck*)

Standalone Paranormal Romance

Wolf in Sheep's Clothing

Keeping Her Pride

Warriors of Galatea

Metal Wolf

Metal Dragon

Metal Pirate (forthcoming)

Metal Gladiator (forthcoming)

Made in the USA
Columbia, SC
23 April 2024

34812097R00219